HOLDOUT

ALSO BY JEFFREY KLUGER

NONFICTION

Apollo 13,
with coauthor Jim Lovell

*The Apollo Adventure: The Making of the Apollo Space Program
and the Movie* Apollo 13

*Journey Beyond Selene: Remarkable Expeditions Past Our Moon
and to the Ends of the Solar System*

Splendid Solution: Jonas Salk and the Conquest of Polio

*Simplexity: Why Simple Things Become Complex
(and How Complex Things Can Be Made Simple)*

*The Sibling Effect: What the Bonds Among Brothers and Sisters
Reveal About Us*

*The Narcissist Next Door: Understanding the Monster in Your Family,
in Your Office, in Your Bed—in Your World*

Apollo 8: The Thrilling Story of the First Mission to the Moon

FICTION

Nacky Patcher & the Curse of the Dry-Land Boats

Freedom Stone

YOUNG ADULT NONFICTION

*To the Moon!: The True Story of the American Heroes
on the* Apollo 8 *Spaceship*

Disaster Strikes!: The Most Dangerous Space Missions of All Time

Raise Your Voice: 12 Protests That Shaped America

HOLDOUT

A NOVEL

JEFFREY KLUGER

DUTTON

DUTTON

An imprint of Penguin Random House LLC
penguinrandomhouse.com

LIBRARY OF CONGRESS CATALOGING-IN-PUBLICATION DATA
has been applied for.

ISBN 9780593184691 (hardcover)
ISBN 9780593184707 (ebook)

Printed in the United States of America
1st Printing

BOOK DESIGN BY TIFFANY ESTREICHER

With love to Elisa and Paloma,
my sweet, wise, and courageous daughters

HOLDOUT

CHAPTER ONE

Walli Beckwith had no way of knowing that she probably had just under an hour to live. If she had known, she likely could have calculated exactly how *much* under an hour it was. By now she understood well-nigh all there was to know about how a spacecraft at a particular distance with a particular mass moving at a particular speed behaves, so she could also understand precisely when the one coming at her would arrive and what it would do when it hit. But the spacecraft was, at the moment, keeping all that a secret from Beckwith, as well as from the other two crew members aboard the International Space Station. If a mindless machine with no one aboard could be said to be acting with devious intent, this one was—and its intent was to kill them all.

The machine that was threatening to end the crew's lives would also make a mess of an experiment Beckwith was conducting, one that she'd rather looked forward to completing but now probably never would, what with death all at once on the day's menu of events. For most of the morning, she had been working in the station's Zarya, or Sunrise, laboratory—one of the five modules the Russians had contributed to the football-field-size, fifteen-module station. Lost in the experiment, she jumped when a voice suddenly called out to her over the station's intercom system for a routine status check. Most communications aboard the station were conducted publicly, over speakers and microphones arrayed throughout the modules, sparing the crew from having to wear headsets all day.

"Are you all right back there, Walli?" the voice, belonging to the station commander, Vasily Zhirov, called in Russian-accented English.

"All good," she answered.

"You didn't catch the shit bug?"

"Not yet," Beckwith said with a laugh.

Zhirov's English was better than Beckwith's Russian, so that was how they typically communicated. Still, he chose his moments to speak in Russian, and for "shit bug," which was how he always referred to the *E. coli* intestinal bacteria that was used in the lab studies, he used "*dermóvaya zaraza*." In either language, the term was one of the many ways Zhirov had of waving off the science that was conducted aboard the station, which, as far as he could see, was busywork compared to the more challenging business of simply keeping the huge ship flying. When the experiment involved salmonella, Zhirov called it *kurínaya bolézn*, or chicken sickness, and any studies involving the five mice aboard the station were *krysinie ígri*, or rat games.

Earlier in the morning, Beckwith had been running *E. coli* studies, but she had finished up that work and was now starting on an experiment with meningitis bacteria, a more important job since it was being done in pursuit of a better treatment for the disease; it was the kind of experiment that made her feel her time in space was being especially well spent. As she worked, she could listen in on what Zhirov and the other Russian aboard, Yulian Lebedev, were doing.

The station had been shorthanded for the past two weeks, ever since the last three-person crew had returned to Earth to make way for the next. The newcomers would be arriving in ten days, filling out the crew manifest to the more typical six. Before they arrived, the station needed to be resupplied. An unmanned Progress cargo vehicle had been launched from Russia's Baikonur Cosmodrome in Kazakhstan two days ago and was scheduled to arrive and dock with the station at just after 11:00 this morning, station time, which was pegged to Greenwich Mean Time.

Docking a Progress had its perils. Without a pilot aboard, it relied on a computer to execute the delicate pas de deux of approaching and linking up with the station. But computers were imperfect, and for that reason, Zhirov and Lebedev, the two Russians aboard, who presumably had a better understanding of the Progress than the one American, would be in the nearby Pirs, or Pier, module, a downward-facing pod barely half the length of the school-bus-size Zarya. The nose of the Progress would fit into a port on the Pirs, a routine procedure that had been conducted uncounted times before. Still, the two cosmonauts would be monitoring the Progress's approach and could take over and fly it in by remote control if the automatic guidance system failed. The dual Mission Controls in Moscow and Houston would be listening in on the procedure, but it was Zhirov and Lebedev who would do the piloting if a problem arose.

Beckwith had little doubt that the likes of those two would bring off the docking without incident. Lebedev was a first-time cosmonaut and a quiet sort, but over the course of the last two years of training together, she'd come to see him as the best pure engineer she'd ever met. People liked to say that he could take the entire Russian portion of the space station apart in his head, redesign it, and put it back together better than it had been before. That had seemed like nothing more than the kind of hyperbolic praise ladled out to promising

3

rookies until Beckwith saw Lebedev do just that—staring at a busted evaporator or a broken-down air scrubber, regarding it this way and that, then finally nodding once as he sorted out exactly what it needed and fixing it within minutes.

Zhirov was another order of exceptional altogether. He'd been to space five times before, putting together 780 days off the planet as of this morning's count. He'd already made it clear he was aiming for a full thousand, and at this point, he would need just one more flight after the current one to get there. It was all but certain he would, what with the press attention it would garner. The Russians were already working on a publicity campaign for what they would call the "*Zolotáya Tysyacha*," or the "Golden Thousand."

Zhirov had earned his thousand. He was widely considered the most gifted natural pilot in the Russian space program, a master of the three-person Soyuz spacecraft—which he adored. It was so light, so responsive, so zippy a ride up and so buckingly wild a ride back down that anyone who had ever been at the stick of one would never want to fly anything else. Zhirov liked to boast that while the other two crew members in a Soyuz were expected to assist the commander during flight, he could fly the thing with two cabbages in the other two seats.

Beckwith was proud of her own 153 days in space, accumulated over the course of a two-week space shuttle mission early in her NASA career, a three-month space station rotation three years ago, and the seven weeks she'd spent aboard the station on this rotation. But they felt like little more than a long weekend compared to Zhirov's total. She was thus delighted to have been assigned a full six months this time around.

Now, as Zhirov and Lebedev monitored the approaching Progress, Beckwith went about her laboratory work. A freezer tray of meningitis floated in front of her; she extracted one sample vial and broke its seal carefully, half listening to the call-and-response chatter between the cosmonauts and the ground. She could tell that the Progress was drawing closer.

"Target at forty-five, closing at twenty-six," Lebedev called to Moscow Mission Control. They spoke in Russian, but it was pilots' Russian, and in that, at least, Beckwith was fluent. During the docking, it would be Zhirov's job to monitor the approach data as it changed, Lebedev's job to announce it to the ground.

"Copy your forty-five and twenty-six," Moscow answered.

The changing numbers were also reassuring numbers. At this moment, the Progress was forty-five kilometers, or twenty-eight miles, below and behind the station, approaching at twenty-six meters per second, or fifty-eight miles per hour. Throughout the docking, both numbers would get steadily smaller as the Progress drew closer and moved slower. Beckwith glanced at her watch. The Progress would have to slow to a few meters and then a few tenths of a meter per second in order to come in slowly enough to insert its prow into the station's docking collar safely. Still, at the speed it was traveling, it would close most of the distance fast, and under normal circumstances the whole exercise would be over in less than forty-five minutes.

As if in recognition of that narrow window of time, the patter between the station and the ground took on a brisker clip.

"Forty-five kilometers, closing at twenty-four," Lebedev said.

"Forty-five and twenty-four," Moscow echoed.

The speed then slowed to twenty-two meters per second, then twenty, then eighteen, and then just fifteen. And then it did something it very much was not supposed to do, which is to say it did nothing at all.

"Holding at fifteen," Lebedev said.

Three seconds passed.

"Holding at fifteen," Lebedev repeated.

"Copy your fifteen," Moscow said. Even through the air-to-ground static, Beckwith could hear that the voice from Moscow had tightened. Several seconds elapsed with only the communications hiss playing through the station's intercom.

"And now twenty," Zhirov said, taking over Lebedev's callout role. His tone was hard, almost a snap.

Beckwith looked up. Zhirov couldn't mean twenty. Twenty meant that the Progress was accelerating—precisely what it wasn't supposed to do, precisely what no incoming vessel was ever supposed to do at this close range when it was heading for the huge, slow, barely maneuverable station.

"Repeat please, station," Moscow requested.

"Yes," Zhirov said. "Twenty."

Beckwith stopped what she was doing. Zhirov spoke again.

"Twenty-three," he said flatly, and then, "Twenty-eight."

"Go to manual override, station," Moscow called.

"Copy, override," Zhirov answered. Beckwith waited to hear Zhirov say that the override had worked, that the speed had been braked. But Zhirov did not say that.

What he said instead—flatly, tonelessly—was: "Moscow, we have no hand."

That was the call Beckwith had dreaded. "No hand" was a term of Zhirov's own devising. It was the one he first used during pre-flight training when the simulation supervisors threw him just this scenario—a Progress vehicle speeding toward the station, its onboard computer, backup systems, manual control, and every other intended fail-safe having in fact failed. A commander without a hand on his ship was a commander in the worst kind of trouble.

Beckwith sprang toward the end of the Zarya lab that led to the docking module, then doubled back—her open vial of meningitis still in her hand and the sample tray floating where she'd left it. She forced the top back on the vial, banged it back into place in the tray, pivoted toward the freezer, and clumsily slid the tray inside, slamming the door too hard, then slamming it again when it failed to catch. Then she kicked herself off a bulkhead, shot toward the lab exit, and dove down into the open hatch of the Pirs, which was just below her.

When she entered, Zhirov and Lebedev had their backs to her, facing the module's instrument panel and the small windows that looked down toward the planet. Through the windows, Beckwith could see the dark shape of the Progress approaching against the white of the clouds. It was just three kilometers away now, or a little under two miles, and big enough for her almost to make out its shape, though at that distance, the twenty-three-foot-long multiton vessel still looked relatively harmless. The view on the monitors in front of Lebedev and Zhirov told a different story. One showed the Progress as seen from a camera on the far larger station; the other showed the station as seen from the Progress. On the screen, the station resembled nothing so much as a vast butterfly, its two giant solar arrays forming the butterfly's wings, dwarfing the chain of fifteen linked modules between them that made up its body. The Progress was closing on it like an angry wasp.

"Vasily," Beckwith said, announcing her presence.

Zhirov, his hand on the useless control stick and his eyes fixed on the screens, nodded without turning.

"Target is accelerating, Moscow," he said levelly. "We are at thirty."

Beckwith did some hurried calculating and swallowed hard at what the numbers told her: Thirty meters per second meant that the Progress was up to sixty-seven miles per hour. An impact, if one was to occur, would now take place in just three minutes. Lebedev, as if following her ciphering, confirmed it three seconds later.

"One hundred seventy-seven seconds," he read out. The images on the twin screens grew bigger.

"Station, recycle please," Moscow called up, ordering Zhirov to, effectively, reboot the guidance system by switching it off and then back on again.

"Recycle," Zhirov commanded Lebedev, who flicked the appropriate switches in front of him off and then on. Zhirov tried his control handle—and the images on the screen continued to grow.

"No hand, Moscow," Zhirov said.

"Recycle again please," Moscow said.

Lebedev complied and Zhirov tried the controls.

"No hand, Moscow," he said.

"Again, station," Moscow ordered. Again Lebedev tried.

"Moscow-we-have-no-hand!" Zhirov said in an impatient staccato. "We will evade." He then turned back to Beckwith. "Walli, thrusters," he ordered.

"Copy, Vasily," she said, then flew from the docking module and made a sharp turn into a larger adjacent module the Russians called the Zvezda, or Star, where the station's thrusters were controlled. She threw the breakers that powered the system and feathered the control handle to determine if it was engaged. Thrusters made no noise in space, but within the ship, the power of their exhaust vibrated through the walls and was very much audible. Aboard the American space shuttle, thrusters went off with a sound like a shotgun that left no mistake they were functioning. On the station, they produced a much softer whoosh. Walli heard the whoosh. During routine station maneuvers it was actually a pleasing sound. Today it signaled only looming disaster.

"Engaged, Vasily," she said grimly through the open intercom system.

"Pitch up and yaw starboard," Zhirov ordered, telling Beckwith, effectively, to raise and bank the station.

"One hundred and thirty seconds," Lebedev said.

"Roger," Beckwith said and obeyed, but her stomach turned over at the particular evasive maneuver Zhirov had ordered; it was an acknowledgment that a collision was unavoidable. The station turned lazily and could not easily get out of harm's way in time. Instead, the pitch and yaw would simply reposition it, putting one of the great solar wings in the path of the Progress and avoiding damage to any of the modules that made up the main body of the butterfly, which could lead to a lethal depressurization. Zhirov was trading a mortal wound for a flesh wound. The station lurched upward and to the right.

"Ninety seconds," Lebedev said.

"Walli, more!" Zhirov called.

Beckwith jerked the thruster handle again; the little jets outside whooshed in a higher, more urgent register. The station struggled up and away.

"Thrusting," Beckwith said.

"Copy," Zhirov acknowledged.

"Seventy-five seconds," Lebedev announced.

Moscow, helpless to do anything at all, remained silent.

For the next thirty seconds, the crew worked wordlessly, Beckwith driving the station, needing no more instruction from Zhirov to know that every degree she moved the huge vessel was a degree less damage the onrushing Progress might do. Suddenly, however, she felt a hand on her shoulder and she looked around. It was Zhirov.

"I will do this," he said. "You get in the spacecraft."

Before Beckwith could respond, Lebedev called out, "Forty-five seconds."

Beckwith fired herself toward the module exit. "Get in the spacecraft" was the station's agreed-upon command for "Abandon ship." It was the last command, the all-is-lost command, the command Beckwith had trained to respond to but had never really thought she would hear—least of all on a flight commanded by Zhirov.

She shot from the Zvezda module and into an upward-facing module known as the Poisk, or Explore, where the Soyuz spacecraft in which the three of them had arrived seven weeks earlier was docked. She yanked open the Soyuz hatch, then dove inside the spacecraft toward the center seat, Zhirov's seat, pushing aside the heavy pressure suits that had been left in place like empty effigies.

Beckwith quick-flipped a long row of breakers on the instrument panel and felt a flicker of relief for the first time since the emergency had started as the panel lights blinked on and the interior fans whirred into motion. The Soyuz lifeboat seemed fit. She reached for the switches to engage the life-support systems and the engines, when all at once the thrusters outside screamed rather than whooshed, as Zhirov's violent maneuvering caused the station to lurch again. Beckwith's head snapped backwards, cracking against the hard ridge of the spacecraft seat. Her hand went instinctively to the site of the pain, and she felt a slick of blood.

"Twenty seconds!" she heard Lebedev call through the rising sound of the thrusters outside.

That was followed by "Fifteen seconds." Then, "Nine seconds." And then, as the station bucked upward one more time, a final "Four seconds!"

A moment later, Beckwith was aware of only three things: a bang first; a hard, violent lurch to starboard next; and a sudden, knifing pain in her ears. She clapped her hands over both sides of her head and doubled forward, rocking in pain. She stayed like that for what was surely just seconds but felt like much more. Then she held still, steadied her breathing, and through her hands covering her ears could faintly hear the station's emergency Klaxon sounding everywhere. That cleared her mind and steadied her thinking—and the circumstances fell into place.

The Klaxon sound was the collision alert. The starboard swerve meant a portside hit. And the lightning bolt of pain meant the hull of one of the modules had been breached and the station was depressurizing. Still, while the circumstances were worse than they ought to be, they were better than they might have been.

If the breach had been a fatal one, Beckwith would have been deafened first as her eardrums ruptured and dead directly after as the station's atmosphere exploded completely away. As she was neither—yet—she knew she had things to do. She crawled out of the Soyuz, batting aside storage bags, flight plans, and other drifting items that had been knocked loose by the collision, and exited the upward-facing Poisk module—closing the hatch behind her to prevent any further depressurization. She pushed off quickly to the downward-facing Pirs module, where Lebedev was and the impact had likely been. She immediately collided with Zhirov, emerging from the Zvezda module.

"Walli!" Zhirov exclaimed. He took Beckwith by the shoulders and then by her head, turning it this way and that. He came away with blood on his hands from her slowly leaking wound. He wiped it on the leg of his pants.

"Your ears," Zhirov said, his voice sounding muffled. "You can hear?"

"Some," Beckwith answered.

"The same," Zhirov said. The depressurization had caused the air in their inner ears to expand painfully and grow trapped there, stopping just short of causing them deafness—for now. Zhirov looked toward the Pirs module, where Lebedev was. Both of them dove for the open hatch and stopped cold at what they saw: Lebedev was floating in mid-module, unconscious, blood running from his right ear. They lunged toward him and grabbed him, and Zhirov began shaking him and slapping his face.

"Yulian!" he shouted. "Yulian!"

Lebedev's face was pale and his lips were blue. Beckwith lifted one of his eyelids with her thumb. The white of the eye was shot through with the deep red of burst blood vessels. This was how a man who was dead of vacuum asphyxiation looked. Beckwith turned to Zhirov and then quickly turned back as Lebedev stirred.

"Yulian, Yulian!" Zhirov shouted, louder this time. It was his implacable calm in moments of crisis that had set him on his path to his Golden Thousand, but at the moment, there was little of it in evidence. Lebedev muttered something and his eyelids fluttered open; he turned away from the fluorescent lights directly in front of him. He could see, and, from one ear at least, he apparently could hear.

"Yulian!" Zhirov shouted again, this time in joy, and grabbed Lebedev in a clumsy hug.

Through Beckwith's own clogged ears, she heard both the ongoing sound of the Klaxon and a high whistle along with it. She turned in the direction of the whistle and saw a small mound of debris—papers, packing material, a pair of jumpsuits, and more—wadded up against a misshapen portion of the bulkhead. This, she knew, was where the Progress had hit. The hull had ruptured, the air had begun to rush out, and any loose detritus in the module had then streamed toward the hole and, in effect, stopped it up. Their lives had been saved by junk. But the whistling was the sound of air still slowly escaping. Beckwith grabbed Zhirov by the shoulder, then pointed to what she'd seen.

"Out," she said. "Let's go. Now."

The lucky patch would hold only so long. When it worked loose, the catastrophic depressurization would resume. Zhirov nodded his understanding and, in an unaccustomed moment of obedience to a subordinate, swam toward the module hatch, pushing Lebedev ahead of him. Beckwith followed, and when all three of them were out, she slammed the hatch and sealed it. The module was wrecked, but the wound in the station had been cauterized and the interior atmosphere elsewhere was secure. The Klaxon sounded heedlessly on.

Zhirov led the way to the larger Zvezda module and threw a switch on the instrument panel, shutting off the alarm. In the silence, a low, steady roar continued inside Beckwith's head, the result of her damaged ears.

Lebedev opened his eyes, saw Zhirov, and muttered simply, "Vasily." Zhirov smiled and Lebedev smiled back. The commander then passed Lebedev on to Beckwith and keyed open his air-to-ground channel.

"Moscow, station," he said.

There was no response.

"Moscow, station," he repeated. The air-to-ground loop emitted a loud crackle.

Zhirov frowned and looked out the window. The collision had left the station in a slow, wobbling spin, and the Earth was passing by outside at a sickening angle. If reliable radio contact was going to be reestablished, he would have to bring the motion to heel and allow the antennas to establish a lock with the ground. He grabbed the thruster controls and carefully began to work them, slowly nulling out the rate of spin. Eventually, the communications link crackled to life.

"Station, Moscow," came the call. "Station, Moscow. Confirm your status please."

"Moscow, station," Zhirov answered. "Impact with vessel. Pirs hull is breached, station is stable. Crew is four-two-four."

Beckwith looked at him, struck by the phrasing. Zhirov was an old-school cosmonaut—deeply mindful of the Soviet traditions—and he was speaking old-school code. Ever since the earliest Soyuz landings, recovery crews would open the hatch and call out the status of the crew members on a one-to-five rating. Five meant healthy and well. Four meant some injuries. Three and two meant serious injuries. One was the code that a crew member had died. Only once in history had a one been heard—in 1971, when Soyuz 11 depressurized during reentry and a grim recovery officer had opened the hatch after the spacecraft made an otherwise perfect landing, then turned and reported hoarsely: "One-one-one."

Today's "four-two-four" was vastly better but not remotely good. Moscow and Houston would call an end to any mission with so battered a crew. No NASA voices were on the line, but they were surely patched into all of the air-to-ground chatter, and a small delegation of five NASA representatives was always on hand in Moscow Mission Control, just as a similar delegation from Roscosmos—Russia's NASA—was always stationed in Houston. Any order that came up from the ground would come by agreement from both sides, and there was no doubt what that order would be.

"Station, prepare spacecraft for return," came the command from Moscow. "Stand by for entry time and coordinates."

"Understood, Moscow," Zhirov said. Lebedev closed his eyes, and Beckwith slumped. Her ears would recover within a couple of days—she was certain of it. So would Zhirov's. But the ground could not be as certain, and in any event, Lebedev was fit only for a hospital—as quickly as possible. Zhirov ticked his head in the direction of the Poisk, where the Soyuz lifeboat was docked. Beckwith swam toward the module hatch and opened it up, and then Zhirov and Lebedev followed.

When they were inside, she floated back into the attached Soyuz and wrestled out the crew's three pressure suits. Zhirov turned and shook his head.

"No suits. If Yuli has lost an ear, the helmet pressure could take the other," he said. "And if he flies without a suit, so do I."

Beckwith smiled. "And so do I," she said. It was a risk. If a spacecraft depressurized on reentry, a suitless astronaut would die. Zhirov rarely broke a rule or cut a corner, and when he did, it was always the right call, the honorable call. Today it was a call that respected the oneness of the crew.

She pushed the suits out of the way, collected Lebedev, who was slumped against a bulkhead, dried blood streaking his face, maneuvered him into the Soyuz, and began buckling him into his left-hand seat.

"Thank you very much," he said with a weak smile. Lebedev was a man to whom courtesies mattered, and old-school or not, he showed particular politeness to women.

"Quiet, Yulian," she said. "No *boltovnyá* from you."

Lebedev smiled at both Beckwith's use of the approximate Russian word for "babbling" and her perfectly miserable pronunciation. Beckwith then emerged from the Soyuz.

"Shut it down, Vasily?" she asked.

"Shut it down, Walli," he responded, then hailed the ground. "Moscow, station," he said. "Proceeding with evac power-down."

"Copy, station," Moscow responded.

Beckwith kicked off for the station's American segment. The evacuation power-down was the final step before a crew abandoned ship. It required that the lights, air scrubbers, water recyclers, and other life-support equipment be shut off in order to save power. It also called for every hatch on every module to be closed and sealed, preventing a stationwide depressurization in the event of a collision with a meteor or another piece of flying ordnance. The station had already been clobbered once today. Another hit could be the end of it.

She followed the drill—throwing switches, slamming hatches, locking down a station she realized she might never see again. She worked hurriedly but sorrowfully—an astronaut bringing a failed mission to a sudden close—then shook off the gloom and refocused her mind. She had to power down not just the eight modules built by the Americans but also the two that had been provided by the Japanese and European space agencies, the Kibo and the Columbus laboratories. That part took all of her concentration because, despite her training, she was simply less familiar with them than she was with the American machinery.

"Walli!" Zhirov called. "Time is short."

"Copy!" she answered.

She focused her thinking, powered down the Kibo and Columbus as best she could, and slammed their hatches as she had on the American modules. The station was secure, and less than ten minutes after she'd left the docking module, she returned. Zhirov had by now powered down the Russian end of the station and was waiting for her. He and Beckwith both moved toward the open hatch of the Soyuz, and Beckwith stopped, offering a nod to the commander and gesturing for him to enter first. Zhirov floated inside and buckled into the center seat.

At that moment, Lebedev caught his breath and grabbed his injured ear. A fresh trickle of blood ran down his face. Zhirov turned Lebedev's head, examined his ear, and gave his crewmate a reassuring pat on the knee.

"Soon, Yulian," he said. "We will have you in a hospital soon."

He turned to Beckwith and gestured at her to hurry. Beckwith complied and dove in. She sealed the station's hatch so that it wouldn't depressurize when the spacecraft undocked, then sealed the Soyuz's own hatch. She settled into her seat and buckled her restraint harnesses. The Soyuz felt comparatively roomy without the crew's bulky suits, reminding Beckwith of the hours she'd spent in the simulator on the ground.

She sat for a moment with the thought of the ground—the feel of soil, the smell of the air, the return to gravity, all so much earlier than she had planned. Then, despite herself, she thought of other things that the ground held—the things at a particular spot that could easily be seen when the station flew by at a particular point in its orbits. She dismissed that image, but it swam right back. She tried again, but it returned again, so she decided to let it stay where it was, turning it this way and that, considering its various angles and implications. The sorrow she had felt just moments ago at the idea of having to bid farewell to the station had been misplaced—a little trick her mind had played to keep her from embracing what she knew she had to do. She had already contemplated it well; she just wished she didn't have to do it so soon. But she couldn't control the timing; she could control only the doing, and she knew what that doing called for.

Wordlessly, then, she punched open her seat restraints, floated back up, opened the Soyuz hatch and then the module hatch, and drifted back into the station. Zhirov, who had been trading coordinates and entry angles with the ground, looked up with a start.

"Walli!" he said. "What are you doing?"

"I have something to tend to, Vasily."

"It can keep."

"It can't keep."

"What is it, then?"

"I left the bathtub running."

"*Ne shutítye!*" Zhirov snapped. *No jokes.*

"*Ne shutítye*, Vasily," Beckwith responded seriously. "*Ne shutítye*, but I am not leaving."

"What do you mean, you're 'not leaving'?"

"I'm not leaving."

"You cannot stay."

"I can."

"You must come home."

Beckwith shook her head no. "I won't come home."

"Walli . . ."

"No." She stopped and chose her words. "I would prefer not to," she said.

It was an expression that had settled into her brain years ago—a turn of phrase used by a bookworm friend in high school who'd picked up so much of her language from literature. The friendship had long ago ended, but the phrase was something of a parting gift that Beckwith would employ herself when the situation seemed to call for it. She always thought it had a gracious quality to it—and a cunning one too. The conditional tense—that deferential "would"—suggested that she might be willing to change her mind if this or that circumstance were different or this or that condition were met. But the circumstances were unlikely to change, and while she certainly had her conditions, no one was likely to meet them. So her return to Earth was really out of the question.

Zhirov looked at her wonderingly and changed his tone. "Walli," he said, patting Beckwith's empty seat. "Be a good cabbage and come inside."

Beckwith laughed, despite the circumstances. "I can't, Vasily. I know I must come with you, but I won't." She shifted her glance to Lebedev. "And you can't wait for me to change my mind."

"This is not something you can do, Walli," Vasily said.

"It's not something I *can't* do, Vasily. I'm Navy. You're Navy. It's honor; there's no decision to be made in that."

A silence followed. Zhirov held Beckwith's eyes fast and read something in them—sorrow and anger and implacable resolve. And then he understood. Three nights earlier, he'd sensed something amiss in his station hours before the crew's usual wake-up time and drifted from his sleep pod to find Beckwith staring out a window when the station was over that same Earthly spot that was on her mind this morning.

"It's a bad business, Walli," Zhirov had said quietly, startling

Beckwith as he floated up behind her. "But it's their business, not yours." He'd peered outside and down toward the ground, following Beckwith's gaze. "*Their* business," he'd repeated, looking back at her.

Beckwith had nodded. "All right, Vasily," she'd said. But she had not meant it, and he had known she'd not meant it. What Beckwith was doing now, he realized, should have come as no surprise to him at all. At that moment, they both jumped as Moscow hailed the ship.

"Station, Moscow. Please provide update on power-down."

Zhirov, still not taking his eyes from Beckwith, keyed open his mic. "Station is powered down. Commander and Flight Engineer One have ingressed spacecraft."

"And Flight Engineer Two?" the ground asked.

"Flight Engineer Two has not ingressed."

"Why?"

Zhirov almost—*almost*—smiled. "She would . . . prefer not to."

"Say again, station."

"Flight Engineer Two would prefer not to ingress."

"What is her reason?" Moscow asked.

"She did not tell me."

"Does she have a reason?"

Now Beckwith keyed open her own mic. "I do, Moscow."

"What is the reason?"

"I will explain that later. But right now Flight Engineer One is injured and needs a hospital."

"Lieutenant Commander Beckwith," Moscow said, the mention of military rank an apparent attempt to invoke military obedience, "this is a violation of flight rules."

"Yes, it is."

"You will never fly again."

"I suspect I won't."

There was a muttering at the end of the line, and another voice, an unmistakably American one, broke in. "Walli," the voice said, "Flight Supervisor Copper speaking."

Copper was Lance Copper, one of the NASA observers in Moscow's Mission Control. He had always been addressed simply as Lance, but from the moment he arrived in Russia, he began going by his flight supervisor title. In a place where he had no actual authority, the label seemed his talisman. Beckwith had disliked the man from the moment she met him.

"Beckwith here," Walli said.

"Please ingress the spacecraft, Walli."

"No."

"You are ordered to ingress the spacecraft, Walli."

"I would prefer not to."

"You will please do as you are told."

"I should do so, but I will not."

Another forty-five minutes elapsed—an excruciating forty-five minutes for the suffering Lebedev—as the station sailed into the half of its orbit that Mission Control in Houston oversaw. Flight directors came on the line, deputy administrators came on the line, the NASA administrator himself came on the line—beseeching, ordering, threatening in turn.

To each, Beckwith made her decision—her preference—clear. She spoke crisply, hurriedly, aware that every minute the Soyuz lingered in place was another minute of suffering for Lebedev. At last, Zhirov ended the argument.

"The conversation is over now," he told Houston, aware that Moscow was listening in. "The spacecraft is leaving."

Wordlessly, Beckwith nodded her thanks to him. She leaned inside the Soyuz, gripped Lebedev's knee, and then shook Zhirov's hand. Zhirov took Beckwith's hand in both of his.

"*Beregí sebyá*, Vasily," Beckwith said. *Be safe.*

"*Bud' úmnoy*, Walli," Zhirov answered. *Be smart.*

Beckwith slammed the hatch, and before long, the Soyuz had popped free, drifted off, and headed toward the atmosphere and home. After it was gone, she glanced at her watch. In less than four hours, the station would once again sail over the spot on the ground where the trouble lay. She would be at the window to watch when it did.

CHAPTER TWO

Three days earlier

It was a few hours past sundown when Sonia Peanut waded into the jungle and made her way to the clearing about three hundred yards from the camp she shared with more than forty other people from multiple other countries. Most of them knew the reason she was venturing out tonight—and that reason was to set a fire. Fires were hardly welcome in any part of this particular jungle, but hers would be small and controlled and, to her way of thinking, poignant and important. And she had all that she needed to light it readily at hand. There was paper in the clearing and kindling in the clearing, and she would light them first and then feed the blaze logs that would burn brightly and beautifully.

The logs would be mahogany, though Sonia would never cut it fresh from trees even if she were able, which she wasn't. She did not know how to use an ax and was entirely unwilling to go anywhere near one of the ugly, roaring chain saws the loggers used. Had she ever been tempted to try, she would probably have been unable to wrestle one of them into her control. At five feet and exactly one-half inch tall—not a millimeter more, not a millimeter less—she had long looked sideways at big, heavy, dangerous machines. She suspected they regarded her the same way—eager for her to try to master them so they could wrestle her right back and throw her about. She wouldn't give them the pleasure.

Still, there was a fair amount of mahogany to be had lying around, all of it from dead trees toppled slowly by nature or violently by the loggers. She and the others in her camp had brought the logs here and stacked them in the big, open space that had been cleared by hand centuries before and kept clean ever since—swept free of leaf debris and other flammables. Fires would be lit here, but they would never spread past here.

Sonia was looking forward to lighting her fire tonight, partly because of the person she was lighting it *for* and partly because she simply liked the way mahogany burned. She swore there was something about the color of the flame that she saw nowhere else—a faint shimmer of violet so different from ordinary violet that it seemed to be straining to become another color entirely. No one else in the group she lived with could see it, and at least a few of them doubted that she could either. She didn't blame them. The color she saw looked as if it lived at the high, far, exiting edge of the visible spectrum, a final, discernible flicker of electromagnetism, just at the point of hurrying off into the X-ray and gamma ray frequencies where all energy vanished from view.

This was hardly the first night Sonia had visited the clearing. She came here every few nights, depending on the condition of the sky and the turning of the Earth. Two nights earlier, she had been here, but as soon as she arrived, a low gray-black bank of clouds appeared and then exploded into rain. She waited out the deluge under her poncho, protecting the firewood with a plastic tarp while alternating her gaze between the sky above and the smartphone in her hand, spinning and spinning a little globe on the screen a few tiny degrees of arc back and forth. But the screen degrees played out too fast and the clouds parted too slowly and she ran out of time and trudged off disappointed. Tonight, however, the air was clear and the stars were out and the sky was stunning. So she set out from camp for the clearing once more, and this time she did not come alone.

Wading through the brush with her was the boy she knew as Oli—which she pronounced with a long *o*, rhyming with "goalie." His proper name was Kauan—or Hawk in his native Guarani, the language of one of the three hundred tribes indigenous to the Amazon. It was a perfectly fine name, but even Kauan's own father called him Oli now because the boy took such extreme and giggly pleasure in it. He was just five years old, and the wind-chime laugh that sometimes came out of him when someone called him that was one his father said he'd been born with and then seemed to grow out of by the time he was four. The name brought it back.

It was Sonia who gave Kauan his Oli nickname, and it happened not long after she got her Peanut nickname. There were two Sonias in the group that arrived in the rain forest seven months ago. They were about the same age and they studied at the same medical college back home in Texas, but there was no mistaking who was who. The other Sonia was as elegantly tall as Sonia Peanut was kinetically short. One evening, back in the jungle lodge, after the day's work was done and beers had been passed around, the other members of the team took to guessing the height difference between the two. Both a tape measure and then a laser measure settled the question, putting the tall, lithe Sonia at six feet, one-half inch, not a millimeter more, not a millimeter less—or a precise and perfect foot more than the compact, kinetic Sonia. So little Sonia got the name Sonia Peanut—or Caca-huète in the French that was preferred by most of the others. Big

Sonia became Sonia the Elder—though she was actually three months younger than Sonia Peanut. The French called her Sonia Aînée, which Sonia Peanut Americanized to Annie.

Kauan always addressed Sonia Peanut by her proper name, but never quite got the pronunciation right. The *y* sound that the *i* made in "Sonia" seemed to flummox him entirely, and he accorded it its own syllable, pronouncing the name "So-*nee*-ya." All the same, he loved her Peanut and Cacahuète nicknames, and when he first heard about them, he collapsed so hard into his wind-chime laugh that he quite literally fell over, repeating the names over and over again until Sonia scooped him up and began tickling him in the ribs, calling him "Pignoli Nut"—an even smaller, tougher nut than a peanut and a name that seemed to suit him. That made him laugh so hard he had to squirm out of her arms, run a few yards away, and pee in the grass. Then he ran back, jumped into her arms again, and asked her to call him Pignoli Nut forevermore. She agreed, though she shortened it to Oli, which was fine with him since they both knew what it meant.

On the night Sonia planned to light the fire, Oli scampered and tumbled after her as she made her way to the clearing, refusing when she tried to pick him up and help him. He actually appeared to prefer his clumsy way of getting about. Even on clear ground, he tripped and rolled as much as he walked and ran; a road map of cuts and scratches always crisscrossed his skin and would likely be his lot through childhood. When the two of them made it to the clearing, Sonia turned to him and clucked her tongue in concern. He had badly scratched his arm on a low bougainvillea, and a trickle of blood was running down to his elbow. Breathing hard, obliviously happy, he did not notice.

"Oli!" Sonia said, affecting a sternness that both of them knew she did not mean, as she knelt and took him by the shoulders to look at his arm. He tried to wriggle free and she held him tighter. "*Mitā!*" she said this time, trying for a scolding "Boy!"

They communicated in a polyglot mess of English and Guarani, as well as French—because it was the language of Sonia's group—and they included some Portuguese too, because it was the language of the surrounding nation. Oli managed all of them agilely, and in this case, it was Sonia who was left staggering and stumbling behind. Once more she snapped "*Mitā!*" and this time her concern caught his attention. He stood still—or relatively so—bouncing on the balls of his feet.

"Let me see that," she said in their shared tangle of tongues, pointing at his wound.

He seemed to notice it for the first time and extended his arm. She swung her pack off her back and pulled out her first aid kit, then opened a sterile gauze pad and began dabbing at the cut.

"Does this hurt?" she asked.

"No," he answered—lying. She dabbed again, harder, at a fragment of something in the wound. He winced, and before she could ask again, he said, "No, it does not hurt."

She smiled. "OK," she said. "But I think this will, so hold still for me."

She removed an antiseptic alcohol wipe from the pack, and he began to pull away. She tugged him gently back and applied the wipe to the cut. He produced a small whimper, which he tried to cover. She bandaged the wound, then opened her arms and wiggled her fingers, signaling for a hug. He obliged.

"Brave boy," she said, and kissed him on the head.

Sonia glanced at her watch, saw she still had a few minutes before she had to light her fire, and took advantage of the moment to give Oli a fast exam. She and the rest of the group had come here to help when twin epidemics—first of influenza and then of chicken pox—had torn through the tribes in the southern regions of the Brazilian rain forest. The viruses had been carried in by loggers, who had not cut this portion of the jungle yet but passed through on their way to raze bordering lands. That was all it took for them to shed the viruses to which they were immune but which the Guarani people had never encountered before.

Sonia had just finished her four years at Baylor College of Medicine in Houston and was eyeing a specialty in pediatrics. She wanted to take a year before her internship to work for Health on Wings—properly Santé sur Ailes, or SSA—the largely volunteer French organization that sent doctors and nurses to developing nations and natural disaster sites around the world. She didn't want the Amazon; she'd never much cared for the heat and bugs and humidity of Houston and knew that the rain forest would be an order of magnitude worse. She had in fact listed it last—putting Inuit communities struggling with emerging diseases at the top of her list. She briefly considered withdrawing her application altogether when she was nonetheless assigned to a hospital camp in the Guarani tribal regions, but Sonia Annie had talked her out of quitting, and now she was deeply glad she'd heeded that advice.

There were about fifty thousand surviving members of the Guarani people scattered across the jungle, all of them living in small tribes, scraping by on jigsaw bits of their remaining ancestral land, surrounded by ranches and sugar and soya plantations. Oli's village was home to four hundred Guarani and was located just half a kilometer from the SSA hospital camp—an easy walk back and forth for the doctors and villagers, and an easy run for Oli, at least when he was healthy.

But only recently he hadn't been. The boy had contracted chicken pox first and then the flu—one of the few children in the tribe to have had the poor luck to be hit by both. Toward the end, he'd developed pneumonia and nearly slipped away from respiratory arrest. Sonia had been assigned his case and wound up staying by his bedside for much of his illness, developing a connection to the boy—and he to her—that was all wrong for the dispassion she was supposed to feel as a practitioner, but she could not help herself.

Oli had lost his mother to a cholera outbreak just over two years ago, and while that was well before Sonia knew him, she could recognize the lost and envious look on his face when he saw other children his age picked up and cuddled by their mothers. He once was a boy who had been picked up and cuddled by a mother too, and now he wasn't. That simple mortal arithmetic—going from one mama to no mama—seemed to weigh heavily on him. It weighed less so when he was with Sonia.

Then too there was Oli's way, once he got to know her, of reading her almost eerily well. His father had told him of his belief in the idea of *peteï korasõ*, or one heart—the ability of two people to know each other's moods and feelings and sometimes even thoughts, provided they cared for each other enough; it was a quality of near mind-reading he said he had shared with Oli's mother. Sonia had never experienced such a thing herself, but no sooner had Oli recovered from his illness than he seemed to have developed something of a unidirectional *peteï korasõ* with her, able to climb inside her head, even if she could not climb inside his.

"Don't be sad now," he said to her once when she was privately feeling melancholy and missing home and he ran up to her in the doctors' quarters and attempted to tug her outside to play. She was filling out patient reports on her computer at that moment, and there was nothing she could see that she was doing that signaled sadness, but he read it anyway.

"I feel fine!" he said to her another time when she picked him up for a hug but secretly planned to take the opportunity to check his temperature since she had been anxious that he looked flushed and might be coming down with the measles after an outbreak struck some of the other tribes.

Whether the *peteï korasõ* was real or not, a near mother-child bond had begun to form between Sonia and Oli, one that was all the stronger for one other reason: She very much looked the part. So many of the doctors and other outsiders were Europeans or Americans—pale, with light eyes and fair hair and sometimes dustings of freckles, which absolutely fascinated Oli. But they were clearly from somewhere else. Sonia could have been Brazilian—even Guarani. She was born of an American father and a Mexican mother, but the American part was hard to spot. Sonia's hair was black and thick, and she kept it long, though for fieldwork she braided it and then tied it up to the crown of her head in a businesslike bun. She had the kind of mocha skin that darkened a shade if someone so much as took a flash picture of her; in the jungle sun she was nearly the color of the tribespeople. Her eyes were a brown so dark that she sometimes had to squint in the mirror to make out the pupils. If there was any flicker of north-of-the-border appearance that survived, it was a faint spangling of green, her father's eye color, in the brown of her own eyes. Oli loved the bit of color and called the bright flecks "*hovyū mbyja*," green stars.

At the moment, though, the boy's mind was on the real stars. He squinted up at the sky and then turned to Sonia. "Where is it?" he asked in his language scramble.

Sonia looked up at the curtain of stars across the sky. "It's coming," she said.

He reached toward her pocket for her phone, and she took it out. By now he knew how to spin the little globe on the screen and understood what it was telling him. He looked at the image and pointed to a tiny red dot that, if you focused long enough, you could tell was slowly moving.

"Soon, right?" he asked.

"Soon, yes," she answered. "So let's hurry."

He scurried over to a pile of mahogany logs and selected a small one he could lift. She trailed after him and picked up two larger ones. They carried the logs into the clearing and dropped them there. Oli ran back and collected another small one, and Sonia hoisted another heavy one, and they tossed them on the pile they had made.

"That's all for now," she said. "It should be big enough for them to see us say hello."

She crouched down and handed Oli some newspapers and kindling, and he began tucking them in under the logs as she'd taught him. They worked in silence for a few moments; then Sonia sat up, took a box of matches from her pack, struck one, and it lit and flared. The clearing flashed briefly in the white light of potassium and sulfur, then gave way to the softer yellow given off by the tiny flame. The smell of the powders and, more subtly, of the burning pine of the little matchstick hung in the air. Sonia bent forward to light the paper, and Oli leaned toward her to watch. Then, suddenly, his head snapped up. Caught by the movement, Sonia looked at him in alarm.

His eyes were wide, his nostrils flared. An instant later she noticed the thing that had caught his attention—the sulfur, pine, and magnesium smells were gone, overwhelmed by the industrial scent of diesel on the air. It was followed immediately by the loud sound of crushing and cracking underbrush. Then a hot, bright white light slashed across the clearing.

"Run, Oli!" Sonia shouted, shaking out the match.

Oli didn't need to be told, having already jumped up and bolted for the jungle cover. Sonia tore off after him, caught up to him in half a dozen strides, snatched him up, and sprinted forward. She tore through thickets and vaulted exposed tree roots as best she could, catching her left foot on one, tumbling forward, just barely maintaining her balance and twisting her ankle in the process. She cried out in pain; Oli cried out in fear.

"Hang on!" Sonia shouted.

The sound of crashing and crunching grew louder, angrier, as if entire trees were being ripped from the soil. The stink of diesel was now everywhere—and so too were the blinding white lights, coming from all directions, washing out Sonia's vision like the midday sun. She plowed ahead blindly, caught her other foot, tumbled forward again, and twisted that ankle too, and Oli cried out once more.

"I have you!" she screamed.

It was too far a run to the Guarani village, and even if it had been closer, that was the last place Sonia and the boy would be safe. If the crashing and crunching and bright lights and diesel stink were descending on this part of the jungle, they'd likely be closing in on the village too. Instead, Sonia sped straight on, heading toward the SSA camp—offering the safety of the staff as well as of local guards hired for their protection. There were jeeps and trucks too, along with a pair of helicopters that could slip through an opening in the jungle canopy if they flew straight up for 150 feet before peeling away.

Whether there would be enough time for an escape by any of those means suddenly seemed uncertain, however, because now Sonia smelled something worse than the diesel: the smell of burning wood, and not dry wood, not firewood, but the fresh greenwood of living trees. The white light from the huge machines closing in was replaced by a dimmer but hotter yellow of fire, just as the phosphorous and magnesium light had given way to the match light little more than a minute before. Sonia could hear the blaze crackling and see its light rising all around her.

She and Oli burst at last into the clearing of the SSA camp—a cluster of tents and storage sheds and a clapboard hospital clinic. She detected the same fear here that she and the boy were feeling, but it was contained, channeled, disciplined by the drills they had all run again and again. Equipment was being thrown into trucks; staffers were climbing into jeeps and ambulances. Four pilots had leapt into the two helicopters and had already started the engines, the huge machines adding their own stink of diesel to the air and their whipping blades adding their own noise and a swirling wind. Voices were calling out everywhere in the same mix of English, Guarani, French, and Portuguese that Sonia and Oli used.

The Guarani patients who had been occupying the beds in the SSA clinic were being carried into the helicopters, and leading that part of the evacuation was Sonia Annie.

"Annie!" Sonia shouted, running to her. The noise of the helicopter blades drowned her voice and she tried again. "Annie!" she called.

That time her call did carry, and Annie looked at her and waved her away.

"Get back, get back!" she shouted, pointing Sonia to one of the helicopters. "Get on! You have the boy!"

"You need help!" Sonia shouted, trying to break Oli's death grip on her so she could get him aboard the helicopter, but unable to loosen it without hurting him. Nonetheless, she continued running toward the clinic building and Annie screamed out—her eyes blazing furiously.

"Don't!" Annie ordered. "Go!"

She pointed a commanding finger at the helicopter and then a warning one at the clinic, and Sonia could see that its jungle-facing side had caught some embers and was beginning to blaze. There was the smell of burning pine again—the fire feeding on the wooden planks from which the clinic was built, with the convection caused by the rising heat and the wash of the blades feeding it fresh oxygen. There were more patients and staffers inside, and Annie and two other medics plunged in to help them.

"No!" Sonia screamed. "No, no, no!"

She made one last attempt to break for the clinic, but now one of the guards grabbed her around the waist and hoisted her off the ground. He was at least a foot taller than she—a full Annie foot—and far stronger.

Sonia kicked and cursed, but it availed her nothing as the man tossed her and Oli—literally, bodily—into the open side of one of the helicopters and slammed its door shut. He banged twice on the side, and the machine lifted itself off the ground and rose quickly through the canopy. Sonia lunged toward the window and looked down in time to see the clinic building—and the people inside, and the entire SSA camp—being consumed by flames.

She let out a wail—a terrible soul-sick sound—and collapsed to the floor. Oli jumped atop her, sobbing, and she tried to gather him in.

At that moment, she felt her phone—which rarely rang in the jungle, but did when it was within reach of a satellite antenna, which the helicopter surely had—vibrating insistently in her pocket. She groped for it, pulled it out, nearly dropped it, then caught it and jabbed a finger at the screen.

Through the earpiece, she could hear a long hiss, a distinctive hiss—exceedingly distant, practically alien, a hiss from far above her. Finally a voice cut through.

"Sonia!" it said, equal parts a command and a plea.

"Mama!" Sonia answered.

CHAPTER THREE

August 21

No one in Moscow Mission Control cared for the sight of Walli Beck-with's face in the moments after she announced her intention not to return to Earth. She had made a wreck of what had started out as a reasonably routine day, and she would likely make a wreck of a lot more days to come. It was almost too much to ask for the controllers to have to endure a picture of her face, four or five times as big as life, gazing down at them from the giant control screen at the front of the room.

It was certainly a nice enough picture: Her dark hair was cropped short as she always wore it in space. Her smile was the one the NASA press office liked to describe as "winning," even after she pointed out to them that the male astronauts were never expected to have any particular kind of smile as long as they could manage at least a simulation of one for the camera. Either way, it really was a singularly infectious smile—one that looked as if she were barely holding back a laugh that any moment was going to slip the traces and break free.

At any other time, it would be a pleasant thing to see, but today the smile was entirely wrong for the mood in the room. Still, the picture was part of the protocol, and the protocol would be followed no matter what.

Ever since the Soviet Union fell and the Russian Federation rose, Roscosmos had done its best to follow NASA's practice of courting the attention of the media, and Moscow Mission Control was helpful in that effort. The big auditorium looked less like a technological nerve center than a grand concert hall—its walls and consoles paneled in dark wood, with plush red theater seats installed in a balcony, affording a view of the complete sweep of the floor below.

In the Soviet era, those seats were reserved for party officials; these days the seats were principally used by the press and the families of the cosmonauts, who would visit the control center for launchings and landings and important events like the docking of a Progress vehicle.

As long as the reporters would be there, Roscosmos didn't want to lose the chance to advertise its work, so while the middle two quadrants of the viewing screen were always filled with a map of the Earth, the orbital track of the station, and streams of relevant data, the left quadrant would be taken up by a photo of the current crew, posing in their spacesuits without their helmets. The right-hand quadrant would list all of the experiments that were taking place aboard the station, highlighting the promise the work held for the betterment of humankind.

Today, the right-hand quadrant, where the experiments were listed, was still fine, but the moment Vasily Zhirov and Yulian Lebedev evacuated the station and the American girl took control, the crew picture became awkward. You could hardly display a three-person crew when two of them were injured and on the way home and only a mutineer remained behind.

"Take that down!" the flight director barked as he stood at his console in the center of the room, pointing at the picture.

Immediately, the left quadrant of the screen went black and the flight director sat down, mollified. A moment later, a much calmer voice filled the controllers' headsets.

"Put it back up," the voice said, from an observer's console at the back of the room. "The girl only."

No one in the control center needed to turn around to know that the speaker was Gennady Bazanov, the director of flight operations. Bazanov's age was a mystery. He had joined Roscosmos as a young man in 1961, the same year Yuri Gagarin became the first person in space. Some said he was a high school student at the time, the son of a party apparatchik, serving as an errand boy while hoping to study engineering. Some said he was actually a freshly graduated engineer. The difference meant he was now anywhere from his late seventies to his mid-eighties. Either way, he was still here today, neither looking nor acting whatever his age was. If Bazanov gave an order, it would be obeyed.

Inside of a minute, the crew picture reappeared, this time re-framed to show Beckwith only. The image of her was even bigger now, expanded to fill the screen; Zhirov's shoulder was still visible to her right. Her smile was as it had been before.

"It stays," said Bazanov, "until she comes home."

There was an audible grumbling among several of the controllers. Bazanov frowned and keyed open his mic again.

"Boys and girls," he began. Long ago he would address what were then the all-male controllers as "comrades." By the time the Soviet Union fell and that honorific no longer applied, he was already among the oldest people in the control room and there were just as many women at the consoles as there were men. So he changed his form of address to something that would stress his near-paternal seniority.

"Boys and girls, we are flying a mission today, nothing more. We will ensure that any cosmonaut or astronaut under our care returns to the Earth safely. Is that understood?"

The controllers craned around, looked at him, and gave him a respectful nod. He nodded in return, then switched to a channel that connected only with ranking Roscosmos officials and the three most senior NASA flight supervisors, all of them seated in the back of the room. When he spoke, he did so far more crisply.

"Join me in the teleconference room," he said. "We will speak to the Americans." He said no more, rose, and exited, and the other officials followed.

.   .   .

In Mission Control in Houston, the mood was little better than it was in Moscow. As in Russia, several members of the space agency brass had gathered in the control center to observe the docking, and as in Russia, many more arrived the moment the morning's crises began to unfold. But unlike the Russian officials, the Americans in the control room were not free to leave.

There had never been a set of developments quite like today's in the long history of NASA. There had been emergencies and mission aborts but never an act of rank criminality. To the flight director on duty, dramatic circumstances called for dramatic steps. As soon as Beckwith seized the station, he made a call that in quiet moments, when he was all by himself and could let his imagination wander, he'd often dreamed of making.

"Go to battle short," he barked, with precisely the tone of command he'd practiced in his head. He nearly smiled at the sound of it.

"Battle short" was an order given during the old Apollo program, when a spacecraft was about to disappear behind the moon for the first time or, more dramatically, to land on the moon. The lives of the astronauts depended on the exercise being conducted with exquisite precision, so the doors to the control room would be locked until the procedure had been completed. What's more, all of the circuit breakers that powered the control center would be frozen in their *on* position. There would be no blown fuses, no flipped circuits to black out the control room at the worst possible moment.

But while battle short was familiar to the old Apollo teams, it was entirely alien to the modern-day controllers, and the flight director's call was met not with quick compliance but with confusion.

"Uh, say again, flight?" several controllers asked more or less at once.

"Battle short," he repeated unhelpfully, then gave up and spelled it out. "Lock it up. Doors and breakers."

With that, the memory of the Mission Control security team was jogged. The room was locked, and for a while it all seemed new and bracing, until it started to seem silly, not to mention uncomfortable. The building's restrooms were located outside of Mission Control proper, and while back in the Apollo days you usually knew when the critical maneuvers were coming and could take care of matters before the battle short was called, this morning it had come as a complete surprise.

After a while there was a lot of fidgeting going on at the consoles, and it came as something of a reprieve when Moscow called, asking for a teleconference. That would require that the NASA brass be freed from the lockdown—and everyone else too.

"All clear," the flight director announced with disappointment in his voice. "Release doors and breakers."

The senior officials half walked, half ran from Mission Control, made whatever comfort stops they needed, and then gathered one floor above in the teleconference room, where the main screen was already receiving a test signal from Moscow. A second, smaller screen was receiving a feed from Washington, where the NASA administrator, Joe Star, would be joining the conference from the agency's headquarters.

Star was new to the job, appointed just a year and a half before, when the incoming president had been inaugurated. He had no background in astronautics or aeronautics. He had, instead, made his reputation and fortune in the cattle and meatpacking industry, and he had a keen eye for business—the kind of eye the new president thought the space agency needed. Plus, he was a generous donor to the party, and the president leaned on him hard to accept the NASA posting. Plus, there was that name.

"You're going to be an astronaut one day," his friends and relatives had said and said and said again when he was growing up. Then, when it became clear his career was not going in that direction at all, the refrain had changed. "You should run NASA one day," they'd say. And now he did.

The officials in Houston arrived in the room and took their seats, and the screens flickered to life. From Moscow, the scene was of a similar conference table, with Bazanov at the head, Roscosmos officials occupying most of the seats closest to him, and the three ranking NASA observers seated the farthest away. In Washington, Star sat alone at a conference table. He did not care for the look of things—Bazanov flanked by his team, while he sat by himself. He did not care for the unspoken imbalance in space power either.

The Americans may have led the construction of the space station, but at the moment, the Russians' Soyuz was the only way to get there and back. Just recently two private companies—the aerospace giant Arcadia, based in Seattle, and the upstart CelestiX, out of Los Angeles—had begun flying crews to and from the station. But Arcadia had been grounded for months by a labor dispute and CelestiX had just suffered an explosion of a rocket on the launchpad—an accident that cost no lives but ate a $1.8 billion Saudi Arabian Mars probe. The company was certainly not going to be permitted to fly crew until it sorted out the cause of the accident. The Russians thus had the whip hand as the only ride in town—and the only way to fetch Walli Beckwith home.

Star began the teleconference the way international protocol demanded he begin it, with an apology on behalf of his country. But straight from the gate he bungled it.

"I would like to open by saying to our Soviet friends—" He caught himself and stopped. "To our Russian friends . . ."

Even before the Russian translation of what Star had said was complete, there was no missing the problematic word. Bazanov visibly winced. So too did Lance Copper, the head of the NASA team in Moscow.

Star pressed on. "We deeply apologize for the behavior of our astronaut. We do not know why she took the actions she did this morning. We are looking into it, questioning her friends, her family, her colleagues. And we will be talking to her."

Bazanov stayed silent, listening to the translation and at the end simply nodding—a bit too regally for Star's liking, but never mind.

"Her behavior is perhaps criminal?" Bazanov asked, in English.

That surprised Star. It was entirely true that Beckwith had probably broken a whole raft of international laws, but opening with a diplomatic club like that seemed excessive. Bazanov, however, had grown up in the old system, and showing the club first was the way business was conducted. Once you'd done that, you could put it away since the room now knew you had it at hand. He went on more amiably.

"But it's much too early to talk about punishment, and with a bit of good fortune we never need to discuss it," he said, now speaking in Russian. "Is the girl . . . sick?" That was how the American translator repeated it, but Bazanov had actually chosen the word "*nezdoróvaya*," which was the somewhat softer-sounding Russian for "unwell."

"Sick?" Star asked.

"Crazy, a lunatic," Bazanov said. *Psikh, sumasshédshaya.* Never mind the decorousness.

"Not that our medical teams detected, no," Star answered. "Dr. Boysen?" he asked, directing his question to Charlene Boysen, the space agency's lead flight surgeon. She was in Houston, he was in Washington, but he inclined his head at precisely the proper angle so that his image on the screen was looking directly at her. Star might not know much about astronautics, but he had participated in enough cattle-industry conference calls to know how to play the proper cameras and make the proper eye contact. Boysen was prepared and had Beckwith's medical file in front of her.

"There is nothing in our records that indicates any psychological imbalance," she said. "Lieutenant Commander Beckwith performed exceptionally well during her five years of aircraft carrier duty and on both of her previous spaceflights. She had performed equally well on this flight too."

"Until this morning," Bazanov said dourly.

"Until this morning," Boysen conceded.

"Perhaps then she needed a man," Bazanov said.

"I beg your pardon?" Boysen answered, not pleasantly.

"I beg your pardon," Star echoed, but much more congenially, even inquisitively. He flashed another well-placed glance—this one more of caution—directly at the flight surgeon.

"We have our submarine rule," Bazanov said with a shrug. "You do not."

Star was appeased. The old Soviets never put a naval officer in command of a nuclear submarine unless he was married and, preferably, had children. A man with so much military authority, in control of an invisible vessel with unimaginable destructive power, could easily go rogue. Best he had a family at home that would suffer for his mistake. The Russians continued to apply the rule to all naval commanders and to their cosmonauts too; the Americans never had. Beckwith was not married, had never been married, and had no children, as her NASA biography clearly would have revealed to the Russians.

"Mr. Director," Star said, "NASA has flown unmarried astronauts for years without a problem. We flew them to the moon in fact."

The mention of the moon was tactical. Americans went there; the Russians didn't. In the right circumstances it paid to remind them of that.

"And you have flown many married astronauts too," Bazanov mused, almost as if he were puzzling out a problem.

"Yes . . ." Star said.

"Which kind of astronaut stole the spacecraft?"

Star frowned. Bazanov smiled. He glanced down at a sheaf of papers in front of him.

"The question, of course, is why Lieutenant Commander Belka 'Walli' Beckwith did what she did this morning," Bazanov said. He read Beckwith's full name and title from the top sheet of paper—including her proper first name. It was a Kabuki signal that he was working from an official dossier on Beckwith that Russian intelligence had, in just the past hour, made available to him.

"We do not know her reasons," Star admitted. "As I said, the space agency and other government officials are investigating it even as we speak."

Bazanov said nothing for a moment and glanced back at his papers. He turned to the second page and then looked back up.

"Is it this business of the Consolidation, do you think?" he said.

"It has nothing to do with the Consolidation," Star said immediately.

"Our research shows she has been outspoken on this issue. She mentioned it in speeches and in interviews and to you as well, Mr. Administrator."

Star was struck. Beckwith had indeed spoken to him about the Consolidation, but the conversation had been a private one. Still, in the world of spycraft, both sides had ways of knowing things they had no business knowing, and this was just one more example of that dark art. Star sidestepped the matter.

"People all around the world have been outspoken on this issue," he answered.

"People all around the world did not have a space station at their disposal," Bazanov said.

He turned his hands palms up as if out of ideas. Star said nothing for a second or two, but in that brief silence he said more than he wanted to say.

· · ·

It was quieter than it ought to have been aboard Walli Beckwith's space station. The pumps and fans and whirring computers were audible in the background as they always were—the soundtrack of the station that never fell silent. But the other sounds—the bumping of human occupants, the chatter among them—were entirely gone. That was to be expected. What Beckwith hadn't anticipated was a similar, near-total silence from the ground. Nobody, it seemed, wanted to talk to her.

There was little inquiry from Houston into the state of her ear, no confirmation from Moscow of Zhirov's and Lebedev's safe landing—though if they had had a problem, she knew the ground would have told her. Beckwith could understand the ground's pique, but outlaw or not, she was an injured astronaut completely alone aboard a damaged ship. Both the cable and broadcast networks were surely reporting the story by now, along with NASA TV, which streamed mostly on its website and dared not go dark today. With so many people following the mission, a little buck-up banter between the astronaut and the ground would be good for appearances. But both Houston and Moscow were maintaining a chilly distance, breaking the silence only when mission rules absolutely demanded it.

"Comm check, station," the capsule communicator, or Capcom, in Houston called, obeying a mission rule that required regular voice confirmation at least once an hour. The link was firm and the line was clear.

"Reading you five-by," Beckwith responded.

"Crew status, please."

"Crew is stable," Beckwith said. She rolled her eyes at the formality of the question, but she echoed the third-person construction anyway.

"Copy," was the only reply. Beckwith knew the voice as well as she'd ever known any voice in her life, but something was off about it today—its flatness, its tonelessness.

"That really you, Jasper?" she asked.

"Affirmative, station," came the clipped response.

Jasper was Lee Jasper, an astronaut who entered NASA in the class directly after Beckwith's and was easily as agreeable a man as had ever been to space. He was deeply proud of his Southern heritage, and when someone would ask him where he was born, he'd simply say, "South, Deep South. Go to the toe of Louisiana and keep going."

The answer made no sense, both since that would put his birthplace in the Gulf of Mexico and because a simple check of his NASA bio showed he was really born in Greensboro, North Carolina—in the northern part of what wasn't even the southern Carolina. But Jasper was so pleasant a fellow that nobody ever thought to question his harmless Dixie fib.

He and Beckwith had met at the Paris Air Show when they were both flying military jets—she for the Navy, he for the Air Force. They had drinks on their first date, dinner on their second, and wound up sleeping together on their third through eleventh. Jasper was equal parts gentleman and wild man in bed, which was what Beckwith looked for in a man. The key was how that man balanced those two qualities—and Jasper balanced beautifully.

Both Beckwith and Jasper, however, were eyeballing careers in space, and she worried that would be harder if she were entangled with anyone—especially another flier. So shortly before applying to NASA, she broke off the relationship.

"It's the job, Jasper," was all she could offer by way of explanation.

At the time, Beckwith was assigned to the USS *Dwight D. Eisenhower*, and Jasper, his pride stung, decided that was the real reason the romance had ended. "Nobody ever got hot thinking about Ike," he'd say to Beckwith in the years to follow. "If you'da been assigned to the *Yorktown*, we'd have three kids and a house by now."

Jasper got married, got his house, and got two of those kids, but after eight years, the marriage busted up. "It's the job, Walli," he explained when he told her what had happened.

The two of them had remained fast friends ever since. Jasper typically addressed Beckwith as "Walli Bee," seeming to feel that if everyone else called her by her one Walli nickname, he needed a warmer, longer one of his own invention. Beckwith called him by his surname in response, simply because it so seemed to capture him. Today there was none of his genial nature in evidence. He was a by-the-book pilot, and, friendship or not, he couldn't overlook the fact that there was nothing by-the-book about what Beckwith had done.

"Flight surgeon instructs you to report any problems if they develop," he said now.

"Copy that," Beckwith answered. She groped for something else to say, but Jasper spared her the effort.

"Houston out," he said. If they'd been talking on the phone, he'd have slammed down the receiver.

Beckwith floated in place for a moment, feeling extraordinarily alone—which made sense—and uncertain of herself as well, which she typically wasn't. Absently, she ran her right thumb over the inside of her left wrist, just underneath her watchband, which made her feel a bit better. That spot on that wrist was part of the reason she was here today at all.

Throughout her childhood, Beckwith had never objected to her real name, Belka. She didn't object even when she learned that it had been borrowed from a dog—something she was told just after she turned four. The fact that the eponymous Belka was a girl dog made it easier to take. Beckwith shrugged it off when she was in third grade and her classmates inevitably—and, to her way of thinking, belatedly—took to calling her "Belcha." It was a variation on her name she'd come up with years before, and she found it clever; she'd been waiting for the other children to tumble to it too.

But what Beckwith especially liked about her name was that her parents meant it as the highest possible tribute. They had met in the early 1960s when they were both finishing their doctorate degrees in engineering at Caltech—her father one of 107 men in the program and her mother the sole woman. Their goal had been to land jobs at NASA and Caltech's Jet Propulsion Laboratory in Pasadena, working to build unmanned spacecraft that would fly to the moon and the planets. They were both hired fast.

Like so many other Americans, they had fallen hard for space a few years earlier, when the Soviet Union launched Sputnik, the first satellite. But unlike most Americans, who loathed and feared the Soviets, the Drs. Beckwith openly admired the Russian space program's combination of ingenuity and pragmatism, and the extraordinary machines those twin qualities produced.

Russian missiles and spacecraft were so simple, so plug-ugly, so heedless of aesthetics and so mindful of function, that they came back around to being a strange kind of gorgeous. Let the Americans exhaust themselves building their ships out of lightweight, thin-walled metal that held together only because of some magic of welding and stress-point science. The Russians would be just as happy to hollow out a giant cannonball, put a chair and a man and a few controls inside, and fire it all off on top of the biggest missile they could dream up. That was the kind of solid engineering that transcended the vulgarity of politics.

When the Beckwiths' daughter was born, in the mid-1970s, after the Americans had won the race to the moon, they wanted to give her a name that would honor the Russian way. Valentina, the first name of the first Russian spacewoman, would have been too provocative in an era in which the Cold War was still hot. But there were always the Russian dogs, which flew to space before the people.

Russian space dogs were like Russian spacecraft—mongrels, with not a shred of pedigree, but with toughness to burn. And they had irresistible names: Laika and Strelka and Belka and Mushka and Damka and Bobik and more. They were all females too, both because they were more tractable than males and because it was easier to design space diapers for them. The Beckwiths chose the name Belka for their daughter, liking the way the first name paired up with the last name, giving the whole affair a nice alliterative bounce.

So Belka Beckwith sallied into the world, grew a bouncing confidence to go with her bouncing name, and took to engineering just like her parents had. She, however, decided to study at the Naval Academy and earn her military commission along with her diploma.

Beckwith thrived at Annapolis, graduating second in a class of 1,964 students—behind only a perfectly humorless grind of a midshipman who was promptly assigned the nickname Tube, for no other reason than it seemed ignoble and was certain to annoy him. Despite her best efforts, Beckwith could find nothing remotely interesting about Tube save for something about his breakfast, which every single day for every one of the four years they were at school included two slices of white toast, which he would, on alternating days, eat with either apricot jam, butter, or cream cheese—or sometimes entirely dry. It took Beckwith until late in her first year to notice the pattern and until early in her fourth to make sense of it.

"Tube!" she exclaimed one morning at breakfast, slapping her hand on the table and startling the other midshipmen. "It's alphabetical: apricot, butter, cream cheese, dry! *You're alphabetizing your toast!*"

Tube turned to her expressionlessly. "Yes," he said, and then turned away.

Upon graduation, Beckwith and Tube both applied to fly jets, and both were assigned to the Naval Air Station in Pensacola, Florida, for training. Tube washed out, and the last Beckwith heard, he had wound up in a policy-making office at the Pentagon. Beckwith, by contrast, certified in pretty much every jet she decided to try—and she tried an awful lot of them. She spent the next five years happily flying off the *Eisenhower*, attaining the rank of lieutenant commander in the process. Eventually, when NASA was accepting candidates for a new class of astronauts, she applied and was accepted.

In Beckwith's new role, she wanted a new name, one she'd been considering for a while. That name would be Walli, and if anyone didn't recognize straightaway why, that person didn't actually deserve an explanation.

The name, of course, was a tip of the hat to Wally Schirra; Schirra was one of the original seven astronauts and, to Beckwith's thinking, the best of the seven—the best of the five-hundred-some people who had ever gone to space for that matter. It was Schirra who flew ninety combat missions over Korea in an F-84 Thunderjet—a plane so slow and leaden that it needed nearly two miles of runway before it could hoist its bulk into the sky. The other pilots called it the

"Ground-Loving Whore," but it was Wally's whore and he adored it. Half the reason he flew so many missions was just so he could ride the thing as hard as he could and feel it ride him right back. That was the way Beckwith decided to fly her bad-boy jets, for exactly the same reason.

Schirra's innate feel for flying machines was what gave him the piloting mettle to command all three of NASA's first generation of spacecraft—the one-man Mercury, the two-man Gemini, and the three-man Apollo—making him the only astronaut to hit for that cycle.

On his final mission, in command of Apollo 7, he led what amounted to nothing short of a cosmic mutiny, tearing up the overly complicated flight plan that had been written by the NASA ground pounders and running the show his own way. He was in command of a brand-new spacecraft and would not risk the safety of his crew conducting a lot of unnecessary science when the purpose of the mission was simply to make sure the ship was fit to fly.

By every single measure of military and space program protocol, Schirra was wrong. But he was right by the more important pilot's code of making the correct call for his vessel and his men.

It was that certainty that Beckwith most admired in Schirra. During her Navy days and her first flight in space, aboard the shuttle, she carried along a small white laminated card reading "WWWD"—*What Would Wally Do?* After Schirra's death, in 2007, she tossed the card away and had the letters tattooed on the inside of her left wrist. On all of her spaceflights, the question the initials asked was always somewhere in her mind. If she could answer it when the situation called for it, she guessed she'd get along just fine. This morning, she hoped, she'd answered it right.

In the silence filling the station, Beckwith busied herself undoing the partial power-down she and Zhirov had executed before the

49

Soyuz set sail. She drifted from module to module, opening hatches, turning on lights and fans, like a vacationer returning home from a long trip. She did not even bother checking her food supplies. There was enough aboard to sustain six crew members for a minimum of ten months, and that was assuming they all ate three full meals a day. Beckwith was a light eater in space, and most of the food had a shelf life of pretty much forever. The station was similarly oversupplied with oxygen, which, with one person aboard, was similarly being underused. And most of the water on the American segment was reclaimed and recycled and for practical purposes never ran out. Beckwith could live here for years and years.

The ground, she knew, would be able to monitor all of her power-up procedures on Mission Control's environmental consoles, and could even observe her using the video cameras arrayed throughout the ship if they chose. Small red lights on each camera would indicate when it was switched on. Beckwith looked up, and for now at least, she saw no red.

When she was done with the power-up, she returned to her sleep pod to see if the storm she'd created on the ground was truly bad enough to earn the affable Jasper's ire. The sleep pods in the American segment were enclosures about the size of a phone booth with accordion doors and a cocoon-like sleeping bag tethered to a wall. Each pod had two laptop computers bungeed to the wall facing the sleeping bag. She logged onto one of the computers, opened up a browser, and prepared for the slow, dial-up-quality connection, which was the only thing possible from space to Earth. When she finally connected, her eyes widened.

"HIJACK IN SPACE," read the headline on CNN, with a smaller "Rogue astronaut seizes station" underneath.

The characteristically buttoned-up Associated Press was more reserved: "Crisis in Orbit; Station Commandeered."

The New York Times held its fire too: "Space Station Evacuated; Lone Astronaut Disobeys Orders, Remains Behind."

The *New York Post* let fly: "CARJACKED!"

But it was London's *Guardian* that was the most succinct of all: "WHY?" it read, above a picture of Beckwith taken at a preflight press conference in Baikonur. The picture happened to catch her glancing to the side in the middle of a blink, which left her looking either nuts, drunk, or shifty. She suspected they went through a lot of pictures before they found that one. Still, the newspaper's question was reasonable—and it was one she knew she'd have to answer soon.

Finally she attempted to log onto her own web page. NASA encouraged astronauts to make liberal use of social media, but Beckwith had always thought it a waste of time. Still, to keep the public affairs people happy, she had allowed a NASA intern to build her a page, which she updated only occasionally. Most days she had no more than a few dozen visitors at any one time. Today, she was inundated: More than a hundred thousand people had visited the site in the first ninety minutes after the accident. That figure was climbing, in real time, as she watched.

She scrolled a bit more, then had a thought. She opened her search engine and typed a few words into it. The results appeared, and she smiled her winning, infectious, almost-laughing smile. The phrase "I would prefer not to" was burning down the internet.

CHAPTER FOUR

The first thing on Vasily Zhirov's mind when his Soyuz spacecraft thumped down on the ground in the plains of Kazakhstan was getting back out of Kazakhstan as fast as he could. The second thing was avoiding the dumplings they were going to make him eat before he left.

Getting out of Kazakhstan fast would allow him to get to Moscow fast—and Moscow was where Zhirov needed to be. One of his crewmates was injured, another had mutinied, his space station was broken, and his mission was over—or at least Roscosmos would say it was over. But Zhirov had other ideas. He had signed on to serve for a full six months, and only seven weeks had passed since launch day. If he had to command his mission from a control room in Moscow, he would, but he still had to *get* to Moscow.

The dumplings, however, would have to come first.

Zhirov and Lebedev had hit the ground outside the city of Zhezkazgan, the southernmost point of a triangle on the Kazakh Steppe within which most returning Soyuz crews landed. Just what the welcoming city would be for any returning Soyuz depended principally on the angle of reentry and the weather on the ground. The cloud ceiling today was barely four hundred feet in Arkalyk, the western-most point of the triangle, and it was even lower in Karaganda, the easternmost point. So Zhezkazgan it was.

There were no people more enthusiastic than the Zhezkazganis when cosmonauts fell out of the sky near their city. And there was no cosmonaut who excited them more than Zhirov. By pure chance, the reentry variables had lined up to send him to the city on the last three of his space station missions, and now he was coming for a fourth.

In short order, Zhirov and Lebedev would be choppered in to the Zhezkazgan airport, where they would be greeted by a little cere-mony. There would be speeches by local officials and a presentation of Russian nesting dolls—hand-painted with the cosmonauts' like-nesses. Local girls dressed in traditional green-and-yellow costumes would stand decoratively in attendance during all of that. Then they would step forward to offer the cosmonauts trays of food—nuts and dates and especially sweet fried dumplings. It all would be pleasant enough except that people coming back from months in zero-g typi-cally have a hard enough time fighting just to stay on their feet and hold down whatever the last thing was that they'd eaten in space. The mere thought of nuts, dates, and dumplings would be enough to make them lose both battles.

All returning cosmonauts might get the local greeting, but none of them would be watched as closely as Zhirov to make sure he was feeling the local love. Even after an emergency reentry like today's, Russia—always sensitive to its delicate relations with Kazakhstan—would expect him to play the grateful hero at least briefly. Lebedev would be spared the ceremony.

Much more worrisome to Zhirov throughout the entirety of the twenty-three-minute plunge to Earth was the matter of Walli Beck-with. It preoccupied him as he felt the gravity load of the high-speed reentry and as the parachutes deployed and jerked the spacecraft violently. It was only the sudden impact in the loose scrub and hard soil—which was always tooth-rattling even with the chutes and a small burst from braking rockets to slow the fall—that pulled back his focus.

"Spacecraft is on the ground," Zhirov announced into his mic. "Recovery team, please inform us of your status."

"Eight minutes out, Vasily," came the response in Zhirov's headset from the lead helicopter. Even through the rotor noise in the background, Zhirov could recognize the voice of the recovery team commander, Sergei Rozovsky.

"Why eight?" Zhirov challenged.

He knew even as he said it that it was not a fair question. On such short notice, it had been impossible to assemble the full complement of helicopters, spotting planes, and all-terrain vehicles that usually made up a recovery crew. Eight minutes out for a shorthanded team scrambling to a touchdown site was something of an achievement.

"On our way," was all Rozovsky said in response. *Mi v pyti.*

"Understood," Zhirov said. "Thank you."

Eight minutes later, to the second by Zhirov's watch, he could hear the *whup-whup-whupping* of the chopper blades overhead and a moment later a hand banging on the side of the Soyuz. A ladder knocked against the spacecraft, and the hatch on the top of the module opened. Rozovsky's face peered down at the cosmonauts. It was a round, genial, almost jolly face, and it was the first face returning cosmonauts had seen during sixty recoveries over the past fifteen years. When Russian media would ask Rozovsky how he had endured so long in such a punishing line of work, he would typically answer, "*Mi vipolnyáem chërtovu rabótu*"—more or less, *We do the fucking job*—which is why Russian media finally stopped asking the question.

Today Rozovsky did not look jolly. He cast a practiced glance at Lebedev and his brow creased, and then he turned to Zhirov.

"How are you, Vasily?" he called down into the spacecraft.

"We are fit," Zhirov responded. "Crew is five-three."

"You reported four-two."

"I was wrong. I am unhurt, and Yulian is improved. We are five-three. Announce it please."

"I will not," Rozovsky said.

"Sergei," Zhirov said, "please do this for me."

Rozovsky paused, then nodded. "Crew is five-three!" he called over his shoulder. "Bring them out."

Rozovsky's face vanished, and more recovery officers clambered up the side of the Soyuz. They lifted Lebedev out first, handing him carefully to personnel on the ground who loaded him onto a stretcher and hurried him to a waiting helicopter.

Zhirov was next. After several months in orbit, he would usually accept the indignity of being extracted from the spacecraft, placed on a portable chair, and carried to the helicopter. But Zhirov had been aloft for just seven weeks and he'd abide no such coddling. He was lifted out, but he waved off the chair and began striding to the helicopter on his own. He lasted just four steps before the combination of gravity and the damage to his inner ear got the better of him and he staggered. He accepted the supporting arm of a recovery team aide but no more. They reached the helicopter and he climbed aboard.

By the time the one-hour flight to the Zhezkazgan airport was over, Zhirov was feeling better—a little. Lebedev was lifted from the helicopter and carried to a Roscosmos hospital plane waiting on the tarmac just a few dozen yards from the helicopter. Zhirov hopped down to the ground, and the recovery aide began steering him to the plane as well.

"This way first," Zhirov said, pointing to the airport building. He called out to the crew carrying Lebedev: "Take him aboard. I will be back. Five minutes." He hurried off with the aide at his side before he could hear any objections.

When Zhirov entered the airport building, the welcoming ceremony crowd stampeded toward him. They surrounded him in a great crush, taking his picture, shaking his hand, hugging him when they got enough room. Zhirov smiled, accepting the greetings, until security guards parted the crowd and the local officials and costumed girls were shown through.

The Zhezkazgan mayor made a short speech and presented Zhirov with the nesting doll. There had not been enough time to hand-paint one with his face, and while there was indeed a cosmonaut on the front, Zhirov could not make out who it was exactly. It resembled Neil Armstrong, the American. He beamed at the doll and thanked the mayor.

The three costumed girls then stepped forward. They smiled shy smiles. The eyes of two of them glistened with tears. Each held a tray of the sweet fried dumplings. Zhirov plucked and ate one from each tray and closed his eyes briefly as he did, with the look of a man focusing on the fineness of the flavor. When he was done, he smiled warmly at the girls—all of whose eyes were now teary—took another moment to admire his nesting doll, and then waved and turned and walked unsteadily back out the door.

When he got back to the hospital plane, he climbed aboard and took a seat next to Rozovsky. A doctor approached to examine him, but he waved her off.

"Later please," he said, and turned back to Rozovsky. "Are there assets at the airport?"

"Assets?" Rozovsky responded.

"In Moscow. Transportation."

"Yes. There will be an ambulance to take you and Yuli directly to the hospital."

"Yuli will go alone," Zhirov said. "I am going to Mission Control, and I will need a government car."

"You can't do that," Rozovsky said. "You're hurt."

"You may send the doctor with me if you want," Zhirov said. "I would also like a change of clothes, and by the time we arrive I will perhaps be able to drink tea and eat a meal."

"Be sensible, Vasily."

"I am being sensible," Zhirov said. "I am in command of a spacecraft and I have a crew member on board. I believe I know what she is trying to do, but I have no idea how she plans to do it."

With that, Zhirov closed his eyes and reclined his seat. It was nearly 1,800 miles to Moscow, and he could use the three-hour nap.

CHAPTER FIVE

August 22

The president of the United States could not quite decide on his feelings toward Walli Beckwith. She was a nuisance and a criminal, but also an opportunity and a gift. His administration had been in office for more than a year and a half now and had been awfully slow breaking from the gate. There had been few meaningful legislative achievements and no significant foreign policy deals. A small-bore national emergency—one that could not remotely be blamed on the president but could be seen as being quickly and decisively resolved by him—might be a restorative thing right about now, especially given his claimed management acumen, which had been at the heart of his campaign for the White House. It was not an empty boast.

He had come to office after one term as governor of Oklahoma, but he had achieved his greatest successes in private industry, having made his fortune in agribusiness. That was how he had come to know Joe Star and how he knew at least four of his top cabinet appointees, who worked variously in ranching, livestock trading, and meat processing. The media immediately dubbed them the Cattlemen's Cabinet, which was either a compliment or not depending on which news outlet was using the term. The president chose to take it as a tribute to his administration's rugged cowboy competence, but that would be a hard image to maintain if the cattlemen could not ride herd on a single rogue spacewoman.

The message he sent to his cabinet in a round of calls in the first hours of the emergency was thus a simple one: Settle this fast. The one person he didn't phone directly was his attorney general, outsourcing that call to one of his aides, and his reason was simple: He simply couldn't abide her. She was the one woman among the cattlemen and, in fact, had nothing to do with cattle. Instead, she was a career prosecutor—and a lethally good one, having served three terms as New York County district attorney. For her first campaign, she ran under her full name, Constance T. Polk. She had grown up in a stern family and was given a parochial school education, both of which taught her discipline, a steely integrity, and a tidy formality.

In her first term in office, she hit hard and hit fast, bringing down a whole pack of Wall Street bad guys, including one whose dodgy hedge fund had actually, theatrically, bankrupted a private orphanage. Polk was a savvy enough politician to know she had been handed about as Dickensian a story line as any DA could hope for and was not surprised when the *New York Post* soon dubbed her "Killer Connie." The *Daily News* began publishing a running tally of all the people she'd put on trial—calling them "Connie's Cons." By the time she ran for reelection, her campaign materials needed to read simply "Connie!" She won 81 percent of the vote that time and ran unopposed for her third term. There was not a defendant on the planet who liked facing off against her.

There was a lot about Polk that chafed the president—her confidence, which to him looked like cockiness; her frankness, which to him read as abrasiveness. It didn't help either that at least a few of the president's business associates had been swept up in Polk's various investigations. But there had been the predictable clamor for at least one woman in the cabinet, she was popular with voters, and his chief political adviser had lobbied hard for her, so he'd chosen her.

When he did not call her directly after Beckwith's act of space theft, she called him. When he didn't respond, she called again forty minutes later, then again thirty minutes after that. Finally he agreed to come to the phone.

"Lieutenant Commander Beckwith is breaking the law," she announced with no preamble.

"I don't doubt it," the president responded.

"She's breaking a lot of laws, actually."

"How many?"

"That will take some work to determine," Polk answered. "But they're not just American laws. A great many nations have jurisdiction in near-Earth space, and she has taken actions that may open her to criminal liability around the world."

"And?"

"And she needs to know that," Polk responded. "I would like your authority to speak to her directly."

"That's up to NASA."

"Sir, you direct NASA."

"And NASA directs the space station."

"How satisfied are you," she asked pointedly, "with how they've handled that responsibility today?"

The president sighed. This was how all of his calls with Polk seemed to go. "Connie," he said at last, "Lieutenant Commander Beckwith just stole the space station and defied direct orders to come home. I'm not sure reading her the law will make any difference."

"Sir," Polk said, "it will if I'm the one to read it to her."

. . .

On her first full day in command of the International Space Station, Beckwith decided to let herself sleep in—or at least try to. The station's workday typically began at 8:30 A.M.; crew members got up at 7:30, but Beckwith usually set the alarm on her watch for 7:00 since it always took her a bit of time to get her internal motor up to working speed. Today she treated herself to setting no alarm at all. It did her little good. She awoke at barely 6:00—which meant a longer-than-usual day and one, she suspected, with very little to do. That suspicion was confirmed.

The astronauts' daily schedule was always uploaded the night before onto tablets they could carry with them throughout the day. The sequence of experiments, maintenance chores, meals, and exercise periods was broken down into fifteen-minute increments and written out across the screen like a day's TV listings. A red indicator marched across the screen in real time. If your completed tasks kept up with or outpaced the indicator, you were having a productive day. If you fell behind, the ground would know. The lead instructor on the first day of training for Beckwith's incoming astronaut class took pains to disabuse the eager young plebes of whatever glamorous image they had of their new positions.

"Your job in space will be chasing the red line," he said. "Nothing less, and often nothing more."

Today, when Beckwith logged onto her tablet, there was no red line, no schedule, nothing.

"Houston, station," she radioed down. "I'm getting a negative reading on the activity log."

"Copy that, station," the Capcom replied.

It was not Jasper this time, which was just as well. Beckwith had been more troubled than she'd expected by his deliberate chill. But the current Capcom seemed no more warmly inclined.

"Please upload at your convenience," she said.

"Flight director has no orders for you at this time," the Capcom said. "We will forgo the day's schedule."

Beckwith frowned. Houston really did want nothing to do with her, but she was pleased to realize that that didn't rattle her. She didn't know if Zhirov believed her when she mentioned the matter of honor to him, but she had meant it. Before she ever laminated her *What Would Wally Do?* card, she had laminated the Naval Academy honor code. She couldn't help it. She loved the code. The first-year students were required to commit it to memory, and Beckwith did, but she wanted to keep the card with her all the same.

"It's eighty-five words, Beckwith," her first-year roommate had said to her. "Remember it and then forget it."

But that was the point—the sublime leanness of the eighty-five words. The code had the fat-free simplicity of a haiku. Its meaning was clear, its rules direct, but there was a certain modest poetry to it all the same: Midshipmen would do what was right, stand up for principle, "tell the truth and ensure that the truth is known"—the second "truth" a lyric force-multiplier for the first. The eighty-five words ticked off the relevant virtues with such declarative power that to Beckwith they felt less like moral goals than laws of science.

Now, with or without the red line, she knew that since she had chosen to stay at her post, she must also *tend* to her post. The schedule uploaded to the tablets every morning might have included all of the experiments and other scientific work that the crew would have to perform, but not the business of routine maintenance—which was simply an understood part of the space station workday. Air filters needed to be cleared, pumps needed to be recycled, coolant systems needed to be checked. Then too there were the five mice in the five small cages in the American Destiny lab that needed to be cared for lest they languish or die.

Beckwith loved the mice. There had been six at first, but one had not survived the transition to zero-g. She had wrapped its small body in gauze, sealed it in a plastic sample bag, and stowed it in one of the lab freezers. Had the uncrewed Progress cargo vehicle docked as planned, it would have been unloaded first, then repacked with station trash and sent on an incineration plunge through the atmosphere. Beckwith had planned to tuck the mouse inside too—affording it the dignity of a decent cremation and allowing the single ounce of organic chemicals that had been all there was to its body to return to Earth.

The other five mice adapted to weightlessness better. Some preferred to cling to the floor of the cage since that was what constituted *down* when they were on Earth. Others clung anywhere at all, as long as they could stay in one place.

And one loved to fly. He was a male—Beckwith had worked with them all long enough to tell the difference—and he would spend a fair share of every day climbing up one wall of his cage, kicking off to the opposite one, and furiously pedaling his feet in what looked to Beckwith like an attempt to pick up speed. She named the mouse Bolt. This morning, after making herself a breakfast of rehydrated eggs, a pouch of hot coffee, and one of cold juice, she started on her maintenance chores, which took just over two hours, saving the mice for last. When she had gotten them fed and changed their water, she turned to Bolt and did one thing she'd never done before: She opened the top of his cage to let him fly free.

Beckwith had no doubt what the little creature would do when offered the chance of escape, and he did just that—kicking off a side of the cage and shooting straight for the opening. In the vast space of the lab module, he had nothing within reach to stop his forward trajectory and he began his usual pedaling motion, this time backwards, as if to slow himself down. Beckwith raised an open hand in front of him and his nose bumped gently against her palm. She slowly moved her hand away and he hung motionless in space, looking left and right, up and down. Beckwith then gently tapped him on his rump, sending him drifting forward in the direction of the lab module's small porthole. The window was on the bottom side of the station and was at that moment filled with the sight of the eastern edge of the Mediterranean Sea. Beckwith stopped Bolt's motion again, and then the two of them looked down at the planet.

"Beautiful, isn't it?" she said.

The mouse did not respond.

"It's the Mediterranean," she added.

The mouse did not respond.

A moment later, both of them jumped as a voice from the ground cut through the silence.

"Station, Houston."

"Copy," Beckwith said, sounding cross at the interruption.

"Please stand by at 2100 hours station time for an audio conference with Washington."

That would be 9:00 P.M. station time and 5:00 P.M. Washington time, but at the moment, it was barely 11:45 in the morning aboard the station, or 7:45 A.M. on the East Coast of the United States.

"That's still more than nine hours away, Houston."

"Yes, but Washington requested that you be informed now."

"Why?"

"To organize your thoughts," the Capcom responded. "That's how it was put—'to organize her thoughts.'" Before Beckwith could ask, the Capcom spared her the trouble. "They didn't say any more than that."

The line fell silent and Beckwith and Bolt turned back to the window, but for Beckwith the mood was broken. The mouse continued to watch as the Mediterranean Sea slid by below.

.　.　.

Within an hour of arriving in the Mercado field hospital in eastern Bolivia on the night of the fire, three days before Beckwith commandeered the space station, Sonia Peanut kicked a wall and broke a toe. She had already been hobbling on her two twisted ankles, and now a new blaze of pain shot through the small bones of her right foot. She was rearing back for a second kick when a nurse got hold of her and wrestled her under something close to control.

"Those bastards!" Sonia spat, looking in the general direction of the entire nation of Brazil.

The nurse agreed that they were bastards.

"I'll make them pay!" Sonia added.

The nurse agreed that Sonia surely would.

Sonia was unappeased, kicking wildly at nothing at all, and another nurse appeared and convinced her that perhaps a half milligram of a little tablet that looked like Xanax or Valium or some kind of benzodiazepine would make her feel better. Sonia refused, but the nurses pressed, and as much to make them go away as anything else she agreed to swallow it. The minimal dose of the mild pill hit her empty stomach and small frame almost immediately, and her mood changed from a molten rage to an exhausted grief. She dropped into a chair with her face in her hands, rocking and sobbing, and the two nurses looked at each other, wondering if the little pill had really been a good idea, then deciding that it probably was because the new girl at least had quieted down and wasn't breaking any more bones. They removed her shoe and taped her toes. The girl barely noticed, lost in her sorrow.

The helicopter ride from the Guarani lands across the Bolivian border and to the eastern edge of the Mercado National Park had taken close to two hours—and they had been grueling hours. The hospital was a designated SSA safe zone—close enough to the violence in Brazil to make it possible to get back and forth more or less easily, but located on the other side of an international boundary line, which provided legal if not always actual protection. There were seven patients from the clinic hospital aboard the two helicopters—three with tuberculosis, three with pneumonia, and one with an unknown infection that had nearly killed him twice. None of them should have been moved, all of them required constant attention, and at least a few had likely lost family members who had come to the clinic to visit them that evening and become caught in the fire before they could escape. There had been twelve patients in the clinic beds before the blaze reached the wooden building. The five not aboard the helicopters had probably died as well.

Sonia checked her phone every ten minutes during the flight. On nights like tonight, the SSA posted casualty lists quickly, the better to keep scarce doctors from searching for survivors where there were none to find, freeing them up to get to the places where they could do some good. The camp had burned fast, but the list was coming slowly, and Sonia felt her head go light and her stomach turn over as she concluded—rightly, she was convinced—that it was simply taking longer to find and identify all of the bodies. The fire had surely been intended not just for the SSA hospital but also for the nearby Guarani tribal lands, which meant a great many people would have lost their homeland and at least a few could have lost their lives. She glanced about for a bucket in case she needed to vomit and found one just behind the pilots' seats; the mere fact that it was there helped her collect herself. She spent the rest of the flight comforting Oli, who alternately sobbed and stared blankly forward.

Before he and Sonia set out for the campfire site that night, Oli's father had left the tribal village to visit his mother—Oli's grandmother—in the clinic hospital half a kilometer distant. She had been the last in the tribal group to have contracted the chicken pox infection that was stubbornly hanging on in the jungle, and had been having a hard time shaking it. Both Sonia and Oli knew that his grandmother and father had probably been in the building when the fire broke out. They had no way of knowing if either one of them had escaped.

When they at last arrived at the Mercado hospital in Bolivia, it was to a storm of activity. There had been three other fires in three other tribal reserves in the southern jungle that night, and five other SSA helicopters had already arrived and were unloading patients and doctors. Sonia hopped down from the helicopter with Oli in her arms and badly underestimated how far the distance was to the ground. That plus the extra forty-five pounds that was the boy caused her to hit with a thud, and her ankles twisted yet again.

"Mother*fucker!*" she barked.

The shout startled Oli and also drew the attention of a guard who trotted over with his gun slung over his shoulder. He asked Sonia her name and she told him; he asked Oli's name and she gave him that too, the full and formal Kauan.

"*¿Es su hijo?*" he asked in Spanish. *Is he your son?*

"No," Sonia answered truthfully.

"*Entonces dámelo.*" *Then give him to me,* the man said.

Sonia didn't quite follow his Spanish, especially over the roar of the helicopter blades, and neither did Oli, but they both understood when he reached for the boy and tried to grab him from her arms.

He immediately began to wail and thrash, and Sonia clutched him tight.

"Take your hands off him!" she screamed.

"*Si no es suyo . . .*" he began to explain. *If he isn't yours . . .*

"Take your hands off him!" Sonia repeated.

At that moment, from about ten yards away, Sonia heard someone shouting, "Stop, stop, stop!" She turned, and a woman she faintly recognized from the first time she was here—seven months ago, at the beginning of her rotation when she had arrived for orientation—was sprinting toward them. She was a third-year resident—or maybe a second—and she was training in surgery. Her name was Myra—or maybe Mia. The woman came skidding to a stop in front of them and looked squarely at the guard.

"She's right; don't touch the boy," she said. "He's my son."

Sonia looked at her wide-eyed. "He is *not* your—" But Myra or Mia cut her off.

"He's my son," she repeated emphatically, looking fixedly at Sonia, who was too stunned to respond. "Or," the woman named Myra or Mia went on, "he's hers." She pointed to a doctor hurrying by and shouted out to her.

"Gisele!" she called. "Is this your son?" She inclined her head to Oli. The woman smiled.

"Yes. I'm glad he made it." Then she hurried off.

Mia or Myra then looked squarely at Sonia and spoke very deliberately. "Are you sure this boy is not yours too?" Sonia knew what answer she was supposed to give, though she had no idea why she was supposed to give it. But she did so all the same.

"No, I'm not sure," she said. "Actually, he *is* my son."

Mia or Myra then turned to the guard and spoke in high-speed Spanish that left Sonia entirely behind. The guard looked piqued, then confused, then just plain exhausted.

"*¡Pues, bueno!*" he snapped, not sounding as if he thought anything was *bueno* at all. He stalked off with a parting glare at Sonia, who was utterly flummoxed.

"It's fine now," the other woman said.

"What just happened?"

"Children who come in without family are separated and processed individually. If an adult does claim to be the parent but doesn't have the proper documents—and no one here does—the detaining guard must take an affidavit. That lasts two hours. If there are two people making a claim, it's two more hours—and so on." She shrugged. "He's supposed to be off duty in fifteen minutes."

Sonia smiled a deeply grateful smile. "Thank you," was all she could say, and then added a tentative, "Myra."

"Mia," the woman said. Sonia nodded an apology and tried to take a step forward, but her right ankle gave way and she bent and grabbed it in pain. "Steady," Mia said, taking her elbow and standing her back up. "Let's go inside."

As they made their halting way forward, Sonia could at last look around, and was startled at the scale of what she saw. When she had been here before, the Mercado field hospital was already big—an enclosed compound with a dozen patient tents, one free-standing clinic, and one surgical building. Now it had at least quadrupled in size, stretching across an area that was the equivalent of two football fields. Sonia counted nine buildings, with a tenth under construction, and could only guess at the number of tents. Electrical cables snaked across the grounds, leading to innumerable generators; sanitation trucks, pumping in fresh water and pumping out waste, were parked at various spots outside the perimeter.

The boundaries of the camp had changed too. The first time Sonia was here, they had been marked by nothing more than stakes and wire forming a makeshift fence. Now that had been replaced by a cinder-block wall perhaps seven feet high, completely surrounding the nearly two acres of land with only one opening big enough for people and small vehicles to pass through. The temporary camp was becoming very much a permanent one.

"When did all this happen?" Sonia asked, gesturing generally at the entire complex.

"Just after the Consolidation began," Mia responded. "It was . . . necessary." Sonia nodded tightly.

The overall atmosphere within the walls was faintly bazaar-like, with people swarming everywhere, about a third of them fieldworkers and two-thirds forest people—refugees and patients. Sonia could loosely understand Guarani when she heard it spoken, as well as a scattering of Yanomami words, and that was it. But if she didn't know all the other local languages, she could at least pick out some of their differences—in tones and inflections and distinctive glottal stops. There were at least three hundred tribes and three hundred languages across the more than one million people who lived in the jungle. They all seemed to be represented here.

Sonia looked down at Oli to see if he was disturbed by all of the activity, but he had in fact—and at last—fallen asleep. She freed up one of her arms, held him tightly with the other, and reached into her pocket for her phone. The casualty list had still not posted. Mia saw and understood.

"It'll come," she said.

At last they reached a building with a sign that said, "Pédiatrie, Pediatrics, Pediatria." There were two dozen beds inside, about twenty of which were filled. Some of the children were sleeping, some were simply staring, all were utterly silent. Oli breathed steadily and peacefully in Sonia's arms.

"May I take him?" Mia whispered.

"Yes," Sonia responded, matching Mia's tone. She passed the boy off, and Mia noticed the crisscross of scratches on his arms and legs. She looked at Sonia questioningly. Sonia shrugged. "Normal for him," she whispered with a weak laugh.

Mia passed Oli to another doctor, who took him to an examining table, lightly swabbed his scratches, and took his vitals. Oli remained asleep, and Mia caught Sonia's eye and nodded to one of the empty beds, a corner of its blanket already turned back, with a little pink plush toy next to the small pillow; it looked like a pig. The room was softly lit, and a fan in each of its corners kept it cool. Sonia smiled. Mia walked her to the door and pointed to the general infirmary building only about ten yards away.

"Get those ankles looked at. Can you make it on your own?" Mia asked.

Sonia nodded. "Come get me when he wakes up," she said.

Mia agreed, and Sonia hobbled to the infirmary. As soon as she entered, a nurse saw her struggling and hurried over to help her, but at that moment, Sonia's phone vibrated and she grabbed it with a shaking hand. It was the casualty list. She punched the icon on her screen, and the little color wheel spun and spun and spun some more as it slowly fetched the file. At last it opened.

Fifteen people had died in the clinic tonight, ten of them Guarani, five of them doctors and staffers. Annie was among the dead. So was Oli's grandmother. So was Oli's father. The entire population of the Guarani village had been scattered into the jungle.

It was then that Sonia kicked the wall and broke her toe, and it was then that the nurses gathered her in and gave her the pill and tended her foot. After all that was done—and after Sonia had rocked and cried—she reached for her phone one more time and pecked out an email, blinking at it through a blur of tears. Within four minutes of her sending it, the phone rang. She picked it up and once again heard the hiss from far, far away. When it cleared, the voice came through.

"It's Mama," the voice said. "Talk to me." And Sonia did.

.   .   .

After that long call on her first night in the Mercado camp, Sonia slept little, curling up as best she could in a canvas chair next to Oli's small bed and drifting in and out of a restless doze. Oli, on the other hand, slept the sleep of someone who had no capacity left to do anything *but* sleep—lying on his back, his left arm slung over the side of his little bed, his head mostly off his pillow. It was as if he had been dropped from the ceiling while sound asleep and simply maintained whatever position his loose limbs and lolling head had assumed on the bounce.

When he at last woke up the next morning, the first thing he saw was Sonia in her chair, watching him closely. He shimmied over on the bed, making room for her. She climbed in beside him and held him. Then she got him up and showed him where the communal bathroom for the girls and boys was, but he wouldn't go in without her. She brushed his teeth and washed his face, which he fought, and gave him breakfast, which he didn't eat. Then she walked him outside, away from the constant noise and buzz of the pediatrics building, through the crowds swarming everywhere, past the seven-foot wall and toward a tiny grove of barrigona palms about thirty yards away— far enough for privacy, close enough that the hospital would be just a few seconds' sprint away if trouble came from the jungle.

Then she told him in their shared tangle of tongues what had happened—that his father had died, that his grandmother had died, that his village was no more. He reacted mostly by not reacting at all. The child was spent, wrung out, already cried out. What's more, the empty look on his face confirmed Sonia's suspicion that he already had known everything she had just told him. Perhaps he had known from the moment the clinic caught fire, from the moment Annie, in her final act, had ordered them into the helicopter and then dove into the flames. Perhaps he had slept so long partly to avoid the dawn—a dawn in a world in which he was now parentless.

Sonia had nothing to offer him. There was no changing the fact that he was an orphan; no changing the fact that the mortal arithmetic had found him again—that he was a child who had had one papa and now had no papa. She could not undo that equation for him. She could only hold him—and promise him she would not leave him for as long as he needed her. So she did promise him.

And she promised herself something too: The night before, in her wall-kicking rage, she had spat the words "I'll make them pay" in the direction of the people who had caused such devastation. Having said it, she decided, she would have to do it.

. . .

Attorney General Constance T. Polk was nothing if not punctual, and at 2100 hours to the minute, station time, on the day after Walli Beckwith committed her cosmic crime, the call came in from Houston. This time the first voice Beckwith heard belonged to Lee Jasper.

"Station, Houston," he said.

"Jasper, station," she responded, tweaking him for his earlier frostiness. But he would not be tweaked.

"Please stand by for the administrator," he said.

"Roger," Beckwith answered, mildly relieved. She hadn't known what to expect from the call, but Joe Star scared no one.

"He will be joined by a NASA house counsel, who will be there for your assistance," Jasper went on.

"Roger," Beckwith said, more interested.

"And they will be joined by the attorney general of the United States."

That got Beckwith's attention. She certainly knew of Polk and she respected Polk. As with most people, that also meant she was eminently capable of fearing Polk.

"Understood, Houston," she said, no longer especially interested in teasing the one person she'd speak with today who bore her only minimal ill will.

"Patching you through to Washington now," Jasper said. Then, despite himself, despite his pique, despite his desire, just this once, to hide his affable Southern honey, he just couldn't. "Good luck, Walli Bee," he said.

She could have cried. "Thank you, Jasper," was all she trusted herself to say.

There was a full minute of air-to-ground hiss as the connection was made, and then the familiar voice of the NASA administrator came on the line.

"Lieutenant Commander Beckwith?" he said.

Star never called her that; he addressed all of his astronauts by their first names and had readily accepted that Beckwith would be known as Walli, even if her paycheck would read Belka. But now, she suspected, he was performing for the attorney general.

"Hello, sir," she responded. She rarely called him that either, but she would honor the tone he was establishing for today's interview.

"I am here with Jerry Ullage, NASA house counsel," Star went on. Beckwith liked Ullage; he had stood by the astronauts in various dustups with NASA over speaking fees and book rights and other means by which they might try to make some real money after their life of working for government pay was over.

"Hello, Jerry," she said.

"Hello, Lieutenant Commander," he responded. *Him too*, she thought with an interior sigh. She would address him formally for the rest of the conversation.

"And Attorney General Polk is here as well," Star said.

"Madame Attorney General," Beckwith said, not waiting to be addressed.

"Lieutenant Commander," Polk responded.

"The president asked the attorney general here today to see if there is a way to resolve the current . . . circumstances," Star said.

"I would like that," Beckwith answered.

"Let's begin, Lieutenant Commander, with why you've taken the actions you've taken," Polk said. "There is a great deal of speculation about that, and the president has asked me to try to determine your reasons. Perhaps when we know them, we can do something about them."

Beckwith smiled. There was a great deal of speculation indeed. Earlier in the day she had opened up her browser and scanned the news online. Various sites had aggregated the prevailing guesses and ranked them. The leading theory was that she was, as Bazanov had suspected, simply crazy. Close behind that was terrorism—that the destruction of the station was somehow imminent. Following that was the increasingly popular theory that she'd committed a terrible crime on Earth—at least one dead body was usually involved. And after that came the theory that this was simply a wonderful bit of performance art. Beckwith was especially partial to that one. Few people mentioned, as Bazanov had, the matter of the Consolidation.

"I'm not quite ready to disclose my reasons," she now responded to Polk.

"Why is that?"

"Ma'am, I'd prefer—" she began, but Polk finished for her.

"Not to."

"Yes, ma'am."

"Will there be a time you'd be prepared to have that conversation?" Polk asked.

Beckwith smiled. "Yes. As it happens there will be: tomorrow at exactly 10:22 A.M. eastern time. That will be 2:22 P.M. station time." She then added, "I will establish voice contact with Houston about ten minutes early just to be sure."

"Can you reveal the reason for so specific a time?"

"Due respect, ma'am, but that will be clear at 10:22 A.M. tomorrow." She turned her attention to Star. "Mr. Administrator," she said, "will that conversation be carried live on NASA TV?"

"I expect it will be," he responded.

"I need to *know* that it will be," she said, "or the conversation can't take place."

"Lieutenant Commander," Star said, "you're not in a position to make that demand."

"Mr. Administrator," she began. "Joe, I have your space station. I think I am."

Polk cut off that line of argument. "I will speak to the president about the broadcast. I'm certain he will agree to your condition, though he will insist on a seven-second delay so that you can be silenced if you try to incite violence."

"I will not incite violence, but I accept that condition," Beckwith said. She had, in fact, fully expected that condition.

Polk then tacked another way. "Lieutenant Commander, remind me: You did not resign your naval commission before joining NASA, did you?"

"No," she said, "I have remained a naval officer."

"And as such, you are required to obey commands from superior officers."

Ullage interrupted: "Walli, you can feel free not to answer that question." He had reverted to her first name. She liked him for a reason.

"I understand that, but I don't mind," she said. "Yes, I am aware of the chain of naval command."

"And you're aware that the president sits at the top of all military chains of command," Polk said.

Beckwith had anticipated this too. "Yes, I am."

"Accordingly," Polk said, "I am authorized by the president to order you to return home with no preconditions."

"Even if I were inclined to do that, I couldn't," Beckwith said reasonably. "There is no spacecraft attached to the station at present."

"That can change in as little as a week," Star said. "The Soyuz that was going to bring up the next crew was being prepared to launch then anyway. The crew can't fly as long as the station is in unstable hands—those are the words the Russians themselves used—but the ship can fly empty and automated on the way up and bring you down the same way."

Beckwith grimaced at the "unstable hands" business, which Star probably intended; the administrator was decidedly displeased with her and was not above indulging in a cutting remark. But she also felt terribly guilty for denying the next crew their mission. She knew all three of them and knew how hard they'd trained for it. For that reason as much as anything else, she responded impolitically, with a verbal slap of her own.

"The Progress was supposed to fly empty and automated too," she said sourly.

"All the same, a Soyuz will be launched and you will be expected to help dock it and to board it," Star said. "Walli, you're in very real legal jeopardy. Come home and a lot of it could go away."

"I can't do that, sir," she responded.

"You realize this exposes you to a court-martial," Polk said.

"You needn't respond," Ullage interjected.

She ignored him. "I do realize that," she said.

"And there's more," Polk went on. "You're familiar with the Outer Space Treaty of 1967?"

It was an elementary question and an insulting one—probably calculatedly so. The treaty was a fundamental and early subject of astronaut training. "Of course I am familiar with it," Beckwith answered tersely.

"And you're equally familiar with the 1998 intergovernmental agreement signed by all of the space station's partner nations?"

"Yes."

"And you're familiar with the language?"

"Walli . . ." Ullage warned.

Beckwith shook him off. "I studied both in detail, yes."

"Then you probably remember Article VIII of the 1967 treaty," Polk said, "which states that any nation that launches an object into space, and I'm reading here, 'shall retain jurisdiction and control over such object, and over any personnel thereof, while in outer space or on a celestial body.'"

"Again," Beckwith said, "I studied it in depth."

"Then you know it means that you are subject to prosecution in the United States when you return to Earth as well as in Russia, since your crime was carried out in the Russian segment—a crime committed for no apparent reason."

Beckwith tightened her lips. It might have been Polk's tone, so smooth and supercilious, or it might have been her dismissal of Beckwith's exceedingly good reasons for doing what she was doing—the *honor* in what she was doing—but either way, in that moment she decided that she disliked this woman. And that, in turn, made her sloppy.

"One final thing, Lieutenant Commander," Polk said. "Did you decide before you left the ground to take the action you did?"

"Walli," Ullage said sharply, "this is *not* a question you should answer."

Beckwith barely heard him. "No," she said.

"When you were aboard, then?"

"Yes."

"But you couldn't have made the final decision to act until that morning, after the accident, as your crewmates were preparing to leave."

"Walli!" Ullage now fairly shouted. "Stop!"

"That's correct," Beckwith responded, ignoring him.

"Oh, Walli . . ." she heard Ullage softly mutter.

"During the power-down, you shut off systems in all of the modules on the American end of the station, including the Japanese and European ones?" Polk said.

"That's what the procedure calls for, yes."

Polk then let the air fill for just a moment with the ship-to-shore static. When she spoke, it was with an unmistakable edge of a person savoring a victory.

"Lieutenant Commander," she said, "you flew under the authority of the United States, you committed your crime while on the legal equivalent of Russian soil, and you formed your intent on Japanese and European soil."

Beckwith said nothing. Polk pressed on: "There are twenty-two partner nations in the European Space Agency. Japan, Russia, and the United States bring us to twenty-five. And the 1998 agreement makes extradition among all of those countries mandatory in the event of a crime committed in orbit—even to countries with which the United States does not ordinarily have extradition agreements. This means you are currently subject to prosecution in more jurisdictions than most international drug traffickers. You could spend the rest of your life traveling from country to country, courtroom to courtroom, and jail to jail. I doubt you would live long enough to stand for all twenty-five of your trials."

Beckwith considered that very real prospect and blanched. Polk, famously, never bluffed. Facing the legal wrath of the US and Russia had been one thing; adding the wrath of nearly two dozen more nations was another matter entirely. For a moment, Beckwith was unable to locate her voice. Then she did.

"Ms. Polk," she said, "I ride rockets for a living. Before that I flew jets. Onto carriers. In the dark. I'm accustomed to risk. This interview is concluded. You will have answers to your questions tomorrow morning."

"Lieutenant Commander . . ." Polk began.

"Station out," Beckwith announced, and cut the line. Then, before her courage could fail her, she opened up her home page and told the world what she had told the attorney general: that she would have something to say at 10:22 A.M. the next day.

CHAPTER SIX

Of course it was about the Consolidation. It had always been about the Consolidation. Half the world was talking about the Consolidation, and Walli Beckwith had been talking especially loudly. But she had more reason than most to be as worked up as she was because she had a daughter caught up in the deadly mess—and yet, at the same time, she didn't.

Technically, Walli Beckwith had no daughter at all, and at forty-four years old, she probably never would. What she had was a niece, her very first blood-niece, and since Beckwith had had only one sibling and he had had only one child and now he was dead, that first niece would forever be her only niece.

Beckwith's brother was three years older than she, and she had looked up to him in all things. Their parents had named him like they had named her, in a loving nod to the business of space. In his case, the name was Karman, in honor of Theodore von Kármán, the Hungarian aeronautical genius without whose studies of hypersonic airflow modern rocketry would have been impossible.

Karman Beckwith, unlike his parents or his sister, was uninterested in engineering and instead went to medical school, specializing in pediatrics and, once he graduated, shipping out to work in the jungles, first in Africa and then in Southeast Asia. He met his eventual wife there, a Mexican doctor with the serendipitous first name Carmen and the last name Bravo-Castillo. Karman adored the homophonic coincidence of the Carmen part of her name and the heroic huzzah of the Bravo-Castillo. That, plus her dark beauty and incandescent intelligence, led him to propose to her within four months of their meeting. She accepted, and after three years in the field, they moved back to the United States, took jobs at the pediatric center of the Mayo Clinic in Minnesota, and soon had a baby girl. The child looked entirely like her Latina mother and not a lick like her fairer father, which was absolutely fine with both parents. They named her Sonia Bravo-Beckwith.

But Carmen would not see Sonia grow up. Years before, in northern Cambodia, she had contracted a case of drug-resistant malaria, and the parasite had lurked in her liver, where all malaria likes to hide. It flared up once after Sonia was born, then again a year later, then again eighteen months after that, and during that third bout, it killed her. Sonia was not yet four. She and a devastated Karman moved to Houston at Walli Beckwith's insistence. She was now off-ship and working for NASA, keeping more or less ordinary hours so she could help raise her niece.

Walli Beckwith had been with Carmen the day she died. Carmen had asked her to be as much of a mother to Sonia as she could, and Beckwith had agreed. But she was still surprised—and seized by guilt—several nights later at her brother's home when Sonia awakened, crying convulsively, clutched Beckwith in a near death grip, and called her "Mama." At first Beckwith assumed Sonia was crying out for Carmen, but when she repeated it several more times, it was clear that at that moment, at least, Beckwith *was* Mama.

The next morning, Sonia was back to calling her "*Tía*," as she always did, but over the years that followed, whenever the girl was feeling deeply sad, deeply in need, she'd come back to Mama. Karman and Sonia and Walli agreed that it was all right, that it actually honored Carmen's wishes. And now and then, when Sonia was older, if Beckwith would send her a note or a birthday card in which she wanted to convey particular love or an email in which she had occasion to scold, she would address her as "Daughter," which Sonia quite liked. But Beckwith would render the word "Dauhter," hedging the spelling and thus the relationship in deference to Carmen, but embracing it too in obedience to Carmen.

When Sonia grew older and chose to become a doctor, Beckwith both celebrated the decision and fretted about it. The girl had a sandpaper toughness to her that never seemed fully in keeping with the healing arts. Instead, Beckwith worried, Sonia might at some level be seeking to replace her lost mother by *becoming* her lost mother. It was not unheard of—or so the psychology studies Beckwith looked up online seemed to agree—and it often ended badly, with an offspring ill suited to a parent's career winding up trapped there by misguided sentiment.

That fear was allayed the moment Sonia began medical school and attacked her studies with a lioness' ferocity. She might or might not ever develop a gentle bedside manner, but she tore into the book work and the lab work and the endless memorization of the Latinate medical terms in much the way Beckwith herself had worked at Annapolis.

"*Tía*," she said to Beckwith after her first year as a med student, "I see why Mama loved this."

That might have closed the circle, might have completed the long journey from loss to redemption that Sonia had been making since the death of her mother. But before her second year in medical school could even begin, she and Beckwith again found themselves grieving a loss when the Houston police appeared at their door to tell them that Karman had been killed in a bicycling accident while pedaling in a lane in the northeast part of the city that was supposed to be closed to vehicles, but could not be closed to one vehicle that had jumped a divider because the driver was reeling drunk. Beckwith received a summer leave from NASA, and she and Sonia huddled close and mourned as one.

They took walks in the city's arboretum and Sesquicentennial Park, visited the Houston aquarium because they liked the dark rooms with the blue-violet lights in the tanks and the soothing, bubbling sounds of all of the little ecosystems keeping all the little fish alive. They lingered over long dinners, sometimes staying silent, sometimes crying together. Finally, after three months, the five-foot girl with the huzzah last name marched back to medical school, and the astronaut named after the street-tough pup jumped back into training, and they both pressed on as best they could. And then, three days before the collision in space that could have cost Beckwith her life, the same near-daughter almost lost her own, in the fire that killed fifteen people in the jungle but spared her.

The Brazilians themselves—or at least the Brazilian government— did not speak much about the increasing number of jungle fires, and when they did, they spoke of them clinically, as an admittedly messy part of a larger project they decorously described as "the Consolidation." It was a name and a policy dreamed up and executed by the new Brazilian president, Jair Bobo-deCorte.

The president's hyphenated surname struck plenty of people as openly comical, and his opponents in the media promptly dubbed him a clownish man with a name that suited him. But Bobo-deCorte himself was actually delighted with the name, guessing that it nicely rounded out his edges—making it easier for him to go about the decidedly sharp-edged ideas he had for his country.

Bobo-deCorte had made his fortune in the Amazon jungle, first in ranching, then in lumber, then in farming, and most recently in hydroelectric-dam construction. He built each of those enterprises individually, then gathered them together into a single multinational giant—one that he actually named Multinacional Gigante.

But a businessman was subordinate to the government, and the Brazilian government was largely subordinate to its president—and the president who preceded Bobo-deCorte was no friend of the industries that had made Multinacional Gigante so *gigante*. The Amazon rain forest could take only so much, he would argue. By US estimates, it was losing the equivalent of one New Jersey—or 8,700 square miles—every year to burning, clear-cutting, and dam building. At that rate the entire jungle could be razed to stubble within a generation.

"A Amazônia é o jardim do mundo"—the Amazon is the world's garden—the Brazilian president would promise on his trips overseas to the United Nations or to this or that conference in Paris or Geneva. The Europeans would applaud and the UN would applaud, and Bobo-deCorte would grumble to his aides that a garden is useless if you don't pick the fruit.

So even before the fifth year of the Brazilian president's six-year term was done, Bobo-deCorte declared that he was running to become the next president. He promised that he would spend his yearlong campaign visiting all twenty-six of Brazil's states, driving himself in his own weathered van.

Anyone who had tried to drive Brazil's notoriously poor roads—especially the ones that cut through the Amazon—would tell you that was a fool's errand. Brazilian roads ate cars alive. But Bobo-deCorte didn't have just one weathered van; he had six, and they were actually brand-new. They were exactly the same model and year, as well as the same shade of bivouac green, with dashes of chrome and faux leather seats. It would not be hard to weather them by hand, however—claw hammers, ball-peen hammers, and nails would do just fine. Pliers could loosen chrome and leave strips of it bouncing and slapping as the van moved. Salt, water, bleach, and vinegar applied in just the right spots could cause just the right amount of decorative rust. And Mexican serapes bought cheap in import market stalls could be used to cover the elegant upholstery.

Deface and drape all six vans in just the same way, stash them in garages all over the country, and it would be a simple matter for the candidate to fly from city to city in a private jet headed for a private landing strip, pick up one of the vans, which would be waiting for him on the tarmac, and drive straight to a rally. Dirty shirts were kept in a satchel in each van for Bobo-deCorte to put on during the ride, along with plastic bags of soil and road dust he would spread around his neck and streak across his forehead. When he arrived at the rally, he would hop out of the van and climb onto the hood in front of the crowds who would already be assembled, having waited hours for the man who had driven a day and a half just to be here with them.

Bobo-deCorte on the hood of a van with a microphone in his hand was a thrilling thing—passionate, fierce, seductive. His followers were his *parceiros*, his partners, he told them, and they had work to do together. They would get that chance: Bobo-deCorte would win the presidency in a landslide, with sixty-six million votes, out of a total ninety-eight million cast.

Almost immediately, the Consolidation began. The great resources of the rain forest were being commercialized by a patchwork of companies in a patchwork way, and now they would all be gathered together under a government authority that would advance their interests jointly. Roads would be cut where they needed to be cut; jungle would be cleared according to where the agriculture minister determined the best farmland was located, not according to where the environment minister said the impact would be the least. Even better, Bobo-deCorte promised, the Consolidation would not be a Brazilian project alone. Neighboring countries whose borders included portions of the Amazon would be invited to participate in what he promised would be a bold multinational alliance.

It was all achievable, Bobo-deCorte would promise, but ever and always there was the problem of the tribes—and the tribes were everywhere. There did not seem to be an acre of forest, he complained, that wasn't near them, or set aside for them, or somehow said to be essential for their survival. Dam a river upstream and there was a tribe affected downstream. Dig a mine on private land and the runoff would poison tribal land. It was exactly the kind of interference with the jungle's natural order that had already turned the Guarani tribal lands into scrub and wasteland.

The one million indigenous people were little more than a demographic blip next to the 209 million people making up the nation as a whole, but to Bobo-deCorte they were a blip that needed to be eliminated. "It's a shame the Brazilian cavalry hasn't been as efficient as the American cavalry," he would lament to his cabinet, musing that the United States needed barely a century to clear eighteen million indigenous people off the North American continent, while Brazil could not handle a fraction of that in the south.

The cabinet would shift uneasily when Bobo-deCorte said that—and not just because even for his most febrile followers, such murderous thoughts seemed best left unsaid. The fact was, the South Americans actually had been as efficiently lethal as the cavalry to the north. The trouble began the moment the Europeans first established a toehold on the continent in the fifteenth century, bringing with them diseases like smallpox, which they spread unwittingly, and weapons like lances and swords, which they used with deadly efficiency when there was land they wanted to seize. By the middle of the twentieth century—after the Industrial Revolution boosted the global demand for rubber, which fairly ran from Amazon trees—the tribal population of eleven million was down to just a single million, devastated by displacement and disease and two centuries of war with the rubber tappers.

Bobo-deCorte pledged to resolve the problem of that small but stubborn remainder. If Amazon industries could be consolidated, said the president, so too could the Amazon tribes. The vast jungle across which the million indigenous people were so diffusely scattered would be claimed by the state, then set to the torch where needed to turn unproductive wilderness into profitable farmland and ranchland, and the members of the tribes themselves would be gathered into a single population—for their own safety, for their own good—and relocated to lush Brazilian borderlands near Peru, Bolivia, and Paraguay.

The government's deal—relocate voluntarily to fertile new land—was carried to the tribes by official representatives who would travel into the jungle trailed by video crews who documented the friendly way the plan was being proposed. The tribes were not impressed; they had lived on these lands for centuries, and they would not go. Few people had believed that they would. But having been offered an easy route by the government—with that offer captured on camera—they would now be pushed out the hard way. And so the burning began.

.   .   .

Beckwith was on the ground in Mission Control during her last month in the United States before shipping out to Baikonur, Kazakhstan, for her launch to the space station, when the first pictures of the fires being lit in the jungle to clear the land and roust the tribes began streaming down from the station. The bright spots of light could have been wildfires ignited randomly by lightning, except that they flared at fixed times, usually after dark, and burned for precisely two days, often linking into a small necklace of blazes, pushing west—and herding the tribes ahead of them. Nature didn't do that; people did.

"Are we tracking these?" Beckwith asked the flight director on duty when she got her first look at the pictures.

"We're *observing* them," came the hedged answer.

"Are we reporting them?"

"We're observing them."

Beckwith was not remotely alone in seeing what was going on. Every astronaut, flight controller, and administrator in the space center could tell the difference between an accidental fire and a tactical one. So too could the people operating other nations' weather and military satellites. But no country had more influence in the Western Hemisphere than the United States, and the United States was staying mum. The orders from Washington—particularly the White House— were that no NASA images taken of the fires were to be released.

That was what truly enraged Beckwith: the silence, the complicity— that, of course, and the fact that alone among the entirety of the NASA staff, she had a loved one in the middle of the violence in the jungle. She told herself that she wasn't letting her personal feelings color her outrage at the inhumanity that was unfolding, and once in a while she believed that self-fib, but mostly she didn't. Whatever Beckwith's mix of reasons, they were more than enough to prod her to ambush Joe Star in a Mission Control hallway on a day he had come from Washington to Houston for what was supposed to be a round of morale boosting and glad-handing with the space center's employees.

"These are deliberate," she said to him without an opening hello, brandishing a stack of pictures of the fires.

"Yes," Star said evenly. "Of course they are." He kept his eyes on hers and did not look down at the pictures; he had seen them all already.

"Are we sharing them with anyone?"

"We're sharing them with everyone, Walli," Star said. "The president, the Congress, the Pentagon. Then we're required to be quiet about it and let them decide what to do."

"And what are they deciding?"

"To do nothing, as you know."

Beckwith began to respond, but Star cut her off. "You have family down there, don't you, Walli? A niece?"

"I do," she answered.

"You're concerned about her?"

"Of course."

"And you're concerned about the tribes and the jungle and the politics of it all."

"Yes, as I've said."

Star appeared to contemplate these facts. "That's a lot to worry about," he said, affecting a sympathy that didn't really read like sympathy. "It could all become a distraction for you. *Will* it be a distraction for you?"

Beckwith said nothing. Star, they both knew, was threatening her—specifically threatening her mission—and the coded word "distraction" made that unmistakable. A distracted astronaut heading for the space station would never get to go there in the first place. Beckwith, Zhirov, and Lebedev would all travel to Baikonur in a month, accompanied by three fully trained backup crew members. Any one of the second-stringers could be swapped in to fly in as little as a day before launch if a member of the prime crew were ill or unprepared or . . . distracted.

"No," Beckwith said frostily. "This will not be a distraction."

"Very good then."

Beckwith did curb her tongue and did make it to Baikonur and then to space, and as she'd promised Star, she did do her job there. But she had not promised that she wouldn't do *more* than her job once she was off the clock. She used her free time to watch the ground; she saw when the big fires raged and when the smaller ignition fires were lit. She watched too as what seemed to be more-concentrated fires flared at the western border of Brazil, abutting Paraguay, Peru, and Bolivia. Patches of jungle were cleared there, and within days, narrow roads were cut in symmetrical lots in the blackened spaces, looking like they were intended less for lush, open tribal relocation lands than for contained refugee camps—where tens and even hundreds of thousands of people could be kept.

She followed the news stories about the mounting refugee toll too: By her sixth week in space over one hundred thousand tribespeople— more than 10 percent of the entire indigenous population—were now either homeless and dispersed or being housed in what amounted to forced confinement. There had been a scattering of deaths in all the dislocations, and Bobo-deCorte himself had taken to the airwaves to pay his respects to what he called *Os Lamentáveis*—the Lamentables— promising their families restitution, but pointedly not promising that there wouldn't be more dying to come.

In the United States, angry lawmakers in both chambers of Congress introduced bills to mandate intervention in the jungle, with a vote set for September 18, lest the refugee toll soar to half a million and beyond. The United States had stayed out of the bloodbath in Rwanda in 1994, and even years later, the consciences of lawmakers were scarred by the global condemnation that followed the American inaction. The congressional bills represented an attempt both to fix the immediate problem and to get right with 1990s history. Few people expected the bills to go anywhere.

And yet for all the ugliness Beckwith saw through her space station portholes as the jungle floor burned beneath her, there was also the occasional welcome fire, a tiny fire, so tiny she needed a high-resolution ground-surveillance system to see it at all—a fire that was lit just for her. They appeared at agreed-upon times, and they were hard to mistake for any of the other fires on the burning continent. In addition to the familiar orange and yellow of other fires, the little ones always gave off a quivery shimmer of purple first, way up at the high, vanishing edge of the visible spectrum. Beckwith couldn't explain how she could see the purple, though since the only other person she knew who could see it too was her dauhter-niece, she reckoned it was something genetic.

Either way, that dauhter-niece was in danger. And the entire continent was in danger. Beckwith was not so vain as to think she was the only person in the world who could make the devastation stop, but she was not so modest as to deny that from her very particular position, she had a very particular voice. She would use it.

CHAPTER SEVEN

August 23

Sonia Peanut Bravo-Beckwith learned about her *tía*-mama's plan to address the world at about the same time everybody else did. By now there was no newspaper, news site, cable channel, or social media platform on the planet that wasn't devoting a good share of its coverage to the story of the possibly crazy, definitely criminal, and absolutely irresistible astronaut who had stolen the world's only space station and was at last condescending to explain why. The news of Beckwith's intention to make her address at 10:22 A.M. on her third day in sole command of the station pinged on Sonia's smartphone just as it was pinging on every one of the hundreds of other phones in the Mercado camp.

"Beckwith Will Talk," was how the *USA Today* alert that appeared first on Sonia's phone phrased it.

That was followed by *The New York Times*' "Astronaut to Address NASA, World; Will Explain Actions."

The *New York Post* was last with "The Pirate Speaks!"

That real-time pop-up of the breaking news was not at all the way Sonia learned that Beckwith had taken the station in the first place, two days ago—or three days after she and Oli had arrived in the Mercado camp. She got word of that development hours after the fact—about 1:00 P.M. Bolivia time, 5:00 P.M. space station time, nearly five hours after an injured Vasily Zhirov and Yulian Lebedev had floated free of the station in their Soyuz spacecraft, leaving an injured and obstinate Beckwith behind. The Mercado camp had been in an internet blackout for most of that day, something that often happened when the satellite antennas mounted on the backs of a pair of uplink trucks went dark for one glitchy reason or another.

Sonia was in the pediatrics building that afternoon, folding sheets with Oli's help, though Oli's help more or less meant just tangling the sheets—which Sonia then had to untangle and fold, telling him she was "just going to smooth these out a little bit." His willingness to take on the little job encouraged Sonia. For the three days they had been in the Mercado camp, he'd spent his time alternately brooding and crying, trying to come to terms with what had happened to him, to his village and his family.

He had learned from the cradle of the Guarani belief in the Isondú and the Panambi, the glowworms and butterflies that were said to carry the souls of the reincarnated dead. After dark one night he crept from his bed, sneaked outside the pediatrics building, and began scouting for glowworms. His patience was fleeting and he howled in frustration when he was unable to find any after just a few minutes, waking Sonia and Mia, who bolted outside and carried him back in. The next day he slipped away again, only this time it was the butterflies he was looking for. When he at last spotted one but it would not settle onto his outstretched hand, he picked up a broken, leafy branch lying on the ground nearby, swatted it out of the sky, and killed it.

Sonia had anticipated that such rage—in this case, a tiny murderous rage—would come and had tried to get out ahead of it, allowing him to cling as close to her as he needed. Now, on that third day in the Mercado facility, as she and Oli wrestled with the sheets and the camp was sunk in an internet blackout, Sonia at last felt her smartphone vibrate in her pocket and heard a series of pings around the camp, indicating that everyone else's phone had come back online too. With her hands filled with sheets, she ignored her phone, but a moment later she heard someone outside the building calling her name—getting louder each time, meaning he was coming toward her at a run. She and Oli came to the door of the building, saw who it was, and Sonia slumped.

He was a med school graduate from Ohio State who was agreeable enough, but so very eager to please, so very anxious to be liked, that Sonia found it difficult to hold him in any real regard at all. His name was Raymond, and from the time they met, she feared he harbored hopes that she might come to regard him as something more than just another clinic doctor. At first by happenstance and later by design, she had never learned his last name. She suspected he didn't realize that, but she somehow felt that the less she knew about him, the more of a remoteness she could project and the more he'd direct his attention elsewhere. Now, as he sprinted toward her, she was for once intrigued by whatever it was he had to say to her.

"Sonia!" he called, waving his smartphone over his head. "Your aunt! Your . . ." He gasped for breath. ". . . your astronaut."

At last he stumbled to a stop in front of her, panting and able to get out only "Your . . . your . . ." while pointing at the phone.

"What, Raymond, what?" Sonia demanded frantically. "Is she all right?"

"Yes!" Raymond said. "But she stole"—here he paused for a ragged breath—"she stole the space station."

"What the hell are—" Sonia started to ask, but before she could finish, Mia ran out from the infirmary building, also with her phone in her hand, shouting for Sonia just as Raymond had, and shoved her phone, open to CNN, into Sonia's hand.

"Look at this, look at this!" she said.

Sonia looked down and her jaw dropped. "HIJACK IN SPACE," the headline read, with the smaller "Rogue astronaut seizes station" underneath.

"What happened?" Oli asked, grabbing Sonia's leg. "What happened?"

"Something . . ." Sonia said distractedly, looking down at him and then back at the screen. Unable to focus on anything *but* the screen, she reached out and wrapped an arm around him in a reassuring clinch. She scrolled further, from page to page, site to site, now on her own phone as Mia and Raymond did the same on theirs. Finally, after about fifteen minutes, her phone buzzed and rang and she punched the answer button. She heard the hiss, turned to Raymond and Mia, and nodded yes. They leaned in to listen, but Sonia shooed them back and pressed the phone tight to her ear.

"Sonia," she could hear Beckwith say.

"*Tía!*" Sonia answered. "What did you do, what did you do? Are you all right? What did you do?"

"So you heard," Beckwith answered evenly.

"Yes, I heard! Everyone heard! The newspeople say you're a criminal."

"They're probably right."

"That's not funny!"

"It's not meant to be. I know what I did."

"But why? You had to leave! There was an accident! Those are the rules!"

"Sonia, baby, listen—" Beckwith began.

"No," Sonia interrupted. "It's wrong! It's dumb! You're alone up there."

"Sonia!" Beckwith now said more crisply—a tone of address that Sonia had long since learned meant that she was to stop talking. She obeyed, and Beckwith said simply, "Listen to me."

Sonia did listen, backing several steps toward the wall of a building, sliding down it to a seated position, and waggling her fingers for Oli, who came over and settled into her lap, indifferent to what Sonia was talking about, content to hear her occasional "mm-hmm" or "right" or "no" or "yeah." He heard her say "No!" sharply once, and he looked at her with concern. He heard her say, "I do understand," more softly, and he relaxed. At last he heard her say "yes" and "of course" and "I love you too." Then she clicked off and looked up at Raymond and Mia, staring down at her wide-eyed.

"She stole it all right," Sonia said. "And she aims to keep it."

"Why?" Raymond asked.

"She'll explain that soon."

. . .

Beckwith readied herself for her address to the world only three minutes before it was set to begin. It was 2:19 P.M. her time, 10:19 A.M. eastern time. She knew what she wanted to say, she knew how she planned to say it, and so when the time came, she merely gathered up her laptop and her camera and floated into the cupola—a five-foot-wide, seven-windowed dome on the bottom-facing side of the space station, located just off the Destiny lab. It was the cupola that was used for the most—or at least the best—photography of the Earth. The bright blue of the morning Pacific Ocean sprawled out 250 miles below her, filling the left-hand side of her field of vision. The green-brown stretch of western South America, cut by the white of the snowcapped Andes, glowed as the prenoon sun cast westward-pointing shadows across the breadth of the Amazon.

"Houston, station," she radioed down.

"Station, Houston, reading you five-by."

The link was good, the transmission was clear, but the person on the mic was unfamiliar. Beckwith recognized the voices of all of the astronauts who would be manning the Capcom station during the mission, even if she could not always connect them with a name, and this voice did not belong to any of them. Military intelligence, she suspected, an officer who knew the language of space but also the business of espionage—just in case that was Beckwith's game today.

"Are we wide?" Beckwith asked.

"Wide?" the ground answered.

"Is this conversation broadcasting live?"

"Yes, Lieutenant Commander," came the response. "NASA TV is carrying this feed, as are all of the networks."

"Good," Beckwith said. She glanced down at some notes she had scribbled on a card, but she had reviewed what she wanted to say so many times she had fixed it all firmly in her head. She collected herself and began.

"Hello," she said to what she rightly assumed was a planetwide audience below. "Twenty-two years ago, I took an oath as a commissioned officer in the United States Navy and promised to 'bear true faith and allegiance' to the Constitution. I aimed to keep that promise."

She paused, looked at her watch and then out her window. Time was short. She went on.

"The thing about the Constitution, though, is that it may have been written for the United States, but its principles are universal. Bearing true faith and allegiance to them does not mean ignoring them outside our own borders. In the past few months I have betrayed my oath. I spoke out—a little—when I saw something wrong, but speaking up a little was not enough. So I will do more."

She let a long air-to-ground hiss fill the comm channel, long enough for Houston to grow concerned that the downlink had been cut.

"Station?" called the stranger on the Houston mic.

"Stand by one," Beckwith answered. She looked out the window. A dull orange glow and ugly smudges of black were unmistakably evident at more than two dozen spots in the thick canopy of the Amazon, rolling in from the east. Each second, they drew nearer, more vivid. She raised her camera and continued speaking.

"I am in the cupola of the International Space Station, the greatest spot in the greatest flying machine ever built. I am moving east at a speed of four-point-nine miles per second. In ten seconds I will be crossing over lands of ruin and death. More than a hundred thousand people who began this year living peaceful lives have now been scattered in a storm of fire and violence. An uncounted number have lost their lives in that storm. There will likely be many more fires and many more deaths. The jungle itself is approaching its own death. Burn away just another bit of what's left, and the rest will collapse."

She leaned forward, aimed her camera, gathered the sweep of the burning jungle into her frame, snapped her picture, and spoke again. "In a moment I will post a picture of what all that devastation looks like from here."

She released her camera, let it float where it was, pressed her palms against the windows, and looked down again. "I will come home," she said, "when we have put an end to the project that is causing damage so great it's visible from space. On September 18, just under four weeks from now, the United States Congress will cast a vote either to stop the slaughter or allow it to continue. The people must gather in Washington on that day, by the hundreds of thousands, by the millions. And they must not leave until those in power do what is right. I hope to help lead that fight—and I hope you will *allow* me to help lead it. Meantime, I will be watching the jungle from here. I will warn when I can—and I will show the world what I see. For now, station out."

She cut the comm line, uploaded her picture of the Amazon disaster, and watched her website. It was immediately stormed by people seeing and sharing the image around the world.

Far below, on the ground, the entirety of Beckwith's transmission could be heard on a radio in a pediatrics building in the Bolivian jungle. A knot of doctors and even some of the children gathered around it. On the floor, closest to the radio, sat Sonia, cross-legged with Oli in her lap. He looked up at her.

"Your *tía*-mama?" he asked her.

Sonia nodded.

"She's in space now?"

She nodded again.

"Is she coming home?"

"Not now," Sonia said. "Not for a while."

CHAPTER EIGHT

Beckwith had known there would be a great deal of noise from a great many people all over Washington and the media about what she had done, but she had not quite imagined the white-hot blast of it. She was alternately compared to Benedict Arnold, Rosa Parks, Ethel Rosenberg, Eleanor Roosevelt, Axis Sally, and Susan B. Anthony. She got two Lizzie Bordens from an elderly couple interviewed on TV in a Springfield, Massachusetts, diner, as well as numerous Joan of Arcs on numerous college campuses—which was inevitable.

The more measured members of the media—especially the science and legal reporters—took a more cool-headed approach. What Beckwith had done was surely a crime, but it was well short of the hijacking or act of terror that a lot of people were calling it. The space station was flying through its orbits as it always had, and Beckwith couldn't raise or lower that orbit by so much as an inch without NASA and Moscow knowing it and overriding her from the ground. As long as she continued performing the important work of cleaning and maintaining the station's essential systems, one reporter argued, she was less a hijacker than a lighthouse keeper—one who might have refused to leave the lighthouse when she was told, but a menace to no one.

Precisely that comparison was put to the White House press secretary during the briefing he called within an hour after Beckwith signed off. He was having none of it.

"This is a $100 billion lighthouse with both global and national security implications," he said. "Lieutenant Commander Beckwith has broken the law. She can't stay in space forever, and when she comes home, she's going to jail—probably for a long, long time."

The press secretary repeated the familiar notion that America "was not the world's policeman" and could not be expected to wade into conflicts if other countries wouldn't. But in this case, America was in fact the only option. The press secretary knew it, the president knew it, and Beckwith most certainly knew it.

United Nations intervention in the Amazon would require unanimous approval by the body's Security Council, and that vote was wired before it could even be held. There were five permanent members of the council—the United States, Great Britain, France, Russia, and China. France and Great Britain were in favor of intervention. Russia didn't care either way except insofar as it could cast a vote that would annoy Washington, and since the president had already made it clear the US was opposed to any action in the jungle, Moscow declared that it would vote in favor. China was immovable. It had forged a quick and close business relationship with the Bobo-deCorte government, was pleased with the strategic toehold that was buying it in the hemisphere the US considered its own, and was not about to interfere with anything Brasilia might be up to. The US too would vote an immovable no.

NATO could have no role in the fight because it had no dog in the fight, since Brazil was not a member of the thirty-nation organization. If there were to be an intervention at all, it would fall to the

Organization of American States, many of whose thirty-five member nations were indeed agitating for action. But here too there were problems. The group included big players like Canada, Argentina, Mexico, and Brazil, as well as tiny ones like Barbados, Belize, and Guyana. But militarily, none of them were much more than dickey birds on the rhino's back of the United States. While the OAS did regularly run collaborative military-readiness exercises, they were "collaborative" only in the sense that the US military organized the drills, provided most of the hardware and troops, and sent its generals out to tell everyone else what to do. For now, an actual war in the Amazon was not something the American generals were permitted even to consider endorsing, much less leading. It was only the September 18 congressional vote that could make a difference, which was why Beckwith chose that single target.

"She's not dumb," the US president said to his aides with grudging admiration as he watched Beckwith's broadcast. The date of the vote had been set only days earlier, and Beckwith had seen its potential and pounced on it immediately. "She's a criminal, but she's not dumb."

If Beckwith was indeed a criminal, however, she was an awfully popular one. Over the course of just the first few hours after her broadcast, more than fifty groups were established around the world in support, including three dozen in the United States alone. They went under a variety of names—March on Congress, Stop the Killing, Save the Tribes, and Rainforest Peace. At the University of Oklahoma College of Law, in the president's home state, a group and a website had been set up to gather in all of the disparate organizations, to aggregate, coordinate, or, as Jair Bobo-deCorte would put it in his darker, deadlier way, to *consolidate* their efforts. The group was dubbed, simply, the September 18 Coalition, and it was growing by the hour. Bobo-deCorte himself would envy Beckwith's appeal.

. . .

Jasper got to Boondoggles Pub at 11:20 P.M. Houston time, at the end of the day on which Beckwith had called Earth. He needed barely four minutes to make the three-mile drive east along NASA Parkway to the pub—much faster than it typically took for after-shift drinks when he was working the 8:00-to-4:00 cycle at Mission Control. There was always traffic at that time of the day; there was none at 11:20 P.M.

Jasper looked around the place as soon as he arrived, grateful that he saw no familiar faces since he had no wish at all for company. Just to be sure, he made straight for the bar and took a seat at the far right end, with several open seats to his left. He hailed the bartender and ordered a Cutty Sark on the rocks. He smiled. Cutty had been Wally Schirra's drink, which meant it was Walli Beckwith's drink, which meant that Jasper, who typically didn't care which brand of whiskey he drank but very much liked the ritual of sitting down at a bar, wagging two fingers, and ordering the same drink for himself and a lady friend, made it his drink too. After that, he learned to prefer his Cutty—partly because of the taste, mostly because of Beckwith.

He opened up his phone and typed the first few letters of an email address; the field quickly populated with Beckwith's—something the algorithm had long since memorized. "You there?" he wrote in the subject line. In the body of the email he simply typed another question mark. It was close to 4:30 A.M. station time, fourteen hours after Beckwith had made her address to the world. If Jasper knew this woman—and Jasper did know this woman—she'd be awake already, especially after so eventful a day.

The email first made its speedy way through Jasper's carrier, then its much slower way through NASA's security filters, and at last sped up to the space station 250 miles overhead. The response fought its way back down via the same route in reverse and eventually popped into Jasper's inbox.

"Here indeed," Beckwith wrote. "Where else would I be?"

Jasper smiled. "I heard your broadcast today," he replied.

"I was nervous," she answered.

"I didn't notice."

"Thank you."

Jasper took a swallow of his Cutty. "Walli Bee?" he typed.

"Yes?" came the response.

"You mean this thing, right? You mean to stay?" He knew the answer. He was stalling.

"Yes," she wrote. "Of course."

"You know this could mean jail? Actually, it WILL mean jail."

"I know that."

"Walli Bee?" he typed again.

This time the delay in her response was longer than could be accounted for by the air-to-ground system. She was stalling too.

"Yes?"

Jasper plunged ahead. "Is this about Kandahar?"

"No," came the immediate response.

Jasper began to compose his thoughts, but before he could, Beckwith answered again.

"Yes," she typed. "A little."

He had not needed the answer. He knew it was about Kandahar, and it was probably a bigger part than Beckwith was admitting.

When Beckwith was flying jets off carriers, it was agreed among the pilots that she didn't so much pilot her planes as gallop them. Pilots who galloped their planes were said to fly them with a sixth sense, as if the machines were living things, understanding what their hidden tics and hiccups were, and how to coax the very most out of them in the very worst situations. Beckwith could do all of that, and what she understood especially well was a plane's range. The manual might tell you that you could get 1,458 miles out of a Boeing Growler with a full tank of fuel, or 2,069 out of a Super Hornet. Try to go farther than that when you were over open ocean and you'd drop $70 million worth of US Navy property in the drink. But that was only if you believed the manual more than you believed what you felt when you were in the seat. Beckwith very much believed what she felt.

She could tell if a freshly serviced plane had been poorly tuned and was not flying at its best, or had been well tuned and could fly more nimbly and be pushed farther than the manual said it could. "Walli Bee," Jasper had once said to her, "you can fly on nothing but fumes and ladyballs." She took it as the finest compliment he'd ever paid her.

But that kind of instinctual flying wasn't allowed on one of her last combat runs before she left active service to join NASA, when she and a flight of five other Super Hornets were on a surveillance mission over Afghanistan, taking off from the *Eisenhower*, which at that moment was stationed in the Arabian Sea due east of Oman. There had been multiple insurgent strikes around Kandahar during the previous month, and more than 150 civilian lives had been lost. Beckwith's group was flying low, looking for hostiles and their vehicles, equipped with Sparrow air-to-ground missiles that would eliminate the threat of another attack before it could begin.

They'd been flying for hours and were all low on fuel, reaching the drop-dead cutoff point before they wouldn't have enough to make it back over the sea and out to the carrier. They made one last pass over the Kandahar-Bamiyan Highway, near a commercial area that was close to a school, a wedding venue, and a hospital. All three of these extremely soft targets looked clear and the flight commander had just given the order to return when suddenly, to Beckwith's eye, all *didn't* look clear. A slow-moving truck had left the highway and was moving in the direction of the school. The truck was on a commercial road but draped for desert camouflage. Beckwith didn't like a single thing about it.

"Swinging back around," she radioed the commander.

"Negative," he responded. "Break off and follow."

"Possible trouble here, sir," she pressed.

"There'll be trouble *here*," he snapped, "if you don't break off, Lieutenant Commander."

"Sir, it's a truck—" she began, but he cut her off again.

"You are out of fuel, Lieutenant Commander! You will break off."

"But there's a school—"

"You *will* break off!" the commander shouted this time.

Now, at last, Beckwith obeyed. Defying a direct order in a combat zone would be a court-martial offense. She wheeled around, rejoined the group, and spent the entire fifty-eight-minute flight back to the ship pleading with circumstance, with chance, with the random fates of war, to spare the school from the attack she was certain had happened.

It was not spared. The school had been one for girls and it was fully attended that day. Only minutes after Beckwith had turned and flown off, the truck pulled up and thirty-two of the students, along with their young teacher, were killed in a spray of automatic weapons fire and the blasts of multiple grenades. The next day, another flight of Super Hornets went back in search of the group responsible but found nothing. Even if they had, nothing would have changed the arithmetic of what had happened: Beckwith had seen what was coming, was in possession of a jet and the weapons that could have saved thirty-three lives, and she did not act; she did not act because, at bottom, the threat of punishment and the loss of her career had stopped her, had rendered her obedient.

She would tell herself that it was the commander's order that was to blame. Jasper would tell her that too when they spoke by phone one day later when the after-action report was back and the girls, some of them as young as six, were identified. And it was true. She was not permitted to disobey a command. But she was *able* to disobey it if she had chosen. She didn't choose—and so the girls died.

On that very day, Beckwith promised herself that if she were ever in such a position again, she would not break off, no matter the consequences. She told Jasper of that resolve; to say it aloud would make it harder for her not to hold herself accountable when the time came. Now it had.

"Walli Bee," Jasper typed, sitting in his seat at a bar that was slowly emptying of its last customers, "this isn't the same thing."

"It's close enough," Beckwith answered.

"You're in very real jeopardy."

"So are the people down there."

Jasper contemplated how best to respond, but Beckwith preempted him, "Where are you, Jasper?"

He smiled. "I'm having a Cutty. Having a Cutty with you and Wally."

Two hundred and fifty miles overhead, she smiled too. "I'm glad," she wrote. "It's late. Finish your drink, take a sip for me, and go home."

They both signed off, and Jasper took a final swallow of his Cutty. Over the last two days, Joe Star had sent him a pair of emails that he'd read but ducked. No one in NASA knew the details of his and Beckwith's past, but plenty of people had long since figured out that there had *been* a past. Star wanted to know if Jasper, with his intimate knowledge of who Beckwith was, had any ideas about what might best persuade her to come home. Jasper had not been sure he had anything to offer. Now he did. He scrolled back through his emails, found Star's latest, and responded.

"Give her what she wants," he wrote. "Give her what she wants and she'll come home."

. . .

The president had been glaring at national security reports all morning. They had been included in his daily brief, which he opened at just after 8:00 A.M. By 8:05 he was in a foul mood from which he hadn't emerged for hours. After each of his meetings he'd pick up the security report and narrow his eyes at it menacingly. His aides had gotten used to this—his habit of returning and returning to some report or bit of news that had displeased him, staring daggers at it and defying it to transform itself into something more to his liking.

Today the news that was troubling him was dispatches from aid workers and independent humanitarian groups on the ground in South America. The reports revealed that displacement and refugee totals had now climbed to more than 150,000, about half of whom were wandering the jungle while the other half had been herded into the western border camps that no one even pretended anymore were "lush tribal lands"—even if the Brazilian government continued to use the phrase.

The cable channels and the editorial pages that had been calling out repeatedly for the president and the US military to intervene had only gotten louder, now that they had Beckwith to whip them up, but he remained immovable. First of all, he didn't necessarily trust that the reports from the jungle were solid. The sources were unreliable— amateur fieldworkers and do-good volunteer groups, all of whom, he believed, had every incentive to inflate the refugee totals. The president's National Security Council had told him that its own estimates did track those of the aid groups, but he was still unpersuaded.

What's more, there was the president's stated and, for better or worse, sincere aversion to mixing in foreign wars. He had wanted to call his policy America First—he actually pleaded with his advisers to *let* him call it America First—but even before he ran for office, the phrase had accumulated more baggage than a steamship and his campaign manager threatened to quit if he used it. His aides focus-grouped alternatives, and to the president's exceeding annoyance, American Objectives was the easy winner. "Sounds like a hedge fund," he grumbled. Still, that was the term his voting base liked, and whatever the policy was called, the no-foreign-wars promise remained popular with a solid majority of them.

But there was a more troubling side to the American president's aversion to getting in the way of the Brazilian president's policies—or at least that's what his opponents claimed. When it came to disdain for indigenous peoples, the critics argued, the two leaders were of one dark mind. That was a reputation the American president had brought on himself.

It was when he was serving his single term as governor of Oklahoma that the yearlong protest staged by the Sioux Nation against the construction of the Dakota oil pipeline across their native lands played out. The then-governor had penned an opinion column for the *Oklahoma Tribune* opposing the protesters and supporting the oil company. He had made no secret to his aides of his disgust with the idea of what he called a "ragged tribe that fancied itself a nation" standing in the way of necessary industrial development. In the first draft of his column he had included the line "We cannot let the stone age stand in the way of the silicon age."

His aides pleaded with him to cut the patently offensive passage, and he acceded—especially after the line was leaked by a disgruntled junior staffer, leading to all manner of blowback from Native American groups. But the then-governor played cute too. In his final draft, which he sent to the paper without his aides' sign-off, the word "stone" appeared three times: once when he called the tribes a "stone in the shoe of progress," once when he accused the tribal leaders of "throwing verbal stones" rather than engaging in a dialogue with Washington, and a third time when he actually managed to get the words "stone" and "age" to bump right up against each other. Ending one sentence with the complaint that the tribes had been "implacable as stone," he began the next with the claim that "age has been a factor in the uprising," with irresponsible young people adversely influencing adults. When the editorial ran, supporters of the tribes picked up on the unsubtle dog-whistling, while supporters of the then-governor insisted that such an interpretation was nonsense. The governor himself, pleased with his wordplay, had some sharp words for his staff: "That is the last time you ever try to edit me."

The "*Tribune* incident," as critics of the now-president called it, continued to haunt him. It was partly because of that, and partly as an attempt to appease the activists and the press, that the president now decided to throw his weight, or at least his grudging approval, behind the move by members of both parties to hold their vote demanding military intervention on September 18. The plan was to introduce one bill in the House and a virtually identical one in the Senate, vote on them the same day, and reconcile them quickly, disposing of the matter and sending it on to the White House as expeditiously as possible. With the president's party enjoying a majority in both the House and Senate, the White House had been confident that the legislation would not pass in even one of the two chambers.

But now there were these reports in the president's morning brief, which he just *knew* he shouldn't have read. If they were already being circulated by the aid workers and other groups nosing around the Amazon, they would surely be picked up and run with by the press. And the mutinous Walli Beckwith would surely run with what the press ran with, which in turn would rattle the lawmakers who would have to cast their votes on September 18. Her act of naked criminality was now in its fourth day, and the public was absolutely loving the show.

One network had already begun running on-screen chyrons reading, "The Holdout: Day One," which became day two and three and now day four, and could, as far as the president knew, go on for the rest of his entire term. On another, there was the "Walli Watch," a tagline for regular station updates that affiliates in no fewer than thirty-four markets adopted. The president's political advisers had nothing to offer him except that he should project leadership, stay above the fray, and not engage publicly with Beckwith. But what he was in the mood for was very much to engage with her. And so when his morning meetings were done, he canceled his first two afternoon appointments and called for Connie Polk. He might not like her much, he might already have begun looking for a second-term replacement for her, but she was a knife fighter, and that he very much admired.

"Mr. President?" she said as she entered. He liked the way she always framed it as a question; it was the only bit of real deference she ever showed him.

"Connie," he said airily. "Sit, sit."

He liked the way too that she obeyed, sitting on command. The thought flitted briefly through his head that once he retired he'd buy a dog, name it Connie, and make sure that fact was released to the press.

"What can I help you with, sir?" she asked.

"Beckwith," he answered.

She nodded. "We're working on that. We can prosecute at will once she returns, probably a military court-martial. The Russians are being cagey about their intentions. She'll eventually land in Kazakhstan, so Moscow will have her first, and what happens then is up to them. The Japanese are furious; they spent $6 billion on their Kibo module, and they don't like the idea of a criminal trespassing on it. They'll likely indict her immediately."

"And the Europeans?"

"Hungary, Italy, Poland, Norway, Germany, and Greece all want to prosecute. France is opposed. The other fifteen nations have not yet committed."

"France," the president sniffed. "What's holding the Russians back?"

"They want to tie a prosecution to continued aerospace sales. We keep buying their RD-180 rocket engines, they'll indict Beckwith and then extradite her here."

"Are the engines any good?"

"They'll do," Polk said.

"Have they killed anybody yet?"

"No."

"Then tell them we'll keep buying them."

"Yes, sir."

"Connie," the president said confidentially. He leaned forward and glanced to either side, as if to make sure nobody else was listening.

Polk hated when he did that. It was his client pose, the one he'd assume when he wanted to confide in her as if she were his personal attorney. She had discreetly asked his chief of staff to remind him that was not her role, and the chief of staff had said he would. If he in fact did, the president hadn't absorbed the lesson. He went on.

"This is not a fight I can lose," he said.

"No, sir."

"A war in Brazil would eat my first term, and I'll have nothing to show when it's time for the second. It would be nice to wrap this up quickly, well before the midterms."

"How can I be of help?"

"We could lean on the rocket companies—Arcadia and CelestiX."

"Lean on them?" Polk asked warily.

"Tell them to get flying pronto so I can send someone up to bring her home—the astronaut." He waved his hand, as if mentioning Beckwith's name would only dignify her. "I can't be seen to be sitting here waiting for the Russians to do our work for us."

"Sir, neither company can fly right now. Not with the strike at Arcadia and the explosion at CelestiX."

"Tell 'em I'll nationalize them then. Truman tried it with steel; I'll do it with space."

"Mr. President," Polk said as levelly as she could. "Launching a rocket is an order of magnitude harder than running a steel mill. You'll only look reckless—decisive, but reckless." She added the "decisive" as a balm, hoping it would appease him and cause him to switch tracks. It did.

"Look into her past then—Beckwith's."

"We're doing that. There's nothing there to work with, and what there *is* you want no part of. Naval Academy, fighter pilot, astronaut—hero business."

"What about her family?"

"There's not much. A niece, both parents, a few cousins," Polk answered.

"Husband?"

"She's never married."

"Hmph," the president said with a knowing smirk.

Polk did not respond.

"Look into the parents then," he said.

"I doubt there's anything there either. They're old-school engineers—early space program. Retired in Arizona. They do a little consulting work on the side to stretch their pensions."

"Send someone to visit them anyway—badge-and-earpiece types. That gets people talking."

A great many things Polk would have liked to say went through her head. Instead, she settled for, "Yes, sir."

She rose and turned to leave before the president could declare the meeting over. He raced to catch up. "You may go, Connie," he said, pointlessly.

CHAPTER NINE

Whatever entrance Vasily Zhirov might have wanted to make into Moscow Mission Control when he returned from space was not the one he actually got to make. Zhirov might have been a national hero, but he wasn't above his vanities, and no sooner had he landed in Kazakhstan than his mind shifted to the grand scene that would play out later that evening at Mission Control, when he strode into the room having come straight from an emergency evacuation in space—still carrying some of the cosmic shimmer, still smelling of thruster fuel. There would be hugs; there would be handshakes. He would smile and express his thanks, but he would make short work of the greetings, take a seat at a console, and resume command of his mission. After a full eight-hour shift was done, *then* there would be time to accept the controllers' plaudits with cognac toasts in an adjacent meeting room.

But no sooner had the Roscosmos plane taken off for the three-hour flight from Kazakhstan to Moscow than he knew that was not to be. The Zhezkazgan dumplings stayed down for less than an hour before Zhirov bolted for the plane's lavatory and brought them straight up again. He was back in the lavatory twenty minutes later and then ten minutes after that. By the second half of the flight he simply decided to stay there, sparing the Roscosmos officials the awkwardness of pretending that they didn't notice that the world's greatest cosmonaut, the man chasing the Zolotaya Tysyacha, the Golden Thousand, was having a harder time holding down his food than a pregnant woman suffering from the *toksikoz*—lady sickness.

"It's your ears," Sergei Rozovsky, the recovery team commander, told him during one of the brief interludes when Zhirov was actually in his seat.

"My ears are fine," Zhirov protested.

"They are not. They have thrown off your balance, and the return to gravity is making you sicker still."

Zhirov started to argue but knew that Rozovsky was surely right. When the Roscosmos plane at last landed in Moscow, he tottered from the lavatory and confessed weakly to Rozovsky, "I cannot go to the flight center."

Rozovsky smiled. "No, Vasily, you cannot."

Zhirov gestured to the others in the plane and lowered his voice. "But they can't know."

"They would understand."

"No," Zhirov protested. "They can't know."

Rozovsky nodded, picked up the cabin phone, and muttered into it. He hung up, then spoke a few quiet words to Zhirov, and the two of them exited the plane and climbed down the steps. Zhirov held the handrail in a death grip and waved with seeming ease with his other hand. He reached the bottom and accepted handshakes. And then he and Rozovsky performed their little pantomime.

"Where is the car I requested?" Rozovsky asked crossly as Lebedev was loaded into a waiting ambulance.

"There is no need," said the airport official who greeted them. "Both men must go to the hospital."

"That's not possible!" Zhirov protested.

"That's not possible," Rozovsky echoed. "This man needs to go to the control center."

"I am told this man is sick," the official said.

"I am fine," Zhirov said and took a few conspicuous steps toward the terminal building. Three airport security guards converged and stood—respectfully—in his path. One of them spoke into a walkie-talkie, and a moment later an Air Force officer strode from the terminal toward the group. The two stars on his epaulets marked him a lieutenant general.

"Colonel," he said, shaking Zhirov's hand. The two men knew each other, had spent more than one evening drinking vodka together, and had long since come to address each other by their first names. But announcing Zhirov's subordinate rank would serve the purposes of their charade today.

"Sir," Zhirov said.

"You are to accompany Captain Lebedev and the doctors to the Vishnevsky Military Hospital."

"I have business at Mission Control," Zhirov said. "And I feel fine."

"Your business can wait and you do not look fine."

"But the mission—"

"The mission will run without you for now."

Zhirov, feeling the eyes of the airport officials and now of various tarmac technicians on him, could have wept with gratitude at the general's command. With so large an audience watching, however, he felt that one more protest seemed called for.

"I would prefer to go to the command center, sir." The words were out of his mouth before he even realized what he'd said. He could practically hear the cursed Walli Beckwith's voice in his head.

"You would *prefer*?" the general said, this time with genuine pique; he too had the eyes of the tarmac technicians on him. "I am indifferent to what you would prefer. You will get in that ambulance now—*Colonel.*"

Zhirov did as he was told, climbed into the back of the ambulance, and ultimately spent four days at Vishnevsky, sleeping, trying to eat, and following the developments unfolding in space and in the Brazilian jungle. The news the doctors gave him was encouraging. His ears would heal. The eardrums hadn't ruptured, but the suddenness of the depressurization had caused fluid along with air to accumulate in the inner ear. It would take weeks for it to be reabsorbed. In the meantime he would be grounded, forbidden to fly so much as a low-altitude glider, much less a spacecraft.

Lebedev would not be so lucky. His eardrum had ruptured completely, as Zhirov and Beckwith had assumed straightaway. Even if the doctors could repair it, there were too many other healthy cosmonauts awaiting their chance to fly for Roscosmos to justify assigning a damaged man to another crew. Lebedev's first, abbreviated trip to space would be his last.

The doctors would have kept Zhirov in the hospital for up to a week, but after just four days, he decided he'd had enough. The treatment he was receiving was doing nothing for his ears, and the doctors themselves admitted his hearing would just have to recover slowly on its own—which it was already beginning to do. Beckwith was getting by without all of the medical doting, and he could too. He had listened to her call to Earth and, through news reports, learned of the global following she was developing. There was only so much longer he could remain sidelined. On his fourth morning in the hospital, he dressed in a clean set of Navy fatigues and announced summarily that he was discharging himself. There was no lieutenant general to outrank him here.

When Zhirov at last made his return to Mission Control, it was just after 8:30 on the morning of August 25. The smell of thruster fuel was four days gone, and the very thought of toasting with cognac or anything at all still made his head swim and his stomach turn over.

His reception was reserved: The morning shift change was underway, and at all of the consoles, the outgoing controllers were busily briefing the incoming ones. Zhirov was greeted only by Gennady Bazanov, the director of flight operations, who hurried up the aisle to him.

"Welcome, Vasily Sergeyevich," Bazanov said affectionately, adding a handshake and a warm embrace. He hugged with the strength of a much younger man. "How are you feeling?"

"I'm fine," Zhirov said and caught Bazanov's skeptical expression. "I am improved."

"You should rest."

"I've rested long enough. I should be here," Zhirov said. "Where can I plug in?"

Bazanov pointed him to a console in the back aisle of the room, and Zhirov frowned. The console was fully functional, but it was also a spare, usually set aside for government officials and other visitors.

"You will observe, Vasily," Bazanov said. "No more."

"It's my spacecraft, Mr. Director," he said respectfully.

"Your mission is over."

"My mission is to last six months. We have barely finished two."

"Vasily," Bazanov said reasonably, "you're on the ground; your spacecraft is in the sky. This is not puppetry."

"One of my crew members is still in the sky too," Zhirov answered. "I respect the chain of command. *She* respects the chain of command." He swept out his hand in a gesture that took in the entirety of Mission Control. "There is not a man or woman in this room who knows Walli Beckwith better than I do."

Bazanov had never cared for Beckwith's nickname, believing it ill served the Russian roots of her proper name. "She is Belka," he said.

"With respect, sir, you have just proven my point," Zhirov replied.

Bazanov, who had worked all night along with the outgoing shift, looked away and rubbed his eyes. He had been directing missions from the ground since the flight of Soyuz 10 in April 1971. His second mission, just two months later, was Soyuz 11, when the mournful "one-one-one" was announced by the recovery team at the site of the just-returned spacecraft. All those years and that long-ago sorrow seemed to be weighing on him today.

"If you speak to her, Vasily, you must bring her home," Bazanov said at last.

"I know that," Zhirov answered. "But I can't promise that I can."

"Is she your crew member or not?" Bazanov asked.

"She is."

"Then you will bring her home. But these are my conditions: You will not have an open mic. You will spend today simply observing and listening to the air-to-ground communications. When you do wish to speak to Belka Beckwith, you will request permission, and the flight director will either grant or not grant your request."

Zhirov nodded. "I accept those terms."

"Then you may take the seat," Bazanov said.

With that, the director of flight operations stood aside. Zhirov put on the headset, fiddled with the volume knob, and, before he had even sat down, flicked the call button.

"Flight," he said to the flight director in the middle of the room, "request permission to speak to the crew."

Bazanov shook his head. "Cosmonauts," he muttered wearily. Then he turned and left the room to go home and sleep. He would, the controllers knew, be back before the dinner hour.

. . .

At the same moment Zhirov was getting settled at his console in Mission Control, Beckwith was having breakfast in the Russian Zvezda module. It was just after 9:00 A.M. in Moscow, which meant it was just after 6:00 A.M. aboard the station. She had not been terribly hungry since the day of the accident—mostly, she guessed, because her still-clogged ears left her just light-headed enough to make her feel chronically, if slightly, motion sick. Still, breakfast was an exception.

Beckwith had grown partial to a lot of the Russians' food, especially *tvorog*, a sort of sticky marriage of cottage and ricotta cheese that could be stored dry, rehydrated, and mixed with nuts or raisins or minced dates. Beckwith preferred all three at once. She always felt awkward about cadging *tvorog* from the Russians and would typically wait to be invited for breakfast, which happened now and then. Even alone on the station, she had forced herself to eat the Americans' rehydrated eggs on her first two mornings, but after that she decided that once you've hijacked a spaceship, it seemed somehow beside the point to worry about raiding the kitchen. She was halfway through her first cup of *tvorog* and already contemplating a second when the radio crackled to life.

"Station, Moscow," came the call.

Beckwith brightened at the voice, fumbled the *tvorog*—which went somersaulting slowly toward a bulkhead—and lunged for the talk switch on the nearest panel.

"Vasily!" she exclaimed.

"Walli Belka," he said levelly. He had expected to hear her voice; she had not imagined she'd hear his.

"How are you? Are you well? Your ears?" she asked.

"Better. They hurt a little, I can hear a little. You?"

"The same. And Yulian?"

"He burst the drum. He won't fly again."

"I'm so sorry, Vasily," Beckwith said, feeling genuine sadness both for Lebedev and for Zhirov, who had held the rookie cosmonaut with the fine engineering skills in such high regard.

"Yes," Zhirov answered. "He is a good man. But he cannot now be a cosmonaut." He quickly changed the topic. "You've caused quite a mix down here, Walli."

"Mix?" she asked.

He switched to the Russian. "*Perepolókh*," he said.

Beckwith thought. "Stir!" she finally said. "Yes, I've caused one."

"You're in a lot of trouble."

"Twenty-five countries, I'm told. Tell me you and Yulian will visit me in prison."

"Don't make jokes, Walli," Zhirov said. "And don't provoke your government. They will not change their minds, and they will punish you for what you're doing. A Soyuz will come to get you soon and you should be on it."

"You know I can't do that."

"I know you don't *want* to do that." Zhirov avoided the word "prefer." It had caused him enough trouble lately.

Beckwith said nothing at all, letting the hiss from space speak for her. Zhirov understood.

"Tell me what your work is today," he said, tacking in a different direction. "You may overthrow your government in your free time, but first you must take care of my spacecraft."

Beckwith laughed and consulted her notes. She was about to read out the first few items—changing air filters in Nodes 1, 2, and 3; adjusting humidity in the plant experiments in the Kibo and Columbus modules—when suddenly the hated Klaxon again sounded from seemingly everywhere in the station. It was loud, cutting, startling, even through the muffling caused by her still-clogged ears. The same sound, mixed with the static of the air-to-ground line, cut through the headsets of every man and woman in Moscow Mission Control.

"Walli!" Zhirov called. "What is it?"

"Stand by one," Beckwith shouted over the noise.

She bolted from the Zvezda module, over to the nearest piece of the American segment—the Node 1 Unity module—and glanced at the instrument panel. The red ATM indicator was flashing. Atmosphere—something was fouling the air. In the same instant, another voice, an American voice from the Capcom station in Houston, cut in.

"Ammonia leak, station. Execute shelter procedure. Negative drill. Again, not a drill."

That was followed by Zhirov's voice.

"Ammonia, Walli! Shelter!" he said.

Beckwith didn't have to be told to shelter, by Houston or by Moscow. Ammonia was the likeliest cause of an atmosphere alert and also the worst. It was the key chemical in the coolant system in the American segment and far and away the most dangerous substance aboard the station. Ammonia was deadly to humans and easy to detect by smell—but not until the concentrations rose high enough that death would not be merely possible, but likely and imminent.

"Copy, Moscow; copy, Houston," she said.

Wherever she sought shelter, it would have to be in the Russian segment, where the coolant system relied on simple glycol. The ammonia might have already drifted that far, but it was surely a safer bet than anywhere on the American segment. The Zarya module was closest. She could hunker down there, slam the hatch, and shut out the leak.

"Moving into the Zarya!" she shouted over the screaming Klaxon.

"Get to the Zarya!" Zhirov shouted at the same moment.

In the back of Moscow Mission Control, a door flew open and Bazanov, who had lingered in his office tending to a few stray matters before going home, dashed in. He had a squawk box on his desk with which he always followed the air-to-ground chatter. He made straight for Zhirov's console.

"Is the ammonia confirmed?" he asked.

"Houston confirms it," Zhirov said.

"Get her to the module." He didn't have to specify which one.

"She's doing that."

Beckwith dashed into the safety of the Zarya, slammed the hatch, and secured it. The sound of the Klaxon grew slightly softer.

"Sheltering in place," she called down.

"We're looking for the site of the leak," Houston reported.

"Copy," Beckwith said.

She braced her hand against a module wall and drew some deep, steadying breaths—breaths she hoped weren't filling her lungs with a gas that could kill her. If the leak was real, she might survive it, but somewhere behind the safety of the closed hatch, the station itself was being killed. Ammonia was a stubborn poison, and if enough was released, the station's entire volume of atmosphere would have to be vented and replenished and vented and replenished dozens of times before the modules would be habitable again. With the American space shuttle retired, there was no longer enough lifting power to get that much oxygen up to orbit. The morning had begun with a huge and healthy space facility made of fourteen functioning modules—already one fewer than there should have been, after the destruction of the Pirs. Under Walli Beckwith's stolen command, the module count would be reduced to just four, all in the Russian segment. That was not the way the Naval Academy taught its officers to command a ship.

Beckwith pivoted back to the hatch and yanked its lock latch, and the little door popped open. On the ground the monitors in Moscow instantly reported the pressure change.

"Walli, what are you doing?" Zhirov shouted.

"Damage control," was all she said.

She exited the Zarya, closed the hatch behind her, and shot toward the American segment. Even if there was no way of knowing yet where the leak was, she could still seal off every one of the ten modules on the American side and isolate most of the poisonous gas in the single one that had the problem. She drew a breath, held it, and headed first for the Destiny module, in the middle of the American array. Gas masks were kept in a storage cabinet there to be used during experiments with toxic chemicals.

"Walli, please return to the Zarya," she heard Houston call.

"Walli, I instruct you to return to the Zarya," Zhirov said.

"Copy," was all Beckwith croaked, with the little breath she allowed herself to exhale. Whatever microphone was closest in the public communications system probably didn't pick up her voice.

She reached the Destiny, pulled open a cabinet, grabbed a mask, put it on, and cinched its straps, then moved on through to the far end of the American segment and began sealing off its modules one by one. When she was done, she shot back through the Destiny lab, then stopped herself short, turned back, grabbed the mouse cage that held Bolt, and turned to go. Then she stopped yet again, silently cursed her own cold-bloodedness, grabbed the other four cages that held the mice she had not bothered to name, then flew back to the Russian segment, herding the floating mouse cages in front of her. When she reached the Zarya, she slammed the hatch behind her. The mouse cages dispersed around her, bumping up against a bulkhead and bouncing back off of it. She ripped off her gas mask, drew some clear, gasping breaths, and hailed the ground.

"Station is secure," she reported.

"Confirm," was all Houston said.

"That was foolish," Zhirov snapped. *"Tupoy."* *Dumb.*

Bazanov grabbed Zhirov's headset.

"Lieutenant Commander, you disobeyed an order from Colonel Zhirov, who remains in charge of this mission," he said.

Beckwith didn't have to be told who was speaking. Astronauts and cosmonauts recognized Bazanov's voice.

"Yes, sir," she said. "I did. I felt it was necessary."

"We do not run our missions based on cosmonauts' feelings," he barked and threw the headset back on the console.

As he did that, the Klaxon, which had been sounding throughout the station and streaming through the communication loops in two control rooms in two cities more than 5,900 miles apart, suddenly stopped. The silence was a sweet relief. A voice from Houston then broke the brief peace.

"Atmosphere is stable," the voice said. "EECOM officer confirms acceptable environment and life support."

Beckwith dropped her head into her hands. "What was the anomaly, Houston?" she asked.

"Uncertain at this time. Either a false alarm or a small, transient leak which has sealed itself. Recommend monitoring, as we will do here. But return to nominal status."

Nominal status, Beckwith repeated in her head. *As you were.* Had she not known better, she'd have sworn that someone on the ground had dreamed up a fake emergency just to scare her off the station. But she did know better. The ammonia system and its various sensors were notoriously glitchy, and the false alarm could just as easily have been a real one. She laughed softly—entirely at herself. She was engaged in an act of madness—madness and arrogance; she'd accepted that from the beginning. But now she had to accept that it might be an act of suicide too.

On the ground Zhirov sat back in his chair, looked up at the ceiling, and closed his eyes. He was jolted back by a hard grip on his wrist. He sat up and turned. It was, of course, Bazanov.

"Solve this problem," he commanded. "Bring that woman home."

He turned and stalked back out of Mission Control. In the front of the room, on the left side of the viewing screen, Walli Beckwith, many times larger than life, smiled winningly.

CHAPTER TEN

The United States was never going to go to war at the insistence of an inactive lieutenant commander who, alone among the 7.6 billion people of Earth, was not even *on* the Earth. That was more or less the opening line of a blistering *Wall Street Journal* article, the overall sense of which was quickly picked up by most of the members of the president's party. The intent, of course, was to diminish Beckwith, to make her seem an inconsequential, even comical figure, and after she read the *Journal* story and the commentary it sparked, she had more than a little doubt herself.

"Who the hell does she think she is?" sneered one cable news commentator, with so perfect a blend of amusement and dismissal that, unbidden, the question *Who the hell* do *I think I am?* flitted through Beckwith's head.

There was no question that her following was growing. The September 18 Coalition was now being led by a third-year law student at the University of Oklahoma named Laurel Cady, who was already working as an intern in the Oklahoma branch of the American Civil Liberties Union. She had long been working toward a clerkship in the federal court system and had set herself a goal of at least being short-listed for the Supreme Court by the time she was thirty-eight, figuring that any younger would be unseemly and any older would be a waste of the fifty-some remaining years she fully intended to spend on the bench.

"The law moves slowly," she'd say by way of explanation. "I'll need the time."

Since her undergraduate years, Cady had been fascinated by the history of organized protest in America, most instructively the Boston Tea Party, the Montgomery bus boycott, the March on Washington, the first Earth Day, and, by way of calamitous negative example, the 1968 antiwar march on the Democratic National Convention in Chicago, which turned into a riot. She took a near-technological approach to all of them, reverse engineering them from the moment the last placard was put down—or, in the case of Chicago, the last brick was thrown—to the first moment someone said, "You know what? I've had enough."

Everything, she had come to conclude, was dependent on laying down sprawling public roots—with activists practically everywhere, enraged, engaged, appearing ungovernable, but governed all the same by a twig, branch, and trunk system of local groups answerable to state groups and finally to one national group with one leader at the top of it. And Cady would be that leader. She had already been organizing local protests against the Consolidation throughout Oklahoma City, and the moment Beckwith began a similar protest from the somewhat more rarefied venue of space, she expanded her efforts nationwide.

Working with the most skilled and committed group of students she could assemble on the fly in the university's computer engineering school—plus a handful of employees she cadged from the school's IT department—she oversaw the construction of a website that the engineers promised her was "unhackable, unbreakable, and absolutely bulletproof." She loved that, hugged three of them in turn, and dubbed them her "Kevlar boys." One of them promptly went out and got a tattoo reading just that, only with "boys" rendered as "boyz." By the end of the week, all three had them.

The coalition website was now coordinating the work of ninety-one groups in twenty-one countries and all fifty states. The organizations had raised a collective $9.3 million in small donations, and more was streaming in steadily. By now 1.5 million people had signed up to march in Washington on September 18, with an average of a hundred thousand new volunteers joining every thirty-six hours. In less-organized signs of Beckwith's growing popularity, nine websites were circulating petitions for her to run for president in three years; student activists at Guangzhou University opened an account on Weibo, China's Twitter, in support of Beckwith, using her English name as well as a Mandarin nickname with characters that translated loosely as "Moon Woman Revolutionary," which delighted her enormously; and in most of the West "I would prefer not to" continued to be a lead search term across the Web.

"You're a meme, Mama," Sonia emailed her.

That, actually, was what Beckwith feared. A meme was, by definition, a fleeting thing. She was undeniably having some effect on a handful of representatives and senators from a few moderate districts and states, who were feeling the heat of the protests to come, but it was uncertain how much of a difference that could make. The best Washington handicappers put the current vote in the House of Representatives at 195 opposed to intervention and 170 in favor, with 70 undecided. In the Senate it was a somewhat closer 48 against and 40 in favor, with 12 undecided. Even if the undecideds broke heavily for military action, giving the intervention side the necessary majorities of 218 votes in the House and 51 in the Senate—and *even* if the Senate ran that total up to the 60 votes necessary to overcome a filibuster by the losing side—the president would just veto the bill. It would then require a two-thirds vote in both chambers to override the veto—a vastly longer long shot.

In the unlikely event an override somehow improbably succeeded, the whole bubbling mess could be thrown straight into the lap of the courts. Article I of the Constitution gave Congress broad war-making powers, but Article II gave the president the absolute authority over all branches of the military, leaving it entirely unclear which branch had the final call. That constitutional booby trap was built into the nation's founding document by its Founding Fathers, who either hadn't thought things through entirely or did think them through and took a secret delight at the idea of punking their posterity. For pro-intervention forces, the only answer then would be a veto-proof, two-thirds victory in both the House and Senate in favor of intervention, plus a groundswell of popular American sentiment so great that the president would feel compelled to act lest the nation's business cease to be done.

Creating that groundswell was the job Beckwith had presumptuously assigned herself, and at the moment her tools were more limited than she'd have liked. Her official agency website was a slow and rickety thing, dependent on a series of patches that NASA had applied to internet software it first began using in the late 1990s. The site crashed when its traffic reached one million, which it often did. NASA for now had decided not to take the provocative step of shutting Beckwith's site down entirely lest it inflame her supporters, and instead simply rooted for it to collapse on its own, and quietly rejoiced whenever that happened.

Sonia was aware of the problem, and she suspected she might have a solution in the form of Raymond. He had studied programming before going to medical school, and while he fully intended to practice medicine when he completed his residency, he just as fully intended to get gloriously rich later on, designing uniform systems for electronic medical records, remote prescribing, and data sharing among research institutes. Sonia showed him Beckwith's website, and he looked at it with the piteous gaze of someone regarding a wounded animal. His fingers almost seemed to twitch to get at it.

Sonia straightaway emailed Beckwith and asked her to call at 6:30 that night, once the children in the pediatric ward at the Mercado camp were quieting down for the evening. The space station phone system worked in only one direction—the station could call Earth; Earth could not call the station. Beckwith agreed, and at 6:20 Sonia hurried over to the infirmary, where she knew Raymond would be working. She got no more than a few steps when she heard a voice behind her.

"So-*nee*-ya!" it called. It was, of course, Oli hurrying after her. "Where are you going?"

Sonia turned and crouched, he ran into her arms, and she picked him up. "I have a phone call, and you should be getting ready for bed."

"Who? Who are you calling?"

"Well . . . I'm not making the call actually; someone's calling me."

"Your . . . *tía*-mama?" he asked.

Sonia nodded. "Do you want to talk to her?"

His wide eyes and broad smile answered her question.

The two of them hurried to the first aid tent, and Sonia spotted Raymond entering patient data into a laptop.

"You need to come with me," she said.

"I do?" he asked, looking up and standing hurriedly, almost knocking over his chair—which was precisely the effect Sonia always seemed to have on him.

"Yes, and bring your computer. She may have some questions for you."

"Who?" he asked, then realized what Sonia had to mean. "She . . . the . . . ?" he managed, glancing upward.

"Astronaut," Sonia said for him. "Yes. Try not to sound overawed when you talk to her."

She took his wrist, and the three of them ran about twenty yards away to a small pine storage building. It was usually private, save for the odd person coming in to collect supplies from the shelves, and it was close by the satellite trucks, which meant a strong cell signal— probably the strongest anywhere in the Mercado camp.

The moment they slipped inside and closed the door, Sonia's phone rang. She tapped it open and turned on the speaker function. Sonia said hello, and the hiss from space filled the little shed. Finally a voice cut through the noise.

"Hello, hello," Beckwith said. "You can hear me?"

"Yes," Sonia said. She glanced at Oli, whose eyes had widened again and whose mouth was slightly open. She smiled. She glanced at Raymond—who was mirroring the boy's expression.

"I'm here with a doctor friend, Raymond . . ." She briefly tripped over the blank spot where a last name should be. Raymond did not seem to notice.

"Hello, ma'am!" he shouted toward the phone. "I am a doctor, like Sonia said, and I am here to help." There was a brief pause and Raymond looked uneasy. He raced to fill the gap: "Over," he said. Sonia rolled her eyes.

"Hello, Raymond," Beckwith said.

"Oli is here with us too," Sonia said.

"Hello, Oli," Beckwith responded. "I've heard about you. Are you being good?"

The boy's face flushed and he stammered a few words, and Sonia bent down and put the phone close to him. He seemed to have no idea what to say, and then he did.

"Can you see me when I'm outside?" he asked.

The hiss came through the phone, followed by a laugh. "Not so far," Beckwith said. "Would you like me to look next time?"

"Yes!" Oli said and bolted immediately for the door.

Sonia caught him by the arm. "It's almost dark now," she whispered. "We'll try in the day."

Oli nodded, and Sonia turned back to the phone. "Raymond says he can get you sorted out online," she said. "I'm going to let him explain things to you." She inclined the phone to Raymond, who by now seemed to have gotten himself collected.

"I can fix your website, ma'am," he said. "I'll clean it up and speed it up and weave in a little code to keep it from crashing."

"You can do that?"

"Within limits. The NASA site is a jalopy, but I'll make it go."

Beckwith laughed an admiring laugh and Raymond looked set to swoon, but he held himself together. "You also need a social media presence," he said. "You have no Twitter, no Facebook, no Snapchat, no Instagram."

"I don't like those," Beckwith said.

Sonia cut in, with an all-business voice Raymond sometimes heard her use in the clinic. "You're going to have to learn to like them, *Tía*." He looked at her shocked, but Beckwith sounded unconcerned.

"Copy that," she responded.

"Ma'am," Raymond said, "I can set up an account for you on Twitter right now if you like."

"Will anyone follow it?" Beckwith asked.

Raymond laughed. "You've heard of Beanfinger, ma'am?"

"No, I haven't."

"No reason you should have. They're a San Francisco band with exactly eight songs—all of them terrible. Do you know how many followers they have?" Sonia had seen where he was going and was already consulting Raymond's computer.

"Just over three million," she whispered, showing him the screen.

"Just over three million," Raymond repeated into the phone. "Yes, ma'am. I think people would follow you."

Beckwith sighed a resigned sigh that was audible all the way from 250 miles above the Earth to a pine shed in the Mercado camp in the Bolivian jungle.

"OK, Raymond," she said, "set it up."

"Thank you, ma'am!"

Raymond began tapping at his laptop, which he had taken from Sonia and set on a stack of crates, and then frowned. Beckwith had become so popular that all manner of people had snatched up all variations on her name for themselves. Belka Beckwith and Walli Beckwith and Walli Belka Beckwith and Belka Walli Beckwith and all of the possible combinations with initials had been taken. Finally Raymond added the abbreviation for her naval designation—"Lt. Cdr."—and it took.

"OK, ma'am," he said with a note of triumph in his voice, "You're now 'at Lt Cdr Walli Beckwith.' Please remember to put the 'at' sign first, run all of the letters together, and capitalize the *L*, *C*, *W*, and *B* so it won't look like gibberish. Would you like to try logging in? Your password is . . ." He hesitated slightly. "It's 'Sonia.'"

Sonia looked at him and shook her head in affected exasperation—but she smiled too.

The two of them watched Raymond's screen, and a few minutes later the first tweet from @LtCdrWalliBeckwith appeared. It read: "This is Walli Beckwith in space. I have Twitter now."

Raymond sighed. "We're going to have to work on these, ma'am," he said.

"Yes, Raymond," she answered.

Within forty-eight hours, Walli Beckwith from space would have 3.5 million followers—or half a million more than Beanfinger from San Francisco.

.   .   .

In the first few minutes after signing off with Sonia and Raymond, Beckwith felt optimistic, excited, and almost drunkenly powerful. It was a heady feeling—one she recognized and that she, Jasper, and a few other pilots she knew called conqueror's syndrome. She snuffed it fast. If you were a flier in command of a fifteen-ton machine that was bristling with weaponry and capable of moving at Mach speeds, all that power could make you reckless, stupid, even murderous. Beckwith was in command of a far bigger machine, moving at a far greater speed, and even if it wasn't carrying so much as a single target pistol, it conferred on her a power that was already allowing her to move millions.

She felt the need to use that power now—thoughtfully, soberly—and she knew how she could. In twenty minutes, the station would pass over South America; the angle would be oblique, not an ideal one for viewing, but it might still serve her purposes. She pushed off for the Russian segment.

The United States, Russia, and all of the other station partners had always promised that not a cubic foot of any one of the orbiting facility's fifteen modules would ever be devoted to military or surveillance work, but nobody expected that pledge to last forever. It did manage to stick, for a while, but then four years ago a Canadian company working with the cooperation of the Russians, and the winking connivance of the Americans, had launched an Earth-observation system to the station aboard a cargo vessel. It was ostensibly to be used only for environmental and agricultural monitoring and for that reason the ground had no control over it, lest one or another government try to use it for aerial spying. Of course nothing could prevent Mission Control in Moscow or Houston from colluding with a cosmonaut or astronaut to do a little snooping. Still, as long as everyone had equal access to the new capability—and an equal opportunity to sneak a forbidden peek at everyone else—no one would have an advantage.

The system was attached to the exterior of the Zarya module and consisted of two cameras—one for medium resolution and one for ultrahigh resolution. They were nicknamed Zoe and Ivy, and Beckwith adored them both. The first time she had a chance to try them out, she peered down into Wrigley Field during a Chicago Cubs afternoon game. She could see—from space—that the Cubs were just shy of a sellout that day. Using Zoe and Ivy without clearance from both Moscow and Houston Mission Controls was forbidden, and it was a rule Beckwith had so far not broken. But during her broadcast to Earth, she had promised she would be watching the jungle from space, and the system was indisputably the most effective way of doing that. She drifted into the Zarya and fired up the twin cameras, and no sooner had she done so than Mission Control hailed her.

"Station, Houston," came the call. It was Jasper; in the last twenty-four hours, it almost always seemed to be Jasper. Beckwith wasn't keeping precise track of how many Capcoms were in the current rotation or when they were working their shifts, but it seemed to Beckwith that he was now putting in up to fourteen hours a day.

"Don't you ever sleep, Jasper?" she said.

"Trying to keep up with you, Walli Bee," he answered. "We're seeing some activity on Zoe and Ivy. Can you confirm?"

"Confirm. I'll be working the girls for a little while."

"Procedure calls for you to ask permission first."

"May I?"

"Walli . . ." Jasper said with a note of warning.

"I'll stay out of trouble," Beckwith said, and before Jasper could answer, she muted the line.

Carefully then, she oriented the cameras, took a bead on the ground, and looked with delight as the image they were capturing—the Pacific surf washing up white against the northern part of the long Chilean coast—resolved on her monitor. She focused it more finely, captured a stretch of beach, and while she couldn't quite make out any people, she did manage to see what she believed to be a pair of dune buggies; they appeared to be racing.

She watched as the station quickly crossed the shoestring width of the Chilean nation and into Bolivia, following a sharp northeastern trajectory. The path would take her over northwestern Brazil, and if she managed Zoe and Ivy deftly, she could see a fair bit of the way into the central Amazon too.

As the jungle drifted below her, Beckwith felt a sting of grief at the thick green canopy, scarred in so many places by the bare, scabby patches of char and ash where there had once been trees. Then, suddenly, her gaze shifted. She spun the cameras' high-resolution system to sharpen the image further and then further still. She locked it on a patch of ground near the Brazilian-Bolivian border and her eyes widened. She pulled the image back, scanned east, and telescoped down to another spot. With mounting alarm, she repeated the scan and zoom three more times in three more locations, with the same results. There was hardware, there was armor, there were soldiers, there were fire cannons. She cursed herself for having left her laptop back in her sleep pod. She darted out of the Zarya, back to the American segment, dove into the pod, grabbed the computer, booted up the phone app, and hit the speed-dial tab with Sonia's face next to it. Far below, in the Bolivian jungle, Sonia's phone vibrated in her pocket and she answered it.

"Sonia!" Beckwith shouted. "Baby! Get out of there!"

CHAPTER ELEVEN

Sonia Bravo-Beckwith was unaware that anything terrible was about to happen in the moments before the jungle began to burn. In the days she'd been in the Mercado camp in Bolivia, she'd spent little time outside the pediatrics building at all, tending the children who had been chased from their lands and continued to arrive, exhausted, hungry, sick with parasites, and in many cases suffering burns from fires that had claimed their communities but at least spared their lives. Some of the children, if they were small enough and not infectious, were sleeping two to a bed. Sonia caught naps in the increasingly crowded staff tents when she could and bunked down in Oli's small bed with him at night, since the boy would not go to sleep after dark if she was not by his side.

There was still a cyclone of grief and terror swirling in his head, though she saw only occasional gusts of it. He would stick close to her as she made her rounds, then would return to his bed, sometimes only an hour after he had gotten up in the morning, and fall into a deep, twitching sleep from which he could not be awakened. He once walked beyond the safety of the walls entirely, telling Sonia he was waiting for his father to pick him up. Sonia, unsure how to respond, said she'd wait with him. He looked at her oddly, said there was no point waiting because his father was dead, and walked back into the camp.

But he managed his sorrow in other ways too. The day after he killed the butterfly, he wandered to a cluster of trees and began staring up at the trumpet-shaped flowers growing everywhere on the branches. He was looking for the Mainumby, he told Sonia, but when she asked him what the Mainumby was—or were—he shushed her and told her she would scare them away. So she went back into the pediatrics building, searched the term on her computer, and found that, like the Isondú and the Panambi, the Mainumby were animals—in this case hummingbirds—whose job was to transport good spirits living in flowers back home to Tupá, or God. Perhaps if his father and his grandmother weren't to be found in the glowworms and the butterflies, they might be in the trumpet flowers and the hummingbirds might carry them home.

Sonia had an idea. She hurried to the food tent, boiled water, and dissolved several large tablespoons of sugar into it, then selected a bottle of red food coloring from a collection of colors the kitchen staff sometimes used to bake birthday cakes for the children when there were enough eggs, flour, and other supplies on hand to permit such an extravagance. She colored the water and poured it into a bowl. When she was a girl, this was exactly the mixture her father would use to fill the hummingbird feeder in their backyard, easily attracting the birds, which were drawn by the color and then drawn back when they sampled the energy hit the sugar gave their high-speed metabolism. Sonia carefully carried the now-cooling bowl back to Oli, who was still standing under the tree. He cocked his head curiously when he saw her approach. She set the bowl on the ground, then put her finger to her lips.

"Shhh . . ." she said. "Sit." He obeyed and then she pointed up to the trees. Within minutes, two hummingbirds appeared, drinking nectar from the trumpet flowers but twice swooping down toward the bowl and the giant boy beside it—clearly interested but staying just out of reach. Oli beamed.

For the next two days, the boy spent much of his time under the trees, by his bowl, watching for the hummingbirds and sometimes napping in the warm sun when they weren't about. But each time they did appear, they drew closer and closer to the bowl until finally, to Oli's utter but silent delight, they hovered above it and sipped from it. He gently extended his hand while they drank, inviting them to alight. If they did, Oli told Sonia, that would mean they were carrying his father and his grandmother and they could go back to Tupá.

"Yes," Sonia said to him. "That's exactly what it will mean."

Now, on the morning that Walli Beckwith saw what she saw from space and grabbed her computer to call her dauhter, Sonia stepped outside of the pediatrics building and heard a hoarse whisper from the stand of trumpet flower trees.

"So-*nee*-ya!" it said. Sonia turned to look and her jaw dropped. Oli was sitting on the ground, cross-legged, his right arm extended. A pair of hummingbirds with ruby breasts and emerald heads sat on his hand, drinking from a small pool of the red sugar water in his palm. Sonia clapped her hand over her mouth, and Oli nodded vigorously, ecstatically. And it was at that instant that Sonia felt her phone vibrate in her pocket and, worse, begin to ring, in a frequency that was clearly intolerable to the hummingbirds, which leapt from Oli's hand and took back to the trees. Oli cried out in frustration, and Sonia grabbed her phone and barked into it.

"What!" she said, not caring who was calling and whom she might be offending. She heard the signature hiss and crackle from space, followed by Beckwith's voice calling down to Earth. Only in this case she was screaming down to Earth. Sonia didn't hear Beckwith call her name; that was lost in the static. She didn't hear the "*Baby!*" that followed it, but she did unmistakably hear the "Get out of there!"

"What is it?" she shouted back.

"Fires, Sonia! Get away!"

"How do you—" Sonia started to ask, but the signal faltered and broke.

Sonia stared at the phone, first in alarm, then in annoyance. There was no fire. She scanned over the wall and into the surrounding jungle. It was quiet, even windless, and she smelled neither diesel nor smoke on the air. She turned a full 360 degrees and saw the same calm everywhere. And then, due east, something changed. The faintest flicker of orange and yellow and, above both, a shimmer of violet that wasn't quite violet. Her heart jumped. As she watched, all three colors—the orange, the yellow, and the almost violet—bloomed higher.

Sonia tore her gaze away and bolted for Oli. She hoisted him up and then pivoted toward a small playground that had been set up for the children near one of the camp walls and lit off, knowing that two doctors had herded at least a dozen children there not half an hour earlier. As she ran, she heard a sound coming in from all directions, one that she could not identify and then, an instant later, could. It was the sound of helicopters—many, many helicopters, but not the kind she had heard before. The medical helicopters had a deep, throaty quality to them, and while their roar was fearsome, it promised a certain protective power. This sound was higher, angrier, waspier, promising only menace. As quickly as she recognized what the sound was, she could just make out the terrible machines that were making it—black, small, flying low, approaching the hospital from seemingly everywhere. As her sprint carried her closer to the play area, she could see that the dozen children and the two hospital staffers minding them were standing rooted, staring up at the approaching swarm.

"Children!" Sonia cried out breathlessly. "*Enfants! Crianças!*" The children and doctors turned. "This way, this way, this way!" Sonia shouted, waving her arm forward in the general direction of the pediatrics building. The doctors herded the children forward and they all raced after Sonia.

They ran-stumbled as a group, fighting their way through the crowds of people who had come outside of the hospital buildings and residence tents, looking up at the sky just as the children had been. People who were already outside sprinted to get *into* the same buildings and tents. There was panic everywhere, zigzag running everywhere. There were collisions and cursing and screaming and chaos, the muffled thud of flesh and bone colliding with flesh and bone.

The helicopters now approached close enough and descended low enough that a flag painted on their flanks and undersides was possible to discern. It featured three horizontal bands—black, yellow, and black—with two black stars in the middle yellow band. There was no country that flew this flag, no regiment or militia that wore it. It was a nothing flag, an invented flag, a flag designed to maintain the ruse that the action in the jungle was not the work of one country— much less just one man leading the one country—but a bold initiative by a new alliance.

The armed guards protecting the hospital sprinted toward the opening in the wall, blocking the entry as they'd practiced and pointing their weapons at the sky. They were big men and there were ten of them, and until moments ago they had seemed terribly brave and powerful. Now they seemed useless, silly. The moment they assumed their positions, several of the helicopters turned their noses their way. Their doors flew open, and there was suddenly a series of bright flashes and terrifying bangs on the ground, as the men in the helicopters tossed stun grenades down at the men guarding the opening in the wall—all of whom fell back, temporarily blinded and deafened, the balance systems in their inner ears blasted into uselessness. Three of them vomited where they lay.

The helicopters landed and dozens of men poured out—wearing black-and-yellow camouflage fatigues, all of them with the nonsense flag on the shoulder and chest. All of them carried weapons too. They quickly disarmed the disabled guards, and two of the soldiers moved them, at gunpoint, toward a clearing under a single tree. The rest of the soldiers stormed into the hospital enclosure.

Pandemonium followed, with patients and even some aid workers stampeding in every direction at once—which meant no direction at all—shoving one another, falling on top of one another, more than a few trampling one another. Inevitably there would be an audible crack that to the untrained ear of most of the people in the camp was easy to miss, but to the trained ear of the emergency physicians was the unmistakable sound of a bone snapping—followed by the unmistakable sound of a person screaming—likely from having been stepped on in the crush. Other cracks, gunshots aimed upward, followed, but they merely made the panic worse, and the soldiers who had fired them stopped.

Mia was the only doctor in the pediatrics building and quickly rousted the children out of their beds and toward the wall farthest from the opening. She shoved several beds in front of them, forming a barricade that could be easily tossed aside by one strong soldier with one strong arm, but created a faint illusion of safety for the children. She then positioned herself at the building's door, with her arms folded and her feet set wide and planted. Two soldiers—one of them a tall, broad wall of a man—approached her without words. Their guns were pointed downward, and they flashed something approaching smiles. Mia stepped forward and signaled them to stop. When they continued to approach and were in reach, she stepped toward the bigger man and shoved her hands hard into his chest.

"Páre!" she snapped. *"Eu disse para parar!"* Stop! I said to stop!

The smaller man scowled, but the big man seemed untroubled by either Mia's tone or the hard slap of her hands. She struggled to say more in Portuguese, but her poor command of the language and the high emotion of the moment would not let her form her thought. She switched to English.

"You may not enter this ward," she said.

"I am ordered to enter it," the big man answered in accommodating Brazilian-accented English.

"You have no authority. You are in Bolivia now, not Brazil."

He nodded slightly toward the insignia on his chest. "I am not sent here by Brazil, and I'm here on peaceful business."

Mia jabbed a finger toward the opening in the wall where the guards had just fallen. "Those men would not say it was peaceful."

"Those men had guns; we have more. It was necessary to stop them from taking actions that would have resulted in their deaths." Even at a distance, the guards were visible, sitting under the tree where the soldiers had taken them. "You see? Unharmed," the soldier said. "We mean your children no harm either. We are simply here to provide everyone but the hospital staff safe transit to new residences in Brazil. As you see, there are fires and the journey could be dangerous if they try to make it on their own."

"These are sick babies," Mia said. "They cannot be moved."

"They must be," the soldier said. "And they will be."

Mia took a half step forward, and the guard responded with a slight quarter turn, presenting his shoulder to Mia. He took one step and pushed her easily, though carefully, aside. *"Com licença,"* he said. *With permission.*

He and the other soldier now entered and nodded to the children, who screamed at the sight of them and retreated farther behind the barricade of beds.

"*Bebês*," the bigger man said with a smile that the other soldier tried to mimic. The babies howled louder.

Another voice now came from outside as Sonia ran toward the building with Oli in her arms and other staffers and children close behind her. "What is this? What is this? What is this?" she shouted, breathing hard.

She forced her way into the building, with the rest of the group behind her. The soldiers now found themselves in the center of the ward, facing more than two dozen children and four adults in front of them and behind them. They liked neither the arithmetic nor the positioning. The smaller soldier lifted his rifle in the general direction of Sonia and the group that had just arrived. The children screamed again. The bigger soldier placed his hand on the barrel and pushed the gun back down toward the floor. When he spoke, his voice was harder, less conversational. And he used Portuguese, with not a word of accommodating English.

"We are leaving here soon. We are taking everyone but the medical staff. The rest of these people came from the jungle and if left alone would return to the jungle, to lands that are no longer safe for them. We will take them to new homes, good homes"—he tried his smile—"homes not far from here, in fact, just across the border."

"You cannot do this!" Sonia snapped.

"*Senhorita*, we can do this," the soldier answered. "We are doing it." The smaller man then raised his rifle again, and this time the other soldier did not stop him. "All of the children will come," he said.

He reached to his belt without taking his eyes from Sonia, unclipped a microphone with a coiled wire attached to a transmitter, and murmured into it. He replaced the microphone, held his pose—and his gaze—and inside of thirty seconds, three more soldiers appeared at the doorway and edged their way inside. All of them were armed, and all were pointing their weapons.

Sonia began to speak—and the look on her face made clear it would be a shout—but Mia spoke first. "There are more than a thousand people in this camp. How do you plan to transport them all?" she asked. Sonia looked at her, dumbfounded at her seeming surrender.

"The young and strong ones will walk, in the care of the soldiers and with many stops for rest and food," the big soldier said. "The old and the small will take the helicopters." He tried the smile once more. "Don't worry. Your babies shall fly."

Wordlessly, the newly arrived solders approached the back of the tent. They pointed their rifles toward the ground but tossed the beds aside and pulled and coaxed the cowering children forward as they wailed in protest. Sonia watched, her gaze fixed and furious, as she held fast to Oli, who buried his face in her shoulder. The soldiers exited the tent with the children and began moving toward the opening in the wall and the waiting helicopters. Only the big soldier remained behind. He turned to Sonia.

"The boy," he demanded, holding out his hands for Oli.

"He is not going with you," Sonia said. "He just lost his father, his grandmother."

"We will give him a home, and he will find a new family. He is coming."

"Then take me!" Sonia ordered.

"You are not from the jungle."

"I am," Sonia said. "I am his mother and came here with him." She inclined her face, displaying her features and her color, so close to Oli's own.

"You are lying," he said. He inclined his head to the white scrubs she was wearing with the SSA logo—the initials stylized into the shape of two wings—on the breast and pants leg. "You are a doctor."

He stepped forward, laid hands on Oli, and proceeded to pull him from her. Oli fought ferociously and screamed with an animal howl, as did Sonia. Mia turned away, tears filling her eyes. With one arm, the soldier restrained the small, thrashing woman, and with the other, he took the flailing little boy and succeeded in separating them. Sonia lunged toward him, but Mia pulled her back and held her fast. They both watched until the wailing Oli, held fast in the soldier's arms, vanished beyond the opening in the wall.

. . .

Fifty-six thousand people would be displaced in the jungle that night, with inevitable deaths, though those Lamentáveis—in Bobo-deCorte's decorous phrasing—would never be identified or properly counted. The number of fires *would* be counted: There were at least twenty-two of them, arranged in a lethal crescent from Rondônia, Amazonas, and Acre in the west and north, through Pernambuco and Bahia in the northeast and east, and down through Paraná and Rio Grande do Sul in the southeast. All of them were arrayed so as to push steadily west in a manner that would force anyone living in those parts of the jungle—and there were many, many people living in those parts of the jungle—to flee ahead of the fires' advance. If the retreating tribes weren't overtaken by the onrushing flames, they'd tumble directly into the arms of the refugee camps.

The reaction of the world press to the night of burnings was almost unanimously furious—a degree of media blowback Bobo-deCorte had never experienced before. Whether it was because of the sheer scope of the burnings or because of the American astronaut calling so much attention to his Consolidation was impossible to know, but either way, the Brazilian president called a rare evening press conference to try to get ahead of the story.

Mercenaries who had joined the Consolidation army from Colombia, Uruguay, and Paraguay were by his side, even though they represented nations that had formally rejected Bobo-deCorte's policies.

They did not speak tonight, though they did wear their countries' flags on their sleeves along with the Consolidation flag, creating at least the illusion of a legitimate multinational alliance at work.

The Brazilian president mostly stuck to his talking points, which meant that he mostly stuck to a tumble of lies: Yes, some fires had been tactically lit, but the overwhelming share of the burning was the result of a tragic convergence of three deadly factors—dry brush, poor rainfall, and "rolling lightning strikes," *relâmpagos rolando*, a term that had no genuine meteorological meaning but that Bobo-deCorte repeated six times in his remarks because he liked the vaguely scientific way it sounded and was convinced the domestic press would pick up on it. The next day's newspapers proved him right.

"The American and European newspapers will say that the lightning was really soldiers and the strikes were really planned," Bobo-deCorte said. "I invite the Americans and Europeans to camp out in our Amazon at this time of year in this kind of weather and see how they get by."

Bobo-deCorte also pointed out that the fires were contained quickly, "a sign of our soldiers doing the brave work of safeguarding our land." But fast containment was also the sign of a fire that had been timed and lit with those same soldiers standing by to move in when a designated amount of land had been cleared. It escaped no one's notice either—at least no one in the foreign ministries around the world that had been monitoring the activities in the jungle—that all of the fires occurred on land with rich soil and within reach of major rivers where the Brazilian government had been eyeballing sites for hydroelectric dams.

"If this was lightning," huffed the British foreign secretary, "it was lightning with a degree in civil engineering."

CHAPTER TWELVE

It was easy to tell that the little community in the quiet pocket of Mesa, Arizona, was a space community, provided you knew what you were looking for—though most people didn't. Still, the clues were everywhere.

There were the little white fins somebody had quietly installed at the bottom of a few of the light posts—blunt-cut like the ones on the old Mercury-Redstone. There were the license plates with similar-looking gibberish that read "PICKRN1" or "PICKER3" or "PRING2," all in homage to William Pickering, the New Zealand–born engineer who was the first director of the Jet Propulsion Laboratory in Pasadena in the days when the Jet Propulsion Laboratory started leaving mere jet propulsion behind and began launching rockets toward the planets. Pickering had hired most of the people in the little community when they were young engineers, and long after his death, they honored him still.

Most tellingly, there were the distinctive doorbells that the residents had designed for their homes, which played tunes like no other doorbells in the world: Bach's *Well-Tempered Clavier*, Stravinsky's

Rite of Spring, the Bulgarian folk song "Izlel je Delyo Hagdutin." Every one of those songs made perfect sense—if you knew what you were listening for, though most people didn't—because every one of them and twenty-three more were etched into the celebrated golden records carried aboard the two *Voyager* spacecraft, which the people who lived in the neighborhood had once helped build and launch. Now, more than forty years later, the *Voyager*s were at the edge of the solar system, their records ready to be played by any alien species that might find them and want to learn more about the civilization that launched them.

The two agents from the Department of Homeland Security who rang the bell at the fifth house on the third street in the little community got a fine song too: Louis Armstrong's "Melancholy Blues," which was also etched into the records.

"If they're nice aliens," one NASA engineer had told the press before the launch, "they deserve a little Louie."

The older of the two agents, Agent Hadley, smiled. The younger of the two, Agent Littrow, actually bounced in time to the tune. Hadley waited just a few seconds before ringing the bell again—too few seconds for anyone in the house to have a fair chance of responding—and midway through the second chiming of the song, the door opened.

"Enough," said the man who answered. "I wasn't standing here hoping you'd show up."

The man appeared to be in his late seventies or early eighties; he was an inch or two over six feet and carried that height with a certain stubborn defiance. He'd been a tall man his entire life, and he wasn't going to surrender that now to age and gravity.

"I'm sorry, sir," Agent Hadley said, gesturing to the doorbell. "It's the song."

The man waved it off. "It happens all the time," he said. "I told my wife we should have taken the Hungarian one, but she likes Louie." He regarded the men on his step with passing interest; they were guests he had expected but hadn't been especially eager to see. "I assume you're from the government?"

"Yes, sir," said Hadley. "Homeland Security. I'm Agent Hadley; this is Agent Littrow." Both men produced their badges, and the man examined them and nodded his approval. They put them away.

"And you're Dr. Beckwith?" Hadley asked.

"I'm one of them, yes."

"Dr. Virgil Beckwith?"

"I am. Dr. Mae Beckwith is here too."

He opened the door wider, and a woman his age stepped forward and shook the agents' hands.

"You should come in off the step," she said to them.

"I'll wait out here, ma'am," Littrow said, casting a glance up and down the street and adjusting an earpiece connected to a little coil of wire that ran down the left side of his neck.

Mae smiled. "You think my daughter is going to pull up in her car?"

"No, ma'am," Littrow answered.

Hadley intervened. "It's just protocol," he said. "Someone watches the street. I know it seems silly, but it's department rules."

The Beckwiths looked at each other, an agreement passed between them, and Virgil opened the door the rest of the way. Hadley stepped inside and closed the door behind him. He looked around, taking in the living room.

A television mounted on the far wall was turned to the news, but the sound was muted. The screen was filled with a scene of a protest on the Arizona State University campus, in support of Beckwith and against the Consolidation. "Walli Watch: Day Ten," said the slug in the upper-right corner of the screen. There was a countdown clock next to it that at that moment read eighteen days, thirteen hours, eleven minutes, and sixteen seconds until the moment at 9:00 A.M. eastern time on September 18 when Congress would take up the legislation mandating intervention in the Amazon.

"I can change it if you like," Virgil said, "but it's on all the local channels."

"No need," Hadley said. He felt a slight chill, looked up, and for the first time noticed an array of eight rotary fans, two per wall, evenly spaced, all mounted just below the ceiling molding and pointed down toward the room. They were connected by a webwork of cables, which ran to a control panel near the television. It was just under ninety degrees outdoors; it felt twenty degrees cooler inside, but Hadley could neither feel nor smell the sharp edge of refrigeration that came with air-conditioning. He looked curiously at Virgil.

"Mae's handiwork," he said.

"I don't care for the air conditioner," she said. "We keep one running in the bedroom—this is Arizona, after all—but if you know how to handle your air, that's all you need."

Hadley glanced toward a hallway at the end of which was an open door leading to a bedroom. Four more fans lined the hallway walls near the ceiling, connected to more cables. He glanced at the control panel near the television.

"May I?" he asked.

Mae smiled agreeably, and he approached the panel and turned one of its three knobs. The fans throughout the house nodded in response. The other knobs moved them in two other axes and a series of sliding switches controlled the speed of their blades. A thermometer on the panel read seventy-one degrees.

"Her PhD was in airflow and wind resistance," said Virgil. Hadley tipped his head to Mae in respect, and she nodded her thanks.

"But you didn't come here to talk about engineering," she said. She motioned Hadley to sit. He motioned for them to go first, and the Drs. Beckwith pulled up two straight-back chairs from the nearby dining table—the only two straight-back chairs—and sat. Hadley had no alternative but to settle into a settee facing the chairs. He sank several inches into the cushions and was left looking up at his hosts. He admired their execution.

"Ma'am, sir," he said, looking from one Dr. Beckwith to the other, "your daughter is in a great deal of trouble, as you surely know."

"We do," said Virgil.

"She faces prosecution in twenty-five countries," Hadley said.

"Only ten have agreed so far," Mae corrected. "The news keeps a tally."

"I would think that was more than enough," Hadley said.

"You would," said Mae. "Belka might hold out for the entire twenty-five."

"I wouldn't joke about this, Dr. Beckwith," Hadley said, dropping the "ma'am."

"I'm not joking," said Mae. "I know my daughter's character, and I would think you would make it your business to know it too."

"Did she tell you what she was planning before she left the United States?"

"No, she didn't," Virgil answered.

"Did you travel to Baikonur for the launch?"

"Yes, we did."

"Did you see her while you were there?"

"Families are allowed to visit in the days before launch, but through glass. The medical isolation," Virgil said.

"Did she discuss her plans with you then?" Hadley asked.

Virgil sighed. "No," he said. "We neither aided nor abetted our daughter on foreign or domestic soil. I understand you are required to raise all this legal business, but we have an attorney and you should move on to any other matter you'd like to raise."

Hadley did not. "Did she discuss her plans with your granddaughter?" he asked and glanced away for a moment to summon up the name. "Sonia Bravo-Beckwith?"

"Yes, that is her name," Virgil said. "No, I have no reason to think Sonia and Belka talked about any of this. As your research surely also shows you, our granddaughter is facing her own kind of danger."

"Yes, sir," Hadley said. "She is in a perilous spot, and our thoughts are with your family."

Virgil nodded wordlessly. Hadley pressed on.

"Have you spoken to your daughter since she's been in space?"

"Yes, we have," Mae answered, "and we have emailed as well. I am certain you know that already, since NASA would surely be tracking any downlinks."

"Yes, ma'am," Hadley said. "But the government only knows the calls are placed. We're not allowed to listen in without a warrant."

"Have you gotten one?" Mae said.

"I'm not at liberty to discuss that."

"Which I assume means you have."

Hadley did not respond to that. "Would your daughter listen to you if you advised her to reconsider her actions?" he asked.

"I'm not sure that's in her nature," Mae said.

"Would you be willing to try if the government asked you to?"

"I'm not sure that's in *her* nature," Virgil said, inclining his head toward Mae.

Hadley shifted directions.

"Has your daughter ever been married?" he asked.

"No, she hasn't," Mae said. "Surely you know that already too."

"Is there a particular reason she's remained single?"

"She's never seen the need for a husband, I imagine."

"Are there any men in her life currently?"

"That's not a question a stranger asks a mother," Mae said.

"Any women then?"

"Nor is that."

Hadley looked away, then reached into his breast pocket and removed a folded piece of paper. He grew formal again.

"Ma'am, sir," he began, "when did you retire from the Jet Propulsion Laboratory?"

"Twelve years ago," Virgil said.

Hadley unfolded the paper and scanned it. "And you both worked there for . . ."

"Forty-four years," Virgil said.

"You have government pensions."

"Yes, we do," Virgil said. "And I suspect that sheet of paper tells you how much those pensions pay us."

"It does," Hadley said. "It also tells me that now and then you supplement your income with outside consulting work."

"We do. It's not uncommon for government engineers after retirement."

Hadley handed Virgil the paper. "Is that a list of all of the companies you've done work for in the past twelve years?" he asked.

Mae and Virgil scanned the list. "That looks like all of them," Virgil said. "They are all American companies, doing private business, and we shared no classified government information with any of them."

"No, no," Hadley said apologetically. "Of course you didn't. I am not suggesting *that*."

He let the emphasis on his final word hang, and Mae appeared impatient. "Finish your thought, Agent Hadley," she said.

"The mere fact that you've complied with all government rules doesn't mean that the Department of Homeland Security would not need confirmation," Hadley said. "That would require reviewing all of the projects you've worked on for all of the companies that have retained you."

"The companies would not like that," Mae said.

"Private firms do like to avoid trouble," Hadley said. "The risk does exist that if it all became too difficult for them, they would choose not to retain you in the future."

The Beckwiths said nothing for a moment. Behind them the television played silently. A reporter was interviewing a student wearing a T-shirt with a picture of a hand with a raised middle finger and the words "I would prefer not to."

Virgil stood with a small grunt, walked over to the sideboard in the dining room, and picked up a model of a spacecraft that measured a couple of feet wide by a couple of feet tall. He lifted it with care, carried it back, and offered it to Hadley. The agent angled his head inquiringly to be certain he could lay his hands on the thing.

"Just be careful," Virgil said.

Hadley took the model and looked at it with open admiration. It was deceptively light, made of balsa or some other type of thin wood, but painted and enamelized to appear metallic. It was exquisitely assembled—plainly hand-cut rather than laser-cut because only a hand could manage this wood the way it had been managed. Where there was a deep flaw in the grain causing a tiny bump at a seam, there would be an equally tiny dimple cut into the adjoining piece to accommodate the irregularity. The spacecraft's delicate antenna components were assembled from shavings of wood that were no thicker than toothpicks. The nameplate on the base of the model read, "Voyager 1."

"You built this?" Hadley asked.

"*We* built it," Virgil corrected. "Mae and I, in the first year after we retired, just to keep our hands busy. And we helped build that one too," he added, gesturing roughly skyward.

"How far away is it now?"

"Thirteen billion miles. Been up there since shortly after Belka was born, and it'll be flying forever."

Virgil took the model from Hadley, walked it back to the dining room, and replaced it on the sideboard. By the time he turned around, Mae was standing and Hadley had taken that as his cue to stand too.

"Agent Hadley," Virgil said, "we know you had to make this visit, but we cannot help you. Mae and I, we've done our remarkable things. Now our daughter is doing hers."

"You know Washington will take steps," Hadley said. "Against her, against you."

The Beckwiths nodded their understanding, and Mae opened the door to show Hadley out. He exited and she shut the door behind him. Across the room, the countdown clock on the silent TV continued to roll.

CHAPTER THIRTEEN

September 3

Whatever the presidents of Brazil and the United States had hoped was going to happen in the week that followed the great burnings of August 26 was surely not what did happen. Jair Bobo-deCorte could tell himself at first that all was going as planned. He had herded the people he wanted to herd and seized the land he wanted to seize and was already deeding the huge, burned parcels to the ranchers, miners, and other developers who would pay richly for the use of what had once been the homes of the now-scattered tribes.

The president of the United States at first seemed too to have gotten what he wanted. Public sentiment in favor of intervention in the Amazon basin had spiked in the first twenty-four hours after the burnings, but then—news cycles being news cycles and distractable Americans being distractable Americans—passions cooled and attentions shifted and the Amazon returned to a matter that was just another nation's business. That helped ensure that, for now at least, the majorities the president enjoyed in both houses of Congress would hold, still backing his policy of standing aside and letting Brazil handle Brazil.

But that was just the piece of the story they could easily see—and wanted to see. If Laurel Cady's studies of the great domestic uprisings of the past had taught her anything, it was that people in power could be badly losing even when they thought they were winning. The Montgomery buses ran indifferently along, with all their rules about which people could sit in which seats—until all at once the pressure built and the lid blew off and everything changed. The colonial tea tax was paid—until all at once it wasn't. And Ohio industries went right ahead pouring their wastes wherever they wanted until one day a river in Cleveland caught fire and twenty million people in all fifty states took to the streets and said enough was enough. The tea drinkers had been grumbling and the bus riders fuming and the twenty million people stirring slowly to action all along, but the people who would feel their wrath paid them little heed.

Now the September 18 Coalition was rising the same way, with more than two million people signed up to appear in Washington for the congressional vote and similar local demonstrations planned in all of the nation's major cities as well as many smaller ones. Cady, a scholar of America's great civil uprisings, was about to become the author of what could be the largest of all.

Alone in space, the holdout astronaut continued to do her part to keep the movement galvanized. Every time the station flew over the jungle, she was positioned at Zoe and Ivy for the entire pass, scanning the ground for the smallest sign of military mobilization. Whenever fires were lit—and many were—she captured images of them at their greatest magnification and resolution and streamed them down to Earth, both alerting the world to what was happening and warning the people in the path of the flames to get away.

"President Bobo plays with matches," she tweeted when a fire looked small and she could afford to be flip.

"Blaze at Tapauá, winds southeast," she tweeted at the first flicker of a bigger fire, with similar notifications following as the attacks moved on—to Juburi or Abunaí or Mamori—and the winds shifted with them.

On a few occasions, Beckwith delighted the activists and infuriated Brasilia when she spotted Bobo-deCorte's helicopters and earthmovers just as they were roaring into position for another attack, and sent those pictures down to Earth. She watched as the machines stopped and then pulled back, and she showed the world the evidence of the retreat.

"Can't hide from the eye in the sky," she taunted the Brazilian president. #CantHideFromWalli, came the hashtag.

The Brazilian forces were, of course, perfectly capable of planning their advances for the moments when the station would not be passing by—anyone in the world could download the same space station app Sonia had on her phone—but the military mobilized slowly and the station moved fast and Beckwith was almost always out ahead of the operations.

The risk did exist that Bobo-deCorte could try to strike back at Beckwith in the worst way possible—through Sonia. But that was unlikely. If the Brazilian president even knew that Beckwith had a niece in the jungle, she was one small figure lost in a vast expanse of rain forest, and the only people who knew her actual whereabouts were the officials from the SSA, who surely wouldn't share the information with Brasilia. What's more, Bobo-deCorte was no fool. He might have the American president's friendship, but that same American president was under growing pressure to crush his Consolidation. Harming or even detaining an American national—to say nothing of the niece of an American folk hero—would force the White House's military hand and bring down US hellfire.

The only way to keep Beckwith and her spying under control was thus a simple if extreme one: NASA could sever her internet link entirely—something that could be accomplished by a single touch on a single icon on the Capcom's screen in Mission Control. But just as Bobo-deCorte dared not mess with Sonia, NASA dared not silence Walli. For one thing, her millions of followers would not abide it, and additional demonstrations had already been planned around the country if the stream of communication from space should suddenly fall silent. The sites of the protests would be the Johnson Space Center in Houston, the Kennedy Space Center in Florida, the space agency's headquarters on E Street Southwest in Washington, and the New York Stock Exchange—simply because any unrest on Wall Street rattled markets, and rattled markets would in turn rattle the president. Similar demonstrations were also planned in front of the Supreme Court Building, in Washington. It was that site that was likeliest to stay NASA's hand.

Already lawyers from the American Civil Liberties Union had gone to work, writing, releasing, and preparing to file First Amendment claims in federal courts in Texas, Florida, and Washington, seeking an immediate ruling that Beckwith's downlink—effectively her means of speech—be restored immediately if it were severed. Beckwith herself had joined in advance as a party to the suits, ensuring that the claim would have standing; so had the students who were organizing the rallies and multiple indigenous-peoples civil rights groups, arguing that Beckwith was their voice and most effective channel for being heard.

Cady appeared in on-camera remotes on various network news shows, sharing a split screen with a NASA spokesman once the word of the ACLU action got out. She had expected this to happen and had prepared for it.

"Astronauts flew for decades before there even was internet or email," the spokesman argued. "NASA is under no obligation to provide them now and could shut the line at will."

"NASA *was* under no obligation to provide them," Cady corrected. "But once a means of speech has been provided, the government—which includes NASA—cannot withdraw it based on its content."

"Is she right?" the newscaster asked the spokesman.

"I'm right," Cady said. "Don't ask him."

She *was* right. A case like this fit so neatly into the apron pocket of the First Amendment that Connie Polk herself called Joe Star and asked him not even to try to muzzle Beckwith. "You'd have a court order demanding you restore the link inside of an hour," she said. "And you'd only make my job harder, appealing the whole thing up the federal ladder."

Eavesdropping on Beckwith's conversations with her parents and Sonia or reading their emails was similarly availing the government little. Agent Hadley had been right that that would require a warrant, and Beckwith's mother had been right in guessing the government had already secured one. But all of the Beckwiths took care to keep their conversations anodyne against just that possibility—simply checking in on one another's welfare. The closest anyone on the ground had come to colluding with the renegade astronaut was when Sonia and Raymond set up Beckwith's Twitter account, which came right back to the First Amendment turf Cady and the ACLU had so neatly covered.

With their hands tied, NASA and the Navy were reduced to formally ordering Beckwith to stop her "unauthorized surveillance of the jungle and dissemination of classified information." The State and Defense Departments, under whose command she did not serve, issued a similar demand—though not making it an order, because they did not have that power.

"I would prefer not to," Beckwith responded. And within minutes, that hashtag, which had already been everywhere since the day she first seized the station, once again swamped the internet.

. . .

There were enough cars in front of the elegant house off Belmont Road in the Kalorama neighborhood of Washington, DC, that Connie Polk figured she had a reasonable chance of slipping inside unnoticed. The press, at least the society press and the political press, were everywhere, but they weren't looking for her. They were looking for the seven-figure campaign donors and the selected lobbyists and dignitaries who would be here for a fundraising dinner tonight. And, of course, they were looking for the president, though he had already arrived and gone inside, as the Secret Service detail outside made clear.

Nobody expected the attorney general to attend. She wasn't on the leaked guest list, which was fine with her because she loathed such cash-for-contact events. But the president had strongly suggested she be here, practically instructed her to be here, and she had agreed, on the condition that she could arrive in a private car with tinted windows and be allowed into the house through a back entrance. A political event like this was simply the wrong look for the job she held. Those conditions were met, and she entered the home through a door that led into a huge chef's kitchen where live lobsters scrabbled in bushel baskets on the floor and institutional-size pots of water boiled on the sprawling range. From there, she was led to a too-bright dining room where about forty guests were being seated. Almost immediately, the president's voice called out to her.

"Connie!" he said. "There's my AG."

She turned toward the table, where he was centrally seated. Joe Star, the administrator of NASA, was to his right, which surprised her. He was largely apolitical, and while he had amassed a fortune in the private sector, it was nowhere near the fortune of the other men in the room. He was here for a reason. The seat to the president's left was empty, and he patted it.

"Come, come," he said, motioning to her. "All for you."

Polk winced inwardly. He'd been drinking—she could see that. A mostly empty glass of bourbon was next to him, and from experience, she knew that it was the only one he'd had. He would accept the wine later when it was poured, but aside from a pantomimed sip if there were toasts, he wouldn't drink it. He knew his limits—one drink loosened him up, and that was plenty. She admired that about him, but she actually preferred him unloosened. She could not reciprocate the near friendliness the bourbon would free up in him, and it would be gone by morning anyway. She took her seat and smiled at him and Star.

"Mr. President, thank you for inviting me," she said.

"Thank you for coming, Connie," he answered.

She said hello to Star, addressing him as "Mr. Administrator." He insisted on Joe; she agreed on the condition that he call her Connie, and the wine was poured.

By the time the appetizer was served, the president got to the point of the invitation, though he addressed his first remarks to Star, not to Polk. "Your space girl is causing me nothing but headaches," he said.

Star seemed to flinch, though Polk couldn't be sure if it was in reaction to "space girl" or "your"—an accusation of ownership Star could probably do without.

"Yes, sir," Star said. "I imagine she is."

"The congressional leadership is leaning on me to figure this out, and the Russians couldn't be happier."

"Beg pardon, sir," Star said, "but the Russians want her off that station as much as we do."

"Your *space* Russians, yes," the president said. "But the Kremlin is happy for anything that makes me look weak—and this does." He changed tacks. "Shouldn't she be starting to crack by now? Isn't she going stir-crazy all alone up there?"

"To the contrary, sir," Star said. "She appears to be having the time of her life."

"Can she actually run the whole thing by herself? Any chance she'll make some mistake and get herself killed?"

He stopped as soon as he said that and appeared surprised at himself. Without looking down, he pushed the bourbon glass an inch farther away. This was why he didn't drink.

"No, sir," Star said neutrally. "She is more than able to tend to the station."

"As I suspected. So what say we bring her home?"

"We are continuing to try to do that. The Russians are sending up a Soyuz to fetch her."

"Any reason to believe she'll actually get in the thing?"

"I doubt it. The demonstrators certainly wouldn't want her to. They're playing this September 18 thing big."

"I bet they'd settle down if she comes home. Connie?" the president said, at last turning to her. "How are we coming on that?"

"Just as the administrator . . . as Joe says, sir," she answered. "She's immovable. Prosecution doesn't scare her, she knows her NASA career is surely over, and we can push the parents only so hard. They're law-abiding people and they're very sympathetic."

"How about we give her what she wants, then?" the president said.

"Sir?" Connie asked.

"Give her what she wants. Look at the polls. She's a hero and I'm eating shit for this."

Two people across the table turned and looked at him. He glanced directly at the bourbon this time, accusingly.

"I try not to worry about the polls, sir."

"You should worry," he said, "if I'm going to keep my job—and you're going to keep yours. So let's back off the parents. And let's ease up on the threats of prosecution. I'll press the Europeans and Japanese to leave her alone, and you can promise her some minor sentence stateside—naval discharge after a court-martial, maybe a few months of base confinement."

"Mr. President," Connie said, "it's the Consolidation, not the punishment, that matters to her. She wants it stopped; she wants *you* to stop it."

"So give her that too," he said.

Now Polk was truly shocked. The president could see that and looked pleased at his ability to blindside her. He went on.

"The pro-intervention polls are rising right along with hers, the congressional majority is wobbling, and I need to get this all behind me. So we let it leak that I'm willing to consider a compromise if Congress approves the intervention. The party will demand I kill the bill once it passes, so we make sure it's veto-proof. Then, for the good of the country and all the rest, I won't drag it through the courts on constitutional grounds."

"I've counted the same votes you've counted, Mr. President," Polk said. "There's not nearly enough to reach the two-thirds to beat a veto. A lot of these party lawmakers will get clobbered at home if they vote for military action, won't they?"

"They will. So the whips and leaders on the Hill had better get moving."

"I'm surprised, sir," Polk said.

"Beckwith will be too, I'd bet."

"What about your American Objectives policy?" Polk asked.

"You mean America First?" the president said with what he intended to be a mischievous smile but struck Polk as more of a leer. "I'm not agreeing to a full-blown war. We keep it light: fire a few missiles, fly a few Thunderbolts over the treetops, see if that scares El Bobo back into his box."

Polk said nothing and looked at the president skeptically. She'd never heard him refer to the Brazilian leader so dismissively before. It was always either a warm "Jair" or a respectful "President Bobo-deCorte." This felt vaguely like a performance to her, and she plunged ahead with the question that immediately presented itself to her.

"Will you actually follow through on all this, Mr. President?" she asked. "Are you telling the truth?"

The president froze, and Polk did too, after a fashion. But it was a question that needed to be asked if she was going to act in reliance on his words. She was a prosecutor, and asking questions was what she did for a living. Today would be no different.

"Yes, Connie," the president said frostily. "I am telling you the truth."

"Very good, sir," she said. "Shall I back-channel the congressional leaders that you'll be in touch with them?"

"Do that, yes," the president ordered. Then he nodded at her briskly, took one more swallow of his bourbon, and summoned a waiter to take the rest of it away. He spoke not a word to his attorney general for the rest of the evening.

CHAPTER FOURTEEN

The Mercado hospital had the look of a place that had been struck by a cyclone. Tents were collapsed and debris lay everywhere; furniture inside buildings had been tipped and tossed, with the contents of shelves and cabinets spilled out across the floors. And then, of course, there was the silence.

The SSA was fastidious about its record keeping, and every time a patient was brought in—or staggered in—an entry was made in the computer system and a name and case number were attached. If anyone left—a child claimed by parents, a husband found by a wife—that fact was recorded too. So were the deaths. As of yesterday, there were 1,243 active names and cases in the system, meaning 1,243 tribespeople in the camp. That plus the 203 SSA staffers made for a huge crowd on the small patch of land.

But the soldiers from the army that wasn't really an army, wearing the flag that wasn't really a flag, were fastidious too. From a rough head count the SSA doctors conducted, and then a much more careful search of the camp, it appeared that every single one of the patients and refugees who had been living there had been rounded up and then marched off or choppered out. The infirmary building was empty, the surviving tents were empty, the scrubby playground that had been filled with children earlier in the day was empty.

Sonia had collected herself only slowly after the giant soldier carried Oli away, unable to get him out of her mind. He was a boy composed of pieces just loosely held together, and the centrifugal spin of this latest terror could pull his loose bits apart. No magical belief in hummingbirds and glowworms could put him back together if that happened. Worse, it was Sonia's own inability to hold him close—her failed grip as she fought the giant soldier—that was the cause of all that.

She returned to the doctors' quarters and collapsed on her cot, consumed by a hot grief and a cold rage—a grief and rage that left her beyond even tears. She was spent. Worse, she felt defeated—wholly, helplessly defeated. Then—only then—did her own words come back to her: *I'll make them pay.*

They had killed Annie. They had killed Oli's family. They had ripped Oli from her very arms. And she was lying on a cot in her quarters, trying to cry. At that, Sonia's sorrow and anger tipped into something else entirely—to an electric sense of furious purpose. She leapt from her cot, sprinted back to the center of the camp, and quickly joined one of the three groups of doctors conducting the search for hidden survivors. She then helped muster teams to repitch tents, pick up furniture, and collect the spilled contents of the cabinets and shelves. The work needed to be done quickly because the staffers knew they would not be alone here for long.

The 1,243 people who had been taken would soon be replaced by another thousand or two and then another and then another. The burnings were not going to stop and the displacements were not going to stop, which meant the people would keep flowing in. The doctors could do nothing but accept them and treat them and give them refuge, and the army that wasn't an army would thus know just where to come to collect them.

"We're going to be a depot," Mia said miserably as she was helping Sonia set the infirmary building to rights late in the afternoon. "We gather them in and the soldiers take them out."

The pediatrics building was the final one they worked on late that day. When they had finished, Sonia looked slowly around at all of the empty beds, coming to rest last on Oli's. Mia followed her gaze, stepped to her, and took her by the shoulders.

"We will find them," she said firmly, then, conceding Sonia's particular grief, added, "And we will find *him*."

"We don't even know where to look," Sonia answered.

"Yes," Mia said. "Actually, we do."

She took Sonia by the wrist and marched out of the pediatrics building and across the grounds to the far wall of the enclosure, where the camp's small communications building stood. An array of dish antennas was positioned on the roof, and a snaking tangle of cables ran along the ground nearby. Two small windows spilled yellow light. When they reached the building, Mia flung open the door, and both women were struck by the energy and industry they found there.

The soldiers had stopped by here briefly—just enough time to yank out cables, disconnect power and computer systems, and prevent the doctors from reporting the attack to the world, at least until the hospital had been emptied and the attackers themselves had vanished back into the jungle. Raymond and a handful of other staffers were busy bringing the entire facility back online. They had already reactivated the generator, and four of the twelve computers that were used both for patient records and for communications were rebooting and flickering to life.

"Server first, server first!" Raymond was instructing a physician's assistant, who was trying to activate a twin-screen computer console and getting nothing but a spinning color wheel on either monitor. "Get that working," Raymond said, jabbing a finger at a cabinet-like piece of equipment and then back at the screens, "and those will work."

He then spun around, about to bark a similar exasperated command to a similarly befuddled-looking infirmary worker, when he spotted Mia and Sonia. He read Sonia's face and spoke without preamble—unknowingly echoing Mia.

"We will find them," he said simply. "There will be fieldworkers at the relocation camps; there will be observers." He pointed at the computers across the room, slowly lighting up. "And there will be reports." Then he turned back around and proceeded to bring one more computer to life.

.   .   .

The news of the president's stunning decision to abide by a congressional vote, stop the burnings and relocations, and bring Beckwith home in the bargain leaked informally before the official leak. He was politically inexperienced enough not just to have discussed a matter so sensitive in as buzzing a hive as a Washington dinner party, but to have discussed it in a conversational tone. There were uncounted people in the room who knew uncounted people in the press, and it was certain that someone would pass the word fast.

When that word did pass, the media jumped on it, reporting it all but universally as a presidential concession and a victory for the rogue astronaut—exactly the spin the administration didn't want to put on the story. The White House pushed back, releasing a statement that it had hoped to get out first, describing the move as "a potential way forward that could serve the twin interests of saving lives and enhancing national security."

But the pundits were having none of it. Commentators in favor of intervention called the president's move a "stunning capitulation" and a "White House surrender." A *Washington Post* columnist described it as "a good start from a weakened president."

The president's own party was even harder on him, with its most industry-friendly factions calling him alternately a coward, a turncoat, a quisling, and, inevitably, Neville Chamberlain, though when the occasional reporter asked them what they meant by that, they could only mumble something about Munich and nothing more.

It was the turncoat charge Beckwith first saw when she awakened that morning to an open laptop in her sleep pod with a headline screaming, "PRESIDENT BOWS TO ASTRONAUT. BASE ENRAGED." She tore through the story, then another, then another, piecing together enough from all of the different takes on the same development that she thought she had a realistic sense of it. It was encouraging news—but encouraging was *all* it was until she learned more. She toggled open her air-to-ground link.

"Houston, station," she said.

"Copy, station," came the voice of a Capcom she did not immediately recognize. Before she could say more, the voice said, "Stand by one." The line went silent, and a moment later, Lee Jasper took the Capcom's place.

"You get your newspaper delivery?" he asked her.

"I did."

"So you heard the word from Washington?"

"I did," she repeated.

"You check your email yet?"

"No."

"You should. Message for you."

"From whom?" Beckwith asked.

"Just read it."

"Copy."

"And, Walli . . ." Jasper began before she could go. "Walli Bee . . ."

"Listening."

"Do what's smart."

"Thank you, Jasper," she answered.

She signed off, turned to her screen, and opened her email. There were dozens of messages in her routine inbox—none of which jumped out at her in any way—but there was a single new arrival in her encrypted directory, which was used for confidential communications with NASA. She opened it with equal parts happy anticipation and creeping dread and then closed her eyes in relief when she saw it was from Jerry Ullage, the NASA house counsel and the astronauts' advocate.

The reports in the press were true, he told her, and she should believe what the president was offering. Connie Polk herself had called Ullage before dawn to talk to him about the outlines of a deal. She stressed that under no circumstances could anything she said be construed as a formal offer since Beckwith was still in violation of multiple criminal laws. A plea agreement could not even be considered until a suspect had surrendered—and Beckwith should make no mistake that her return would constitute a surrender.

Still, Washington, Europe, and even Moscow were aware of Beckwith's growing popularity, and they were, for now at least, reluctant to get crosswise with that. Tokyo was the lone holdout. They would probably file an indictment, but as long as no harm came to their Kibo, they might not seek extradition. If Beckwith simply accepted that she would have to cross Japan off any future travel plans, that problem could go away too.

Polk mentioned the mild penalties the president had raised, adding the inducement that Beckwith could retain her pilot's license so she could earn a living in commercial aviation. Finally, Polk stressed that from her personal reading of the president, she knew he was sincere about being open to compromise on the intervention—not a large-scale mobilization that would halt all the killing and burning, but enough to scare Bobo-deCorte into slowing down and pulling back, creating room for diplomacy to work. Certainly, the congressional vote would have to go the right way, with a two-thirds, veto-proof majority in both chambers approving intervention—since the president's base would abandon him entirely if he didn't veto the measure if he could—and that was by no means assured, what with anti-intervention lawmakers having their own voters to face. But the outlines of a deal were clearly in place.

Beckwith considered Ullage's email and then read through a sampling of messages on her home page and her Twitter feed, nearly all of which were from some of the millions of people who had signed on with the September 18 Coalition. None of them believed a word the president said; all of them urged her to reject any deal. Nothing Beckwith did would satisfy everybody.

All at once, she felt utterly spent, deeply sad, and terribly alone. To her own surprise, her eyes began to fill with tears.

In zero-g, her tears could not fall and instead formed a heavy film in her eyes, which she had to wipe on her sleeve twice before her vision cleared. She collected herself, logged onto her laptop phone, and dialed a number in Arizona. A woman's voice answered.

"Mama?" Beckwith said simply.

"Belkie," her mother said.

"I'm glad you're there, Mama."

"Would you like me to put your father on?"

Before Beckwith could answer, her father picked up an extension.

"Hello, B," he said.

"Pop," Beckwith answered.

"We saw the news this morning, about the president."

"Yes," Beckwith said. "I just learned about it."

"What do you think?" her father asked.

"I don't know. I was surprised—and a little relieved. How would you feel if I came home?"

Her mother answered before her father could. "How would *you* feel if you came home?" she asked. It was what she was sure to say, and it was one of the reasons Beckwith had called in the first place.

"I'm trying to decide that," Beckwith answered. "I feel like I should stay."

"You can't bring back the people who have died already," her mother said.

"I know that."

"Maybe you've done all you can then," her father said. "So now you come home."

"I promised I wouldn't," Beckwith said. "Not without a real intervention—and not until the president actually acts instead of just promising."

"Then that's your answer," her mother said. "You stay."

That too was what Beckwith had expected to hear, but the answer wouldn't stick. Beckwith was not afraid of much, but she did fear herself a little: her ego, her stubbornness, her streak of conqueror's syndrome. The president of the United States had offered her a deal. A nation had shifted at her command. Surely that was enough. Who the hell, she asked herself, did she think she was?

"I think . . ." Beckwith began, "I think maybe I should accept the offer."

"All right, B," her father said.

"Mama," Beckwith asked, "do you agree?"

"I do, Belkie."

"OK then," Beckwith said, with a wan smile she was glad her parents could not see. "I'll make plans."

She cut the connection, radioed Moscow, and asked the Capcom on the console to get Zhirov. He was off-shift, sleeping in the cosmonaut quarters on-site, but the controller went to fetch him. When he came on the line, Beckwith did not say hello.

"Vasily," she said simply, "please send your Soyuz."

"All right, Walli Belka," he answered. "I am very glad."

CHAPTER FIFTEEN

The news of Beckwith's agreement—or concession or capitulation or surrender or victory or defeat, depending on who was doing the reporting—spread even faster than the news of the president's had. She was called a coward by some people, which hurt, and a variety of foul names by others, which didn't. "Turncoat" and "quisling" were again popular, as was "Neville Chamberlain" with the same vague hand wave to Munich. A fair share of people—though well less than half—praised her pragmatism, and that helped, but only a little.

When the station made its next southwest-to-northeast pass over South America, she fired up Zoe and Ivy and scanned the Brazilian Amazon. The relocation camps in western Brazil were now large enough that they cut easily discernible brown rectangles in the green forest canopy, with wide roads running to them like arteries feeding sickly tissue. Estimates from fieldworkers and human rights groups were that the camps were capable of housing a collective 320,000 refugees, and there was every indication that they'd soon be filled to that capacity.

But there were reasons for hope. Since the president's announcement leaked, human rights workers reported that military activity had been paused in numerous parts of the jungle, and from her orbital perch, Beckwith could see just ten major fires burning across the jungle. In an ordinary year, that would be considered an environmental outrage; in the midst of the Consolidation, it represented progress.

Before long, Moscow would begin sending her details on the arrival of the Soyuz, but she knew them already. The spacecraft would be ready to fly in less than two days. Beckwith would be expected to help dock the ship if needed when it arrived. She would be allotted three more orbits, or four and half hours, to secure the station, stow her gear, and review what she needed to know for an automatic reentry.

That was the plan, and that would have remained the plan had one more leak not come out of the fundraising dinner the president had attended at the rich man's home in the Kalorama neighborhood of Washington. He had lingered longer at the dinner than he intended to, deciding to tuck into a chocolate mousse cake topped with vanilla ice cream, and then to allow himself another helping, along with two cups of very strong coffee.

Rich food, a few slugs of caffeine, and attentive company tended to loosen his tongue as much as alcohol did. No sooner did Connie Polk pass up her own dessert, make her apologies for keeping early-bird hours, and leave than the president became loose-tongued indeed. What he said to the aide who had taken Polk's seat was overheard by three different people, who all took the better part of the night to decide what to do with what they had heard, and who all decided the next afternoon that what they would do was leak it to the press.

Not long after Beckwith had made clear her plans to come home, word crashed onto the news sites that what the president was heard to say to the aide at the conclusion of dessert was, "Let this all sit till the space girl comes home. Release a statement that I'll support a veto-proof majority, but back-channel the caucus that they can vote any way they want. That ought to put two-thirds out of reach. The jungle's four thousand miles away, football season is coming, and no one will care by then. With luck we can slow-walk the whole thing till the midterms."

The story was solid and the substance of the quote was reliable, but the three sources took pains to say that while they absolutely heard what they said they heard, they couldn't vouch for every single word. It was an odd hedge since their stories matched perfectly but so did their qualifiers. For the better part of two hours, the firestorm over the president's reversal played out online and on the cable channels. White House staffers insisted that his comments had been taken out of context, while the September 18 Coalition went into full-throated rage at a man whose word could not be trusted to hold for even a single morning.

It was then that things got worse—much, much worse—for the president and his supporters. Because it was then that the busboy who had surreptitiously propped his smartphone on a coffee cart near the presidential table and had set it to record voice and video throughout the dessert released his clip to *Mother Jones* magazine, which promptly shared it with the world. And it was then too that the reason for the original sources' hedging became clear.

Many TV stations bleeped the relevant word in the astounding clip, but rudimentary lipreading made it clear what the president had said. Even that wasn't necessary on the internet, where the clip circulated unedited and was shared tens of millions of times.

The New York Times did edit the video in its online coverage but explained in the accompanying story that instead of the word "girl" in the term "space girl," the president had "used a single-syllable, four-letter vulgarity that refers to a part of the female anatomy."

Other mainstream news outlets used a decorous asterisk in place of the word's single vowel; still others published the word in its full and florid form. The *New York Daily News* trumped them all with the headline on its website and later in its morning edition, which screamed: "P. Calls Walli a C!" The paper's editorial page said it would "leave it to readers to decide if *P* should stand for 'president' or for a single-syllable, five-letter vulgarity that refers to a part of the male anatomy." The White House tried to put out the fire, first saying the clip might be a forgery, then conceding it was real but dismissing it as "just gym talk."

For about an hour after the news broke, Beckwith herself knew nothing about either the president's reversal or his choice of language. Both Houston and Moscow had been unusually silent in that hour—a silence that, under the circumstances, made her suspicious. So she opened her laptop, and the first thing she saw was the *Daily News* headline, mostly because no fewer than 15,000 people had forwarded it to her Twitter feed.

Even in zero-g, with no gravity to pull on a jaw whose muscles had suddenly stopped working, her mouth fell open. She quick-scanned from site to site, confirming what the first headline had unmistakably told her, her jaw then snapping shut and clenching. She watched the busboy's clip three times to satisfy herself that it was absolutely impossible that the president had somehow been misunderstood.

Almost dizzy with fury, Beckwith punched open the line to Moscow, reached the person on the communications console, and demanded to talk to Zhirov. When he had been fetched, she again spoke with no preamble.

"Vasily," she said, "cancel my ride."

CHAPTER SIXTEEN

September 10

Zhirov had no intention of keeping Walli Beckwith's Soyuz on the ground. The plan had been to launch it, and that plan would be followed on schedule—never mind the dirty-mouthed American president. But the morning the rocket rolled out to the launchpad did not begin as Zhirov would have liked.

He watched the train carrying the fifteen-story machine emerge from its hangar, the Soyuz lying flat on an open railcar like a captured deer, its bottom end—its magnificent twenty engines—facing forward. Traveling just a few miles an hour, it would take close to two hours to reach the pad. During an ordinary rollout, Zhirov would watch the train travel only its first few hundred yards and then would light out for the pad at a brisk run that took him along a road near the tracks—his legs carrying him faster than the train was creeping. He would cross the tracks about half a mile from the launchpad, speed-run the rest of the way, and arrive before the rocket did. It was a rollout routine he'd followed many times, one that afforded him a chance for some predawn exercise but still ensured that he would be present to observe the rocket as it was stood up straight—its nose rising from the horizontal, up to forty-five degrees, then to a full ninety-degree vertical. Once the Soyuz was upright, it would be enclosed in its scaffold-like gantry in preparation for launch.

This morning, however, Zhirov stayed an extra fifteen minutes near the hangar to ensure that all was going well and only then set out. He enjoyed his run far less than he usually did, having badly underdressed for the weather, and was relieved when he reached the railroad crossing to find Gennady Bazanov on the other side of the track, standing outside a government car. For a rocket as important as this one, the director of flight operations himself would be present, and he and Zhirov had agreed that they would meet at this spot and drive the rest of the way to the pad together. The tailpipe of the car puffed white smoke in the frigid air—a promise of the warmth that would be found inside.

Just as Zhirov raised his hand to hail Bazanov, however, two security guards stepped forward. Both were young, both were armed, and both had dressed far more warmly than he had, having stood their post for hours so far. Both also instantly saw who Zhirov was, and he registered the flash of both recognition and respect he had long since grown accustomed to seeing.

"I'm sorry, Colonel," one of them said, "but the dog has already walked."

"He never walks this soon," Zhirov protested.

"No, sir," the guard said. "The dog was on time; he is always on time."

Zhirov slumped. The dog was the bomb-sniffing dog. On rollout days he would be brought to the crossing when the train was about fifteen minutes away, just as it appeared around a bend in the tracks, where its twenty lovely engine bells could be glimpsed in the distance.

Once the dog had walked and the tracks were secured, nobody—not the commander of the Cosmodrome, not the chairman of the Duma, not the most accomplished cosmonaut in all the world—could cross until the train had passed. Zhirov glanced down the tracks and could see the rocket approaching.

"Corporal," he said, stressing the younger man's very junior rank. "Look at me." He spread his arms to display his inadequate dress. "Do you know the temperature?"

"It is cold, sir. I'm sorry," the soldier said. "But there is nothing I can do."

Bazanov, watching the exchange from a distance, jogged over while Zhirov hugged himself and jumped up and down in a largely ineffective effort to stay warm. The moment Bazanov neared the tracks, the guard turned to him and repeated the drill that was his sole mission here this morning.

"I'm sorry, Mr. Director, but the dog has already walked."

"Corporal . . ." Bazanov began.

"It's no good, my friend," Zhirov interrupted. "The soldiers are just doing their job."

"I will strangle that dog," Bazanov said.

"He's just doing his job too," Zhirov answered.

Bazanov flashed a glare at the guards, trotted back to the car, opened the trunk, and pulled out an olive drab army blanket. He hurried back to the tracks and prepared to toss it across to Zhirov, but the lead guard stopped him.

"I'm sorry, Mr. Director, but the dog has already walked," he said unselfconsciously, as if it were the first time he'd spoken the words all day.

"The dog was not sniffing for a blanket!" Bazanov snapped. "Blankets do not explode!"

The corporal looked from the fuming Bazanov to the shivering

Zhirov, then at last took the blanket and, with the assistance of the other guard, unfolded it, shook it out, and examined both sides of it. Satisfied that it would indeed not explode, he handed it across to Zhirov, who gratefully wrapped it around himself and waved Bazanov back to his car where he could wait in the warmth.

Not long after, the sleek orange-and-white Soyuz rumbled by. Zhirov watched it go with open admiration—the great Russian space machine, the speedy cosmic sports car. When the train had fully cleared the crossing and had moved to a safe distance, the guards lowered their guns, stood aside, and nodded apologetically to Zhirov. He nodded back and then, on reflection, offered them a crisp salute, which they received with broad smiles and smartly returned.

Zhirov trotted across the track, hopped inside Bazanov's car, and the two of them motored to the pad. When they arrived, they watched in silence as the rocket was slowly raised and began to be prepped for its upcoming journey.

"I'll be glad to see this one fly," said Zhirov.

Bazanov grunted. "It's been given a foolish errand. I am not in the business of providing taxi service for misbehaving Americans."

"She will behave now, sir. She will get aboard and this will end soon."

"She already told you she would do no such thing," Bazanov said.

"She was angry. No one outside of Mission Control heard her say that. She will not have to explain herself if she boards the Soyuz and comes home, and I will see that she does."

"Perhaps you can. Either way, this will be her last chance."

"Sir?"

"Moscow has had enough; I have had enough. If she does not come home, the Americans can solve this problem. There will be no more communications between Moscow and the station except in the event of an emergency. I will order a power-down in the Zvezda, the Zarya, the Poisk—all of the Russian modules. There will be air, but they will be dark and damp. And there will be no more resupply missions. She can live on what she has there and she can live there alone."

"The Americans will feed her."

"Then let them," Bazanov said. "But they can't go get her without a Soyuz rocket, and this one—" He jabbed his finger toward the elegant booster standing on the pad, the now-rising sun glinting orange off its side. "This one is the last one I send until astronaut Belka 'Walli' Beckwith is off my station."

Bazanov spoke the "Walli" with open contempt. Then he turned away, his face flushed.

"I will bring her home, sir," Zhirov promised.

Bazanov said nothing, but put the car in gear, and the two of them drove away from the pad.

. . .

It never occurred to anyone at the White House that a three-minute recording with an eight-second sentence that included a one-syllable vulgarity could eat a presidency alive, but no sooner did the recording of the president's dinner-table remarks go wide than the great devouring began. Snap polls—equal parts unreliable and irresistible—were conducted by all of the broadcast networks and cable news channels, as well as by *The New York Times*, *The Washington Post*, *The Wall Street Journal*, and *USA Today*, and all but the pollsters at the friendly *Journal* saw at least five-point losses in the president's popularity. Beckwith, whose popularity continued its perfectly Newtonian relationship with the president's—moving in equal and opposite directions—saw her approval numbers bounce by the same amount.

The president was left with no good options. He could apologize and recommit to the intervention deal he had offered Beckwith—which absolutely no one now trusted him to honor. Or he could brazen it out and concede that he had lied to her but argue that it was necessary in the interests of national security. That was the course he chose to take, and he decided on his own just how he would take it. During an already scheduled Chamber of Commerce speech that evening, he would apologize for his "dinner-table potty mouth," and he would confess, abashedly, that his wife had instructed him to "put a dollar in the cuss jar every day for the rest of the year."

Then he would turn directly to the matter of the intervention. He would begin with more or less the same speech he'd given during the campaign, opposing America's involvement in "elective wars in others' lands." He would then go on to "deplore the tragic displacement and loss of life in the Amazon" and promise that his administration would "continue to work with the nations of the world to bring the suffering to an end." And then, pointedly, angrily, he would declare that the US government would "not have its choices made or its policies dictated by the playacting and sedition of a naval officer who had become nothing more than an outer space outlaw." With that, he would look roughly skyward, point a scolding finger, and announce, "Never!"

When he actually reached that part of the speech that evening, the partisan audience rose to its feet and cheered, and the clip ran throughout the day on cable channels and websites around the world.

. . .

Raymond's confidence in his finesse with computers and the information that they could gather from the relocation camps in Brazil proved well placed. Within two days of the attack on the Mercado hospital, he had the entire facility's network up and operating, gathering information about impending attacks and the locations of new burnings, as well as processing the new arrivals who were already beginning to stagger into the Mercado camp, chased by the fires.

Just as important was the business of tracking information about the growing population of refugees who were being herded into what were now four fully constructed internment camps, which stood in a cluster at the western border of Brazil and were identified by the four major compass points—*norte, sul, leste,* and *oeste*; north, south, east, and west. Bobo-deCorte wanted to keep what he continued to call "tribal relocation lands" as hidden from public eyes as possible, and when it came to the news media, he did a good job of limiting access. He allowed only friendly interviews and happy footage of native children playing together and native adults working on crafts and peacefully making their traditional meals, all of the videos directed and shot by a single, state-friendly TV station in Brasilia.

The Brazilian president would have liked to leave it at that, but he knew that he also had no choice but to allow human rights groups, as well as medical teams from the SSA, UNICEF, the Red Cross, and the World Health Organization, to visit the camps and ensure the health of the internees. The fragile support he was receiving from friendly nations—Saudi Arabia, North Korea, Hungary, and a few others with similar strongman leaders—would evaporate quickly if the relocation camps began to look the slightest bit like death camps.

With the help of the visiting health groups, the workers at all four camps kept a running census of the internees, identifying them by four metrics: gender, age, tribe, and health status. All of the information was made publicly available in order to help convince the world that the people in the camps were being well accounted for and well cared for. The well-accounted-for part was more or less true, except for one detail: While the names of all of the internees were taken and recorded, they were not released along with the other four descriptions. University scholars knew the most common familial names of the one million Amazon tribespeople, and also knew more or less what their distribution and numbers ought to be. If particular names stopped appearing in adequate numbers, it would be a sign of whole family groups dating back centuries being eliminated.

For Sonia, Mia, and the other doctors in the Mercado camp, that lack of names presented a problem. SSA protocol dictated that the moment patients were taken in for care, the organization remained responsible for them until they were properly discharged. The raid on the camp had hardly represented such an orderly closing of the file on any of the cases, which meant that the doctors were obliged to track the patients' whereabouts so they could continue providing treatment if it ever became possible. Under the current circumstances, SSA officials in Paris might have waived the rule, considering it impossible to abide by, but the SSA workers in the Mercado camp—having lost track of 1,243 souls—felt obliged to honor it as best they could, even without names to guide them.

Sonia and Mia led the effort, and from the moment Raymond established his computer network, they each commandeered a laptop and made it their responsibility to scour the lists from the four camps, looking for descriptions of people who might match any of the patients who had been at the Mercado hospital. Sonia did not even pretend that there was not one description of one Guarani boy she was looking for more closely than all of the other 1,242 people, even if the name Kauan—much less Oli—would never be attached to it.

The reports from the four camps came in only spottily. The record keeping and reporting were best at the eastern camp, where lists were released at least twice a day, once at midday and once just after sundown. The north and south camps were next, always issuing a single reliable report, and always around noon. The western camp was a mess. At best there was a list every other day; it was always a short one—due not to the size of the camp, which was as big as all the others, but simply to poor head-counting. Often some of the data was missing—in one case, an internee's gender, tribe, and health status would be released, but not age; in another, it would be age, health, and gender, but not tribe.

Mia and Sonia would take a first pass at the lists and turn any descriptions of any people who seemed even faintly familiar over to another pair of doctors at two other computers who would cross-index them with the fastidiously kept Mercado database.

"We've got a possible," would come the call from the doctors with the databases whenever three out of four of the metrics matched.

"We've got a likely," was the call when there was a four-for-four match—since while four-for-four was good, there could certainly be more than just one, say, forty-something female Yanomami with low-grade malaria.

And once in a great while there would be a shout of, "We've got a match!" if, say, the health description of the twenty-something male Enawene with burns to the extremities also happened to mention that he was missing the fourth and fifth toes on his right foot due to a childhood accident with an ax—a detail that would surely have been included in the Mercado camp's own exceedingly thorough records.

Sonia did her work as diligently as she could, but her breath would still catch if a list included a child—more so if that child was Guarani and male. She would then look and look and silently plead for a mention of a recent case of chicken pox or flu, but Oli's flu had long since resolved itself, and if there were any faint spots remaining from his bout with chicken pox, they were too small and inconsequential-looking to attract attention, much less a mention. The most she ever got was a "possible."

On the fifth day after the computer network had been set up, well after dark, when Mia and the database doctors had at last gone to bed, Sonia sat alone with her laptop outside the infirmary building, enjoying the evening quiet and reviewing two reports—one from the northern camp and one from the south. Both had come in almost simultaneously during the day, and she and Mia had read them quickly. Sonia found herself wondering if something might have slipped by them. So she called both reports onto her screen again and scrolled through them more carefully, looking once more for a small male child.

There was nothing to be found on either list. She threw her head back and looked up at the sky. It was a very clear, very starry night, and if her *tía*-mama had been passing over, she'd have been able to see her easily. She drew a deep breath of the jungle air and took a fleeting bit of calm from that. And then, suddenly, came a ping from her computer.

She jolted up and looked at the screen. A new report had come in. It was from the western camp—the lazy, cursed, worthless western camp, whose lists were so poor and whose filings so late. She opened the file and saw a shamefully short census of barely thirty names— thirty names in a camp that held at least eighty thousand people. She scanned it fast, with a mix of resentment, fatigue, and stubborn, hollow hope—and then she sat up straight and tensed.

There was a child, a male, under ten years old, the report said. And he was Guarani. And then, in the column labeled "*Saúde*," for health, there were just two words: "*Muitos arranhões*." *Many scratches.*

Sonia looked up—and then leapt up.

"We've got a match!" she cried out to the silent jungle.

CHAPTER SEVENTEEN

Beckwith was in the midst of the day's maintenance work when Mission Control called to tell her that the Soyuz rocket Vasily Zhirov and Gennady Bazanov had sent to fetch her was at last approaching. Had the station been passing over Baikonur when the engines on the Soyuz lit, Beckwith would have been able to watch the show. It could be a striking sight from space—the match flare on the surface of the planet and the rising white contrail behind it. In this case, however, the contrail was following a rocket that was bringing a spacecraft whose arrival Beckwith was very much dreading, so it was probably just as well that she was too far southwest of Baikonur to see anything at all. Usually the time would drag before a newly launched Progress or Soyuz—bearing fresh supplies or, better yet, fresh crew—actually arrived. Today it all went too fast—not least because the trajectory on which the rocket was launched would bring it to the station in a zippy six hours, instead of the two days a rendezvous usually took. Moscow wanted Beckwith off the station and off it now.

"Station, Houston," came the call from the Capcom. It was not

Jasper. "Anticipating Soyuz in fifty-four, thirty-eight," he said—the count referring to minutes and seconds.

"Copy your five-four, three-eight," Beckwith said.

"Expect visual confirmation in eighteen minutes."

"Copy," she responded. "I'll be watching."

Beckwith kicked off toward the Russian end of the station where the Soyuz would be docking. She dove down toward the Pirs module on the bottom side and then stopped herself. The Pirs was wrecked—wrecked and sealed and probably now empty of air, the temporary patch of paper and clothes that had bandaged the breach in its bulkhead having long since worked loose. She turned back around and instead vaulted upward, toward the upward-facing Poisk module, where the Soyuz that took Lebedev and Zhirov home had been docked.

Moscow was hoping to execute the arrival of the new Soyuz entirely automatically, so as to keep the X-factor of the crazy American out of the equation, but in the event of another mishap like the last attempted docking, both she and the controllers knew a human would have to be on duty to intervene. No sooner did she open the Poisk hatch and drift inside than Mission Control—this time Moscow's—hailed her.

"Station, Moscow," said the Capcom.

She had expected it to be Zhirov, and it was Zhirov. Beckwith had little doubt he had been at the Baikonur launch and just as little doubt that, once the Soyuz was safely in orbit, he had hopped a Roscosmos plane straight for Moscow. The three-hour flight would have him back on the ground well before the docking. For once, Beckwith was not happy to hear his voice. She would have preferred an anonymous Russian at the mic, rather than someone whose good opinion mattered very much to her.

"Moscow, station," she responded. "Looks like you sent me a package." Her instrument panel indicated that the approaching Soyuz was forty-eight kilometers—or thirty miles—below and behind the station, closing at thirty-one meters per second, or sixty-nine miles per hour.

"I did," Zhirov said. "Package at forty-eight, closing at thirty-one. We have capture at forty-nine minutes."

"Copy," Beckwith said.

Zhirov was performing the comfortable ritual of the nominal docking: the range-finding, the call-and-response, the predicted time to an agreed-upon result—*capture at forty-nine minutes*. But the cosmonaut was also silently pleading with Beckwith to honor that agreement. The more closely he stuck to the precise routine, the more she might be carried by habit and muscle memory to see it through to its end.

Beckwith followed that script too as the Soyuz closed to thirty kilometers and its speed steadily slowed to twenty-three meters per second. The upward-facing windows of the Poisk made it impossible for Beckwith to see the approaching spacecraft yet, but the camera on the bottom side of the station captured it. The Soyuz drew closer still and moved slower still.

"Target at seventeen and twenty-one," Zhirov said.

"Copy seventeen and twenty-one."

"Sixteen and nineteen."

"Sixteen and nineteen."

"Fifteen and fifteen," Zhirov now said.

"Fifteen and—" Beckwith began and was brought up short. It was when the Progress had slowed to fifteen meters per second at a fifteen-kilometer distance during the previous approach that it had *stopped* slowing, that it had then begun to accelerate to sixteen and eighteen and then twenty-eight and everything had come unraveled. She shook off the memory. This wasn't the Progress, it was a Soyuz, and this wasn't the previous approach, it was now. "Copy fifteen and fifteen," she repeated. And then, to her deep relief, she saw the readout on her screen slow to fourteen.

The Soyuz continued to behave itself, drawing steadily closer and moving steadily slower. It at last matched the station's altitude and then rose above it, climbing a predetermined additional half kilometer and beginning a slow rotation until it was pointed nose down. It hung there motionless. Now Beckwith could see it through the Poisk's upward-facing windows, and the two monitors on her instrument panel showed the same twin perspectives the monitors in the Pirs had shown during the Progress docking: the station as seen from the camera in the approaching vehicle, and the approaching vehicle as seen from the camera on the station. She knew that the screens in both Mission Controls, in Houston and Moscow, displayed the same two views, and, she suspected, the networks and cable channels were airing them too.

"Commencing approach," Zhirov said. "Soyuz to point-four-nine and one." Now just under a half kilometer away, the Soyuz was moving at one meter per second, or 2.2 miles per hour—slower than walking speed.

"Point-four-nine and one," Beckwith repeated.

She alternated her view between the approaching Soyuz outside her window and the images on the screens, but her mind was not on either. All morning, she realized, she had not been entirely certain what she would do when this moment arrived. Accepting the Soyuz—allowing it to dock with the station as she'd been ordered—did not mean she would have to board it.

But Houston was watching, Moscow was watching, and, she was certain, the world was watching too—as was the president of the United States, the man who had insulted her so lewdly and lied to lure her home, which would have led to her mortification if she had believed it and returned to Earth. Letting the Soyuz dock would have very different meanings for those very different audiences. She looked down at the screens. The one showing the view from the Soyuz was now entirely filled with the image of the station, with the Poisk's docking port at the center. The one from the station showed the approaching docking probe of the Soyuz.

"Five and point-three," Zhirov said, as the Soyuz, now just five meters, or sixteen feet, away, crept forward, closing the small remaining distance. "Now four and point-two."

Beckwith said nothing and then made up her mind. She darted to the Zvezda, punched the circuit breakers on the guidance panel, and fired the system up. She seized the thruster controller and yanked it into a hard yaw. The whoosh of the jets sounded through the station walls, and the motion threw her off-balance. On the screens in Houston and Moscow and all over the world, the station slewed hard to port.

"We have you in a yaw, station," Zhirov said.

"Copy that," Beckwith answered.

"Stabilize please."

"Copy," Beckwith said. She held the station steady and watched as Moscow repositioned the Soyuz so that the docking port was back in the center of its sights. Beckwith now hit the thrusters in the opposite direction, and the station slewed hard to starboard.

"Reading opposite yaw," Zhirov said. "Repeat: Stabilize please."

Beckwith ignored him. She could see the jets fire on the Soyuz as it tried to adjust and she hit the thrusters again, jerking back to port.

"Station!" Zhirov barked. "Walli! Stabilize."

Beckwith replied evenly: "No, Moscow."

"No?" Zhirov repeated. "*No?*"

Beckwith looked at the screens in front of her—at the docking probe on the Soyuz and the docking port on the station—and smiled, thinking of the personal-safety course she and the other female midshipmen had taken in their first year at the Naval Academy.

"No, Vasily. No means no," she said. Then, for emphasis, she added: "No on stabilize, no on approach, no on docking."

Zhirov said nothing, and now, to Beckwith's astonishment, she heard Joe Star, in Houston, break into the air-to-ground feed.

"Station, Houston," he said, without bothering to introduce himself. "You have been given instructions from Moscow, and Houston concurs with them. You will comply."

"I will not," Beckwith responded. "I ask that the Soyuz stationkeep. Request that it retreat to one trailing kilometer and maintain that distance pending future instructions. There will be no docking today."

She waited for a verbal response from Star, but none was forthcoming and none came from Moscow either. There was silence on the air-to-ground loop, but she suspected that the lines between the two command centers were crackling. She imagined that some of the controllers were fantasizing about simply dumping the Soyuz, sending it on a flaming plunge into the ocean, and, in doing so, telling the mutinous astronaut to go straight to hell. It's what Beckwith would have been tempted to do if she were on the ground.

But that was out of the question. The twin space agencies could not abandon her—much as they might have liked to do so—since that would mean eventually leaving her to die in space. They could not order her to dock the craft if she refused. Nor could they even contemplate a forced docking, since Beckwith could always override the systems that would be needed to latch the two vehicles together, and either way the odds were too great of another collision—one that this time the world would watch unfold.

Instead, the people on the ground could only comply with her command—*obey* her command. Slowly, the Soyuz retreated, returned to a nose-first attitude, and puffed its forward thrusters until it had backed away a hundred meters, then a few hundred, then a full kilometer. There it stopped, absolutely motionless relative to the station, its running lights flashing as it hung in space.

Beckwith stared at it for a long moment. Then, without warning from either of the two Mission Controls, everything around her changed. The interior lights flickered and went dark. The constant churn of the pumps and compressors and computers around her fell silent, and all she could hear was the whir of a fan, circulating atmosphere throughout the Russian segment. Almost immediately, a chill began to grow in the Zvezda. She hugged herself against it and thought about the mice. Before long, the cold would spread to the American segment too.

CHAPTER EIGHTEEN

September 11

In Mission Control in Moscow there had always been two kinds of quiet. There was the quiet that descended in the time between missions, when the great room was hushed and mostly empty, and there was the quiet that settled over the room during a mission—which wasn't a true quiet at all, but an intense focus on the business of keeping cosmonauts alive in the killing environment of space.

But the quiet in Moscow Mission Control after the people of Roscosmos shut down Walli Beckwith was of a third, entirely new kind: It was a silence of indifference, of abdication. It was a silence that came from having only the most basic of a spacecraft's vital signs flickering across the screens and little more—requiring no focus at all, much less an intense one. If Beckwith radioed down, safety protocols demanded that Moscow respond. But otherwise, Mission Control would have nothing to do with her.

"The goat is at last eating up the wolf," Gennady Bazanov said with a smile as he approached Vasily Zhirov, who was sitting glumly at a half-blank console at the back of the room.

The goat eating the wolf was the Russian equivalent of the pig flying, and it was what Bazanov had always said would happen if he ever spent a boring day in Mission Control. Zhirov frowned up at him.

"Only because we fed it to him," he said.

"It had to be, my friend," Bazanov answered.

Zhirov didn't respond. It was a bad business to make flight decisions based even partly on pique, and that's exactly how this one had been made. Nothing captured that official pettiness better than the crew picture of Beckwith on the left side of the viewing screen.

Despite his support of the power-down decision, Bazanov had insisted that the picture remain in place. It was not so much out of loyalty to Beckwith as it was out of superstition. Crew members' pictures had never been pulled down until they were home, and it would court bad luck to break that tradition now. But when the Russian segment went off-line, the Roscosmos administrator, who outranked even Bazanov, demanded that the picture go with it. Zhirov agreed with Bazanov that the picture must stay and even threatened that if Beckwith's face disappeared from the screen, he would disappear from Mission Control, storm straight out, and denounce the administrator and the entirety of the Roscosmos brass to the press—a press that adored him and had never heard of them.

Finally a compromise was reached. The picture would stay where it was, but it would be grayed out—dimmed a shade like an on-screen computer tab that was technically there but inaccessible and pointless. That, in a lot of ways, was worse.

. . .

Grayed out was exactly how Walli Beckwith felt, all alone aboard her half-functioning space station. It didn't take long before the largely powerless Russian segment grew as chilly as the silence coming from the Russian controllers, with the cold soak from space seeping through the bulkhead. Within forty-eight hours the humidified cabin air had begun to condense out into beads of water along the walls and Beckwith's exhalations frosted up into clouds.

The American end of the station was warmer, but Beckwith did not want to seal the hatch between the two segments to preserve what heat she had. There was too great a risk that the temperature differential on the opposite sides of the closed door would cause the different types of metal that made up the hatch to expand and contract at different rates, jamming the latches shut. Over time, the temperature all over the station thus began to fall. The space station was a ghost ship, and Beckwith its sole drifting spirit, with very little to do.

There was only so much time she could spend on the treadmill without pulling a muscle or exhausting herself, and only so much she could devote to surveilling the jungle with Zoe and Ivy. The station rarely made more than two passes over the Amazon in any twenty-four-hour period, and when it did, the entire flyby was over in minutes. There were few experiments left that needed tending in the American segment and none possible in the dead Russian segment. Beckwith was able to complete basic maintenance work like cleaning air filters in as little as an hour. After that, she was reduced to busywork.

She reflected that she had never much cared for the untidiness of the Russian modules and devoted a couple of hours to cleaning them up for no reason other than the work ate those two hours. The Zarya was a particular disaster, with thawed water and condensation drifting through the air everywhere. It was easily the dampest of the dark and chilly modules. She sopped up some of the mess near the laboratory console with a cloth, discarded it in a garbage bag, and wiped her hands on her pants. Then she was once again at a loss for how to fill her time.

It occurred to her that there was something she very much wanted to do, even if she knew she shouldn't—even if she'd have to ask for help from Moscow and it would likely not be forthcoming. But she'd spent the better part of the past three weeks doing things she shouldn't do and why should now be any different? She opened the communications line.

"Moscow, station," she called.

She was met with silence.

"Moscow, station," she repeated.

Still no one answered. She was about to call again when the line cracked to life.

"Copy, station," came the response.

Beckwith closed her eyes and drew a grateful breath. It was Zhirov, taking over the Capcom duties in the half-functioning Mission Control. Had Wally Schirra himself radioed back from the grave, she could not have been happier.

"Vasily," she said more casually than she felt, "I'm glad you're there this evening."

"I am always here in the evening," he said. He was trying to be cold, brusque, but he achieved just the opposite. He sounded warm, relieved to hear from her. They both knew it. Neither one of them said it.

"Have you decided to come home?"

Have you decided to come home? Just like that. It so captured Zhirov.

"Vasily," Beckwith said. "You know I can't do that."

"You can do that. You have made your point. Your followers will forgive you and your government will listen now."

"It's more than my followers, and my government won't listen."

Zhirov said nothing, and the air-to-ground link hissed and crackled. Beckwith dropped her head in her hands and rubbed her eyes. They stung from lack of sleep, and she stank from nervous energy and need of a wash. She was wrung out.

"Vasily," she said at last, "I've got a headache."

"Take some medicine."

"I need some Russian medicine. Ours doesn't work as well."

"Walli . . ." Zhirov said reproachfully. "That's the wrong medicine."

Among astronauts and cosmonauts, "headache medicine" was alcohol. Officially, there was not a drop aboard the space station, and on the American segment, the prohibition was honored. On the Russian segment, there was official practice and there was actual practice, and Progress supply vehicles routinely came aloft with at least a little unauthorized cargo—brandy and cognac mostly, repackaged in plastic bottles with squeeze-activated nozzles, tucked between authorized bundles of food and supplies. The ranking Russian on any mission would stash the liquor in an undisclosed place to ensure that no one had access to it unless all of the station's work was done for the day and all of its systems were secured. On the ground or not, Zhirov was that Russian.

"Vasily," Beckwith persisted, "it's a very bad headache."

Zhirov sighed. "All right, Walli, go to the Zvezda."

Beckwith kicked off a wall and shot from the Zarya to the Zvezda. Zhirov instructed her where to look—in an orange storage box on the top level of a bookshelf-like structure, next to a picture of Yuri Gagarin that had been taped to the bulkhead. She swam over to the shelf and opened the box. There were three squeeze bottles, containing brandy, cognac, and vodka. Labels had been taped to the front of each container, identifying the type and brand name of each spirit. Beckwith grabbed the vodka and frowned. It was Russian.

"The medicine," she said. "You used to have Polish."

"We used to have Poland," Zhirov answered.

Beckwith laughed. She transferred some of the vodka to a drinking pouch stored in a pocket at a workstation the cosmonauts used as a makeshift dining area. She took a long swallow and let the power of the drink—medicine indeed—seep into her. She would allow herself only a bit, but it would be a soothing bit. Zhirov let her have her moment.

"I cannot answer if you radio down again," he said at last. "Not unless there is a problem or you are ready to come home."

"I understand that, Vasily."

"*Bud' úmnoy*, Walli," Zhirov said, as he had three weeks earlier, before leaving the station. *Be smart.*

"I will," Beckwith answered.

"Moscow out," Zhirov said.

The line cut, and Beckwith floated where she was, listening to the dead hiss coming across the communications line, which was all she would hear from an indifferent Moscow from now on. She took one more swallow of the vodka.

It was at that moment, for the third terrible time in her long stay in space, that the piercing cry of the emergency Klaxon sounded everywhere in the station.

. . .

The western camp just inside Brazil was an utterly miserable place—and Sonia Bravo-Beckwith was determined to get there as fast as she could. If you watched the news only on Bobo-deCorte's preferred state-controlled station, which plenty of Brazilians did, the four camps looked nothing short of lovely. And the fact was, they were—provided you didn't look too closely.

All of the camps were actually two camps: There was the sprawling mass of tents and lean-tos, smoky open stoves and non-flush latrines—an ugly expanse in which tens and tens of thousands of people were crammed. Then too there was a smaller, public-facing showpiece camp. It was these camps that the visiting dignitaries, journalists, and TV crews were shown—and they were quite a thing to see.

There were children playing soccer on the freshly lined grass field and others in the movie tent watching American cartoons. There were art classes for adults and pop-up libraries with books in English, Portuguese, and Spanish, as well as computer lessons for anyone who was interested because in the era of the Consolidation, the tribes would be absorbed into modern society, making their contribution to the larger continental enterprise and leaving the wild at last. There were, too, the food tents serving fresh vegetables and rich native stews and the snack carts with their sliced mango and fried plantains.

The simple wraps and other clothes the tribes typically wore had been taken from them, and Western clothes—shorts and T-shirts with counterfeit logos and misspelled brand names—had been given to them instead. There was a New York Yankees shirt with a New York Mets logo and "York" spelled "Yorq." There was a *Star Wars* shirt with *Star Trek* characters and a *Sesame Street* shirt with Bert and Ernie labeled "Ben and Eddie." The new clothing, the government explained, was the first part of the tribes' "assimilation." Counterfeit branding or not, from the look of things, the people were assimilating well indeed.

"Paradise!" ran the headline on the front page of the state-affiliated newspaper in Brasilia.

"Theresienstadt Novo"—*New Theresienstadt*—answered the opposition newspaper. The headline was a deliberately searing one, a reference to the ghetto and work camp the Nazis established in what is now the Czech Republic during World War II, which was similarly prettified into nothing short of a spa town for a Red Cross visit in 1944 before returning to its actual purpose of either working internees to death or shipping them farther east to concentration camps in Poland.

It was the Red Cross, UNICEF, SSA, and other health workers who saw the truth—though they had no way of proving it. Before they even came within sight of the camps, Consolidation soldiers conducted body searches and confiscated smartphones, cameras, and anything else that could capture a telltale image of what was taking place inside. On a handful of occasions, they pulled doctors aside for strip searches, when a metal detector was triggered by an artificial knee or a permanent bone pin—despite the doctors' pleas for decency and promises that the implants were the reason the detector sounded. The searches were conducted in the open, in full view of the guards and other health workers—the latter of whom looked away out of respect.

Still, nothing could stop the health workers from whispering about what they saw to the press, and they did—reporting the poor food, the running sewage, and the diseases, especially cholera, that were the true face of the camps. Argentina and Chile, both opposed to Bobo-deCorte's rule, threatened to fly military surveillance planes over the camps to see what the conditions were inside, and activists in Bolivia and Paraguay made their own attempts to reveal the truth, trying to fly drones over the camps. Consolidation officers had anticipated that, however, and deployed marksmen to shoot the drones out of the sky before they even reached the camps' airspace.

Finally Bobo-deCorte declared that if the outsiders didn't stop trying to look in, he would have no choice but to have the camps covered—roofing them over with massive canvas tarps that would trap both jungle heat and body heat, turning them into filthy sweat lodges for the people forced to remain there. Deployment of the tarps actually got started in the western and southern camps before Argentina, Chile, and the activists promised to call off their actions. Much of the world thus still believed the prettified pictures of the showpiece camps more than the warnings from the medical and human rights communities.

The instant after Sonia shouted her discovery of the boy in the western camp with the wonderful telltale scratches, she slammed her laptop shut, tucked it under her arm, and began sprinting through the camp and calling out for Mia and Raymond. Mia appeared at the opening of the darkened pediatrics building, wearing only a long T-shirt and underwear, her hair mussed and her expression unfocused. Sonia had clearly awakened her. Raymond, who had not yet gone to sleep, appeared from the communications building, where he spent more and more of his time so that he could be on hand to keep the whole underpowered, stapled-together network running. Sonia came to a stop in front of Mia, and Raymond hurried over to join them.

"I found him!" Sonia shouted excitedly.

"The boy?" Mia asked, still cloudy with sleep.

"The boy?" Raymond echoed as he reached them both.

"Oli, yes," Sonia said.

"Oli, sorry," Raymond responded.

Sonia opened her computer and scanned the screen, looking for the one-line listing on the roster. She found it.

"Right here!" she said, pointing to it. "Boy, Guarani, under ten, and this." She pointed to the comment under "*Saúde.*" Raymond tried to read it aloud.

"*Mui . . . muitos,*" he began.

"Many scratches," Mia finished for him. "Sonia," she said, "that's not a lot to go on."

"Who else could it be?" Sonia demanded.

"A lot of people," Mia said. "There are thousands of Guarani, hundreds of boys, and Oli's just five. Do you know how many more children there could be between that and ten?"

"What about the scratches?"

"It's the jungle," Mia said. "I have scratches, *you* have scratches. And the children certainly have scratches."

"No," Sonia said emphatically. "This is him. I *know* it's him."

"If it is, then at least you know he's safe," Raymond ventured.

"Not in that camp he isn't," Sonia said. "You've heard the stories."

She turned to face Mia. "I'm getting him out," she declared. "I'm getting him out, but first I'm getting *in*."

"What do you mean, 'getting in'?" Mia asked.

Sonia stopped and smiled inwardly. She had promised herself she would make the bastards pay—the bastards who had killed Annie, who had killed Oli's family. And now she could—and she would.

"I'm getting into that camp and I'm getting out, with Oli and with video of what's really going on in there."

"Can't be done," Raymond said. "You've heard what they do with doctors they even think are carrying phones."

"I'm not going in as a doctor," Sonia said. "Raymond, give me your shirt."

"What?" he asked.

"Your shirt, off with it. Give it to me," Sonia said.

Raymond, perplexed, did as he was told, stripping off the Baylor University T-shirt he wore most days and handing it to Sonia. He was skinny but broad-shouldered, and the T-shirt was an extra-large. Sonia put it on, and it hung hugely and loosely around her. Then she undid her bun, unbraided her hair, and shook it loose around her. Finally she leaned down, gathered some dirt from the ground, and—in an unknowing impersonation of Bobo-deCorte applying road dust before a rally—streaked it across her face.

"I'm going in as a Guarani refugee," she said. "And I know how to get there."

She looked toward the opening in the wall surrounding the complex, then beyond it to the grounds outside where the guards stood and where the helicopters were parked. She would go where she needed to go.

CHAPTER NINETEEN

The alarm that was screaming inside the International Space Station made itself known in different places and in different ways. Within the station, it was inescapable and everywhere. It knifed through the hearing of the one human and surely the five rodents on board in a way that both inflamed and insulted, and it was designed to do just that.

Beckwith shot from the Zvezda, toward the Node 1 module, where she saw the same red light flashing at her that she had seen once before—the cursed atmosphere light. She smashed her hand down in the direction of the round, plunger-like kill switch to silence the alarm, missed, and came down on the corner of the console instead, stabbing the meat at the base of her palm. She drew in a pained hiss of air and grabbed at her wounded hand with her good one, but not before she saw the first red pearls of blood appear. The Klaxon screamed on.

"Fuck!" she exclaimed, punched down on the plunger again, this time with both hands balled together, and shut off the hideous racket. Then she shook out her injured hand in an involuntary effort to manage the pain and instead succeeded only in scattering a little constellation of blood droplets in all directions. She sprang back to her sleep pod to fetch a bandage before she bloodied up the station air completely.

Hundreds of miles below, the problem that set off the Klaxon was making itself known in a similarly insistent, if not nearly as jarring, way, flashing in a semaphore of emergency lights on multiple consoles in both Houston and Moscow. It was in Houston that the alarm was received first and responded to first, as an atmosphere alert began to blink at the flight director's station, as well as at the stations of the Capcom, the flight surgeon, and the electrical, environmental, and consumables manager—or EECOM.

"We got atmosphere here," the EECOM controller announced into his headset.

"Copy your atmosphere," the flight director answered. At the moment, the flight director on-shift was Glynn Hampton, a three-decade veteran of NASA who had been occupying the center seat in Mission Control since the early days of the shuttle program.

"Copy here too," answered the Capcom.

"Bring her online," Hampton ordered.

"Station, Houston," the Capcom called. There was no answer. "Station, Houston," he repeated, but still nothing.

"Watch for the ammonia," the flight surgeon, Charlene Boysen, called.

"I'm not getting that," the EECOM answered, then immediately reversed himself. "Reading it now."

"Call her again," Hampton ordered

"Station!" the Capcom announced more emphatically. "Respond if you read."

High overhead, Beckwith did read, but Houston would have to keep. She had done a hurried, sloppy job of bandaging her hand, leaving paper wrappers and adhesive backings floating everywhere, and she still had to grab a towel to wad around her hand where the blood continued to seep.

She kicked off a bulkhead, fired herself as fast as she could toward the Destiny module, once again gathered the mice up, and this time shoved the cages into a large beta-cloth storage bag so as to spare herself the clumsy business of trying to herd them all as they floated free. Then she doubled back to her sleep pod and pulled out her Naval Academy hoodie and her Houston Astros sweatshirt. She and the mice then sped to the Russian segment, where she slammed the hatch behind her and sealed it shut. If it jammed from the cold, she'd deal with that later. She struggled into both shirts—her breath condensing again—and reached for the nearest hand mic. The other, ambient microphones had been shut off in the power-down.

"Houston, station," she said, and then added, "Moscow, station."

The Capcom in Houston answered first. "Reading you, Walli. Status please."

She recognized the voice—sort of. It belonged to an eager young astronaut whose name she could not for the life of her remember at the moment—something French, she was sure. She knew the timing of the rotations at the Capcom station, though, and knew that the current shift was almost up. Jasper would be coming on next, and she could picture him in the back of the auditorium, rocking on the balls of his feet and waiting to seize the console—especially now that there was a problem to solve. But at the moment she was happy even for the voice of the nameless rookie.

"Sheltering in place in the Zvezda," Beckwith answered.

"Good. Stay there."

"Copy that. I'm assuming ammonia," she said.

Lagrange, she suddenly remembered. He was something-or-other Lagrange.

"EECOM thinks it's ammonia, yeah," Lagrange answered.

"No false alarm this time?"

"Doesn't look like that. Still checking."

At that moment, the EECOM cut back into the Mission Control communications loop, which the controllers could hear but Beckwith couldn't. He had been consulting with his technical team and had nothing good to share.

"Flight, EECOM," he said.

"Go, EECOM," Hampton answered.

"Confirming breach in pump on P6, inside the IFHX. Consistent with ammonia. This one's no false alarm."

"How fast is the leak?"

"I've seen faster, but only in sims. No joy here, flight."

Hampton silently cursed. The ammonia network, which cooled the station, worked via two sets of piping, one of which carried ammonia and one of which carried water. The water picked up excess heat within the station and transferred it to the ammonia, which radiated it into space. Much of that transfer took place inside the IFHX—or the interface heat exchanger—a piece of machinery about the size of a large steamer trunk. If an ammonia pump had broken, it would contaminate the IFHX, which would in turn contaminate the atmosphere of the station.

The problem was not insoluble. The ammonia system was complex enough that the station's designers knew they needed backup hardware on board in case of a malfunction. For that reason, there was a replacement IFHX that could be swapped in for the broken one. But both of the units were located on what was known as the P6 truss on the outside of the station, part of the scaffolding that held the solar panels—and it was a distant part of that scaffolding. If the panels were the wings of the butterfly, and the Russian segment where Beckwith had sheltered was near the butterfly's head, the pump was located at the end of the right wing. Making the repair would require an EVA, or extravehicular activity—or spacewalk. Beckwith had never taken a spacewalk. Hampton, the flight director, keyed his mic back open, still excluding Beckwith from the loop.

"What are our options, EECOM?" he asked. "Can you shut down the pump?"

"It already shut itself down. Doesn't fix the leak."

"Can you seal the IFHX?"

"Too late for that."

"So what else have we got?" Hampton asked.

Lagrange, the rookie Capcom—the eager Capcom—jumped in. "She has to go EVA," he said. "It's what the book says."

"The book doesn't have a seat in this room," Hampton said.

"It's the only way to fix the problem."

"Beckwith's not trained for EVA."

"She can learn," Lagrange answered.

"That ain't how it works, son," Hampton said. Hampton almost never used "ain't." When he did use it, it was in situations exactly like this, and what he was really saying was, *Do you have any idea what you're talking about?* And never before had anyone heard him tack a "son" to it. Lagrange fell silent and Hampton went on.

"EECOM," he called, "how long till saturation?"

"At the current rate of leak, ten hours," the EECOM responded.

If the EECOM had had no joy to report before, he had even less now. Saturation was the point at which enough ammonia would have soaked into every crack, socket, and porous surface inside the American segment that no amount of atmospheric venting would ever clear it. That half of the station would forever be uninhabitable. Before Hampton could respond, Beckwith called down.

"Houston, station," she said.

"Copy, station," Lagrange answered.

"Confirm ammonia?"

"Yes, confirmed."

"How bad?"

"Bad."

"What's the saturation number?"

"Ten hours."

"That's certain?" she asked.

"That's certain," the EECOM, who was listening in, said on the loop to the Capcom.

"That's certain," Lagrange radioed up to space.

"Well, that's it, then," Beckwith responded.

"Say again, station?"

"That's it. I go EVA, right? I go, or we lose the station."

Lagrange the rookie did what no one in Mission Control was ever supposed to do when a veteran flight director like Hampton had been shown up: He turned around in his seat to look at him. Hampton glared back.

"Fine," he said on the closed loop to the controllers. "She stole it, now she can save it." He keyed open the link to the station. "Copy, Walli, you go EVA." Then he toggled open his line to his counterpart in Moscow. "Station to full power," he said, then added: "Please."

"As you wish," the Russian flight director answered, sounding very much as if he'd have preferred that circumstances did not require him to do as NASA wished.

Five minutes later, the Russian modules on the station came back online. At the front of Moscow Mission Control, the grayed-out image of Beckwith flashed brightly back to life.

. . .

The news broke wide and fast that more than ten weeks after climbing aboard the International Space Station and three weeks after seizing control of it Walli Beckwith was going to go outside. The tabloids loved it. The fact that the walk would have to begin within hours meant it would all be over before the morning editions came out, but the editors did what they could online.

"WALLI WILL WALK!" read the headline on the *New York Daily News* site. The paper would have used two-hundred-point type on its front page, so it did the same on the site. That meant scrolling far down before reaching the actual story—which was perfectly fine. The paper had made a business out of writing headlines that could make news all by themselves.

The *Boston Herald* went further, opting for straight drama, no ice, free-poured: "LIFE OR DEATH FOR STATION—AND BECK-WITH." By morning, newspapers around the world would be able to run physical headlines on physical paper, reporting which of those two binary outcomes had in fact occurred.

The TV networks made their own contributions, immediately running countdown clocks to the time the EVA would begin, which was just over two and a half hours after it became clear that one would have to take place. On college campuses and in volunteer offices across the country where the September 18 movement was being co-ordinated, televisions were turned to the news and left on, with people stopping their work every time there was a fresh development in the unfolding story.

At the Mercado hospital in the Bolivian jungle, the news came late. There was yet another glitch with the satellite uplink trucks, rendering the smartphones around the camp temporarily silent—cut off from the world beyond the jungle. Sonia was sitting at a table in the dining tent scouring census lists from the four camps that had already been downloaded and saved, looking for any description of any internee who might sound even more like Oli than the one she had. She was all but certain that she had the right person, but *actually* certain would be better.

It wasn't until ninety minutes before the EVA was set to begin that the satellite signal flickered back to life and her phone, lying on the table next to her computer, buzzed and lit. The words "Beckwith to Take Spacewalk" filled the screen. She snatched up the phone and read the first story in scanned chunks of paragraph. She looked at her phone log. Beckwith had tried to call her three times in the past hour—all when there was no signal in the camp. Now it would be too late. The news sites were reporting that by now, she would be preparing to climb into her suit. She would surely not have her computer with its phone app near her.

Sonia opened her email, and there was a single message from Beckwith: "You may have heard that I have to go outside and run an errand. Do NOT worry. I'll call as soon as I get back. Love."

Sonia jumped to her feet and ran to the infirmary building that had the only TV in the camp. A handful of doctors and workers whose phones had lit up with the same news were clustered around it, watching the live feeds from NASA. When they saw Sonia, they parted and made room for her. She nodded her thanks and took a position in front of the screen, standing silently with her arms folded.

At the White House, the president had his seventy-inch flat-screen TV in the dining room adjacent to the Oval Office turned on and was standing before it with a fixed expression and folded arms, unknowingly mimicking Sonia's pose. He had summoned Connie Polk to join him, along with Carl Bart, his chief political strategist. Joe Star had been in Huntsville, Alabama, for his annual administrator's roundtable with the employees at the NASA facility there, and was now en route by air to Houston so that he could be in Mission Control in time for the EVA to begin. He was being piped in to the White House by conference call, and the crackling of the connection from the government plane was evocative of the air-to-ground link from space.

"What's her status, Joe?" the president called out to the phone, his eyes not moving from the screen.

"Status, sir?" the voice of Star asked through the speaker.

"This leak . . ."

"The ammonia."

"Yes, the ammonia. How serious is it?"

"It's very serious," Star answered. "The newspeople are telling it right."

"Could it kill her?" The president asked the question baldly, with his eyes still on the TV. Polk and Bart turned to look at him, but he did not react.

"Ammonia is poisonous, and spacewalking is very dangerous," Star answered. "It's more dangerous than people know, and Beckwith is not well trained for it. She is in peril no matter what."

"And what if she dies?" the president asked. Star said nothing—either because he had no answer to such a question or because he somehow intuited that it wasn't meant for him. It wasn't. "Connie," the president now specified. "What if she dies?"

Polk kept her voice emotionless. "I imagine we will bury her at Arlington National Cemetery, sir, assuming we can recover the body," she responded. "She is a naval officer."

The president turned away from the screen, his eyes betraying the flicker of irritation Polk ever and always raised in him.

"I mean if she dies and the station is permanently poisoned from all of the ammonia," he said. "Do we abandon it? Are we on the hook to the other countries for making the whole thing uninhabitable?" Polk looked at him disbelievingly, and he seemed to feel an unaccustomed need to explain himself. "I'm sorry, Connie," he said. "These are things I need to know."

"I have not looked into the question of liability," Polk said. "But I

imagine that yes, the partner nations might seek some kind of restitution."

"How much would that be, Joe?" the president asked. "What did
the whole thing cost?"

"Well, sir," the administrator's voice answered, "nobody knows."

"Nobody *knows*? How is that possible?"

"We say $100 billion, including the cost of all the shuttle flights
that shipped the parts. But it's been six administrations since it all
started. No one ever kept track. Either way, that's only the American
share. If the thing is wrecked, expect the partners to come to us for
up to another $100 billion."

"Carl," the president now said, turning to Bart and adopting the
tone a superior uses to a true employee, not to government officials
like Polk and Star whom he may have appointed to their jobs but who
pledged their oaths only to the government.

"Sir," Bart responded with a corresponding tone indicating that
he knew his place precisely.

"If she dies, what happens to this business she started?"

"The intervention thing?"

"Yes, the intervention thing."

"It becomes unstoppable, I'm afraid. She's a nuisance alive; she's a
legend dead."

The president nodded. "All right," he said, "then let's make sure
she fixes our station and comes home safely."

"Which was always our plan," Polk said with a tone that was both
declaration and incredulous question.

"Which was always our plan," the president repeated.

CHAPTER TWENTY

Joe Star was not kidding that Beckwith wasn't well trained to walk in space, which wasn't quite the same as saying that she wasn't at all trained—but close. Like all astronauts, she had logged plenty of hours in a facility NASA called the Neutral Buoyancy Lab, which was just a fussy way of saying something very simple. In this case, the simple thing was nothing more or less than a gigantic swimming pool—202 feet long and 40 feet deep, filled with 6.2 million gallons of water. Sunk at the bottom of it were exact replicas of every module that made up the station, which astronauts, sealed inside NASA space-walking suits and equipped with breathing gear, could use to learn the basics of EVA work.

Beckwith hated everything about the training—it was slow and exhausting and did a lousy job of replicating the true friction-free, zero-g environment of space. What's more, with competition fierce for what were relatively infrequent spacewalks, she had never yet been assigned to one and had thus not had the more intensive training that would have truly equipped her for the work. For all of the aggravation of the swimming pool work, she still had come away without the adequate skills.

Now NASA had no choice. If they wanted to save their space station, they'd have to send Beckwith—ill-trained or not. The moment after Glynn Hampton grudgingly approved the walk and Beckwith signed off with Houston, she drifted from the Zvezda to the upward-facing Poisk module, where she'd refused to let the Soyuz dock. Cosmonauts beginning spacewalks typically exited from the downward-facing Pirs, but the Pirs was wrecked and would never be of use again. That left only the Poisk—and that was a problem. For one thing, the hatch of the Poisk was smaller than the Pirs's, meaning a tighter squeeze in an already bulky suit. Worse, while there were two very new EVA suits stored in the off-limits Pirs, there was only one, an older one used as a backup, in the Poisk.

Beckwith floated into the module, sealed the inner hatch behind her, and regarded the exhausted-looking suit. It was appallingly dirty—smudged with grease and gone half gray from constant handling. And now that she examined it with the unforgiving eye of someone who was going to be depending on it for her life, she noticed that the thing was frayed at some seams. That didn't mean the three-layer garment would spring a leak. It was the innermost layer that was meant to be airtight. Still, the suit didn't inspire confidence. It also smelled truly, hideously awful. Spacewalking was a hot, exhausting business, and a lot of sweat had been lost in that suit over the years.

On the ground, Houston and Moscow were now fully online and fully engaged with each other, with all of the consoles—especially the EECOMs'—swapping data from one side of the world to the other. The Russian EECOM noticed changes in pressure and airflow in the Poisk and radioed that information to his flight director, who passed it on to Houston. It was clear where Beckwith was and what she was doing.

"Station, Houston," the call went up from the Capcom. Lagrange should have had a few more minutes on-shift, but having run afoul of the flight director, and with his rotation almost up anyway, the rookie had surrendered the console early—to Jasper.

"Copy you, Jasper," Beckwith answered.

"Checking out your formal wear?"

"Affirm," she answered. "Smells like dog."

"Don't blame me. I only wear American-made."

"Station, Moscow," a voice interrupted.

It was Zhirov. Beckwith smiled. *I've got both my boys!* she thought, but didn't want to say it out loud. Then she decided she very much did want to say it.

"I've got both my boys!" she radioed down.

"Here to serve, ma'am," Jasper said.

Zhirov cut back in. He was in no mood for play.

"Station, we're counting eighty-seven minutes till egress," he said.

"That's eighty-seven—eight seven?" Beckwith asked.

"Affirm," Zhirov answered.

She was surprised. Eighty-seven minutes was far sooner than she had anticipated. "What does the book allow for IFHX swap-out?" she asked.

"Once you're outside, four hours," Jasper answered.

"And we've got ten till saturation," Beckwith said. "Figured that meant two and a half hours for suit-up and egress."

"Roger that, Walli Bee," Jasper answered. "Thinking here is that you'll need more time for the actual swap-out."

Beckwith frowned. "I can do this work," she said.

"Affirm, but you haven't been *trained* for this work."

Beckwith knew he was right, but she didn't much care for the low expectations. "Understood," she answered. "I'll be ready."

For the next hour, Houston and Moscow tag-teamed with the

station, alternately coaching and quizzing Beckwith on what she'd need to know to get outside, do the work she had to do, and come back alive. The time she'd spent in the Houston pool did leave her reasonably confident she could navigate her way around the exterior of the station, even to as remote a spot as the P6 truss on the end of the butterfly's right wing. If she lost her way—which was possible in an environment in which there was no up or down and she was creeping along so huge a machine—there was the equivalent of street signs to help her: arrows and labels on the exterior of the station pointing the way to various modules.

Beckwith was also adept at manipulating the kinds of tools that were necessary in zero-g. In space there's no such thing as turning a bolt in the ordinary way, since a hard twist to the right would simply turn the astronaut's body to the left. Instead, the tools worked with squeeze handles that didn't produce any action-reaction problems.

Of greater concern to Beckwith was the IFHX itself. She knew the units were big and unwieldy, and she knew that before she wrestled the new one into place on the station, she'd have to wrestle the old one off and back to a berthing spot so it could be anchored safely out of the way. Jasper had trained with an IFHX mockup in the Houston pool, and he walked her through what she'd need to know. He was frank with her about how hard she would find the work.

"You're going to hate that big, ugly box," he said.

The bigger challenge, in many ways, would be the spacesuit. Beckwith had practiced only in NASA EVA suits, and there were three of them stored in a docking node in the American segment of the station. But the American segment was contaminated, and even if Beckwith ventured down there with a gas mask, the suit would be unmanageable. It was a multipart garment, which had to be put on one piece at a time and required at least one other person to assist.

The Russian suit was a whole different matter. It was both brilliant and ridiculous, both invention and contraption. The first time Beckwith saw one demonstrated at the Gagarin Cosmonaut Training Center, outside of Moscow, she'd had to stifle a laugh. The suit was grandly called the Orlan—for sea eagle—which only made it seem more comical. Then she watched a video of an actual cosmonaut getting dressed in an Orlan in zero-g—a job he did on his own, in less than ten minutes, before heading outside—and she had to concede the genius of the thing.

The key to the Orlan was that it was only a single piece and you didn't so much dress in it as climb aboard it. The backpack was hinged at the top and could be lifted up to create a wide entry hatch. Once a crew member had slipped inside, a lanyard hanging near the left hand could be pulled to shut the hatch. A lever on the right side locked it. The life-support equipment was in a chest pack, with a readout screen on top that could be seen through the visor of the helmet.

Ports and hoses and other controls on the front of the pack were labeled in Cyrillic—*backwards* Cyrillic, since the only way to see them was with mirrors on the wrists of the suit. Cooling fluid ran through tubing in the suit's interior at a temperature of 46.4 degrees Fahrenheit, which, given that the suit would be used for heavy physical labor often in the direct glare of the sun, was barely enough to keep it comfortably cool. Even with the crude air-conditioning system cranking, the average cosmonaut lost at least three pounds in sweat during an eight-hour walk—hence the ripeness of the suit Beckwith would be climbing into today.

But there was no denying the genius of the Orlan. The Russian technician who had given the visiting NASA astronauts the demonstration Beckwith had attended seemed to sense the Americans' amusement and ended his presentation with a declaration that was impossible to argue with.

"We've had 107 exits and 107 entrances," he said. "Those numbers have always matched."

Beckwith thought of the technician now with an apologetic appreciation. She stripped off her work pants and short-sleeve shirt and pulled on the one-piece, sweat-absorbent long underwear that was necessary if the Orlan suit was going to be bearable at all. The underwear, at least, was fresh—still in the plastic bag in which it had been delivered by an earlier Progress vehicle.

Then she opened the back of the ungainly Orlan and peered inside. It was dark and dank and entirely unwelcoming. Attached by a cord to the wall of the module was a ring-bound manual with numbered instructions for getting into the suit. It was in Russian, but there were illustrations too, and Beckwith guessed she'd be able to make some sense of them. At that moment she noticed a red light flickering to life high up on the bulkhead, mounted on the module's closed-circuit camera. Zhirov's voice came across the communications loop.

"No book, Walli," he said. "It won't help."

"The procedure is for you to ask before you turn that thing on," she said.

"The procedure is for a senior officer to be present during suit-up and egress," Zhirov answered. "I'm present now. No book. Listen instead."

Slowly then, going from the manual Zhirov kept stored in his head, not on the page, he walked her through every step she would need to take to board the Orlan safely. He warned her about the clamminess of the inner layer.

"You'll think it's wet. It's not," he said.

She climbed inside, realized he was right, and nonetheless grimaced at the wet that was not wet.

"Now pull the lanyard," Zhirov instructed. Beckwith did, but the backpack did not close. "Firm grip," Zhirov said. "Yank it hard enough to rip the cord off."

"But we don't want to rip the cord off," Beckwith answered.

"You won't. Pull it hard."

She pulled—hard enough to rip the cord off and then harder still—and the backpack slammed shut. The air inside the suit compressed, enough to pop her ears and remind her of the post-collision pain that had filled her head weeks before.

"It hurts?" he asked.

"Yes."

"It's supposed to. You're all right."

She pulled on the lever on the right side—hard enough to break it off—and the pack locked with a loud, declarative snap. Beckwith was sealed inside—enclosed in a human-shaped spacecraft within a vastly larger actual spacecraft. For the first time since she had donned her first spacesuit, during her earliest days of training, she felt a small flash of fear—the locked-down claustrophobia that pilots and astronauts were never, ever supposed to feel. They all did at first, a little, which was why the greenest rookies always consumed more suit air during training than the veterans. All the same, she scolded herself. She was wearing no biosensors, but Zhirov seemed to know what she was experiencing.

"A rest now. Sixty seconds," he said, through a helmet radio that automatically engaged when she locked the hatch. And then he added: "It is a good suit, Walli Belka."

Beckwith closed her eyes, focused her thinking, and slowed her breathing, and at precisely the sixty-second mark—not a second more, not a second less, according to the oversize watch attached to the right wrist of the Orlan—Zhirov came back online. He talked her through the steps to power up the coolant, pressure, humidity, and electrical systems. She played the switches on the front of the suit, glancing at the backwards Cyrillic in the mirrors but paying attention mostly to Zhirov—and watched the instrument panel on the top of the chest pack flicker to life. As it did, she grew more confident—the way she would when she climbed inside an entirely new jet, powered it up, and realized that no matter how unfamiliar this cockpit was, every jet was more or less the same as every other jet, and she hadn't found one yet that she couldn't fly.

"It's a good suit, Vasily," she said when she was done.

"It is."

"Still stinks, though."

"It does."

What was left to do Beckwith knew how to do, since spacecraft were, in some ways, all the same too. She would have to depressurize the Poisk module so that the vacuum inside would match the vacuum outside, a necessary step to prevent the force of the escaping air from blowing off the hatch when she tried to open it. She let Zhirov walk her through this step too, though she often found she was ahead of his instructions.

The module would take at least thirty minutes to vent fully, and in the meantime, Zhirov handed communications back to Houston. Jasper quizzed her again on the critical steps for the IFHX swap-out, and her answers—crisp, immediate—elicited the whistle he sometimes produced when he was impressed by something.

"Flashy stuff," he said. "Just one more thing: You got working tethers on that suit?"

"Of course," she said. "Two of them."

A pair of heavy cloth umbilicals about eight feet long on automatic retractors were attached to her belt. There was a clip at the end of each that she would use to connect herself to the handholds outside. The procedure called for her to attach both of them, and then, as she moved along the station, to detach one first, advance it farther ahead, reattach it, and then do the same with the other. That way she would always be connected to the station by at least one.

"Good," he answered. "Soon as you get outside, use them."

"That's what the procedure calls for."

"Just remember to do it immediately."

"I'm not gonna float away, Jasper," she said.

"Do it," he answered. "You'll want to."

At last, thirty minutes later, the Poisk module was fully vented. Beckwith unsealed the outer hatch, edged it open, and peered outside warily. The badly trained astronaut would now begin what had to be decidedly good work.

. . .

At the very moment Beckwith was looking at the great sweep of nothing outside her spacecraft, the world was looking at her looking at it. NASA had rigged cameras at various points along the exterior of the station so that controllers could monitor the crew's work whenever any of them ventured outside. The video feed would stream not just to Mission Control but also to NASA TV, both on the Web and in the few cable markets that carried the station. Watching EVAs as they happened had become something of a compulsion for a certain space-drunk demographic—offering the slow-motion, addictive pleasure of watching bass fishing or chess tournaments—and NASA was happy to feed the need. For Beckwith's spacewalk, the demand was massive, and all of the networks and news channels picked up the transmission.

After taking in the scene outside, Beckwith would have to position herself so that she emerged from the station feet first; the next glimpse the world thus got of the space adventurer was a pair of boots slowly emerging from a round hatchway.

"Looking good, Walli Bee," came Jasper's voice, smooth as Southern Comfort. "Got you about halfway out now. Slow and easy."

Beckwith edged out a bit farther, then farther still, then felt her hands cross over the doorjamb of the open hatch. Then, with one tiny, final slide, she was outside.

She had hold of the nearest handrail, still facing the open hatch. When she was sure she had her purchase, she turned slowly around, still holding on, and looked her fill. In front of her, above her, everywhere around her was the trackless reach of open space. Off to her left was the glinting spot of the Soyuz spacecraft, motionless in the void a kilometer away, where she had ordered it parked. To her right was the forbiddingly remote spot she had come out here today to reach—the P6 truss—which at the moment seemed the same kilometer distant. She finally, tentatively, looked down at the blue-white vastness of her home planet far, far below. She felt a sudden rush of vertigo, an unaccustomed mortal terror. She could not fall. Her forebrain knew it; the physics guaranteed it. But her lower brain, her binary brain, the brain in which things were either good or bad, safe or deadly, could make no such distinctions—and it told her with a desperate certainty that she was about to plunge and die. She grabbed her safety tethers and clipped them both to the handholds.

"Good," she heard Jasper say in her earpiece. "Smart."

She looked up toward the red light of the nearest camera and offered Jasper a shaky smile. He could not see her through her helmet's tinted faceplate. She knew that, but she smiled all the same.

"All right," she said, waving off her momentary swoon and forcing herself to look back down and stare at the cloud tops hundreds of miles below. This time they did not rattle her. "I've got some ground to cover."

"Copy," Jasper said. "Take your time. No rushing."

Beckwith—not rushing—turned back to face the station and made her way carefully along it, inching across the Russian segment module by module, unclipping and clipping her tethers as she went. It was close-up work, just like in the NASA pool, as she shimmied from handhold to handhold, foothold to foothold, at last reaching the final Russian mating adapter in the center of the station.

That brought her to the scaffold structure that was the central truss, and she began edging toward the station's starboard wing, the right wing. There were eight copper-brown solar panels making up the wing on just this side of the station, held in place by trusses of their own—acting as the bones of the wing. Each solar panel—a full 112 feet long by 39 feet wide—contributed to the football-field scale that NASA always used as a point of comparison when bragging about the station.

"We have us a big machine here," Beckwith radioed to Jasper.

She made her way more sure-handedly along the structure now, reading off the onboard road signs as they counted off the numbered trusses—P1, P2, and beyond. At last she reached the P6 truss, where the failed, faithless IFHX was attached—big as a large steamer trunk, just as it had been described. Somewhere inside it, a bit of piping likely no wider than a little finger had ruptured, strained beyond its tolerance by the constant hot-and-cold cycle as the station orbited from the sunlit side of the planet to the nighttime side and back again. She scowled at the useless thing. The replacement unit was ninety degrees away, on the bottom side of the truss, facing Earth.

"The Eagle has landed," she radioed down.

"Roger," Jasper answered. "Pull that busted box off first."

"Copy," Beckwith said.

She reached into her bag of tools, each of which was connected by its own tether to the top of the bag, and made quick work of disconnecting the electrical cables. She might have never practiced on an

IFHX in the NASA pool, but all of the cabling systems on the exterior of the station worked more or less the same way.

The bolts that secured the unit to the truss were another matter. Undoing them required a squeeze wrench, but in the heavy, inflated gloves, even the lightest squeeze meant an effort. What's more, what she had feared might happen with the hatch separating the Russian and American segments of the station had apparently happened with the bolts: Unevenness in the expansion and contraction of the metal parts caused them to jam tight. Beckwith tried first with her right hand—the pain of her bandaged wound not making things easier—and then added her left. Slowly, very slowly, the first bolt gave and tumbled off into space. Jasper saw it glinting as it went.

"Let those go. We don't need 'em."

"Copy," Beckwith said as she went to work on the second one.

That one gave and the next one did and the one after that, but with each bolt, she felt her respiration picking up and sweat soaking through her inner garment. The faceplate of her visor began to grow fogged. The Moscow EECOM, monitoring the airflow in Beckwith's suit, called a warning to NASA, and Jasper radioed it up.

"You're gonna suck all your air up, Walli," he said. "How's the visor?"

"Lousy."

"Slow it down, then."

Beckwith steadied her breath and went to work on the last bolt. It was absolutely immovable. She squeezed with one hand, squeezed with both, winced at the pressure on her wounded right hand, and shifted her grip repeatedly. Finally she felt the bolt give a tiny bit.

"Getting there," she said through gritted teeth. "Getting there, getting there, getting there." The bolt edged open a bit more and then more still, and now Beckwith's jaw ached too as she clenched it hard.

"Little bit more," Jasper encouraged.

Beckwith gave it one more torturous squeeze, and finally the wrench closed fully, the bolt spun free, and it tumbled off to join the others in the void.

"Got it!" she exclaimed.

"Copy that!" Jasper cheered.

Beckwith wrestled the IFHX off its bracket, moved it around to the bottom side of the truss, and prepared to strap it into place with cable fasteners that were already connected to the truss for that purpose. But while the IFHX was weightless, it still had plenty of mass, and Beckwith misjudged that bulk as she swung it into position. The unit, moving with more momentum than she intended to impart to it, easily broke free of her exhausted grip and went tumbling away.

"Damn it!" Beckwith snapped, just managing to stop herself from saying something much worse on the global TV hookup. On the screens in Mission Control and on TVs and computers around the world, the big, clumsy unit somersaulted lazily away, catching the sun and glinting it back.

"That one ain't in the manual, station," Jasper said.

"Affirm, Houston," Beckwith responded with irritation. "Apologies for that."

"Never mind. We don't need the thing anyway."

"Still . . ." Beckwith muttered, cursing herself.

Now, much more carefully, judging the mass more precisely, she detached the replacement IFHX from its mooring spot and moved it slowly back to the bracket that had held the broken one. She shoved on it to get it seated, but she succeeded simply in pushing herself back and away instead. She hooked the toe of a boot into a foothold and then the other boot into another foothold, straddling the box, then wobbled it from side to side. Slowly, it began to settle into place. When it was seated, she withdrew fresh bolts from her tool bag and bolt by bolt secured the unit, silently thanking the wonderful squeeze wrench for spinning so much more easily and cooperatively when she was fastening than when she was unfastening. Still, she gripped mightily as she finished each bolt, securing the unit as tightly as she could. Finally, with aching hands, she reconnected each of the electrical cables. When that was done, she stuffed the tools back in her bag, closed the flap, and simply hung in space at the end of her safety harnesses, utterly spent.

"IFHX in place," she said exhaustedly. "Cabling attached."

"Copy that. Stand by one," Jasper said, then toggled to the Mission Control loop. "Flight, she's done."

"EECOM, she's done," the flight director responded.

"Copy that," came the response.

With that, the EECOM began configuring switches and sending commands that would activate the IFHX unit that, until just moments ago, had been a cold, dead box of weightless mass. Signals came back, indicators flickered on, a few more commands went up and a few more obedient confirmations came back, and then, finally, an array of ammonia system lights on the EECOM's screen began to glow a happy green.

"We're online!" the EECOM exclaimed.

"Copy!" the flight director answered.

"Walli," Jasper called, "you done good!"

Beckwith smiled, closed her eyes, and allowed herself another few moments of effortless float. Then she made her long, slow way back across the trusses and the Russian modules and finally arrived at the Poisk module. She tumbled back inside, slammed the hatch, and repressurized the module. When it was once again habitable, she yanked the lever on the right side of the suit, the backpack popped open, and she squirmed out. A rainstorm of sweat droplets followed her, easily the expected three pounds.

Within minutes, the headline "BECKWITH SAVES STATION" or some variation of it had flashed on televisions and websites around the world. The president saw it, the attorney general saw it, the people in the Mercado hospital in Bolivia saw it. Sonia, who dropped into a chair surrounded by hospital workers and cried with relief, saw it. Beckwith, however, saw none of it. She stripped off her sodden union suit, washed up as best she could, pulled her dry work clothes back on, and slid into a sleep pod in the Zarya module. She did not move for the next nine hours.

CHAPTER TWENTY-ONE

September 15

If Sonia was going to make it to Oli, she'd have to rely on the pilot with the missing ear. She had met him shortly after she arrived at the Mercado hospital and respected him straightaway. His name was Jo—without the *e*, as she could see on the name tag on his jacket. It took a while before Sonia got a look at Jo full-on and learned his economically spelled name. He was the pilot of the helicopter that had evacuated her from the burning Guarani camp, and for most of the flight to the Mercado hospital, she'd seen only the back of his head. On the right side, a patch of hair was missing—perhaps four inches across—as was the bottom half of the adjacent ear. The scar that remained, especially on the scalp, had the shiny, waxy look of a burn.

Sonia never got a chance to talk to him when she tumbled out of the helicopter at the end of the flight, so early on her second day in the camp, she'd gone looking for him, wandering out to the area beyond the wall where the helicopters were parked and the pilots idled between missions. She came up behind them as casually as she could, looking for the man with the telltale scarring. When she found him, smoking a cigarette near his helicopter, she circled around to the front of him, noticing as she did that he had a patch on the shoulder of his jacket that read "Operation Enduring Freedom." It was the official name—the marketing name—of the American war in Afghanistan, the same one in which her *tía*-mama had flown.

"I wanted to thank you," she said.

He exhaled a long stream of smoke, but turned his head far to the right to spare her the cloud, which Sonia took as a sign of good manners.

"For what?" he asked.

"For getting us out of the fire."

"Just my job, sugar," he said. "Fly the machine and land it safe." Sonia smiled—and took no offense at the "sugar." It seemed in keeping with the cigarette. And with the scar.

"You're Navy, right?" Sonia asked. "Not Air Force?"

She had flown with Beckwith on numerous occasions—often in sports planes and twice in helicopters—and always noticed an almost mechanical crispness in the way she worked the stick. If Sonia stared at it too long, the hand looked unsettlingly robotic, like it didn't belong to a human at all. She asked about it once and Beckwith simply explained that it was "the Navy way—no wasted movement." Sonia saw the same mechanical crispness in Jo's wrist too.

"Yes, ma'am," he said. "Two tours in Afghanistan. It got me this, since I noticed you looking," he added, gesturing to his injury. "Antiaircraft. Bailed out but left a piece of me behind."

"I'm sorry," Sonia said—about both the injury and the unseemliness of having stared at it so obviously.

"Others got it worse."

Sonia nodded with sympathy. "My mama flew in that war," she said.

"I thought she was your aunt."

"She is, but sort of my mama too," Sonia answered before realizing that she had never identified herself to the man. "How did you know who I am?"

"People talk," he answered. "You're famous here."

"It's my mama who's famous."

"Close enough for you to catch a piece of it," he said. "She's making a lot of noise up there."

"I think that's the idea," Sonia said.

"If I were her commander, I'd have her in irons," Jo said; Sonia frowned. "But if she were *my* commander, I'd follow her into hell."

Now Sonia smiled. "I suspect she'd agree with both sides of that," she said.

After that initial conversation, Sonia would make it a point to visit Jo at least once a day, sometimes just to talk, sometimes to fetch him a plate of hot food from the kitchen instead of the cold sandwiches and shrink-wrapped field rations that the pilots ate when they were on duty and awaiting orders to fly. Those flights came a lot in the days following the attack on the Mercado hospital. It was impossible to predict exactly when the helicopters would be dispatched, but there seemed to be a certain metabolic rhythm to it. The jungle would spike a fever as an attack was launched, a fire was lit, and a tribal group was driven off.

It typically took a few hours after that for the surviving tribes-people to be chased toward the four resettlement camps, often with other helicopters—the kind that were painted black with the mean-ingless flag and the wasplike buzz—flying low over them, herding them toward choke point roads cut in the jungle that would further lead them toward whichever camp was closest to the fire. It was only then that word would go out to the Mercado hospital and the other SSA field units that sick or burned or otherwise injured people had arrived at one of the camps and that medical aid was needed as quickly as it could be dispatched.

Both Sonia and Raymond volunteered repeatedly to ride along on the flights, but they were turned down summarily. There was only so much room aboard the helicopters, and there were too many fully certified field doctors available to justify wasting a spot on anyone with just four years of medical school. On one occasion Sonia appealed to Jo directly, asking him to let her hop aboard at least when he flew to the western camp, adding that she was looking for the small boy who had been with her when she arrived.

"Can't do it," Jo answered. "I'm sorry about the boy, but I can't take any four-year plebes, and especially not you."

"Why not me?"

"You're strictly no-fly, sugar—on a list all your own."

"What?" Sonia snapped.

"Orders from SSA brass," he said. "You're an international incident just waiting to happen. Your auntie's making trouble in space, Washington's pissed off at her, Russia's pissed off at Washington for flying her in the first place, France is pissed off at everyone, and you're a part of it, like it or not. Even El Bobo's afraid of something happening to you. Nobody wants any part of that hair ball."

Jo shrugged a helpless shrug and Sonia spun and stormed back to the hospital, but she kept a close watch on the camp communications system all the same. Every time an attack happened, it would be through that network that word would first come that doctors were needed *stat*. For days after Jo's refusal to let Sonia fly, the calls had always come from the northern, southern, or eastern camps. Then, finally, late in the afternoon on September 15, an attack hit again, and this time the communications system flashed with the word that the call was to the west. Sonia sprinted out from the communications building, and Raymond, understanding exactly what she was up to, took off after her. They passed through the opening in the wall, into the noisy whirlwind of the helicopters spinning to life, and made straight for Jo.

"Take me!" Sonia demanded.

"No!" he shouted over the motor roar. He looked at Raymond. "Take her back!" he ordered.

"It's not up to me," Raymond said.

"It's not up to him!" Sonia echoed.

"Girl . . ." Jo began to say, when all at once there was a crash to his right as a dolly that was loading medicine and equipment onto the helicopter tipped and spilled its contents. Jo turned toward the sound, and Sonia took advantage of the moment, vaulting catlike from the ground into the crew portion of the helicopter, joining the three doctors and the copilot who were already there. Raymond followed her. Jo spun back, fixed them with a glare, and thumbed them both out. Sonia stood, arms folded, and shook her head no. Raymond mirrored her. At that point, the helipad commander on the ground waved his right arm in a circling motion over his head and shouted out to all five helicopters, "Go, go, go!"

Jo looked at him, then flashed his glance back to Sonia and Raymond.

"Out! Now!" he ordered them. They did not budge.

"Go! Now!" the commander shouted at Jo, who hesitated. "I said *now*!" the commander repeated.

Jo spat at the ground, jumped aboard the helicopter, and pointed a finger at Sonia. "We're gonna talk, girl!" he said, then turned to Raymond. "You too, son!"

Then he climbed into his seat and gunned the engine, and the helicopter hoisted its bulk off the ground and wheeled toward the distant western camp.

. . .

Even four days after Walli Beckwith risked her life to save the world's only space station, that world could not quit talking about her. No one had an accurate count just yet of the exact number of people who had watched the spacewalk, but the networks were boasting that they put up something in the vicinity of Super Bowl numbers—and that didn't include the tens of millions who watched online.

The nation's newspapers uniformly hailed Beckwith a hero; almost uniformly their editorial pages also argued that while she had clearly done wrong in remaining in space when ordered to come home, all—or at least some—of that should be forgiven now. The *Daily News* actually went with that headline: "ALL IS FORGIVEN," once again in two-hundred-point type. *The New York Times* made the same point, more clinically, in the analysis it ran with its lead piece: "Legal Authorities Discuss Amnesty for Astronaut."

There was, too, the unfolding news about the masses converging on Washington—with the anticipated crowd now exceeding 2.7 million for the September 18 vote. More quietly, there were the reports leaking out of Washington that the Department of Defense now sensed the ground shifting sufficiently on Capitol Hill—especially after Beckwith's heroic spacewalk—that the president might actually lose the congressional vote by a veto-proof margin. Even members of the president's own party were beginning to fear that the public would not stand for a protracted, yearlong battle through the federal court system if the White House sought to pursue one—so if Congress demanded intervention, the military would have to be ready to mobilize immediately.

Already the Pentagon was reviewing plans for the kind of action that would be required in a jungle conflict in which hostiles and innocents would be hopelessly commingled. A mosh pit like that would require both air power to cut off roads and destroy weapons and equipment depots, and boots on the ground to separate soldiers from tribespeople. Word had gotten out that Army paratroopers from the 82nd Airborne Division at Fort Bragg, in North Carolina, and the Screaming Eagles at Fort Campbell, in Kentucky, were mobilizing to provide that ground presence.

Airborne surveillance sorties and tactical strikes when troop movements were spotted would be needed too, which would require an aircraft carrier to be in position. The USS *Eisenhower*—Beckwith's old ship—had been in port for retrofitting at the Naval Air Station in Pensacola, Florida, and had been scheduled to redeploy to the Indian Ocean on September 10, but was instead still at anchor, due to "ongoing maintenance issues," according to a Department of Defense release. It was just the kind of vague explanation that no one in Washington was likely to believe. Florida was a handy place to store a carrier that might suddenly need to shift to the waters off the coast of Brazil.

Beckwith was reading all of this news on multiple sites this morning, but it took her a long time to get through any of the stories. The blue-white light of the tablet all at once seemed to fatigue her vision, and, more troubling, she was suffering from a persistent headache that had begun more than twelve hours ago. It had grown from a low and stubborn pulse last night to something sharper and more insistent this morning.

For the first time since she'd been aboard the space station, she had to admit she'd begun to feel claustrophobic. The IFHX had been repaired, and she had stopped the ammonia leak before complete saturation of the American segment would have made it permanently uninhabitable. But that half of the station was still contaminated and would remain off-limits until the air in the modules could be put through the flushing and repressurizing cycle at least two or three times, a procedure that could be conducted only when no one was aboard. Beckwith was thus still restricted to the Russian modules, where she had remained in lockdown for the four days since her spacewalk, a confinement that was beginning to wear on her.

In Mission Control, Charlene Boysen, the flight surgeon, noticed the change in Beckwith's mood and worried that stray ammonia might somehow have fouled the circulation system on the Russian side as well and was starting to have its poisonous way with her.

"How's your breathing, Walli?" she asked when she radioed up for one of her twice-daily medical checks. Since the ammonia leak, the flight director had permitted an exception to the rule that all communications go through the Capcom. This was a doctor-patient exchange and he would allow it.

"Fine," Beckwith answered. "Clear; no shortness."

"Any forgetfulness?"

"No."

"Nausea?"

"No."

"Headaches?"

"Negative. Again," Beckwith answered.

But that last, of course, was a lie. She knew she should mention the headache to Boysen and she almost did, but she decided against it. She wasn't coming home until after the march in Washington and the congressional vote on the intervention no matter what. All she would do by bringing a medical problem up now would be to invite a lot of questions. Besides, she figured, it would be the rare person who could go through what she'd gone through over the past few weeks and *not* come away with at least some symptoms of stress.

But it was getting harder for Beckwith to tell herself that stress could cause a headache like this—and reading only made the pain worse, especially reading on an illuminated computer screen. Even with the brightness of the screen dimmed, Beckwith still found she had to stop reading and close her eyes every few minutes, lest her head begin to throb and her vision begin to double slightly.

She decided to busy herself another way. The stories she had read in *The New York Times* and *The Wall Street Journal* and on the major cable sites had reported on regular surveys of lawmakers on Capitol Hill and had identified thirteen representatives and eight senators from moderate states or districts who were openly opposed to intervention but were feeling the heat in town halls and constituent calls to change their minds. Beckwith could make things hotter for them still. Shaking off her pain as best she could, she logged onto the House and Senate websites, where contact information for all of the Capitol Hill offices was listed. An email from space could easily go overlooked in a lawmaker's overloaded inbox. A phone call, with the signature hiss and delay of a transmission from space, and Beckwith's voice—which was by now familiar to anyone who had watched her initial broadcast to Earth or was following the air-to-ground feed on the NASA site and the cable channels—would get some attention. So Beckwith began calling, starting with the eight senators who had been mentioned in the *Times* and elsewhere.

All of the conversations went more or less the same way. Beckwith would identify herself when the phone was answered and the receptionist would ask, "You're the astronaut?"

"I am," Beckwith would reply.

"You're in space *now*?"

"I am. So might the senator be available?"

"I'm sorry, ma'am," the receptionist would say. "He isn't. I can tell him you called. Can he, um, call you back?"

"No, that's not possible," Beckwith would say. "But tell him I'll call again."

"Can you just . . . do that?"

"Absolutely," Beckwith would answer. "Government's dime."

Beckwith made good on that promise. It took her little more than an hour to phone all eight senators' offices—and get nowhere at all with any of them. She called them all back in the next hour, with no greater luck, and then a third time in the third hour. She posted updates of her telephone campaign on her website and Twitter feed, naming all of the senators, listing their phone numbers and email addresses, and ending all of the posts with the hashtag #TakeMyCall. Each of her tweets was retweeted hundreds of thousands of times, always with a second hashtag: #TakeWalli'sCall.

Finally Garry Oro, the senior senator from Arizona, did take the call. He was a loyal member of the president's party and had already declared himself immovably opposed to intervening in the Amazon. But he had also broken with his party on occasion in the past and rather liked his maverick rep. The cable news channels had been staked out in the hallway outside his Washington office since early morning. Answering the phone the next time Beckwith called—and releasing a press statement announcing that he had done so—might help take the media pot off the boil.

"You're making my life miserable, you know," he said to Beckwith after he at last allowed her call to be patched through to him and they had exchanged hellos.

"I'm trying to do just that," she said. "But I'll stop if you'll change your vote and persuade some of your friends to do the same."

Oro laughed. "I can't do that, but I admire your persistence."

"Thank you."

"You're Navy, of course."

"Yes, sir, I am," Beckwith said.

"So am I," Oro answered. "Officer, but not Annapolis like you. ROTC."

"A commission is a commission, sir."

"That's kind of you to say."

"Senator Oro," Beckwith said, "you know this Consolidation business is wrong."

"Yes," he answered, with a candor that surprised Beckwith. "It's immoral and it's tragic. But I also know it's none of our business."

"The voters are starting to say otherwise."

"I don't listen to polls," Oro said. And then, unexpectedly, he laughed at himself. "Do you believe me?"

"No, sir," Beckwith answered. "I don't."

"Officer to officer, you shouldn't. Still, I've announced my vote."

"Will you change it?"

"No."

"Will you at least *think* about changing it?" Beckwith asked. Oro didn't answer. "Officer to officer," she added.

"You're a lieutenant commander?" Oro finally responded.

"Yes."

"I retired as a lieutenant."

"So I . . ."

"You outrank me, yes. If ROTC taught me anything, it's that I must always consider any counsel I get from a superior officer."

"I would very much appreciate that, sir," Beckwith said.

"It's the least I can do, ma'am," Oro answered.

The astronaut and the senator then said their goodbyes and ended their call. Beckwith smiled at the sweet and simple reasonableness of what had just taken place. After weeks of so much anger and heat, it was a relief. She once again felt the sense of contentment that being in space could give her. All the same, it would be awfully nice if she could shake her headache.

CHAPTER TWENTY-TWO

September 16

Yulian Lebedev was hoping to slip into Moscow Mission Control unnoticed. Zhirov might have expected a hero's greeting for himself when he made his first entrance into the room after returning from space, but Lebedev had never seen himself as a hero, and he preferred not to be greeted like one. What Lebedev wanted and what Lebedev got, however, were two different things, and the moment he opened the door at the back of the grand auditorium and stepped inside, a controller seated at a console nearby sprang up and began to applaud. Other controllers turned, looked, and did the same. Lebedev was paler, thinner, moved tentatively, and wore a collapsible cane at his belt that he could have opened and used if he needed it—though it was not in his nature to lay so much as a hand on the thing and actually admit to that need.

Either way, he was there—though later than expected. A burst eardrum can be a reasonably easy thing to get over, unless an infection results, leading to inner ear damage, which in turn leads to loss of balance, vertigo, and a cascade of other problems. All of that had happened—was still happening—to Lebedev, and the military doctors were unanimous that they could not yet get to the bottom of the problem and that he should not leave the hospital until they had him fully sorted out. But Lebedev was adamant that he had had enough, and that if he couldn't be in space, he belonged where he could continue to serve in some capacity with the rest of his crew, and that meant in Mission Control. Roscosmos was unanimous that he should be there too.

As the grounded cosmonaut made his unsteady way into the auditorium and the controllers stood and applauded, the ones closest to the door mobbed and hugged him. Zhirov, along with Bazanov, joined the scrum.

"Get back, get back. Give him room," Zhirov said to the other controllers as he fought through them and grabbed Lebedev in a bear hug. "Yuli, you are beautiful!"

Lebedev hugged him back, but tottered slightly in the process and braced himself against Zhirov. "I am not beautiful, but I am here," he said.

"That's good enough," Zhirov said. He called out to the room, "Flight Engineer One is present. Crew is complete. Status five-five-five." On the third "five" he gestured toward the picture of Beckwith on the left side of the giant screen. At that, at least a few of the controllers stopped applauding.

Zhirov and Bazanov steered Lebedev to an observer's console and pulled up chairs next to him. They purposely sat first, sparing the injured cosmonaut any sense that they would remain standing in case he needed to be helped into his seat. Lebedev acknowledged that kindness with a tiny nod and sat. The other controllers returned to their stations.

"You are well, *druzhók*?" Bazanov asked, using the colloquial endearment he might have directed to a nephew.

"Terrible," Lebedev said. "But better. Still, I won't fly."

Bazanov shrugged. "I don't fly," he said. "But I serve. You can serve."

"Perhaps," Lebedev said.

"No 'perhaps,' Yuli," Zhirov said. "You will work. When do the doctors want you back?"

"Every night, for now."

"Then they can have you every night. In daylight we need you." Zhirov looked at Lebedev sternly.

"All right, Vasily," Lebedev said. "I will serve."

"Then you'll start right away," Bazanov answered.

He summoned a controller and ordered him to bring strip charts from the past ten days of the mission—printouts of critical telemetry that had been streaming down from the Russian side of the station before, during, and after the power-down. If Lebedev was truly going to serve, he would do so in the capacity in which he was especially well qualified—as the cosmonaut who could disassemble the entire Russian half of the station in his head, rethink its systems, and put them back together better than they had been before. In all the years the station had been flying, none of the modules had ever been shut off in flight and then brought back online. The entire Russian segment had just been put through that sleep-wake cycle, and it was now connected to an American segment that had turned entirely toxic. There was no shortage of small breakdowns that could cause in the Russian systems. If they were there, Lebedev would find them.

He bent over the strip charts while Bazanov and Zhirov lingered close at hand. Lebedev asked a question or two—where in the data stream this or that step in the power-down had occurred—then returned to the charts and before long had no questions at all. Bazanov smiled. Lebedev was an old-school engineer—his favorite kind—and old-school engineers preferred their data in the durable form of ink and pencil on paper, not in the passing flicker of numbers on-screen that lasted only until they vanished entirely and were replaced by other numbers.

For the better part of two hours Lebedev studied the charts, circling and underlining portions in red grease pencil and slipping torn strips of notepaper between pages to mark key spots. Then he pushed away from the console and stood. He saw Bazanov and Zhirov at the back of the room and nodded to them, and they hurried over. He gestured to the strip charts.

"There is nothing about the crew here," he said. "There is nothing about Belka."

Zhirov looked at him questioningly. "She is not wearing biomed sensors, and she has been talking to Houston much more than us."

"Then we should talk to Houston and then we have to talk to her," Lebedev said. "We have to do that right away."

. . .

Beckwith was sleeping when the tag-team calls from Moscow and Houston came in. Moscow was first, radioing up with a clipped command: "Station, respond and report." It was Zhirov calling, but at that point, his usually welcome voice was nothing of the kind. Less than fifteen seconds later came the second call: "Station, Houston." It was something-or-other Lagrange on the line, whose interruption she welcomed even less.

Sleep had been nearly impossible for Beckwith for more than twenty-four hours now—though not for lack of trying and not for lack of exhaustion. She had climbed into and back out of a sleep pod in the Russian segment four or five different times, convinced that this time she must be so fatigued that she would simply pass out before she even closed her eyes. But she never did.

The headache was one reason—easily the worst reason—but so was the fever she felt like she might be running. She would know for sure if she took her temperature, but if she did that and found out she was sick, there was little she could do about it anyway. So she took some aspirin and then some ibuprofen, and while that made her feel a little bit less feverish, the pain in her head remained unchanged. Worse, more and more her vision would double up as if she were drunk. Perhaps it was a migraine; people said that migraines could make you see double. Beckwith had never had a migraine before, but people also said that sometimes you didn't get your first one until you were in your forties. Or maybe people hadn't said that; she really didn't know.

While she was getting the aspirin and ibuprofen from the Russian medicine bin, she'd dug through it looking for something much stronger, half hoping she wouldn't find it—but she did find it. She couldn't read the Cyrillic, and the English translation was so poor that it was impossible to know what was inside the package without the aid of pictures. But the pictures were there, and they told her what she needed to know. There was a tiny human form with little lightning bolts near the head, back, and legs—the lingua franca for pain. There was a sleepy-looking face with half-closed eyes—which always went with the lightning if the drug was any good. And there was a red slash through a steering wheel and a martini glass, which sealed the deal. She was tempted—sorely tempted—but she decided to put off such high-octane medicine as long as possible and for now try to sleep instead.

It was then that the one-two calls came in from Moscow and Houston. This time she had almost, *almost* fallen asleep before she was disturbed. She hit a switch opening channels to both Mission Controls at once and barked a simple "What!" in response. She sounded annoyed. She wanted to sound annoyed.

"Uh . . . report status, station . . . please," said an uncertain Lagrange.

"Systems on this side of the hatch nominal," Beckwith said. "It's up to you guys to tell me what's happening on the other side."

"Crew status, not systems status, station," Zhirov demanded. Lagrange might be rattled by Beckwith's pique; the Russian commander wasn't.

"Crew was sleeping, Vasily," she said, moderating her tone. "Or at least trying to sleep."

Zhirov did not respond immediately, but his mic was open and she could hear him muttering to someone. At last he asked, "*Have you slept?*"

"Yes," she answered.

"When was the last time?" he pressed. Beckwith didn't respond and Zhirov repeated himself. "Walli, when was the last time you slept at all?"

"It's been a while, Vasily."

"Copy. Stand by."

Zhirov clicked off and Houston clicked on.

"Station, hold for flight surgeon," Lagrange said.

"Say again?" Beckwith asked.

"Flight surgeon, station. Please hold."

Charlene Boysen toggled open her communications line, but Glynn Hampton, the flight director, gestured to her to wait. Then he spoke to Lagrange. "Kill the public loop," he ordered. Immediately, the audio dropped out in the press booth at the back of Mission Control, as well as on NASA TV and any commercial stations that might have been carrying the feed. This was one doctor-patient call he wanted to be truly private. He nodded at Boysen to proceed.

"Station, flight surgeon," she said. "Please report your medical status—any and all symptoms."

"Status is good. No symptoms to speak of."

"Station," Boysen began, and then amended: "Lieutenant Commander, this request can come through naval chain of command as an order if you'd prefer."

"That won't be necessary," Beckwith said. "A little bit of a headache is all."

"And you said sleeplessness."

"And sleeplessness."

"Yet you're sleepy."

"Yes," Beckwith said, "I am."

"Any fever?"

"Some."

"Vision?"

"Twenty-twenty," Beckwith answered.

"Twenty-twenty *single or double*, Lieutenant Commander?"

"Double," Beckwith conceded. "Just a couple times."

"And I imagine you're not hungry?"

"No," Beckwith answered. Now, at long last, she felt a prickling along her skin—not of fever, but of fear.

"All right, station," Boysen said. "Please stand by."

The flight surgeon muttered into her headset to the two younger doctors in her backroom support team, then got up and took a few steps to the flight director's console. A moment later the other doctors entered Mission Control and gathered around Hampton as well. They knew this was not ammonia poisoning; the symptoms were all wrong, especially the fever. What they had to determine was what it was instead.

In Moscow Mission Control, a similar scrum had formed around the spot where Lebedev sat with his strip charts, red grease pencil, and scrap-paper placeholders. Bazanov was with him, as were three other engineers from Moscow's own back rooms. They had brought with them other strip charts of the power-down and power-up procedures. Lebedev had torn through all of them too, making more red marks, flagging more pages.

He had been grilling the engineers about each of the flagged pages, and the answers they gave him had been more or less to his satisfaction. But now he'd gotten to the lab racks in the Zarya module.

"Did you cut all power to the lab?" he asked.

"Of course not," the lead technician in the group of three answered.

"What did you leave running?"

"All essential equipment."

"The refrigerators?"

"Of course."

"The freezers?"

"Of course."

Now Lebedev yanked open one portion of the strip chart and pointed a finger at a few lines on the page. "*These* freezers?"

The three men leaned in and looked. One of them turned the chart slightly toward himself. He closed his eyes and swallowed.

"Those two appear to have gone off for the period of time the modules were powered down, but they're operating again."

Lebedev fixed the man with a stare. "What is stored in those freezers?"

The engineer flipped urgently through his own thick pile of documents and found what he was looking for. He appeared relieved.

"The first one is empty," he said. "Awaiting resupply."

Lebedev drew a wary breath. "And the other?"

The engineer scanned down the page and his eyes stopped on a line. He blanched.

"*And the other?*" Lebedev repeated.

"Meningitis," the man said. "*E. coli* and meningitis."

Bazanov hit his fist on the console desk, immediately opened a back-channel line to Mission Control in Houston, and was put through to Hampton. The twin heads of the twin centers spoke briefly and then Hampton spoke quietly to the doctors around him. Boysen returned to her console.

"Station, surgeon," she called.

"Copy, surgeon."

"Walli, come home."

"I . . . what . . . ?"

"Come home. Now," Boysen said.

Beckwith sounded weary—very, very weary. "I would prefer not to," she said.

"Cut the room," Boysen ordered. Hampton nodded, and immediately the audio loop went silent in Mission Control as it had in the pressroom and on the TV feed.

"Walli," Boysen asked, "have you been in the Zarya module?"

Beckwith was mystified. "Yes, of course, yes," she said.

"Since the power-down?"

"Yes."

"Did you touch anything? Anything wet?"

"Everything in there is wet," Beckwith said. "I cleaned up as best I could."

"Walli, come home," Boysen now repeated. "You are very, very sick."

"I can't be—" Beckwith said, then stopped herself as a flood of images came rushing back to her from the day of the accident: The cap on the meningitis vial that she may have snapped on badly. The high, sharp sound the vial made as she banged it back in the tray. The freezer door that she slammed, that didn't catch, that she had to slam a second time—and that still might not have caught. And the wet mess she had so recently sopped up from the air with a cloth and her bare hands, then wiped on her pants. Her stomach turned over.

"The freezers were off, weren't they?" she said hoarsely.

"Yes, Walli, they were."

"I have meningitis, don't I?"

"Yes, you do," Boysen said. "Come home or you will die. I can almost certainly promise you that."

CHAPTER TWENTY-THREE

September 16

The flight from the Mercado hospital to the western camp in Brazil was a particular kind of awful for Sonia and the other doctors in the SSA helicopter, one that would have been easier to tolerate if it had been possible to draw a clear breath—which it wasn't. Jo had warned everyone aboard that they would need to "strap in, hang on, and probably throw up," and two of the doctors did need to lunge for a bucket and bring up whatever they'd had to eat that morning in the first twenty minutes of the two-and-a-half-hour flight. Sonia had no such problem, but Sonia had not eaten that day—or much at all since Oli was taken.

Part of what made the flight so grueling was the altitude at which the helicopters had to fly—little more than treetop level, to stay out of the way of the wasp helicopters that seemed to be everywhere, looking for evacuees who had fled the burning patches of jungle. Flying low meant a constant lurching, as the hot, rising air of the fires lifted the helicopter up and intermittent cool pockets dropped it back down. No matter the exact altitude, the cabin was continually filled with choking smoke from the tree cover burning everywhere below.

"Lay low, breathe slow!" Jo would order when the smoke got too thick.

"Take your seats and enjoy the flight," he'd call when the air had cleared a bit.

At some point during one of those clearer moments, Sonia reached for her phone and clicked onto her email. She had made Beckwith two promises when she had come to the jungle: that she would survive her time there and that she would always let her know exactly where she was. She now summoned up Beckwith's email address and typed "Promise #2" into the subject line, then in the body of the text wrote: "Flying to the western camp." She added, faking a jauntiness she didn't feel, "Hello again, Brazil!" Then, faking nothing, she signed off with, "Keep an eye on me, Mama."

She hit *send*, and the message, riding the electromagnetic updraft of the helicopter's satellite link, went straight to space. Sonia put the phone back in her pocket, hoping to feel the vibration of a return message, but before it could come, the helicopter flew through another dense smoke bank, distracting her from anything other than simply trying to breathe and remain conscious. She lost the second of those two battles and for the remainder of the flight hovered in a state of nauseated near-blackout, returning to full awareness only when she felt the hard thump of the copter skids hit the ground in Brazil. When she jolted awake, she noticed two things: a swirl of activity outside the door of the helicopter and Jo's voice barking orders.

"Hit the deck, hit the deck!" he shouted to the doctors. "Go, go, go!"

People trained in medicine might not have been accustomed to the ways and the language of the military, but they obeyed them all the same, climbing over Sonia, who had yet to orient herself fully, and leaping to the ground.

"Be careful, be careful!" Raymond said to them.

He helped Sonia up, and the two of them jumped out. They immediately joined the rest of the doctors, unloading crates of medical supplies and stacking them for transport into the camp. Three other newly arrived helicopters approached, variously bearing the insignias of the SSA, UNICEF, and the Save the Children foundation.

About fifty yards away stood a tall iron gate, spiked at the top, which should have looked forbidding, except that it was painted a bright yellow, white, and green—each bar and spike alternating in color—surrounding a compound of pretty clapboard buildings, incongruously landscaped with lawn and flowers. It was a showpiece camp, a phony camp, one of the "Theresienstadt Novos" the press had reported—built and beautified to fool the world, only at the moment it would have fooled no one. The gate door had been swung open, and injured, smoke-choked people from the jungle and the helicopters were staggering in. A large tent—striped red and white as if it were meant for a circus—stood just inside the gate, its front flap opened and the chairs inside tossed and tipped. A cartoon—*The Little Mermaid*, Sonia noticed—was incongruously playing on the screen. If children had been watching it, they were no more.

"Sonia!" Raymond shouted. He and the others had been unloading boxes and moving them in a fire-brigade handoff, and she had broken the flow.

"Sorry, sorry!" she said, taking a box and nearly dropping it, having not realized how heavy it was.

She focused on the work, receiving, passing, stacking the crates, her eyes burning from the dust kicked up by the blades of the choppers everywhere, her ears ringing from their roar, and her braid whipping side to side, occasionally smacking and stinging her face.

She squinted, looking around, pointlessly she knew, for a little boy, five years old, with a crisscross of scratches everywhere on his arms and legs.

Doctors and other hospital workers hurried past. Sonia leaned toward them, calling out, *"Bebês? Crianças? Garontinhos?"* Then, "Babies, children, little boys?" Then, struggling for still more words, *"¿Dónde los . . . los . . . ?"* until all at once she felt a hard hand on her shoulder and turned to see Jo looking down at her angrily.

"None of that!" he said. "You came here to work? Then work! Look around!"

She obeyed, and for the first time understood the true scope of what was happening in the jungle tonight, the scale of the injury and human displacement that was unfolding. Fire seemed to be rising everywhere; people were staggering in from all sides. There would be deaths here before the sun rose, and there would be sorrow too, as the people who did survive would lose children or parents or husbands or wives.

"You're a doctor!" Jo shouted over the helicopter roar. "Do your job!"

Sonia nodded, and Jo turned and began helping to unload more boxes. Sonia did the same—all the while scanning around her, looking for the child who was nowhere to be seen.

. . .

There was actually a bit of good news tucked inside the very bad news of Walli Beckwith's meningitis diagnosis. The disease comes in two forms—bacterial and viral, both of which were infections of the layer of tissue surrounding the brain. The viral variety generally had to run its course, but bacterial meningitis—which was the variety in the vials being studied aboard the space station—could be cured with antibiotics and corticosteroids. The problem was that if you didn't get properly dosed in as little as twenty-four to forty-eight hours, the disease could just as easily kill you. That was especially so if you were fatigued and your immune system was worn down—twin conditions that afflicted nearly all space station astronauts eventually.

Beckwith had antibiotic tablets aboard the station—and they were powerful ones too, but they weren't nearly as finely targeted as the ones doctors on Earth would administer intravenously. She did not have corticosteroids, and she most definitely did not have the CT scan or spinal tap equipment that would be needed to diagnose her disease properly and prescribe medication doses precisely.

As Boysen continued to interrogate Beckwith about her symptoms—neck stiffness, absence of thirst—Moscow and Houston were doing what they could to conduct that diagnosis on the fly and at a distance. Electronic copies of all of the lab reports on the precise strain of bacteria that had been sent aloft were transmitted to NASA and were read and translated by bilingual members of the Houston medical team. Those reports contained worrisome news: A weak bug would not do if your goal for sending it to space in the first place was to develop a strong medicine against it—without the so-called forcing factor of gravity getting in the way of the work. So a particularly robust meningitis strain had been selected. Beckwith's confidential medical records—especially her blood labs, antibody levels, and immune system function—were scrutinized for clues as to how she would stand up under that kind of bacterial assault. Those files were sent to Moscow for reverse translation and similar study.

At length, the Capcom came back on the line, and again the person on the mic was Jasper. The air-to-ground feed was being carried live to the world.

"Walli Bee, I'm told you caught a little something," Jasper said without preamble.

"Nah," Beckwith said. "Navy doesn't get sick."

"Mostly that's right," Jasper said. "Still, better let us have a look at you to be sure."

He then filled her in on what she needed to know about her condition—hedging nothing. She had to get to a hospital; she needed the scanning and spinal tapping and laboratory tests that could never be performed in space. The doctors knew exactly what bug she had and they knew the course it could take. They weren't kidding about how quickly it could be lethal.

"You have to come home, Walli Bee," Jasper said at last. "The Russians are working on entry coordinates and your ride is waiting outside. Wave it in and climb aboard."

"I can't do that, Jasper," Beckwith answered. "Soon, not now."

"Soon ain't soon enough. The doctors say twenty-four to forty-eight hours. This thing can kill you that fast."

"I need two days. Just till the eighteenth. When the vote is done."

"You can't afford that."

"Two days, Jasper."

"Now, Walli."

"Two days."

"Two days is your forty-eight hours right there!" Jasper shouted, startling the room. "That's your limit. These doctors aren't fucking around!"

If Jasper remembered that his voice was going out to the world, he didn't care. The networks let it go; the viewers heard it live. Beckwith too seemed unconcerned with what people did or didn't hear.

"And I'm not fucking around either, Jasper," she said levelly. "I'll take the meds I have on board. They're good; they have to help some. I'll dock the Soyuz just in case. But until the eighteenth, I will not go near it."

Jasper did not answer her—and at the moment he couldn't. The astronaut-Capcom who knew Beckwith so well and cared for her so deeply that he had nicknamed her nickname—needing a "Bee" that was all his own to capture the depth of his feeling—had thrown off his headset and stalked out of the room to collect himself. The flight director nodded to the rookie Lagrange, who put on the headset and reclaimed the console.

.   .   .

Nobody knew exactly how many people were living in the western camp at the border just inside Brazil—and nobody was really trying to find out anymore, at least not officially. It had been close to a week since a formal count had been issued, and at that point it was 82,000—a troubling number since it also represented the total official capacity of the camp. In the days since, however, the jungle burnings and land clearings had not slowed, and thousands more dispossessed people had been herded through the gates.

The general who oversaw the camp would give regular interviews to the members of the press who were permitted to attend—a group that was limited to the official government-friendly Brazilian media, as well as reporters from Colombia, Uruguay, and Paraguay, the three nations whose unauthorized mercenaries had joined the Consolidation. The general always wore the black-and-yellow uniform with the black-and-yellow confederation flag, but his Portuguese-accented Spanish made it clear he was answerable only to Brasilia. No matter how he spoke, the job he did at the daily gatherings was an easy one.

"How is the health of the people here?" the friendly Brazilian press would ask.

"Their health is excellent."

"And how is the food they are given?"

"The food is excellent."

"Are they happy to be here?"

"They are happy and they are relieved to be out of danger."

Things got tougher—a little—when the marginally less pliant Colombian, Paraguayan, and Uruguayan reporters would get their turn, especially when they were asking about the population of the camp. But the general did a serviceable job of answering in a way that was no answer at all.

"How many people are living in the camp now?" a reporter would ask.

"The camp's capacity is eighty-two thousand people."

"Is that how many are here?"

"The camp is now full."

"Yes, but how full?"

"Its capacity is eighty-two thousand people."

"So that's how many are here?"

"As I say, the camp is full."

It was a clumsy bit of spin, but perfectly sufficient for an official who faced only cooperative reporters at home and could easily wave off the few journalists pestering him from what he considered vassal states.

The doctors from SSA, UNICEF, Save the Children, and elsewhere who actually worked in the camp estimated the population at a hundred thousand or so, growing by a thousand or two a day—and the place had become every bit the swamp of disease and despair that such an unclean and overcrowded facility could not help but be. Indeed, before long, the general would not even be able to hold his press conferences in the showpiece camp because the spillover of people from the main camp was so great that the once-prettified grounds had nothing left to show off at all. The soccer fields were crowded with refugees who either needed medical care or simply could not find a spot in the main camp. The food tents were now medical tents; the snack carts had been picked clean and toppled on their sides.

The pilots from the Mercado hospital hopped back in their helicopters to return to Bolivia within an hour of dropping the SSA workers off. Jo was among them, and he deliberately left without a goodbye to Sonia or Raymond, sorely angry at both of them for forcing him to bring two such inexperienced aid workers to so perilous a place. If he intended that as a sober-up slap to Sonia, he didn't succeed. She was fully aware of and prepared for the sickness and death that stalked the western camp, and the twin missions of getting Oli out of so dangerous a place and exposing that sickness and death to the world were the very reasons she'd come here.

Raymond was another matter. He had come to the western camp only because Sonia had come—a fact that was already causing her an uneasy feeling of responsibility for his safety. He had been looking around anxiously from the moment they had climbed down from the helicopter, and it was clear that if he wasn't flat-out terrified, he was something awfully close.

"It looks like we're here for the duration," he said to Sonia, blanching as he watched Jo fly off.

"So are they," Sonia said, jerking her thumb in the general direction of the main camp.

"I know that," Raymond said, abashed. "I know."

"I'm sorry," Sonia answered sincerely. Raymond was kind and smart and would be a good doctor, but he would never be brave. It did not make her respect him less—not *much* less, at least—but it did make her feel that she would have to be more tolerant of who he was.

The job the two of them were assigned at the camp was in keeping with their limited field experience. They did not have the speed, skill, or unflappability of people who had been doing this kind of on-the-ground work for years. Instead, they were put on triage duty, passing through an exit at the rear of the showpiece camp and making the short walk to the high gate at the front of the main camp. There the internees who needed medical care would present themselves—at 8:00 A.M., 4:00 P.M., and midnight. Sonia and Raymond were expected to be there at all three times, and the scene chilled them. Some of the internees had burns that needed dressing; others had open or infected wounds. It was impossible to tell at a glance which people were running fevers or suffering from malaria or tuberculosis or other diseases. The smells coming from the camp were overwhelming—a mix of sewage, sweat, and the far more menacing odor of dying or infected flesh.

The people cried out to be selected for the short walk to the showpiece camp, where the doctors would care for them; the guards beat the fence with the butts of their guns to force them back. Raymond and Sonia were allowed to select no more than forty internees at a time—and chose the sickest or weakest or oldest or youngest or simply the ones who were at the front of the crush.

And during each visit, Sonia looked for Oli. Every small child she saw drew her eye instantly; every time the round face or little body resolved itself into someone else's, she irrationally resented the child for being the *wrong* child—and scolded herself for such lack of charity. On a few occasions she called out for him, sometimes shouting "Oli," sometimes "Kauan." Never did she hear a "So-*nee*-ya!" in response. The last time she called, a guard stalked over to her, clearly angry. Raymond interposed himself between them.

"She'll stop," he told the guard, then spun to her. "Please stop," he whispered. Then he turned back to the guard. "It's fine. Go, go," he said. The guard did not move. "Go!" Raymond snapped, with genuine anger. He added a dismissive hand gesture that could not help but offend the guard, but seemed to surprise him so much he could think of nothing to do but obey.

Sonia smiled. "Thank you, Raymond," she said, at his small and unexpected act of courage. Raymond faked an it-was-nothing shrug.

CHAPTER TWENTY-FOUR

September 17

If Sonia was going to get inside the main camp and show the world the horror within, she knew she would have to do it fast. The congressional vote was one day away, and if anything could move the lawmakers to cast the right vote, the decent vote, it would be visible evidence of what they were voting to stop. She would make her move today, she decided, during the 4:00 P.M. visit she and Raymond would make to the camp. The guards who had worked the day shift were tired by then, impatient to leave, and the afternoon medical check was the last item of their workday before they were free to retreat to quarters. Sonia would be likelier to be able to slip in then and hope to be extracted when Raymond returned for the nighttime shift. She would enter the camp carrying just two things: her smartphone—well concealed under loose Western clothes—and a pocketful of oleander leaves.

Sonia described her plan in detail to Raymond early that morning—and he hated every little thing about it.

"You're going to get yourself killed," he said.

"Not if I'm smart," she answered.

"The plan *itself* isn't smart!" he snapped.

"You worry too much."

She explained the plan to another young doctor too, a graduate of the University of Pittsburgh named Lindsey. She would need his help as well, and when she told him what she was contemplating, he—unlike Raymond—loved every little thing about it.

"Woman, you're brilliant," was all he said.

Long before the 4:00 P.M. shift arrived, Sonia began preparing her either mad or ingenious plan, packing a shoulder bag with a pair of ill-fitting shorts and an oversize T-shirt taken from the supply building in the showpiece camp. The shirt said "Detroit Pistons" across the top, with the logo of the Seattle Seahawks beneath it. She and Lindsey and Raymond would leave the showpiece camp at 3:45 as was typical for the 4:00 P.M. visit, and if anyone asked why they needed a third set of hands, they would say it was because they anticipated bringing back four or five small children who were too sick to walk and would have to be carried.

When 3:45 arrived, no one did ask and they left the camp without incident. They walked together most of the way to the main camp, but when they were within twenty yards of it, they split up, with Sonia remaining behind, concealed by jungle cover. Raymond and Lindsey proceeded alone to the terrible gate, with its terrible sights.

"¿*Com permissão*?" Raymond asked.

The two guards gestured both of them forward with the butts of their guns, and Raymond and Lindsey approached, as the desperate people inside pressed against the gate. The selection of the sickest was made as it typically was, with one of the guards unlocking the gate while the other watched and the designated forty were pointed out and allowed to exit.

When about twenty had been chosen, Lindsey stepped away and, in full sight of the guards, removed a smartphone from his pocket and began scanning the camp as if he were recording it. He wasn't. The phone, which belonged to one of the doctors on staff, had long since stopped working after having been blown out while trying to take a charge from the camp's notoriously unstable electrical system, which regularly surged and ebbed. The guards had no way of knowing that, though, and the moment they saw what Lindsey appeared to be doing they sprang toward him.

"*Sem telefones! Sem telefones!*" they said in unison. *No phones! No phones!*

One of the guards knocked Lindsey to the ground, while the other grabbed the phone, tossed it in the dirt, and smashed it with the same rifle butt with which he had just made his welcome gesture.

"*Eu sinto muito! Eu não sabia! Eu sou novo!*" Lindsey pleaded in well-accented Portuguese and well-playacted contrition. *I'm sorry! I didn't know! I'm new!*

The guards yanked him up roughly and one of them picked up the remains of the phone, grabbed Lindsey's wrist, and slapped it into his open palm, drawing blood where the broken glass cut skin.

"*De volta ao trabalho!*" he ordered. *Back to work!*

Silently, as all of that was playing out—as the guards' attention was fully engaged—Sonia, now shoeless, dressed in the T-shirt and shorts, with dirt spread across her face and arms and legs, leapt from her jungle cover and sprinted toward the camp. She ducked around the twenty people who had been chosen so far, slipped past the open gate, and entered the horror within. Raymond, watching from the corner of his eye, saw her make her move. He and Lindsey, obeying the guards' command, resumed their work, selected their next twenty, and left with the entire group for the showpiece camp. The gate of the main camp was closed and padlocked.

. . .

The eight hours Sonia would spend in the western camp were eight hours in a hellscape. She saw diseases she recognized—malaria, cholera, measles—and ones she could not identify: skin lesions and pallor like nothing she had seen in a textbook; people flush and sizzling with fever, but when she asked them what other symptoms they were feeling, they said none. She saw burned flesh, infected wounds, limbs that would surely be lost. She removed her shirt, wearing only her brassiere underneath, and tied it round her mouth and nose, both to protect herself from infection and to reduce the smell of rot and filth. More than once she skidded in a slick of sewage.

She recorded it all—in short bursts so as to keep the file small and make it easy to send to the world. And all the while she looked for Oli, called out for Oli, asked people if they had seen a such a boy, one with *muitos arranhões*, as if scratches would be noticed here. There was no sign of any such person.

As the moon rose and approached the point in the sky that the meteorology websites Sonia had consulted before she left the main camp had said it would reach around midnight, she returned to the main gate of the camp. The crowds had already begun to gather there, awaiting the doctors, whose arrival was still about half an hour away. Half an hour was what Sonia needed.

Staking out her place near the gate, she reached into her pocket and removed two of the oleander leaves. It was a pity she did not have the flowers themselves. They were pretty, pink, wide-petaled things. She remembered seeing them at a wedding once and being so struck by them she asked what they were. But the leaves were a different matter. She put them in her mouth and chewed; they were bitter, awful, evolution's method of warning animals to stay away lest they pay. Sonia was one such animal, but she was one with a plan to follow, and

269

so she chewed the leaves, reducing them to a thick, miserable pulp so as to release as much of their terrible chemistry as possible. Then she swallowed them.

Within thirty minutes, her gut wrenched and knotted with a force and violence that made her cry out. Within another minute, she was vomiting more explosively than she ever had in her life. It was while she was bent over, retching and emptying herself onto the ground, that she heard the voices of two men, American men—the voices of Raymond and Lindsey. She heard the gate rattle open and heard them mutter to the guards as they made their selection. The first person they chose was the vomiting woman wearing the Detroit Pistons shirt with the Seattle Seahawks logo. Clearly someone so ill needed medical help fast.

Raymond and Lindsey summoned Sonia forward and she staggered out of the gate, but the guards stopped her. More than one person had tried to fake illness by inducing vomiting with two fingers, and they were too clever to be fooled by that pantomime.

"*Este está realmente doente!*" Lindsey said. *This one is truly sick!* He bent over Sonia, who was lying just outside the gate, rolling and moaning.

"*Não!*" one of the guards answered. *No!*

Raymond rifled through his medical kit, pulled out a skin thermometer, and trained it on Sonia's forehead. It registered 39.5 degrees centigrade, or 103.2 Fahrenheit—more of the awful power of the oleander. Raymond looked up at the guard with an expression that said, *Satisfied?*

Lindsey looked at the guard and asked, "*Satisfeito?*"

The guard glowered but waved Sonia forward, and she crawled out of the way, vomiting in the soil, while the other thirty-nine of the sickest were selected.

. . .

It took only two hours after Sonia was extracted from the main camp—writhing in pain and convulsed by a stomach seeking to empty itself of contents that were no longer there—before she was well enough to send her email to her *tía*-mama. Antiemetics and an anti-toxin specific to the poisons in jungle botanicals relieved her symptoms quickly, and as soon as they had done their job, she sent the four minutes of short-burst video she had collected to Beckwith, as well as to *The New York Times, The Washington Post, The Wall Street Journal,* and CNN. All of the news outlets would post it soon enough, but *being* news outlets, they would have to confirm its authenticity first. Sonia's *tía*-mama trusted her dauhter, watched in horror what she had sent her, and posted it on her website and Twitter feed immediately. Not only had she scooped the *Times,* the *Post,* the *Journal,* and cable; at this point she had a bigger audience than all of them, so anything that went out on her platforms beat anything that went out on theirs.

The outrage over the video was immediate. The United Nations, the European Union, and the Organization of American States—with the grudging agreement of the US president—issued formal condemnations. The White House followed with a hedged statement read by the press secretary and released online with strategic italics, declaring that "the conditions depicted in the video, *if authenticated,* are entirely unacceptable and not in keeping with the humane standards to which the United States holds itself and seeks in its allies."

The late-to-the-game *Times, Post,* and *Journal* alternately called the scenes in the video "a nightmare," "a mortal crime," and "a scene from Hieronymus Bosch." All of them also observed in more or less matching phrasing that the video "raises pressure on wavering lawmakers to cast their vote in favor of intervention."

Beckwith was as pleased as she was able to be about the results of the video. She was hopping mad at Sonia, too, for putting herself in such danger to record it, but at the moment she was far less capable of feeling pleasure or anger than of simply feeling the utter misery of her illness. After she made it clear to Mission Control the day before that she was not going anywhere before the vote on the eighteenth, she had remained in steady communication with the ground. Often it was with Jasper—though he avoided the jauntiness he usually brought to their air-to-ground chatter. He was fed up with her stubbornness in staying aboard even at the risk of her life, and during his Capcom shifts they kept things businesslike.

Beckwith had to admit he had been right about the business of the forty-eight hours—specifically that those hours could spell her end. Her headache had become almost blinding, a thing so acute that she took an almost academic wonder in how her nervous system could produce something so monstrous. Her neck was in so much pain it was easier to pivot her whole body to look at something than to try to swivel her head. She had no idea what her fever was, but it was high enough that at one point, the image appeared to her unbidden of the blood in her veins forming tiny bubbles the way water in a pot does just before it jumps to a full boil. She would have shaken her head to scatter the image—if she had been able to shake her head at all.

Beckwith could not say with certainty how much sleep she'd had in the past few days, except to say that whatever she did get was in brief, accidental bits. She had given up climbing into the Russian sleep pod because she knew that real sleep, true sleep—the deep blue ocean of a full night's sleep—was entirely beyond her. Instead, she would find herself suddenly mugged by sleep. She'd be rummaging through the medicine bin for yet another ibuprofen, and all at once everything around her would go away and she'd wake up to find that the bin and its contents were floating in front of her and that she'd been in a state of blackout for ten or fifteen minutes at a time. The previous time Boysen called for a med check, Beckwith described these interludes, framing them as much-needed naps, hoping that might appease the flight surgeon. It didn't.

"That's not sleep," Boysen said. "It's unconsciousness. And it's not a good sign."

Earlier in the morning, when the ibuprofen—which Beckwith was taking three and four at a time—had temporarily dulled the pain by about half an order of magnitude, she had told Moscow that it might be a good moment to bring the Soyuz in for docking, since she felt that for now at least there was a chance she would be able to be useful if she had to intervene and help guide the ship. Zhirov took the Capcom console and talked her through the procedure as the thrusters on the Soyuz puffed to life and the guidance computers edged it across the tiny one-kilometer distance to the station. Beckwith looked down at the guidance readout in the hope that she could call off the distance and speed and thus prove to Moscow and to herself that she was not quite as sick as she felt. But the readout came back to her doubled and blurred, so Zhirov called out the numbers and she merely repeated them back.

When the Soyuz was just a few feet away, Beckwith looked at it through the small porthole on the Poisk almost longingly, picturing the cockpit seat where she would buckle herself and close her eyes and fly away and then wake up on Earth in a hospital bed with a pillow under her pounding head and an intravenous line in her arm bringing her the sweet comfort of the drugs that would heal her. The Soyuz docked without incident, a light bump and the reassuring snap of the docking latches confirming it was where it should be.

"We have capture," Beckwith said.

"Copy capture," Zhirov answered.

Now, half a day later, on the night of the seventeenth, as millions were gathering in Washington for the congressional vote the next day, Beckwith could take the pain and exhaustion and kaleidoscope vision no more. She floated back to the medicine bin in the Zarya module and dug through it once more for the blister pack with the lightning bolts and the sleepy eyes and the forbidden steering wheel and martini glass. She broke one of the blisters, removed one of the pills, grabbed a water bottle with a squeeze nozzle, and hailed the ground.

"Moscow, station," she said.

"Copy, station," Zhirov answered.

"Vasily, I'm going to close the shades."

She had no idea who on the planet below might be listening in on the air-to-ground loop, and so she used the slang coined by an earlier cosmonaut when he had taken one of the tablets for a migraine headache and had warned the rest of the crew to take them only if they had absolutely no alternative. The feeling of curling up in the dark, cozy room that was the buzz of the drug would be just too tempting.

"That's a good idea, station," Zhirov answered.

Beckwith looked at her watch and set an alarm for 12:00 P.M. station time, or about thirteen hours away. That was a long time to sleep, but she needed every hour of it. When she at last woke up, it would be 8:00 A.M. East Coast time on the morning of the eighteenth, one hour before Congress would convene.

"Call me at 1200 hours," she instructed. "If I don't respond, call again until I do."

"Copy, station," Zhirov said. "Wake-up call at 1200."

Beckwith took the pill, closed her eyes, and floated in place, picturing the drug spreading through her bloodstream and bringing her the sweet relief of painless slumber. She drifted toward the sleep pod, slid inside, and within minutes felt a warm wooziness come over her.

"Moscow, station," came her voice across the air-to-ground loop. She sounded happy.

"Copy, station," Zhirov answered.

"Vasily," she said, "you're a nice friend."

Zhirov smiled. "Copy, station."

"And this is a nice spaceship."

"Copy, station."

"Yes," Beckwith said, "it's very nice."

"Walli?" Zhirov said.

"Mm-hmm?"

"Go to sleep now."

Beckwith said nothing. Through her open mic, Zhirov could hear the steady sound of her breathing.

.   .   .

The wake-up call Beckwith had requested came just when she asked, at 1200 hours station time. She'd been asleep for the solid thirteen hours she'd hoped for, and while she was not wearing biomed sensors, she had left her mic open and her breathing and occasional turning and shifting remained audible on the air-to-ground loop. Zhirov found the sound reassuring, and he suspected that all of the controllers in both Moscow and Houston did too.

As Beckwith had predicted, she did not answer when he first called. He tried her again two minutes later, then two minutes after that. She finally answered on the third call.

"What, what, what?" she said. She sounded groggy, thick-tongued. In the background, Zhirov could hear her watch alarm sounding.

"Station, how are you feeling?" Zhirov asked. Beckwith muttered something, but Zhirov could not make out what it was. "Station, turn off your watch," he said.

The alarm stopped and Beckwith spoke again. "What time is it, Vasily?"

"Twelve-oh-eight hours."

"I mean in Washington."

"It's 8:08 A.M. How did you sleep, Walli?"

"Fine," she muttered.

"How do you feel?"

"Horrible. Horrible."

Beckwith remembered absolutely nothing from the moment she fell asleep until this very moment, but all that rest had availed her nothing. Her disease had marched on as she slept. Her headache was still blistering, her vision still doubled, her neck still immobile. Even with the lights off in the Russian module, the bit of Earthlight streaming through the porthole made her squint. And she was just as exhausted as she had been before she'd gone to sleep.

"Walli?" Zhirov said.

"Hmmm . . ."

"Hold for Houston. I'm patching in the flight surgeon. I'll stay on the loop."

Beckwith said nothing, the line hissed and then clicked, and then the hiss went to a two-note harmonic. Both Mission Controls were now on the line.

"Station?" came the voice of Charlene Boysen.

"Copy," Beckwith answered.

"Moscow still here," said Zhirov.

"Copy."

"We can speak in confidence, Walli," Boysen said. "Air-to-ground channel is open to keep the press distracted, but they're getting only static. Your mic is on a private loop."

Beckwith grunted in response.

"Has there been any change in your status, station?" Boysen asked.

"Generally worse."

"Any new symptoms?"

"Affirm."

"Nausea?"

"Affirm."

"Walli, do you have a rash?"

Beckwith looked up and down her arms, but only quickly. The light of the module was too much to bear.

"Negative, Houston."

"Everywhere, Walli," Boysen said, "not just the parts you can see easily."

Beckwith groaned, rolled up her pants legs as far as she could and saw nothing. She peered down the front of her shirt and her chest was clear too. Then she lifted up the bottom of the shirt and was jolted. An angry patch of red was spreading across her abdomen and wrapping around to her back.

"Houston," she said, "affirm on the rash. Abdominal."

"Walli," Boysen now said very deliberately. "What is the date?"

"It's September 15," Beckwith answered.

"Are you sure of that?"

Beckwith hedged and covered. "I mean the sixteenth, the sixteenth," she said quickly.

"It's September 18, Walli. What is your rank?"

"I am a Naval Academy graduate and I was commissioned an ensign." As she said it, she knew it was right and yet it was wrong too. Then things came clearer. "Now I'm a lieutenant commander."

"Who is the president?"

Beckwith got that one right.

Boysen let a moment lapse, and Beckwith could hear her partially covering her mic and muttering to someone off to her side. Then she came back on the line.

"Station," Boysen said, "it is the flight surgeon's conclusion that crew status is critical. The flight director concurs. You are out of time."

Beckwith had suspected that Boysen would say that, and she'd known that when she did say it, she would phrase it in the third person, since that was the language of the training protocols. She closed her eyes against both the light and her swimming vision, but even in the darkness everything continued tumbling. The pain in her head was everywhere; it was a thing with form and weight and presence. She thought of the word "critical." *Crew status is critical.* And she knew it was true. She was quite likely going to die.

"Houston," she said.

"Copy, station."

"Vasily?"

"Yes, Walli."

"Tell me about the reentry coordinates."

In Mission Control in Houston, Boysen sat back and released a deep, trembly breath of relief. In Mission Control in Moscow, Zhirov punched the air in triumph and flashed two thumbs up to Bazanov across the room. Then he collected himself and spoke.

"Copy that, station," he said. "We have two entry windows in the next twenty-four hours. One opens up in . . ." He glanced at the Mission Elapsed Time clock in the front of the auditorium and did a fast mental calculation. ". . . in six hours and fourteen minutes. The next is roughly eleven hours after that."

"And tomorrow?" Beckwith asked.

Boysen cut in, "Station, you can't wait until tomorrow."

"The vote in Washington is this morning," Beckwith said. "It starts in less than an hour. It could go on all day."

"Do you want to be alive to know the results?" Boysen asked. Her tone was sharp, angry. "You are out of time!"

"Yes," Beckwith conceded, taking her head in both her hands and trying to contain the pain. "I understand."

Zhirov proceeded. "The first window brings you down near Zhez-kazgan; the second takes you to Karaganda, but there's heavy cloud cover there."

"So it's Zhezkazgan," Beckwith said.

"Yes, it is."

"In six hours."

"A little more, but yes," Zhirov said. "And, Walli, one more thing."

"You're flying me ballistic," Beckwith said.

"We're flying you ballistic," Zhirov confirmed.

There had been little question from the outset that whenever Beckwith came home, Moscow would order a ballistic reentry, which was what was called for if a crew member with no experience commanding a Soyuz was in the center seat. But if there had been any doubt, the fact that the crew member was mortally ill sealed the question.

Ordinarily, a Soyuz would reenter the atmosphere at a comparatively shallow angle, tweaking its route to roller-coaster its way down in a rising and falling trajectory. That would bleed off speed and keep the gravitational load to no more than four g's, so that an astronaut like Beckwith, who weighed 138 pounds on Earth, would feel as if she weighed 552 pounds. Lying prone in a Soyuz couch, she would feel that weight distributed across her body, which would be easier to take than if she were sitting straight up, but it would still be like trying to fly under a quarter ton of rocks. The problem with such a nominal reentry was that if anything went wrong with the descent, the commander would have to take over and fly by stick, which was out of the question today.

The alternative was to fly at a steeper angle of descent, dropping through the atmosphere like a stone in a well. It was faster and it was all but foolproof; the entire crew could be asleep, and the ballistic reentry would still deliver them safely to the steppes of Kazakhstan. The Soyuz 11 crew had been dead, and their landing was still spot-on. But a ballistic reentry meant a load of eight g's or more. Beckwith's 138 pounds would now become 1,104.

"You're prepared for this?" Zhirov now asked her.

"I've eaten more than ten g's in the centrifuge, Vasily."

"Not when you're sick."

"The physics is the physics," Beckwith said. "So I have six hours and now"—she glanced at her watch through one eye—"twelve minutes."

"Copy. But boarding the Soyuz will be earlier, in four hours."

"Then I have those four hours to work." Beckwith opened her laptop slowly, clumsily, and launched her browser and her email.

"You should rest, Walli," Vasily said.

She agreed with him. Spending four hours at her bright, screaming screen seemed unthinkable. But she had arrived at this point after weeks of grinding effort, and all of that would either succeed or fail in Washington today. She could still send the occasional tweet to whip up the Washington crowd or pressure a wavering lawmaker, and she surely wanted to watch the congressional vote as it unfolded. She dimmed the brightness on the screen as low as it could go and still be visible and turned the sound on the computer down the same way.

"I'll rest on Earth," she said to Zhirov.

"Copy that," Zhirov answered. She was coming home; he would allow her anything else she needed. "Moscow out."

At his console, Zhirov leaned back in his chair, stretched his arms, and shook out his hands, feeling a month's worth of tension beginning to uncoil. His long, broken mission was at last about to end. He felt a hand on his shoulder, looked up, and saw Gennady Bazanov standing above him. He sat back up.

"That was good work, Vasily," Bazanov said. "She will be home soon."

"It will be a relief," Zhirov said.

"It will," Bazanov agreed. He hesitated. "But you cannot be here."

"I don't understand."

"You may be in the room. You will yield the microphone." Bazanov inclined his head up the center aisle. The Capcom who was not due to begin his shift until much later was there. He walked down the aisle toward the console. Bazanov then turned back to Zhirov. "You know Belka Beckwith too well," Bazanov said. "The reentry will be difficult; there is no room for sentiment."

He held out his hand for the headset; Zhirov hesitated and then removed it and handed it over.

"Thank you for your very hard work," Bazanov said to Zhirov.

"It was my responsibility as the commander of this mission," Zhirov said.

With that, he turned and strode up the aisle. In the back row, Lebedev was at work at a console, studying the glyphs on his strip charts, monitoring the data points on his screen.

"Yulian," Zhirov said in a low tone. Lebedev looked up. "Please finish what you are doing and come with me."

Lebedev asked no questions. He made a few final notations in red grease pencil, squared and neatened his stack of papers, and stood. There were more than six hours left in his mission, and his commander had just given him an order. The two men wordlessly left the room.

CHAPTER TWENTY-FIVE

At about the same moment her *tía*-mama was waking up feeling utterly awful, Sonia was waking up feeling surprisingly well. The oleander had done its terrible work quickly and left her system just as quickly—thanks to the small dose she'd been sure to take, the medicines she'd been given when she returned from the main camp, and her own stubborn constitution. She woke up this morning with both an unexpected appetite and a stubborn worry.

Going by the space station app on Sonia's phone, it had been more than twenty-four hours since the station had last made a clean pass over the Amazon, which meant that it had been more than twenty-four hours since Sonia's *tía*-mama had gotten a look at whatever violence might be mobilizing far below her. Bobo-deCorte's generals were now completely wise to the space station's routes and flyovers; that meant they had known that the twenty-four blind hours were coming and could plan for them. If they were going to launch an offensive, today would be a very good day for it.

As soon as Sonia woke, she went outside and scanned the horizon in a full 360 degrees, looking for the orange or yellow cast in the sky that would signal a fresh blaze or even the violet that would mean an even fresher but ready-to-bloom one. To her relief, she saw nothing. She glanced at her watch and saw she now had less than forty-five minutes before she and Raymond would be making their 8:00 A.M. visit to the main camp—no need for Lindsey since there was no ruse to pull this time. She hurried over to the food tent, gobbled down an energy bar, and drank two glasses of milk, needing very much to replenish everything she'd lost yesterday. Then she left the tent and prepared to join Raymond in the infirmary, tending to patients for half an hour before they had to go.

It was on her way to the infirmary that she was stopped cold. Far off to the west, at least eight miles away, where the horizon began at this elevation, she saw a shimmer of ultraviolet rising and spreading. She stood completely still and blinked several times to refocus her eyes and ensure she wasn't imagining it. She wasn't.

"Fire!" she shouted to no one in particular—and no one in particular turned and looked where she was pointing. "¡Fogo!" she added, and then "¡Fuego!" and at that, the people milling through the camp and gathered on the soccer field did turn and look and squint—and they saw nothing at all of the shimmery purple. Then suddenly they did see, as the purple gave way to an explosion of orange and yellow and the inky shadow of smoke. On the ground—unlike in space—a fresh wind from the west also carried in the smell of the burning forest, with the blaze unmistakably approaching fast.

At that, the people in the showpiece camp screamed as one and broke for the eastern gate, where the guards, who had been patrolling lazily in the hot morning sun, sprang into position, blocking the opening and brandishing their guns in the direction of the terrified internees. The guards had been prepared for this—had been told a fire might be coming today—and had braced themselves to contain the stampede that was now unfolding.

The timing made sense—from Bobo-deCorte's point of view at least. With the American politicians planning their vote this morning, it was possible their army could be arriving at any time, and the Brazilian president was determined to fortify his gains before that happened. The fires in the east, in Brazil, had pushed the tribes west, toward and through the gates of the four resettlement camps as he had planned. But tens of thousands of them had broken from the flow, sweeping wide of the camps, making straight for the border and pouring into Bolivia. Once the fires in the east stopped, the people would pour back into Brazil and try to retake their lands. So now it would take westward fires, on Bolivian lands, to push them back into Brazil and back toward the camps. The fires would be lit fast and extinguished fast—as soon as the tribes had been moved. The Bolivians would be furious, though Bobo-deCorte was prepared to remind them that they were also perfectly welcome to thank him for the land he'd cleared for them to use for ranching and farming.

That was the plan, and it might well have worked as neatly and quickly as had been imagined had the weather not turned and the wind not shifted—blowing much harder to the east than anticipated. The fire, breathing deep of the fresh gusts, followed the wind in that direction, devouring scrub and forest in its path, spitting embers that flew ahead of it, lighting daughter fires hundreds and thousands of feet away, all moving directly toward the Brazilian border and the western camp.

Raymond and the other doctors in the infirmary building, alerted by the screams of the people rushing the gate, poured outside just as a fresh gale swelled and a bright orange-and-yellow halo rose on the horizon, spraying a shower of sparks, which spread and ignited everything ahead of them. The blaze was still six or seven miles distant, but it was advancing by the second.

Without needing a command, all of the doctors, including Sonia and Raymond, took off in a dead run in the direction of the main camp. The swarm of people on the soccer field was still surging in the opposite direction, retreating from the blaze and heading for the heavily guarded east gate. The SSA group fought their way through them, struggling toward the rear of the showpiece camp. It was gated here too, but there would be no soldiers, as none of the internees were trying to escape into the very teeth of the fire. The doctors passed through the rear gate, and when they did, it seemed as if they had entered a living oven, as the heat climbed higher the farther they ran. Sparks danced around them everywhere, a stinging rain that singed them when it landed on skin and popped into miniature blazes burning dry grass when it hit the ground. The front entrance of the main camp was just twenty yards away, and the sight that greeted the doctors was hellish.

The camp was backlit by fire that now loomed high into the sky and reached around to the north and south—flaming arms appearing to try to gather in everything in their path, including the camp itself. Fire whorls spun from the ends of the arms, skittering along the ground in all directions. The guards who were supposed to be here had abandoned their posts but left the gate locked. The fencing that surrounded the camp was well anchored, thick-wired, and tightly woven to make it hard to climb and impossible to topple even by a crowd so huge. The fence was twelve feet high and topped by a coil of barbed wire. The gate was sturdier still—a barred iron door secured with two separate padlocks. The people trapped inside pressed against the wire and bars, crying out for help.

The western edge of the camp had now been reached by the fire, igniting tents and the occasional pine storage building. People were being burned—it was impossible for them not to be, though impossible, too, to know how many. On the other side of the fence, the doctors could already see some of them—their flesh scorched black or red—as they were passed hand over hand, above the heads of the crowd. The injured adults were hoisted and heaved from person to person. The injured children and babies were literally tossed. All were laid on the ground on a clear patch of land directly inside the front gate—burnt offerings to the doctors if they could only get inside. The SSA team rushed the fence and began to climb it from the outside, finding toeholds and handholds where they could. The people inside did the same, but the barbed wire at the top made it impossible for anyone on one side simply to cross over to the other.

No one, however, was trying to do that. Instead, the prisoners began gathering up their injured, swaddling them in blankets to protect them from the barbed wire, and passing them from person to person up the fence. The doctors mirrored them, forming a similar chain on the other side to pass the injured down. The handover at the top was slow and terrible; the blankets—and, worse, the burned flesh of the victims—often caught and dragged on the barbs. Some of the people cried out; those who had lost consciousness did not. Each time a person was laid on the ground outside the fence, the blankets were tossed back over for the next.

Sonia was the first up the fence, scrabbling easily to the top and halfway leaning over the barbed wire, points of blood dotting her shirt where the barbs pressed and cut her flesh. She was self-evidently too small to muscle any of the adults across, so the children and babies were handed her way. Raymond was part of a different chain, next to Sonia's, midway down the fence, collecting the injured prisoners from the doctor above him and passing them down to the one below.

In the distance now, Sonia could hear a high, waspish whine and looked off toward the horizon, where a vast flock of black shapes approached through the sky. They were, surely, the Consolidation helicopters; nothing else made that angry sound. And they were surely coming to extinguish the wildfire the soldiers themselves had lit, as was their practice after the tribespeople had been driven from their lands and into the camps. In this case, though, whether they would be able to contain the huge, wind-fed blaze was impossible to say. The government in Brasilia clearly understood the severity of the problem, and the helicopters were accompanied by heavier, larger firefighting airplanes.

Sonia pulled her gaze from the helicopters and bent back over the fence, reaching down for an injured baby who could not have been more than a year old and had burns on its arms and legs. She could not tell if the baby was a boy or a girl; she could tell that either way, it was badly undernourished. Year-old babies should not be so light she could hold them so easily with one hand. She passed the baby off to the doctor directly below her on the fence, looked back over for the next child—and then her head swam at what she saw.

A child had been laid on the ground at the inside of the gate. He was a boy. He looked to be about five. His upper body was terribly burned, the remains of his shirt little more than a few scorched scraps. His limbs hung loose with the unmistakable slackness of the dead. And his legs, brown, unburned, were covered with a merry crisscross of scratches.

Sonia released a terrible animal howl. She did not hear herself; she was not conscious of herself. She was conscious only of a huge internal gulf, one that as soon as it appeared was filled by a pain so deep it almost had mass. She howled once more and people turned to look. She howled yet again and then lost her grip and fell the twelve feet to the ground. There was a loud cracking sound as a bone in her right wrist snapped clean in two. She did not feel it. She pounded the ground with both her hands, the broken wrist flopping hideously. She was aware, faintly, of someone bending over her, trying to stop her pounding, saying her name over and over again. It was a man. It might have been Raymond. She wrenched herself away and screamed some more and pounded the ground some more. And then she was aware of one other thing—a sound as high as the wasp sound, but sweeter, softer, better. She heard it again and then again and then it resolved itself into a word.

"So-*nee*-ya!" it called. And once more, "So-*nee*-ya!"

She raised her head and scanned about, and just on the other side of the fence, dressed in little blue shorts and a too-big T-shirt, with his small brown fingers clutching the wires and a merry crisscross of scratches on his arms and legs, was a different boy, an unburned boy, a boy who came into the world as Kauan but who would forever be Oli to her.

Sonia jumped up, pushed off the person who was holding her— vaguely registering that, yes, it was Raymond. She sprang for the fence, climbed it one-handed, rolled over the barbed wire, barely feeling the tattooing of wounds it was leaving across her body, and half climbed, half jumped down to the ground.

And then, broken and bleeding, sobbing and gasping, she rose to her knees and held open her arms, and Oli sprang into them. She held him fast and rocked him slow and repeated his nickname over and over, and he hugged her back and he said her name too. Sonia kissed his hair and smelled the wood smoke in it.

Holding Oli in her single, undamaged arm, she rose unsteadily to her feet, hobbled toward the other boy, the burned and murdered boy, the one with the crisscross of scratches who had not been spared the way the living boy she was holding had been. She dropped to her knees beside him, leaned forward, and kissed his scorched and blackened forehead.

"I am so, so sorry," she whispered to him. That was the last thing she was aware of as the world fell away and she slipped into the painless bliss of unconsciousness.

.   .   .

The Speaker of the United States House of Representatives was frowning at his chamber. Standing on the dais, running his eyes across the historic room, he could see even without a roll call that he did not remotely have a sufficient head count for the vote he needed to hold today—on the bill formally known as H.R. 5898: An Authorization and Mandate for Military Pacification of Contested Regions in and Around the Amazon Basin in Cooperation with Partner Nations. It was informally known simply as the Intervention Bill. All of the 435 House members were present in Washington, and all of them had shown up in their offices—early, even, which quite astonished the Speaker—to be on the floor at precisely 9:00 A.M.

But it was now past 9:00 and most of them were no-shows so far. Part of the problem, surely, was that cursed video from the Amazon. None of the members of the president and Speaker's party much wanted to discuss it, but it was all that the press would want to ask them about the moment they poked their heads out of their offices to make their way to the House chamber. It would be awfully hard to defend voting against a bill that would put an end to the horror that was captured in those four minutes of video, and none of the members wanted to try. The other likely reason they were all running late was that they were doing precisely what the Speaker had done this morning, which was to find the nearest TV—in his case in the cloakroom off the House floor—to watch the dramas unfolding in the streets of Washington as well as in space.

The coverage of the demonstrations and the imminent vote had been constant and often dramatic, as aerial footage taken by helicopters showed the astonishing scale of the crowds that had assembled in Washington. The mass of people was being led by an incorrigible law student the Speaker had been told was named Laurel Cady, who never seemed to leave the microphone on the stage that had been set up on the National Mall, west of the Capitol Building and east of the Lincoln Memorial. In between the speeches she and other pro-intervention activists had been making all day, she repeatedly led a maddening call-and-response.

"The burning . . ." she'd call out.

"Will stop!" the crowd would answer.

"The killing . . ."

"Will stop!"

"The people . . ."

"Will rise!"

"The jungle . . ."

"Will live!"

It had begun forming a rat-a-tat rhythm in the Speaker's head that he couldn't shake. Even when Cady and her crowd weren't chanting, his thoughts and his very footsteps seemed to bounce along in the maddening cadence.

But the astronaut's illness was what people were really tuning in to see. Apart from the few times Boysen and Beckwith spoke privately in a doctor-patient consultation, every bit of the air-to-ground chatter about Beckwith's raging meningitis was being reported—and heard. The very real possibility that she would die in service of an Earthly cause had turned her into even more of a folk hero in the past twenty-four hours than she had been before, with tracking polls showing her approval rating at 77 percent. Meantime, public opinion of the president's plan to kill this morning's bill had continued to slide, with 57 percent of those polled favoring intervention and the bill that would permit it, 43 percent opposing, and an unheard-of 0 percent undecided on the matter. What had seemed like a safe vote for the one-third of the House plus one more member the Speaker would need to deny a two-thirds majority and sustain the president's veto now looked like a political risk.

At last, at 9:35, the sergeant-at-arms approached the dais and confirmed that the entire House was at last in attendance. The speaker nodded his thanks and gaveled the session to order.

"The members will consider H.R. 5898: An Authorization and Mandate for Military Pacification of Contested Regions in and Around the Amazon Basin in Cooperation with Partner Nations," he called. "Will the clerk please read the bill?"

The clerk did just that, briefly taking the dais and reading again the name of the bill and its provisions, specifically citing "Congress's war-making authority, a legislative power equal to or superseding the executive power, including but not limited to determining the time, place, and manner of American military action." That was a claim, not a constitutional fact, one that judges up and down the federal system would surely love to get their hands on but would not get the chance, since approval for a protracted battle in the courts while the jungle kept burning was polling at a vanishingly small 9 percent, as of this morning. Unless the president and the Congress were interested in committing political suicide, today's votes would thus decide the matter: A two-thirds approval in both houses of Congress would mean intervention; less than two-thirds in either chamber would mean none.

At last, when the reading of the bill was done, the Speaker opened the floor for voting. The smart betting still had the bill passing by a predicted vote of 277 to 158—a landslide by most measures, but short of the two-thirds vote of 290 to 145 that would be necessary to override the president's veto. But the prediction might not hold, and if the Speaker lost just thirteen nay votes, the House would have effectively brushed the president of the United States aside and would then send the issue of the intervention across the Capitol, where it could fight for its two-thirds in the Senate.

Almost immediately, the Speaker sensed trouble. Forty-seven electronic voting stations were positioned around the floor—small green, red, and yellow buttons built into the chamber's wooden railings, armrests, and desks. Members would insert an electronic identification card into a slot and vote either yea or nay. Five large viewing screens in the front of the chamber—evocative of the much larger, sleeker screens at the front of the twin Mission Control rooms in Moscow and Houston—would record the members' votes.

Those votes were coming in slowly. The fiercest intervention opponents voted straightaway, inserting their cards and fairly punching the red *nay* button. The most enthusiastic supporters did the same, jabbing at the green *yea*—some of them actually fist-bumping after they did. But even after fifty minutes, just 298 votes out of the 435 had been cast. They broke more or less as they were expected to break— 194 yea to 104 nay so far—still shy of the two-thirds pace needed to beat a veto. Then the voting stalled.

"We're seeing a lot of conferring and muttering there on the House floor, but not a lot of voting right now," observed the CNN anchor.

The Speaker nodded down to his majority leader and whip, who were already working the floor, in an unspoken command that they work it harder and faster. Three more votes popped red on the screen, changing the total to 194 to 107 and bringing the nay side a tiny bit closer to the 146 needed to support the president. Then a whoop went up from the minority party as all at once, at eight different voting stations, eight different yea votes lit up green, pushing the total to 202 in favor and 107 against. Every single one of those votes was from a member of the president's party, and every single one of those members was from a district that had fallen hard for Beckwith and whose voters had been pressing their elected officials to get behind the intervention she was pushing—with the release of Sonia's video only ratcheting up the pressure. Every single one of them also left the chamber as soon as the votes were cast, knowing that somewhere in the White House, the president was watching the broadcast.

"We could be seeing the first real effects of that look inside the Brazilian camp," the anchor said.

Two hundred and fifty miles above, Beckwith herself was watching and pumped her fist into the air.

"You following this, Houston?" she called into her mic. Her voice was barely a croak, but it was a happy croak.

"Not allowed to watch, station. On duty," Jasper said. "But we're getting word. I hear you're doing OK."

"We're doing OK," she echoed.

Still, it was not OK enough to crack the two-thirds ceiling. On the networks, however, the chatter was now that most or all of nine other members whose districts had swung Beckwith's way were likely to switch their votes too. If all of them voted yea, the projected vote total would rise to 288 to 147—only two shy of the needed 290. The mere existence of such a prediction might make it self-fulfilling, with opposition to the bill collapsing in the face of forecasts of its victory.

At that moment, two of the nine members did break, stepping forward to vote yea. Almost as one, the remaining seven huddled, then slipped their cards in the slots at the voting stations and punched the red or green buttons. Five of the seven voted yea. The vote now stood at 209 to 109—with momentum overwhelmingly on the yea side.

But the majority leader and whip did not become majority leader and whip because they were bad at their jobs, and they were deftly working the floor—calling in favors, threatening careers. They buttonholed loyal members to buttonhole wavering members to remind them of the anger of the caucus and donors that would be the wages of a betrayal. A yea vote might mean easier treatment in the press back home today, but it would also mean a nasty fight in the primary election next year.

With that, the defections began to slow. Four representatives in the president's party running in touch-and-go districts who had not voted yet strode simultaneously to four different voting stations. The cameras closed in on them and the newscasters fell silent—and they cast four nay votes at once. On the floor, the opponents of the bill applauded and embraced.

With those votes, the rest of the House members, from both parties, appeared to find their spines—conscious that the TV cameras were watching, conscious that so were the voters, and conscious too that enough was enough and that those same voters wanted the matter settled for good and all. With that, they fairly mobbed the voting stations. The 209 votes in favor surged past 260, closing in fast on the 290 needed; the 113 against moved at more of a creep toward the 146 needed to scuttle the bill, but a little flock of six nay votes came in, and the Speaker allowed himself a brief flicker of hope. That was followed, however, by a larger bunching of nine yeas. The teeter-totter played out until at last the yeas bumped up to 285, and the nays followed to 141. Both sides were five votes from victory—as silence fell in the chamber.

Then, from the back benches, five freshman members from the president's party, five members who had been in Washington for just over a year and knew that one day, at some point in their time in Congress, they might be called upon to cast a vote that would require them to choose between their conscience and their jobs, huddled and murmured to one another. They had all surely hoped they could put off so politically mortal a vote for years, but the matter had arisen today and would have to be decided today. They rose as a group, strode to five adjacent voting stations, slipped in their cards, and almost in unison voted a deciding and quite possibly career-killing yea.

Cheering erupted among the 290 members who now stood on the old chamber floor in veto-proof unison; tears and whoops and hugs and leaping broke out among the demonstrators in Washington; and 250 miles above, a single, sickly astronaut wept in relief and joy. Alone on his dais, the Speaker at last cast his own now-pointless vote, becoming part of the minority that could do nothing at all to change the outcome of what had happened here today.

"The chair votes nay," he declared to the chamber that was not listening. "The measure passes 290 to 145."

Then he rapped the gavel once and hurried out through a side door. In the distance, through the walls and corridors of the grand, historic building, he could just hear the voices outside.

"The burning . . ." the Cady woman cried.

"Will stop!" the masses answered. And the rhythm resumed in the Speaker's head.

CHAPTER TWENTY-SIX

It took two full hours after Sonia cut herself on barbed wire, broke her wrist in a fall, pounded the ground in grief, gathered Oli up in relief, kissed the child who had not survived, and then lost consciousness before she received any medical care at all. There were too many people grievously burned for any of the SSA doctors to tend to someone whose wounds were not life-threatening.

Finally one of the doctors splinted Sonia's arm as well as was possible in the field, then gave her a painkiller, tipping her into a deep sleep that would keep her still for hours. Raymond and Oli stood by her side while her wrist was being wrapped and the medicine was being given; then Raymond lifted her in his arms—she was so small, he marveled, so light for someone who contained such energy— carried her back to the showpiece camp, and found a corner for her in the infirmary building. The cots were all occupied by people who had been hurt in the stampede to the front gate, but Raymond spied a clear spot on the floor near a wall, laid Sonia down, and built a little berm of blankets around her—a boundary that provided no actual protection but would signal to the surrounding crowd that she was to be left alone. Oli climbed in and curled up next to her, his head on her chest.

Raymond then hurried back to the main part of the western camp. The waspish helicopters and the larger firefighting airplanes had done a good job of extinguishing the blaze that had consumed part of the camp, and the Consolidation soldiers even produced heavy metal shears to cut the two padlocks holding the gate closed, allowing the doctors inside. Most of the work the SSA teams were doing involved assessing the worst of the burned and wrapping their alternately blistered or blackened limbs and torsos. Their howls were terrible—as raw as their flesh—and it was a mercy for both them and the doctors when a needle was slid into an arm, sending one more person into an even deeper unconsciousness than Sonia's. None were carried back to the infirmary building in the showpiece camp. There was not nearly adequate care for them there, but there was little to help them here at the main camp either. Without proper hospital treatment they would surely die of infection or dehydration within the next few days.

The only hope for the victims was the helicopters from the Mercado camp and the other nearby hospitals, which had been summoned by radio but would need to fight through the smoke of the surrounding fires to cover the distances from Bolivia and Peru, at least doubling the travel time. When they at last arrived—five of them from Mercado, along with at least three dozen more from other SSA, UNICEF, and Red Cross camps—the doctors began carrying the worst of the injured people over to them and the pilots hopped out to help. Raymond scanned their faces as well as the backs of their heads if they were turned away, looking for the bald patch, the waxy skin, and the missing ear that would indicate Jo. It was just after he had made his third trip to a helicopter helping to load the injured that he spotted him about twenty yards away. He called his name and sprinted toward him, and Jo turned and grabbed Raymond in a surprisingly rough and emotional embrace.

"You're not dead," he said, turning Raymond this way and that looking for signs of injury.

"Not yet. Not hurt much either," Raymond answered.

"The girl?"

"Back at the infirmary. She's banged up but not burned."

"Can she travel?" Jo asked.

"She can. She has to," Raymond said. "She's going to need a surgeon." Jo looked alarmed and Raymond added, "Shattered arm. She'll live."

Jo glanced at his helicopter as the SSA doctors finished loading another burn patient, bringing the total to four so far. "I can fit four more injured with just enough left for you and her." He looked at his watch. "Wheels up in ten minutes. Go."

Raymond tore off for the showpiece camp, stumbling repeatedly on roots and rocks, then barreled through the back gate and into the infirmary building. It was even more packed with people than it had been when he'd left, but his blanket berm had done its work and Sonia had been left alone on her patch of floor. Oli leapt up as he approached, interposing himself between Raymond and Sonia as if to protect her.

"It's OK," Raymond said, out of breath. "We're leaving—all of us." He scooped up Sonia and, with Oli tailing him, ran back out of the building, across the grounds, and back west to the main camp. Jo saw him approach and waved him off.

"The girl only," he shouted. "No locals unless they're injured."

Raymond tried to call an answer but was too winded, and settled simply for shaking his head in a vigorous *no*. He reached the helicopter, and Jo helped him hoist Sonia onto the floor inside. Then Raymond reached down and picked up Oli, but Jo stood in his way.

"I said no locals," he repeated.

"He's coming," Raymond said as Oli squirmed in his arms, reaching for the helicopter door through which he could see Sonia.

"It's the rule," Jo said. "It ain't mine, but it's the rule."

"*What rules?*" Raymond shouted furiously. "*What fucking rules?*" He freed up one arm, restraining Oli with the other, and swept it in the direction of the burned people in the filthy camp. "Do you see any rules here? There are no rules left!"

He stared Jo down and Jo stared back, and then Raymond—smaller than Jo, less battle-tested than Jo—shoved him aside with his shoulder, took two strides to the helicopter, and placed Oli inside. "We're leaving," he declared. "He's coming."

Jo, who had surely allowed himself to be shoved, had allowed himself to be defied, took a final look at the violent, smoldering anarchy all around him.

"OK, son," he said. "We'll go."

"Thank you," Raymond answered simply, then hopped aboard the helicopter and hunkered down with Sonia and Oli as Jo took his seat and the helicopter roared and shook and lifted off.

· · ·

Beckwith watched the House vote on her laptop as it played out. When the intervention measure passed, she cheered so loudly that she swooned from the pain that shot through her head. She closed the lid of her laptop to rest her eyes and within a minute reopened it to watch the Senate vote.

She had found that closing one eye made it easier to focus, as that singled down her vision, but keeping just one eyelid shut was much harder than closing both, and the effort made her headache worse. So she opened the Russian first aid kit, dug about for gauze and surgical tape, and fashioned a patch over her right eye. Her headache was slightly worse on the right and she figured that if she gave that side a rest it might ease the pain a bit. It didn't.

Just as the news stations picked up the feed of the Senate gaveling itself to order, the air-to-ground line crackled to life.

"Station, Houston," came the call.

"Jasper, station," Beckwith responded.

"Congratulations on that vote," he said. It was something he knew he shouldn't say. They were back on open mic, the world was listening, and NASA was an apolitical operation. But Beckwith was his friend, and today that was what mattered.

"There's still the Senate," she said. "They're going to need the same backbone over there."

"How about you let us take care of all that and fill you in as we know? You've got a ride waiting."

Beckwith consulted the clock on the corner of her laptop screen. "Ingress in fifty-eight minutes," she said.

"Moscow wants you to start now," he answered. "They figure you might need more time."

On cue, Moscow, which had been listening on the line, cut in. "Station, please initiate ingress procedure," came a businesslike Capcom voice Beckwith didn't recognize. Clearly, the Russians were in no mood for American chatter.

"Copy," she said.

Ingressing early or not, Beckwith was going to track the events in Washington until the last possible moment. The Senate, she could see, was now officially in session, and the reading of the day's business had begun. The first matter that would receive attention was the intervention, still warm from the House's oven. The bill was expected to pass handily but, as in the early House forecasts, fall well short of the needed two-thirds, with the head count now standing at a projected

57 in favor and 43 against—ten stubborn votes short of the 67 needed. But the drama of her imminent reentry plus the upset victory in the House was causing a lot of political recalculation.

Beckwith pulled on her Houston Astros sweatshirt, which she needed at the moment since her sickness had flipped its polarity from the sweltering side of her fever to the side with shaking and chills. That would not last long, she knew, and she'd need to strip right back down to shirtsleeves as soon as her temperature spiked again. She gathered her laptop and moved toward the Poisk module, passing first through the Zvezda to collect the mice. Hours before, she had transferred them into a single cage, which made them furious at first, as they spent the first few minutes floating about in a swarm, batting one another out of the way. Now, though, they seemed comfortable with—or at least resigned to—one another's company and had gone off to separate corners of the cage, latched on with one paw, and stayed put there. Even Bolt didn't want to float.

"I'm sorry about this, kids," she said. "You'll have plenty of room back in Moscow."

Beckwith used a bungee cord to anchor both the cage and her laptop to the bulkhead inside the Poisk. She closed the hatch leading to the Zvezda and the rest of the station, confining herself and her mice to the one small module at the far end of the giant flying machine. Then she went to work on the hatch on the Poisk's opposite wall—the hatch that led to the Soyuz.

"Commencing hatch opening, Moscow," she called down.

"Copy, station," the Capcom answered. "Doctor says to take it slow please."

Beckwith took mild offense at the suggestion. She was miserably ill, but she'd opened hatches in forty feet of water in complete spacewalking gear during emergency ingress training in the neutral buoyancy pool in Houston. She could certainly manage now.

Only she found that she couldn't. The hatch latch required muscle to move, and even the slightest exertion went straight from her arm up to her neck and head, sending lightning bolts of pain through her.

"Smart doctor," she muttered.

More carefully now, she worked the Poisk hatch, got it open, and was faced immediately with another hatch, which belonged to the Soyuz itself. That one unlatched and swung open much more easily, and she peered inside. The Soyuz was a three-part spacecraft. The hatch opened into the top of a spherical pod called the orbital module, which was used for storage and as a work area when the spacecraft was flying free. The bottom of the orbital module opened into the gumdrop-shape descent module, which was where the cockpit and seats and instrument panel were. Attached to the back of the descent module was the service module, which housed the engines, fuel tanks, and other hardware. Like the trailer end of a tractor-trailer, the service module was neither accessible to the crew from inside nor visible to them through their sideways-facing windows. The Soyuz had the singular smell of a new car mixed with the slight metallic tang of space, and Beckwith felt a surge of warmth for the little vessel that would soon take her home.

"Station—" Moscow began, but Beckwith cut the Capcom off.

"Hold," she snapped. "Stand by!"

At the moment Moscow had begun to speak, the newscaster on Beckwith's laptop mentioned the name of Senator Garry Oro, and she shot back out of the Soyuz to look at the screen. The networks had been alerted that Oro had lingered at his desk this morning until the last possible moment, working the phones and contemplating his vote. Now Beckwith could see the scene outside of his office as he emerged to make his way to the Senate floor. She'd enjoyed the conversation she'd had with him. He'd promised that he would always consider the counsel of a higher-ranking naval officer, and she'd believed him. The reporters swarmed toward him, and he cut them off before they could speak, anticipating what they would ask.

"You will know my vote when I cast my vote," was all he would say.

No sooner had Oro vanished into an elevator than the scene on the screen cut back to the Senate floor in time to reveal a yea vote on the tote board, cast by the senior senator from Nevada. "A significant defection here," called the newsman—and he was right.

The senator was one of the five in his chamber whose anti-intervention state was turning most sharply in favor of military action, and he had clearly made the same calculation the House defectors had: Defying the party today was better than defying his constituents, who would soon enough have their way with him at the polls. A few other votes trickled in over the next minute, and the total on the tote board showed a meaningless but still welcome early count of 5 votes yea and 3 nay. The predicted total vote had switched to 58 to 42, closer but still well short of the necessary 67.

Then, just as Beckwith was about to toggle back on to Moscow, came the thunderclap news that the junior senator from Oklahoma had followed the senior senator from Nevada and voted yea. The actual vote was now 7 yea and 3 nay, with the projection creeping up to 59 to 41.

Beckwith let out with a hoarse cheer, and Jasper immediately hailed her.

"Station, Houston," he said.

"Copy," she answered.

"Moscow says you're ignoring them. Show 'em a little love, please."

"Sorry," she said. "Breaking news."

"Station," Jasper repeated and then shifted his tone. "Walli Bee."

She picked up the change. "Listening, Jasper."

"We're getting the news here too," he said. "We're tracking it. We will not keep you in the dark. But you ain't going to be any damn good in Washington or anywhere else if you don't make it home alive today."

"Copy, Jasper," she said.

"Are you watching your computer there?"

"Affirm, Jasper."

"Turn it off, Walli. Turn it off now. You have a spacecraft to fly."

Jasper, her fine, smart friend, was right. She might never travel in space again. Actually, it was quite likely she never would. She had this one last mission, this one last landing to stick. She was a naval aviator, and she had not been behaving like one. She pulled off her eye patch and tossed it away to float aimlessly about the Poisk. The work ahead of her might demand the depth perception only two eyes could provide, and during the interludes when her vision did not double, that would be possible only with two eyes. Then she turned off the laptop, closed its lid, and left it bungeed to the wall for the next astronaut or cosmonaut who might come this way.

"News off, Jasper," she said. "Computer stowed. I'm on task."

"Thank you, Lieutenant Commander."

With that, Beckwith knew that the rest of her work today would be conducted entirely with Moscow. She set about doing it.

"Moscow, station," she called. "Please talk me through ingress."

The cosmonaut on the mic did just that, reminding her first to load any cargo she needed to bring home. Beckwith smiled; the only cargo she had was the mice. She unhitched the cage from the bulkhead and carried it, along with the bungee cord, into the Soyuz. She anchored the cage to the middle of the left-hand seat and patted it as if she were patting the mice themselves.

"Eight g's, kids," she said. "I'm gonna need you to be strong."

At last she closed and sealed the Poisk's docking hatch, then the Soyuz's own hatch. Then she floated from the orbital module of the Soyuz into the gumdrop-shape descent module and sealed that hatch too. At last, confined to the descent module alone, she settled into the center seat—the commander's seat, the seat that rightly belonged to Vasily Zhirov of the Golden Thousand—and buckled herself in. Tucked into a pocket on the right side of the seat was a plastic pouch that wasn't part of the spacecraft's standard gear. She pulled it out, closed one eye, and read the label. It was vodka, Polish, single-estate. She flipped it over. There was a note on the back. "For after landing," was all it read.

"Vasily," she said aloud to herself, then keyed open her mic. "All right, Moscow, bring me home."

Moscow acknowledged and began reading up the procedures Beckwith would have to follow to power up the Soyuz and ready it for flight. With each switch she threw, each fan that came on or instrument panel display that flickered to life, she felt more and more enclosed by the Soyuz, a part of its ecosystem—dependent on it for her life. It was Beckwith and her spacecraft, and they would take this ride together.

Houston, as always during a Soyuz reentry, would be second chair—there to assist but otherwise to stay quiet. Still, Beckwith now found that she very much wanted to know that Jasper would remain in the Capcom seat throughout her entire fiery ride to the Earth. The idea gave her some small comfort. There was no good way of confirming his whereabouts—not without making it clear that was just what she was doing. But she could always try a little misdirection. She keyed open her mic.

"Houston, station," she called.

"Copy, station," Jasper answered.

"Sorry, Jasper. My mistake—meant to call Moscow."

"Copy, station," he said again. And then he added, "Line's always open." He knew what she was doing; of course he'd know what she was doing. But she realized she didn't mind.

"Station, Moscow," came the call from Russia. "You needed us?"

"Never mind," she said. "Just a comm check."

For the next few minutes, she and Moscow worked further along the checklist toward Soyuz separation—slowly cutting the electrical connections between the little spacecraft and the station, transforming the Soyuz into an independent flying machine. Twice during that call-and-response, Beckwith insisted that Moscow ask Houston to check the doings in Washington. Twice she got back nothing of note; the vote had advanced to an all-but-meaningless 8 to 5. Only thirteen senators had either the courage or the calculation to go on record. Eighty-seven more were still talking, arguing, dealmaking.

"Cowards," Beckwith muttered.

"Stay on task, station," Jasper said.

At last the Soyuz was fully configured, and at last too the station had drifted to the point just over South Africa where a timely separation would put Beckwith on a long arc that would carry her from 250 miles above the Earth to the frigid plains of central Asia. Peering out the small porthole of the Soyuz, she could see the stark blue of the oceans cut by the jagged brown-green of the African coast.

"Station, go for separation in three minutes on my mark," the Moscow Capcom called.

Automatically, the event clock on the instrument panel in front of Beckwith cycled to 3:00 and began counting down. Both she and Moscow held their silence. She scanned about the little cockpit, resting her eyes on the handful of switches and indicators she understood fully, making what sense she could of the others.

"Two minutes," Moscow called.

"Copy two minutes," Beckwith said.

Thirty seconds later, Moscow called again: "Ninety seconds to separation."

Then came the call, "Sixty seconds." Then, "Thirty seconds."

At twenty seconds, Beckwith gathered herself and focused her eyes as best she could on the switch in front of her with the Cyrillic abbreviation "Разд" and the English "Sep." Both "Разделение" and "Separation" called upon her to do the same critical thing.

Beckwith flipped open the plastic safety cover on the switch and hovered her finger above it—maintaining at least a hand's-width distance. Separate two seconds too early above the southern oceans and you'd come down hundreds of miles off target in the Kazakh Steppe.

"Ten seconds, station," the Capcom called. He counted down aloud as Beckwith counted in her head, and at precisely the moment they both reached zero, she pressed the switch and quickly withdrew her hand.

The spacecraft gave an upward lurch as the latches holding it to the station popped free and compressed springs shoved the Soyuz off at four inches per second—or less than a quarter of a mile per hour. To Beckwith, even that tiny acceleration felt liberating, thrilling.

"Soyuz, Moscow," the Capcom said. The change in call sign from "Station, Moscow" was equal parts unmistakable and unremarked upon. "We have clean separation."

"Copy separation," Beckwith responded.

On the floor of the Senate chamber in Washington, lawmakers gathered around a television in the adjacent cloakroom to watch. In Mesa, Arizona, Mae Beckwith reached for Virgil's hand, and they held tight to each other as they watched the coverage alone in their little fan-cooled home. Among the people with the most invested in Beckwith's safe reentry, only Sonia was not watching—at that moment unconscious and in surgery in the Mercado camp's modest operating room.

Beckwith, 250 miles above all of them, enjoyed her quiet drift. Released from the upward-facing Poisk module, the Soyuz rose slowly above the station; the farther it moved, the more of the football-field-size vessel that had been her home for nearly three months fit into her porthole. At first she could see only the Zvezda module, but soon her little window revealed the Zarya, then the Destiny, then the full sweep of the whole huge machine. She gave it a little salute.

After another few minutes, the computers executed a fifteen-second burn of the Soyuz thrusters, pushing her a full twelve miles above and behind the station. With that, the timeline—and time itself—seemed to compress. Beckwith could feel the thrusters nudging the ship this way and that—tiny shifts in orientation, like a sleeping person fidgeting for just the right position, as the Soyuz prepared for the far longer, far more powerful braking burn of its main engine that would slow it below the critical 17,500 miles per hour orbital speed and send it falling toward Earth. Beckwith looked down at the mice's cage, bungeed onto the left-hand seat.

"We're in good hands, boys and girls," she assured them.

Finally the Soyuz found a position it liked—flying rump forward at the precise angle for a precise landing. There was a quick callout from the ground of fuel pressures and temperatures, which Beckwith confirmed with the help of the indicators in front of her that she was able to read. Then there was another countdown, from the same mark of three minutes to ninety seconds to sixty seconds to ten seconds and then the backwards countdown toward zero.

Finally the Moscow Capcom sang out, "Ignition."

"Ignition confirmed," Beckwith said—and she felt every bit of it.

Braking engines were popguns compared to the massive main engines of the space shuttle and the Soyuz rockets that had taken Beckwith to space before, but after months in zero-g, they hit with hammer force. She could hear and feel the engines' vibration through the body of the ship as the sudden deceleration shoved her back in her couch. Her entire body took the blow, but the force—and the pain—seemed concentrated in her head. She emitted an involuntary bark of pain.

"Status please, Soyuz," Moscow called.

"Status nominal," she said.

She realized that she was speaking through gritted teeth—the first sign of an astronaut struggling against gravity. She looked at the g-force indicator on the instrument panel. It read 0.5—or half of Earth's gravity. Nothing at all, except in her weakened, weightless state it seemed like a lot more. Before this ride was over, she'd be flattened by sixteen times that tiny load. The engines burned for their planned four minutes and twenty seconds before they went silent, bringing instant relief from the fraction of a g.

"Shut down," Moscow called.

"Shut down confirmed," Beckwith responded.

Though Beckwith couldn't feel it, she, her mice, and her Soyuz were now in free fall, high-diving from space and aiming for a hard collision with the upper reaches of the atmosphere 175 miles below—which was itself seventy-five miles above the ground. It was at that atmospheric interface that the g-forces would start to climb and an incinerating temperature of three thousand degrees would turn the Soyuz into a meteor—albeit an electronic one with a human being and five mice inside, protected by a heat shield at its bottom.

Before that could happen, the spacecraft had to get smaller, jettisoning the now-useless orbital module on top and the service module on bottom. The loss of the service module would also expose the heat shield, allowing it to protect the ship. Explosive bolts would execute the separations, leaving only the little gumdrop carrying Beckwith and the mice.

The maneuver would kick the ship and thus kick Beckwith and

thus kick her head. When the countdown happened and the bolts exploded, the kick did come, and while it hurt, it was a predictable pain, as it was, in effect, part of the flight plan and thus easier to take.

But then something less predictable happened. "Soyuz, check your eight-ball please," Moscow called.

Beckwith flicked her eyes to the attitude indicator on a screen on the instrument panel: a computerized image of a free-floating ball, scored with hash marks indicating degrees in three-dimensional space, which showed the orientation of her spacecraft. A blue light was flashing at the point on the sphere over which crosshairs were supposed to be positioned. As long as her reentry orientation was correct, the crosshairs and the light should be perfectly in alignment. Now, Beckwith could see, they weren't; the light was up and to the left of where it should be.

"No joy," she said.

"Copy. Reading that here too. Please perform visual confirmation of separation, Soyuz."

"Stand by," Beckwith said. Moscow was asking her to do nothing more than look out her window. She should see both junked modules tumbling away into space, proof that the separations had occurred as planned. She looked—and saw only the spherical orbital module.

"Visual confirmed on orbital," she said. "Stand by."

She drew as close to the window as she could, looking as far in all directions as possible. She could see the Earth, a few stars, and what she guessed might be the station, a very bright star point still in her field of vision. She could see nothing else.

"Negative on service module," she said.

"Copy," Moscow answered and went silent.

The drill now called for Beckwith to do nothing at all for a moment while Moscow determined if the service module had failed to separate and was still attached stubbornly to the ship. If it was indeed still there, the drill would further call for Beckwith to hit the manual separation switch on the instrument panel in an attempt to override any error that prevented the explosive bolts from blowing as they should. All of the people on the ground and the one person in space knew that that was what she would ultimately be ordered to do, but they had to wait for all the steps to be taken and boxes to be ticked. Finally the call came.

"Soyuz, Moscow."

"Manual detonation," Beckwith said, for the second time today jumping ahead of the ground.

"Manual detonation," Moscow repeated.

Beckwith flipped open the plastic cover of that switch, then flicked it to its *detonation* position; it did precisely nothing. She toggled it back and forth a few more times.

"Negative, Moscow," she said.

"Copy your negative," Moscow said. "Stand by."

This time there was no particular drill. Beckwith had felt the bolts exploding earlier at both ends of the ship, which was surely what Moscow's telemetry confirmed. If the service module was still attached, that meant that only some of the bolts connecting it to the descent module had blown clean and at least one had failed. But one was all it would take. Even a partly attached service module would cause the Soyuz to reenter upside down, with the hatch over Beckwith's head at the top of the spacecraft taking the fires of atmospheric friction, burning through and killing her well before the ship ever reached the ground. The heat shield at the bottom of the ship—which was covered by the service module—would remain uselessly pointed up toward space. Beckwith glanced at her altimeter. She had descended to 650,000 feet—or 123 miles—just fifty miles above the atmosphere. At the accelerating pace at which the spacecraft was descending, that collision of machine and air was just six minutes away.

On the ground, TV coverage of the Senate vote was suddenly replaced by the scene inside Mission Control, alternating with a computer illustration of a clumsy two-thirds of a Soyuz, with its descent module in a nose-down death dive and its service module still attached. The legends "Crisis in Space" or "Emergency in Space" or "Plunge from Space" screamed at the top of the various news feeds.

In Mesa, Virgil Beckwith gathered Mae into his arms. In the United States Senate, more than seventy-five senators crowded into the cloakroom and the rest watched their smartphones or tablet screens. In the dining room off the Oval Office, the president of the United States stood before his seventy-inch screen with his arms folded and then nodded to Carl Bart, who was standing as well, for a chair. Bart complied, the president sat, and for the first time in the memory of either one of them, Bart pulled over his own chair and sat in the president's presence.

At precisely the instant the Soyuz was supposed to collide with the atmosphere right side up, with its heat shield facing forward, it instead collided upside down, its hatch absorbing the blow. Beckwith felt the hit and glanced at her instruments. She was carrying 1.5 g's.

"Soyuz, Moscow, toggle separation again," the Capcom called.

Beckwith complied, pointlessly flipping the explosive-bolt switch back and forth. "Negative, Moscow," she called.

Through her doubled vision, the eight-ball on the instrument panel began to gyrate, and she could hear and feel the whoosh of her thrusters firing to compensate. The g-load climbed to 2.5. The weight sat across her chest and arms and legs and horribly in her head.

"Hold tight, Soyuz," Moscow called.

"Hold tight, Walli," Jasper echoed.

Beckwith tried to say something in response, but she could barely choke out the words through a g-load she could now see was 3.4. Through her porthole, she saw an angry red glow of superheated plasma generated by the thousands-of-degrees heat; the hatch above her head could take no more than two minutes of that punishment. The Soyuz bucked wildly one way, then the other, then back again, as the altimeter read 316,000 feet—or just sixty miles over the unyielding Kazakh soil.

And then Beckwith heard something—something that should have been terrifying but wasn't. She heard a clang resonating through the cockpit—the clang of metal on metal. It was—it had to be—her loosening service module, trailing behind her, swinging side to side and banging against the bottom of the descent module. She was surely down to just one or two bolts and they were weakening, melting in the thickening air.

Without thinking, Beckwith reached forward, punched three breakers on her instrument panel, and took manual control of the thrusters. She grabbed the joystick and began to yaw the spacecraft violently from side to side. The banging increased. The eight-ball—both in the spacecraft and on the control panels in Moscow—swung wildly in response.

"Soyuz! Status!" Moscow barked.

"Gone to manual," Beckwith said.

"Negative! Relinquish!" Moscow ordered.

"Negative! Manual!" Beckwith answered.

She continued to slam the control stick one way and then the other. The thrusters fairly screamed in response, the ship bucked harder, the banging grew louder. Somehow Beckwith made out the gravity meter on her instrument panel and saw it rise to 6.2 and felt that force crush the air out of her. She gave the joystick two more violent pulls to the left and to the right.

And then, all once, the noise quieted, the bucking stopped, and the reentry module spun 180 degrees. Where Beckwith's feet had been pointing, her head now was. Where her head had been pointing, her feet were. And much more important, where her overheated hatch had been—facing downward, threatening to burn through—her wonderful, impenetrable heat shield now was. The service module had broken free and tumbled away and the descent vehicle had righted itself.

"Separation!" Beckwith shouted through her mic. "Separation!"

"Separation confirmed!" exulted the Capcom in Moscow.

"Woo-hoo!" came the voice of Jasper from Houston.

Beckwith punched the instrument panel breakers again and returned control of the thrusters to the computer. The reentry was a free fall once more—a beautifully stable, bullet-like plunge through the thickening atmosphere. She looked out her window and saw the red glow brightening as the heat shield absorbed and shed its fires just as it was supposed to. She clenched her teeth and croaked out the g-readings.

"Six-point-five," she said. Then, "Seven-point-one." Then, "Seven-point-eight." And finally, "Eight-point-oh, Moscow."

At last she reached 35,000 feet—or 6.7 miles, no higher than a commercial airliner flies. Beckwith knew what was supposed to happen then and braced for it. At that instant, more explosive bolts fired, this time perfectly and reliably, blowing off the parachute cover near the top of the module. She was jolted violently as the tiny pilot parachute bloomed and billowed, pulling out two larger drogue chutes—which jerked her again. Still, she managed a smile as she saw her velocity indicator plunge from 755 feet per second, or 515 miles per hour, to just 216 feet per second, or 147 miles per hour. It was still a death plunge, but it would get much slower very soon.

"Pilot and drogues deployed," she called.

"Confirm," Moscow said.

With that deployment, the g-meter plummeted too—to a much-closer-to-normal 1.8. The Soyuz continued its high-velocity fall, the air and the chutes bleeding off more speed, until at just 24,000 feet, or 4.5 miles, the huge orange-and-white main parachute deployed—fully, beautifully, floweringly. There was one more violent jerk as the Soyuz slowed to a sweet creep of just twenty-four feet per second, or sixteen miles per hour, and the g-meter displayed a round and perfect and so very Earthly 1.0.

"Main deployed," Beckwith called.

"Copy your main," Moscow said.

"Almost home," Jasper called.

Beckwith cast one more look at the mice. Four of them, including Bolt, appeared badly shaken but intact. One of them was not moving. She looked closer; she was certain it was dead and patted the cage once more.

Then she lay back, closed her eyes, and listened to the almost-nothing sounds around her. She could hear the hiss in her headset; she could hear the cabin fans; and now, in the distance, she was certain she could hear the *whup-whup-whupping* of helicopters. She looked out her window and saw four of them coming, tiny as mosquitoes below and to the west. Aboard one of them would be Sergei Rozovsky—the man who had made sixty-one other recoveries during the past fifteen years, the man who would make this one too because, in case anyone doubted it, "*Mi vipolnyáem chërtovu rabótu.*" *We do the fucking job.*

The spacecraft continued to descend and descend, and the choppers continued to approach. And finally, when the Soyuz was just two hundred feet above the ground, Moscow called, "Brace for impact."

Beckwith rubbed her blurred and exhausted eyes, massaged her throbbing temples, and then took hold of the frame of her seat. The altitude meter counted down to just a hundred feet and then just a few dozen feet and then, finally, to less than three feet above the ground. At that moment, a final set of explosives lit, as six small braking rockets at the base of the ship fired for an instant, slowing its speed to just five feet per second.

Then Beckwith felt a final thump as she hit the ground on the face of a world that she had refused to touch for a long time, but had dearly, dearly missed.

"Soyuz is home," she said and pumped a fist in silent celebration.

CHAPTER TWENTY-SEVEN

Sergei Rozovsky's helicopter was indeed the first one closing in on the spot where Beckwith had bumped down. She had seen just four, coming from the west, but three more were to the east as well. For a ballistic reentry with a grievously ill astronaut aboard, Rozovsky had wanted as much ground cover as possible. The flight-tracking telemetry had been working itself into a sweat trying to analyze what the flapping, banging service module was doing to the trajectory, but Rozovsky, who had participated in five ballistic reentries before, ran different, better calculations in his head and led his group out to a spot within a single kilometer of where the Soyuz actually hit.

Beckwith had remained as still as she could inside the silent, smoking spacecraft. The whole-body muscle tension of the reentry, plus her pounding head, immobile neck, and raging fever were bad enough. But experiencing all of them under the unfamiliar gravity of Earth was wretched. Intermittently, Houston, Moscow, and the communications officer in one of Rozovsky's four helicopters would call, "Crew condition?" or, in the case of the helicopter officer, "*Ekipázh sostóyan?*"

"Five," she'd say to the two Mission Controls. "*Pyaht*," she'd say to the man in the chopper. She knew the code and she knew the calls. She would announce herself the way she wanted and let the doctors prove otherwise.

The mice were a different matter. As best as she could tell, she had four fours—shaken up but fine—and a one. The mouse she had feared was dead was indeed dead. She lay back and closed her eyes again and, in her fever, began imagining burying the dead mouse here on the steppe—having a little ceremony and digging a little grave and planting a little marker, and maybe in the future people would come to visit it and salute it and remember the story of the mouse who died a Hero of the Soviet Union, an award that hadn't even existed since 1991, when the Union itself died. But never mind, the mouse had earned it, and just this once the medal could be given again. She sank further into a febrile dreaminess in which mice were flying and onion domes were rising and Vladimir Lenin was wearing a spacesuit, only it was also evening wear, and either way he had a cape, when at last she heard the *whup-whup-whupping* of the chopper blades nearing her ship. She made an effort through her feverish haze to straighten herself in her couch, which was positioned so that she was still lying on her back.

Through her window, she thought she could see the four helicopters land. Rescue crews scrambled from them and quickly set upon the Soyuz. Beckwith could hear banging on the bulkhead as the wooden bracket was pushed to the side of the ship. Next came the hurried footfalls up the ladder and then the grinding and clanging of the latches at the top of the ship. At last the hatch opened.

The circle of sky that flooded in was a brilliant blue-white, almost searing her eyes. It was followed by an impossibly fresh, impossibly cold blast of air from the steppe. It was wonderful, delicious, the finest air she'd ever breathed—and it revived her considerably. The circle of light filled and darkened, and she looked up to see the face of

Rozovsky—smiling the smile he'd shown sixty-one times before, when he'd cracked a hatch and seen his crew and felt genuine joy at being the first face they'd see in return.

"Hello, Belka!" he called.

"Hello, Sergei," she said in what was mostly a whisper.

"You look terrible."

"Please don't tell them."

"I would give you a three."

"I feel like a two."

Rozovsky turned away and shouted, "She is a five." Then he turned back and gave her his smile. Beckwith could have kissed him.

She gingerly unbuckled her seat restraints and handed the mouse cage up to Rozovsky, who looked at it curiously and passed it on to someone outside. Then he reached low inside, and Beckwith reached high up for him. Their hands locked and he pulled her up, and more hands then reached inside and grabbed her. She was hoisted out into the sun and sat on the rounded top of the spacecraft, her feet on the top rung of the ladder.

She looked around herself blinking, dizzy, swoony. She saw helicopters, off-road vehicles, Russian TV cameras. She also saw four uniformed officers from the Russian Federal Security Service—FSB, in the English initials for the Russian name. FSB was the son of the KGB and the grandson of the Revolutionary-era Cheka. Either way, the men were not a welcome sight. She put them out of her head and turned to Rozovsky.

"What happened in America? In Washington? Is there news?"

"What news?"

"A vote," she said. "In the Congress."

"America's business," Rozovsky said. "I don't know."

The rescue team helped her down the ladder, and for the first time in nearly three months, there was scrub and hard-packed soil beneath her feet. But there was something wrong with it too. It felt like beach sand, sliding and collapsing under her weight and throwing her entirely off-balance. She started to fall and the rescuers caught her. She looked down. The ground was solid; it was she who was not.

A medical team hurried toward her, carrying a collapsible chair. They unfolded the chair, sat her down, swaddled her in blankets, and began taking her vitals. Her fever was spiking at 104.1, her blood pressure was low, her heart rate was accelerated. They gave her a shot of some kind of narcotic painkiller, and Beckwith felt a pleasing drugginess flow through her immediately. They gave her another shot of what she assumed was a first dose of antibiotic. Then they lifted the chair, apparently planning to carry her to the helicopter.

"No, no," she demanded. "I'll walk." One of the doctors began to hush her, actually raising a finger to his lips. She snapped at him, "I will walk!"

They put her down, and she stood up unsteadily, allowing them at least to support her as she began walking to the helicopter. The men from the FSB stepped forward.

"The lieutenant commander is to be taken into custody," one of them said. He spoke first in Russian and then in English. The English was for Beckwith's benefit, but they still referred to her in the third person.

"The lieutenant commander needs to be taken to the hospital," the lead doctor said.

The FSB man nodded. "Yes. But in government custody."

Beckwith addressed them both. "Just take me to the hospital and get me to a phone," she said. She began to try to translate that into Russian, but they waved her off.

"*Da, da,*" one of the doctors said. "Understand."

More rotor noise now roared over the field, and two of the remaining three choppers, the ones that had been sent east, landed with the final one in close pursuit. The FSB man's walkie-talkie crackled to life and he answered it. He muttered for a moment, nodded once, and then turned to Beckwith and the others.

"One minute," he said. "We wait."

The doors of the new helicopters opened and more government officers hopped out; these appeared to be members of the Russian state police. Following them were Lance Copper and three other members of NASA's Moscow delegation. Beckwith had little regard for Copper, but she felt an unexpected relief at seeing him. She waved her hand and called out.

"Over here!" she said. Her voice was weak, the choppers were deafening, and her head exploded at the effort. Copper and the others, not hearing her, trotted over anyway.

The NASA delegation, with the exception of Copper, gathered her in a collective embrace. The two women in the group—heedless of Beckwith's very real infectiousness—kissed her cheek. Copper merely shook her hand, but Beckwith could read his face and he was relieved, happy, to see her.

"It is very good to have you home, Walli," he said.

"It's good to be here, Lance."

"How do you feel?"

"How do I look?"

He allowed himself a small laugh and then gestured to the doctors. "They'll fix you up," he said.

"What happened in Washington?" Beckwith asked.

"I don't know," he said. "I've had other things to contend with today, and I had no phone reception on that thing anyway." He inclined his head toward the helicopter. "And you've got bigger matters to think about." He looked toward the FSB men and the Russian police.

They took a step closer to her and the medical team straightened up, forming as much of a protective buffer around her as they could.

"I'm an American," Beckwith said to the lead FSB man.

"She's an American," Copper echoed.

"Yes, but on Kazakh soil," the Russian responded, "which in this case is the same as Russian soil."

"Our government will allow this?" Beckwith asked Copper.

"Our government doesn't have a choice," he said. "Our authorities are in touch with their authorities, but the Russians won't budge on the arrest."

At that moment Copper's phone rang. He jumped slightly and looked at it in surprise. After a few minutes of sniffing around on the steppe, the phone had finally found a signal.

Copper answered it. Beckwith could hear a faint voice on the other end speaking loudly, quickly. "She's . . ." Copper began to say, but was cut off by the voice. "I can't . . ." he resumed, but was cut off again. Finally he gave up and extended the phone toward her. "It's for you," he said. "From Houston."

She took the phone. "Beckwith," she said.

"Walli Bee!" shouted the voice of Lee Jasper, so loudly that even at the remove of 6,900 miles from Texas to Kazakhstan she had to hold the phone slightly away from her ear. "You did it!"

"Did what?" she asked.

"The vote," he screamed. "The Senate! The opposition folded like a bad tent!"

Beckwith clapped her hand over her mouth, and tears sprang to her eyes. "Tell me, Jasper, tell me, tell me, tell me," she said, her breath catching.

"Seventy-one to twenty-nine!" he shouted. "*Seventy-one to twenty-nine!* Not even close!"

"More . . ." was all Beckwith could get out, crying and laughing at once. "Tell me more . . ."

"Two more of those boys who were getting leaned on by their voters cracked. Then your friend from Arizona . . ."

"Oro . . . ?"

"Oro, yeah. Oro voted yes, and the wheels just came off the opponents."

Beckwith's knees gave out under her, the doctors caught her, and one of them tried to take the phone. She pulled it back but then dropped it, as she felt herself slipping into a near-unconsciousness that was equal parts sickness and painkiller and joy and fatigue.

Had she been able to take it all in, Jasper would have told her more—about the global coverage of her reentry and the calls and emails that began pouring into the senators' phones and mailboxes opposing the Consolidation, supporting Beckwith and demanding that what could be the final wish of an American hero be honored, especially after the release of Sonia's video revealed the truth. Once Oro flipped, the stampede began, with most of the Senate scrambling to get on the right side of the day's events—and the history that would be made. Word was that within twenty-four to forty-eight hours, forces under the direction of the United States and the banner of the Organization of American States would be mobilizing to stop the burnings.

Now, though, Beckwith could process none of that. She was helped back to her feet as a doctor took hold of one arm and an FSB man took the other, and she didn't much care who was helping her as long as they both stayed where they were. The little scrum approached one of the helicopters. and through the open door, Beckwith could see it had been equipped with a hospital cot and more medical supplies and she gave the cot a longing look.

One last time, however, the noise of engines washed over the field and the final helicopter landed. Even before it touched the ground, its side door slid open and two men jumped out and trotted toward her. Beckwith could not remotely make out their faces through her doubled vision and at such a distance. But she recognized their gaits— both of them—which is what happens when you train with people for more than two years and fly with them for nearly two months and get to know every little thing there is to know about them.

"Vasily!" she called as best she could. "Yuli!"

It was indeed Zhirov and Lebedev, who had bolted straight from Mission Control for a Roscosmos flight to Zhezkazgan and then caught the last chopper out to the steppe. They reached her and half collided with her, collecting her into a bear hug and leaving the doctors and the FSB man no choice but to back away. Zhirov, to Beckwith's amazement, had tears in his eyes, which he wiped away roughly on his sleeve. Then he gathered her back in. At last, the FSB man— actually two FSB men now—approached them, with the police officers close by.

"It is time, Colonel," one of the men said to Zhirov.

"Time for what?" he asked.

"The lieutenant commander is being taken into custody."

"She is under my command and I forbid it," Zhirov said.

"She is on Kazakh soil. Her mission is over. Your command has ended."

Zhirov thought. "Then take me into custody too."

"No, Vasily," Beckwith said.

"And me as well," Lebedev said.

"No, Yuli," Beckwith pleaded.

"I conspired with her," Lebedev said to the FSB officer.

"And they both acted under my orders," Zhirov said.

"Colonel, that is not true," the FSB man said, straining for reasonableness.

"If you're right, then Captain Lebedev and I are both lying to a government official during a police action," Zhirov said. "For that too you must detain us."

"It was all my idea," Beckwith said. "Do *not* believe them." She turned to Zhirov. "Vasily, don't be gallant."

Zhirov turned to the FSB man and shrugged. "American," he said. "I would not trust her." He then addressed the group at large. "This is my crew. We flew together, we worked together, and we will take any punishment together."

The FSB men, who were here to do a job, who wanted to get off the freezing steppe as much as they wanted anything else in the world, looked at each other and shrugged. They looked at Copper, who looked away. Then the doctors closed around Beckwith, and the FSB and police gathered around them all, and Beckwith, Zhirov, and Lebedev were loaded into the helicopter. The blades began to whir, the helicopter took off, and the three crew members who had been in space and who were so briefly back on the ground together were in flight once again.

EPILOGUE

The peacekeeping, lifesaving mission known officially as the Military Pacification of Contested Regions in and Around the Amazon Basin in Cooperation with Partner Nations, and unofficially simply as the Intervention, got underway with a speed, efficiency, and pitiless purpose that belied its meandering formal name. The Department of Defense had always pushed back at the canard that it was forever spoiling for war—which it wasn't. But it didn't mind a bit if people believed it was always *ready* for war—which it was—because being ready for a war is the only way to win a war.

No sooner had Walli Beckwith made her stand and the September 18 Coalition formed than the Pentagon, anticipating the action that might be coming, began back-channel talks with thirty-three of the other thirty-four members of the Organization of American States, excluding Brazil. Every single one of the nations—including tiny Dominica, Grenada, Saint Lucia, and Guyana—agreed to be part of an intervention, with the ones capable of providing soldiers and weapons of war doing so and the rest offering food, doctors, engineers, and, in one case, fabric and seamstresses to replace and repair uniforms and tents.

Within twenty-four hours of the congressional votes, the president of the United States appeared on TV and announced that he was approving action that would "save lives, protect the environment, and bring peace to a troubled part of our hemisphere." The USS *Eisenhower*, which had been last seen lingering in Pensacola, wheeled into position near the coast of Brazil for tactical air strikes, just as many had predicted it would.

The Fort Bragg and Fort Campbell 82nd Airborne and Screaming Eagles swept into the fight they'd been rumored to be training for, joined by the Night Stalkers of the 160th Special Operations Aviation Regiment, making targeted strikes on Consolidation forces, pre-scouted by drone surveillance, often intercepting the attackers just as they were moving into position for an attack on a tribe or patch of jungle. Additional Marine and Navy paratroopers descended daily into the jungle to separate the hostiles from the tribes. In places they were too commingled, nonlethal weapons—Tasers, acoustic attack devices, stun grenades, and more—were used. Nevertheless, some innocents were killed. Their names would be taken, records would be kept, and the OAS would compensate their families and their tribes.

Within twenty-one days—two weeks shorter than the celebrated 1991 Gulf War, which had long been seen as the modern-day model of a clean, complex, surgically perfect intervention—the Consolidation was crushed, its make-believe flag hauled down from poles, stripped off of uniforms, and painted over on helicopters. More than five thousand doctors and aid workers were immediately dispatched to the four relocation camps to begin the long and grueling job of treating the sick and wounded, burying the dead, accounting for the missing, reuniting families, and slowly—in a job that would easily take years—moving the survivors back to what was left of the lands that had been taken from them.

Polls conducted of the Brazilian public showed that more than 82 percent of them favored impeaching the president—a popular groundswell that might have had more effect if the Brazilian constitution allowed for impeachment, which it didn't. The country's federal legal system did, however, allow indictments for serious crimes such as murder, and Bobo-deCorte was given a choice of serving out his term and promptly being charged once he was a private citizen again or stepping down immediately and being allowed to flee to Saudi Arabia, which offered him refuge. He chose resignation and flight. His Multi-Nacional Gigante was seized and nationalized and, after a popular contest to pick a new name, was relaunched as O Gigante do Povo—the People's Giant.

Unlike Bobo-deCorte, who ducked imprisonment, Walli Beckwith was headed for jail. She would be the first astronaut ever so disgraced, and it ought to have been something of a humbling experience, but the fact was, she rather enjoyed her time there.

It helped that the jail—to the extent that it was one—was neither in Russia nor in Kazakhstan. Beckwith and her two crewmates had most decidedly been arrested—hustled straight from the Kazakh Steppe to a Kazakh airport and from there to Kubinka Air Base just outside of Moscow, where all three were placed in state custody. Beckwith was taken to a hospital wing, where military doctors finely skilled in bacteriology and neurology took her in hand, and military police—equally skilled at keeping prisoners confined and looking menacing while they were doing so—kept her under guard. Zhirov and Lebedev were held in similar confinement, without the doctors, in officers' quarters on the base.

The course that Beckwith's treatment would follow was well established—antibiotics, steroids, hydration, spinal taps to check for infection levels, and brain scans to look for swelling or tissue damage. And she would be prescribed rest—a great deal of rest. The course of any prosecution for all three of the crew members was another matter.

For all its myriad departments, the Kremlin never had much of a public relations shop, but that didn't mean the people who ran the place were insensible to popular opinion—and there was no mistaking the Russian people's opinion of the latest crew to return from the International Space Station. Lebedev was a wounded hero—the cosmic equivalent of every Russian soldier who had ever slogged through snow, fought while injured, and come home brave, muddy, and bloody. Mess with Lebedev and you mess with all that.

Beckwith was nothing short of a cult figure. She was American—which made her exotic and, much more important, made the mere act of admiring her faintly subversive. It didn't hurt either that she had bested an American president whom most Russians loathed. The fact that she had done so was also a bracing reminder to the Russian people and a sobering one to the Kremlin of what an aroused populace led by a charismatic figure could do. The longer she remained in Russia, the more her message of rebellion would be sent.

And as for Zhirov—Zhirov was untouchable. Even before the recent drama, he was a national icon. After this mission, he was, if possible, even more adored. The icon was now also a cowboy—riding home to Earth with a wounded crewmate, commanding a spacecraft without even having to be in space, and choppering off the steppe at the end of it all with the glamorous American woman on his arm. Beckwith had not remotely been on Zhirov's arm, and if she had been, it would only have been to keep from falling down. But what had actually happened and what it felt like had happened were two different things, and the Russians knew which version they preferred.

Kremlin representatives thus visited Zhirov early in his confinement at Kubinka to see if a deal might be struck. They reminded him that should he be tried and convicted, he not only would be imprisoned but also, worse from Zhirov's perspective, would never fly in space again. They then began with their lowest bid—dropping all charges against him and letting him walk free that very day.

"And Yulian and Walli?" Zhirov asked.

"We will consider making similar allowances for Captain Lebedev," came the answer.

"And Walli?"

"For now, Lieutenant Commander Beckwith must stay."

"Then so will I," Zhirov said.

Moscow might still have pressured Zhirov. The security forces were not above raising the specter of investigating loved ones and friends for corruption, influence peddling, or other vaguely defined crimes, but that would lead to a popular backlash of its own. Ultimately, the Kremlin dispensed with the entire matter with a brief statement:

"Colonel Zhirov and Captain Lebedev performed heroically during their recent mission. After they have completed a short period of rest and debriefing at Kubinka Air Base, they will be resuming their work advancing the nation's ambitions in space. Lieutenant Commander Belka Beckwith is continuing to receive medical attention and when she is strong enough to travel will be free to leave Russia."

"Free to leave," of course, meant required to leave—but the open question was where she would go. The European Union could seek extradition for a range of offenses, but the twenty-seven nations that made up the alliance were also reluctant to tangle with Beckwith and her global popularity. A few hard-line members—Hungary, Italy, and Poland especially—very much wanted to prosecute. Others were either opposed or undecided. The EU thus settled on its own face-saving deal: They would not seek custody of Beckwith while they sent the question to be decided by the European Commission in Brussels.

The commission was famous for needing years to settle matters as minor as import duties on livestock or permissible fat levels in cross-border cheeses, and absolutely no one expected any decision on the Beckwith matter for a long, long time.

All that was left after that were the Japanese—who were still stewing over their Kibo, which to their way of thinking had been sullied by the mere presence of a person committing a criminal act on what amounted to Japanese soil. But the Japanese, like the rest of the space station partners, also recognized Beckwith's global following. In the end, Tokyo back-channeled a message through NASA and Jerry Ullage that Beckwith should consider herself unwelcome in Japan for the next five years, and if she ever did show up after that should behave like any other anonymous tourist. If she accepted that, they'd let the matter drop. It was a deal she snapped up readily.

So it was that after three weeks, when she had largely recovered from the infection that nearly killed her, Lieutenant Commander Walli Beckwith returned to the United States to face justice in the only country in the world that still had a legal beef with her. She left Russia with nothing more than a clean Roscosmos jumpsuit, a few toiletries, and the four surviving mice—which had come from the United States like her and, as far as the Russians were concerned, should return with her.

As Connie Polk had told the president, Beckwith would face military, not civilian justice, and it would be up to the Navy to determine the charges. She faced a general court-martial—the most severe form of court-martial—and the charges were two: failure to obey a command and general misconduct. Both were deadly serious.

Beckwith's trial was brief—which was all it could be. She was candid about what she'd done, and almost every moment of the crimes she committed had played out publicly, across all forms of media, so her intent to disobey an order could not be denied. The prosecutor presented the Navy's case briskly, and with Beckwith effectively conceding the arguments and the evidence, her court-appointed attorney had little to do but plead for a lenient sentence.

The court granted it. She was sentenced to six months of confinement at the San Diego Naval Base, where she would be restricted to quarters after dark but would otherwise have the freedom to wander about the grounds. She would be discharged from the Navy, which, as the court knew, was a form of capital punishment for any Annapolis graduate and would wound her deeply. But the discharge would be honorable, meaning she could keep her rank, benefits, pension, and pride. The terms of her confinement also allowed her to receive visitors.

Jasper was in training for a mission and could manage to fly out to San Diego only once a month, but he kept that schedule faithfully. On the third of those visits he admitted—in his fine, honest, Southern-honey way—that if it had been up to him, he'd have been there every day. Beckwith knew that before he said it—and welcomed it. Her career in government service was now surely over, and with that came a whole new kind of liberating weightlessness.

"Jasper," she said on the last of his visits. "How about I take you to an Astros game when we both get back to Houston?"

"Walli Bee," he answered. "I'd like that just fine."

Sonia visited as often as she could—but it was less often than she'd have liked. She was airlifted straight from the Mercado camp back to the Baylor University Medical Center, where she underwent three more operations on her shattered arm. The small Guarani boy who had left South America with her—a child listed formally on documents under the name Kauan but addressed informally by everyone but immigration clerks as Oli—was another matter entirely.

The boy had to thread an exceedingly narrow immigration needle to be allowed on US soil, but the SSA had made itself adept at doing that threading, having long since learned the medical exemptions and exceptions of dozens of countries that could help get nonnationals across international borders. Oli easily hit a happy trifecta—minor child, refugee of violence, and suffering from an illness that could be treated only in the nation in which sanctuary was being sought. In his case, the illness was trauma and the prescribed treatment was the care of a child psychologist and the reliable presence of his only human object of safety and attachment—Dr. Sonia Bravo-Beckwith. The immigration court granted temporary residency in the pediatric wing of the Baylor hospital, with regular classwork and exercises in peer-group play and socialization.

The American press took a consuming interest in the boy's ultimate dispensation. There was opposition to his remaining in the United States, divided equally among nationalist groups resistant to immigration in nearly all its forms, and indigenous peoples activist groups, who condemned the "cultural elitism" that would allow a child who had been born in the jungle and rightly belonged in the jungle to be claimed instead as an exotic bauble in the custody of an American medical institution instead of a family of origin. That, of course, overlooked the unhandy facts that the boy's family of origin was dead and the jungle idyll in which he had been raised had been reduced to dead char—and that he seemed to be thriving in the care of the hospital.

What's more, Dr. Bravo-Beckwith had already made clear her plans to file for formal adoption, and her *tía*-mama, who, yes, was a criminal serving time in military confinement, but was also an international hero, announced her own plans to sell her home in Houston and move even closer to Sonia's so that she could help raise the boy. During school vacations, they also hoped to take him to a little community in Mesa, Arizona, to visit a pair of old engineers who, after a fashion, could be the boy's great-grandparents and could teach him how to build model spacecraft and tell him about the real ones they had designed that even now were still speeding out across the solar system.

Since American courts decide most custody cases on the basis of what is in the best interests of the child and this particular child seemed quite pleased about all of these plans, there seemed little question about how the matter would be decided, and formal adoption was granted. The government case-workers did insist on monthly visits for at least the first year to ensure the boy was thriving and did ask his adoptive family if they couldn't do something about all of the scratches the poor child always seemed to have.

Sonia received her share of visitors beyond just Oli when she was recovering. Jo came to call once when he was back in the United States, hugging her with relief and worry when he saw the full scope of her injuries, then scolding her angrily for having put herself in such peril in the first place, then hugging her again.

Raymond too visited, very often in fact, and always made a point to visit Oli as well, to the boy's delight. But he preferred his time alone with Sonia and would often smuggle in some cold beers for their visit, which was strictly forbidden by hospital rules and which Sonia considered very brave—grading on the generous curve of Raymond's modest courage. But she came too to appreciate the true courage he had shown in the blazing jungle, underneath the whipping blades of a helicopter, ensuring both her safety and Oli's when they needed him.

"I heard you carried me to and from the main camp after I was hurt," she said one evening during one of his visits when they were alone in the hospital dayroom.

"No other way to get you back and forth," he said. "Besides," he added, affecting a perfectly terrible Southern accent, "you don't weigh nothin'."

Sonia laughed accommodatingly. "Thank you all the same," she said.

They fell into silence, and in that moment of awkwardness, Sonia took a swallow of her beer to boost her own courage.

"Raymond," she said, "I have something to ask you."

"What?" he responded.

"Promise you won't be insulted."

"It's Raymond," he said.

"What?"

"My last name. You've never known my last name."

"That's your first name," she said.

"That too."

"You're . . . Raymond *Raymond*?" she asked incredulously.

"I prefer Ray Raymond, but most folks say the full name."

"How in the world did you wind up like that?"

He shrugged. "My parents liked 'Raymond.'"

Sonia laughed. "Well, Raymond Raymond, I am so happy I know you."

Raymond blushed a deep pink.

Walli Beckwith left the US Naval Base in San Diego six months to the day after she arrived and had no clear sense of what to do with herself. Unlike Zhirov and Lebedev, who had a home at Roscosmos—even if Lebedev would forever be grounded—she was washed up at NASA. She fielded offers to teach engineering at Rice University, San Jacinto College, and the University of Houston. She received no fewer than eleven offers to write a book about her experiences, and most of the deals promised to make her very, very rich. So did multiple offers to join the public speaking circuit. She took the Rice position and accepted one of the less-lucrative book deals because she liked the editor, who saw a little bit more arrogance and a little less heroism than most people did in Beckwith's actions, which suited her fine because she saw things exactly the same way. She quickly set to work in both her new jobs.

And whenever Beckwith had a chance—which usually turned out to be once a year or so—she would visit the scarred but recovering parts of the Amazon basin that she had previously seen only from space. Sometimes she would travel with Sonia, who now and then brought Raymond. Sometimes she would travel with Jasper. Oli remained fascinated by his homeland and his tribe and busied himself learning their traditions and ways—but only from a distance. He always declined to travel to the jungle with Beckwith, until one day, when he was nearly eleven, his curiosity over the land that had birthed him overcame his terror of what had happened to him there and he asked to go.

For that trip, only Sonia, Beckwith, and the boy went, and at his insistence, they visited the scrubby stretch that had been the tribal land where he had grown up. The three of them found their way to the clearing where Sonia used to light fires to signal her *tía*-mama flying overhead.

They gathered some wood, and they set it with kindling and wadded newspaper, and they lit it as Sonia had long ago taught Oli. Then they sat quietly and watched the flames until Oli's eyes widened and he seemed struck by something in the flickering light.

"It's purple," he whispered wonderingly.

"Violet," Sonia corrected. "Keep watching before it slips away."

ACKNOWLEDGMENTS

Holdout is, of course, a work of fiction, but it has its roots sunk deep in the real world. The Amazon rain forest really is vanishing and the indigenous tribes who call the jungle home really are displaced and in profound jeopardy. The government of Brazil, as of this writing, really does appear to be indifferent to—or even hostile toward—addressing these profound wrongs.

The science and engineering in the story are, as well, faithful to the truth, and are a result of extensive research into the Russian and American space programs, and the structure and operation of the International Space Station. In my reporting work for *Time* magazine and my research for this book, I have visited many of the places in which the action unfolds: the NASA headquarters in Washington, DC; the twin Mission Control centers in both Houston and Moscow; the Gagarin Cosmonaut Training Center outside of Moscow; Zhezkazgan, Kazakhstan, and the little airport in which cosmonauts and astronauts are welcomed home; and the Baikonur Cosmodrome in Baikonur, Kazakhstan. Like Vasily Zhirov, I have been stuck on the wrong side of the tracks in the Kazakh cold after the dog has walked.

Some of the emergencies in the book—a near-fatal Soyuz reentry with a service module still attached and an ammonia scare aboard the station—are based on real events. An out-of-control Progress spacecraft really has collided with a crewed space station, though it was Russia's Mir station that sustained the hit—an accident I covered for *Time* magazine back in 1997.

Walli Beckwith's immovable declaration, "I would prefer not to," is a nod to Herman Melville's tragicomic short story "Bartleby the Scrivener," about the legal clerk who will neither work when he is told, nor leave when he is fired, and answers all orders that he do one or the other with the same implacable words Beckwith uses.

The character of Sergei Rozovsky, the leader of the Russian recovery team, is based on Sergei Malikhov, whom I met in Karaganda, Kazakhstan, during the filming of *Time*'s *A Year in Space* documentary. Malikhov, like Rozovsky, is legendary for his work recovering Soyuz crews and, like Rozovsky, explains his success with a dismissive, "We do the fucking job."

The character of Vasily Zhirov is based loosely on Russian cosmonaut Gennady Padalka, who never quite reached the Golden Thousand but has indeed boasted that he could fly a Soyuz spacecraft with two cabbages in the other seats.

I owe a great many people a great deal of thanks for helping to make *Holdout* possible—not least of all the astronauts who were willing to take my calls, answer my questions, and share with me details of life aboard the station and in space in general. They are: Terry Virts, Nicole Passonno Stott, Scott Kelly, Mike Massimino, Ron Garan, Ken Bowersox, and my dear near-*mishpocheh* Marsha Ivins. I am smarter for the time I have spent with them all.

ACKNOWLEDGMENTS

My thanks as well go to the people who made it possible for me to visit so many of the exotic places in which I conducted my research, especially *Time*'s Emmy Award–winning video director Jonathan D. Woods, Roscosmos's Dasha Scherbakova, and Sasha Gorokhova. It is Sasha's winning smile and slip-the-traces laugh that inspired Walli's own.

Numerous people generously lent their time to reading and critiquing the manuscript as it was in various stages of completion. I owe special thanks to my brilliant *Time* colleague Haley Sweetland Edwards, one of the best reporters, editors, and friends a person could imagine; to Jill Santopolo, bestselling novelist and my editor at Philomel Books; and to the wonderful Sylvie Rabineau at William Morris Entertainment.

Thanks as well go to Amelia Weiss, who copyedited the original version of the manuscript with a sharp and discerning eye, keeping my language clear and disciplined when it tried to slip its own traces, and to Alice Dalrymple and Mary Beth Constant at Dutton, who worked the same wonders with the finished manuscript. I am grateful as well to Ella Bouriak and to Robert Fradkin—retired professor of Russian, Hebrew, and Latin at the University of Maryland—for checking and correcting my Russian and ensuring that I was saying what I meant to say; to Marina Lau Peres, for doing the same with my Portuguese; and to Alejandra Kluger, for cleaning up my Spanish. Thanks, too, to my former *Time* colleagues Mark Thompson, for explaining to me how a military mobilization in the Amazon would play out; and Ryan Teague Beckwith, for allowing me to borrow his crisp and perfect surname for a character he'd never met. I hope I have done honor to the family crest.

Most important, my deep gratitude goes to Stephen Morrow of Dutton, who saw the merit in *Holdout* and whose keen edits made it

339

a far better book after it left his hands than it had been before. May we have more chances to do more work together in the future.

As with every book I've ever written (and every book I ever hope to write), my thanks and love go to Joy Harris of the Joy Harris Literary Agency, for reading each version of the manuscript (and there were many), offering her tough-love guidance (of which there was much), and believing in the book through more than a few rough patches. Joy has long been—and will always be—deeply dear to me.

Finally, my thanks and love to my daughters—all day, every day, forever and ever.

ABOUT THE AUTHOR

Jeffrey Kluger is an editor at large at *Time*, where he has written more than forty cover stories. He is the author or coauthor of twelve other books, including *Apollo 13*—which served as the basis of the 1995 movie—as well as two novels for young adults.